DIABLO NIGHTS

An Emilia Cruz Novel

Carmen Amato

"Return in Haste, O Lord" by Miguel Pro Juarez, S.J. Excerpt from *Blessed Miguel Pro*, TAN Books, Charlotte, NC (www.tanbooks.com) used with permission.

2014 CreateSpace Trade Paperback Edition
Copyright © 2014 by Carmen Amato

Library of Congress Cataloging-in-Publication Data
Amato, Carmen
Diablo Nights/Carmen Amato

ISBN
Ebook ISBN-13: 978-0-9853256-5-7
Print ISBN-13: 978-1502715449
ISBN-10: 1502715449

Also by Carmen Amato

Cliff Diver: A Detective Emilia Cruz Novel

Hat Dance: A Detective Emilia Cruz Novel

Diablo Nights: A Detective Emilia Cruz Novel

Made in Acapulco: The Detective Emilia Cruz Stories

The Hidden Light of Mexico City

DIABLO NIGHTS

An Emilia Cruz Novel

The very breath of Hell floats in the air;
The cup of crime is filled by tyrant's hand

from "Return in Haste, O Lord"
Miguel Pro Juarez, S.J.

Note: It is the custom in Mexico to use two surnames. The first is from the father's family and is always used. The second surname is the name of the mother's father. The second is sometimes dropped in conversation and/or to shorten the name in keeping with American and European naming conventions.

Chapter 1

Emilia Cruz Encinos knew that she'd made a mistake. As Kurt Rucker parked in front of the store, she realized how big of a mistake it was.

Madre de Dios. Emilia's heart pounded like a church bell simply at the sight of the place. She would never have asked Kurt to the wedding if she'd known the invitation would lead back to the scene of her first crime.

The store in Acapulco's exclusive El Centro shopping district hadn't changed much in 25 years, except to add an impressively uniformed security guard. As Emilia stared through the car window she remembered the scrolled grillwork protecting the windows and the handsome letters gilded onto the glass. The famous turquoise door stood open and she could see right into the interior of the store. A row of wrought iron chandeliers lit the long and narrow space. The very air seemed to glitter from the flecks of gold clinging to antique statues, the displays of religious medals, and a cabinet of glowing chalices. Even the bishop shopped at Villa de Refugio.

"When you suggested something religious, I asked around," Kurt said as he pulled the keys out of the ignition of his SUV. "Everyone said to come here."

"I don't like the look of this place," Emilia said, trying for nonchalance. The people who recommended stores to Kurt were not people who lived in concrete block houses without air conditioning. "My mother and Ernesto don't need antiques or gold candlesticks."

"I'm not turning up at your mother's wedding with a gift from some neighborhood *mercado*," Kurt warned her. "I'm meeting your entire family for the first time and I'm planning on making a hell of an impression."

"Don't worry," Emilia said. "You will."

Kurt laughed and she experienced that now-familiar jolt of surprise that he was a *gringo* with yellow hair and eyes the color of the ocean at La Quebrada. She didn't know why that should surprise her any more; they'd been together almost six months. They'd met when the Palacio Réal, arguably Acapulco's most luxurious hotel, was the focus of her first big investigation as a police detective. Kurt managed the Palacio Réal, where his penthouse overlooked the ocean at Punta Diamante on the bay's southeastern side. She'd spent the last ten weekends there.

He called it living together. Emilia wasn't sure what she called it.

She still couldn't shake a feeling of unreality about their relationship. She was an Acapulco beat cop who'd fought her way into the detective ranks and Kurt was a *gringo* who lived in a rarified world of foreign tourists and first class wealth. Emilia had told only a few people about Kurt and her forays to the penthouse at the Palacio Réal. She wasn't exactly trying to hide the relationship; she just didn't want to see her own concerns reflected in their reactions when people from the real world found out about the two of them.

Last weekend, when she'd invited him to her mother Sophia's wedding, it had seemed like the perfect solution. Kurt would meet all the important people in her life. Everybody all at once. Over and done with.

With luck, there would be so much noise, excitement, and activity surrounding the happy couple that family and friends wouldn't notice that Emilia's date was blonde, a head taller than anyone else, spoke Spanish with a *norteamericano* accent, and carried himself with a self-assurance that was both commanding and magnetic. If anyone resented Kurt for being a *gringo* and behaved badly toward him, Emilia could say later that they'd been drunk. Sophia would be too busy being the bride to ask embarrassing questions. If she did, Emilia's best friend Mercedes Sandoval would be there to help run interference.

But all week, as Sophia was even more forgetful than usual and intended bridegroom Ernesto looked like a dog kicked to the curb, Emilia had been having second thoughts. And now Kurt had brought her to the Villa de Refugio. It was an omen of disaster.

"Let's go." Kurt unlocked the car doors.

"No, I'm serious." Emilia gripped his arm. "I'm not going in. This store is too expensive."

Kurt raised his eyebrows. "We won't get anything made out of solid gold, okay?"

"I mean it," Emilia insisted. She forced her fingers to relax; they must have felt like a claw digging into him. "Let's go someplace else. You can get them a nice crucifix or a little Virgin of Guadalupe statue and be done."

Kurt shoved the car keys into his pocket and Emilia stared unhappily at the fluid movement of taut muscle under tanned skin. He was so different from Mexican men. Kurt was a former Marine in his country's armed forces who'd fought in wars before deciding to go to college. He ran hotels for a living and competed in triathlons for fun. Even dressed as he was today, in board shorts, an untucked white button-down, and loafers without socks, he exuded confidence and authority. He knew how to both motivate and lead people, as evidenced by the way the Palacio Réal ran like a precision instrument. She'd learned a lot from him and knew she was a better police detective because of it.

"Is this about me coming to the wedding?" Kurt asked. "You afraid they're going to give you a hard time? Pressure you about us getting married someday?"

"*Madre de Dios*," Emilia exclaimed at the unexpected question and jerked her hand back. "Nobody's talking about that."

"Good to know," Kurt said in a neutral voice. "I'm pretty sure that if I got down on one knee I'd feel the wind as you rushed out the door."

"Look," Emilia said, before they went down that road. Most days it felt as if she was already married--to the job. And most days she liked it that way. "Let's go somewhere else to find a gift. Mama and Ernesto don't need anything from this store."

Kurt hit the button to relock the car. "Sure. Just tell me the real reason you don't want to go in."

"I told you." Emilia tried to sound indignant. "I think it's too expensive."

Kurt gave her that steady, confident look that said he knew he would win any contest of wills. "What else?"

"I don't know what you're talking about," Emilia said loftily.

"I don't believe you for a minute, Em. What's going on?"

Madre de Dios. She should have known she couldn't bluff. Kurt was the one person who always saw through her. Emilia slumped in her seat. "I stole something from that store."

"Recently?"

Emilia threw him an eye roll. "No, not recently. When I was little."

Kurt nodded. "How little?"

"Six or seven, I guess." Emilia swallowed hard. After her father died, she and her mother had lived with an aunt, uncle, and two cousins in a tiny apartment above her uncle's car repair garage. Her male cousins were several years older and she'd grown up following them around Acapulco's streets, learning to fight and steal and avoid the pimps and dealers.

"That was what, 25 years ago, Em?" Kurt sounded more teasing than shocked.

"My cousins and I had this thing we did," Emilia said. She clasped her hands together in her lap. Her skin was café against her pale blue knit dress. It was the sort of thing she only wore on the weekends with Kurt, with her hair down instead of in its usual ponytail. She was nominally off duty, but still required to wear her gun and carry her badge. Both were hidden by her white cardigan. "They'd send me in first and I'd cry that I was lost and they'd come in and start yelling that our mother was all upset that I was lost and how great it was that they'd found me. We'd cry and make a lot of commotion. The shopkeepers would get wound up and in all the excitement Alvaro and Raul would pick up a candy bar or some gum. We'd run out and share the loot later."

Kurt glanced out the windshield at Villa de Refugio's elegant façade and the uniformed security guard. "This doesn't look like the kind of store with stuff that would appeal to little kids."

"They didn't have a security guard then."

"Still." He looked at her expectantly.

"I wanted some of those chocolate coins." Emilia said. Reluctance and shame wrapped around her. "You know the kind I mean? Chocolate in gold foil stamped to look like a coin."

Kurt nodded. "I've had a few."

"It was around Christmas time. I didn't want toys or a doll. Only those chocolate coins." Emilia found herself talking through a lump in her throat. "I thought about them all the time. I thought they were real gold. If I got some I could buy my mother a new brain so she would stop crying and forgetting things."

"Tough times," Kurt said.

Emilia drew in a deep breath. It had been years since she'd thought about this episode and it was oddly disturbing to have to confess it to Kurt. He was part of her life now; he had nothing to do with those hardscrabble years of her childhood when she was scared so much of the time. Her mother Sophia had been a teen with a toddler when Emilia's father died, and Sophia's mind had snapped. Emilia became both breadwinner and decision maker as soon as she was old enough. Ernesto Cruz, Sophia's intended, had taken on some of Emilia's role but he was also damaged goods.

"Even then, Alvaro always knew everything," Emilia continued. "He was sure Villa de Refugio had the coins. He and Raul waited around the corner. I went in crying about being lost. I was pretty good at it and could really put on an act."

"Did the store have the coins?"

"Yes. In a bowl on a glass display case by the cash register." Someone walked by the car and a shadow fell across Emilia's face. She'd almost forgotten that it was a sunshiny Sunday in the middle of the dry season.

"Then what happened?"

"A man came out from behind the counter. I guess it was the owner and he must have heard about our tricks because he grabbed me. Yelled that he was going to turn me over to the police and I'd never be seen again." Emilia remembered exactly what he'd looked like; pencil-thin moustache, pomaded hair, and glasses that made his eyes look like those of a giant insect. He'd been eating onions and his breath in her face had tasted like fire. "He was furious. Kept shouting and shaking me really hard. I thought my head would fall off."

"Poor Em," Kurt said. He reached over the console and squeezed her hand.

"I screamed and Alvaro and Raul came in. They tried to pull me away but the owner wouldn't let go and I was nearly torn in two. Everybody was hollering and fighting and the owner kept shouting for help. I was terrified that the police would come and get us all."

"Did they?"

"Alvaro threw down some firecrackers and Raul pulled over the display case. *Por Dios*, what a noise." That was the most vivid part of the memory; the ear-popping sound of the firecrackers, a shattering crash like the end of the world, shards of glass flying everywhere. "The man let go. We got out and ran for three blocks before stopping."

"But you managed to steal the chocolate," Kurt said, still acting faintly amused.

"Yes," Emilia lied and finally returned his hand squeeze. She remembered a little girl's desperate lunge for the glittery things on the floor scattered amid the jagged bits of glass. The shock of what she'd later found clenched inside her bloody fist.

"Must have been a terrible disappointment to find out they were really chocolate," Kurt said.

Emilia dredged up a convincing smile. "It was."

Kurt leaned across the armrest and kissed her cheek. "Tell you what, Em. We'll go in there and buy something that is at least double the value of a bag of chocolate coins. It'll be our way of saying 'sorry' after all these years."

"Face my demons, you mean," Emilia said. There were so many. Childhood memories. Souvenirs of the cartel violence she'd survived as a cop. The secret she carried with her every day.

"That, too." He kissed her again.

"You're such a problem solver," Emilia murmured. She put a hand on his cheek, so that his face lingered near hers, and breathed in the fresh scent of his skin before letting him go.

Kurt unlocked the car again and they got out. The security guard by the turquoise door nodded and stepped aside for them.

"Interesting that you and your cousins all became cops," Kurt remarked as they walked into the store.

"Takes a thief to catch a thief," Emilia replied.

☼

Villa de Refugio was Acapulco's premier Catholic store for good reason. The elegant space was equal parts book shop, jewelry bazaar, antiques store, and art gallery. And all of it was the highest quality, with prices to match.

Artwork hung on the far wall. The paintings weren't ordinary copies of the image of the Virgin of Guadalupe, like in so many religious shops, but original oil paintings of the Virgin, Jesus on the cross, the Holy Family, and the archangel Michael. A long run of glass-topped counter on the right side of the store was bisected by the cash register. One segment of counter was lower than the rest and two red velvet upholstered chairs were pulled up to it for serious shoppers. The left side of the space was lined with floor to ceiling glass-fronted cabinets. Statues, books, boxes, and religious curios of every kind were arranged inside. Another cabinet held items reserved for churches and the clergy; vestments, candlesticks, those glowing chalices.

Besides the security guard, the only staff in the store were two salesgirls, identically dressed in gray skirts and vests, with white blouses and little red bow ties. No cranky men with bug eyes and bad breath.

"May I help you?" The salesgirl who approached them wore a name tag that read "Tifani."

"We're looking for a wedding gift," Kurt said. "Something

very tasteful."

Tifani smiled. "Of course, señor. Perhaps a piece of artwork?"

"Nothing too big," Emilia said hastily. Tifani had the hungry look of a salesperson in close proximity to a well-dressed *gringo*.

They spent time perusing the artwork on the far wall, all of which Emilia vetoed as being too large, too opulent, or too expensive.

The long wall of cabinets looked more promising and Tifani reluctantly followed Emilia and Kurt around as they studied the various pieces. The other salesgirl behind the cash register threw her colleague reassuring looks from time to time. Shadows flickered from the open doorway as people occasionally walked past but no other customers came in, which meant that Tifani could continually direct her attention at Emilia and Kurt.

He was tall enough to reach items from the topmost cabinet shelves and Emilia could almost hear Tifani hold her breath as Kurt took down and studied one item after another; an antique carved statue of the Virgin of Guadalupe, a cross covered with silver *milagro* charms, a diorama the size of a paperback book depicting Jesus turning water into wine.

"What about this?" Kurt took a leather-bound book out of a matching leather box. Both looked worn by time and use. "An antique Bible."

"*Madre de Dios*," Emilia murmured. She looked over his shoulder as Kurt paged through it and found an inscription dated 1790. "Definitely not. This should be in a museum."

Kurt found the price. "Ten thousand pesos."

"I told you this place was too expensive."

Tifani looked crestfallen as she watched Kurt replace the Bible in the cabinet.

Emilia wandered across the room to the glass-topped counters. Small items were tastefully arranged under the glass. Rows and rows of gold religious medals were pinned to cream satin pillows; everything from simple engraved crosses to Virgin of Guadalupe medallions as big as a plate. Crystal, wood, and precious metal rosaries were displayed in open boxes, each set curled in on itself, with the cross on top of the beads. Little rosary carrying cases were set out next to them, ranging from small brocade pouches to palm-sized enamel tins inset with the Virgin's likeness or a vial of holy water.

Most rosaries were dedicated to the Virgin Mary but Villa de Refugio had rosaries dedicated to specific saints like Saint Joseph, the patron saint of families, or Saint Theresa who was known as the Little Flower. The most expensive rosaries were sets of sterling silver beads with matching silver pillbox cases embossed with the silhouette of the Sacred Heart. There weren't any rosaries or cases made of gold.

"May I help you, señora?"

Emilia gave a start. The other salesgirl was standing behind the counter.

Her nametag read Lupita. "I can take out any rosary you'd like to see," she said.

"No, thank you," Emilia murmured. She tightened her grip on her shoulder bag and wandered around a bit more, noticing a row of framed pictures on the wall opposite the velvet chairs. All the pictures were of people standing by the signature turquoise door; a timeline of the famous who'd visited the store, dated by clothes long out of fashion. She recognized the owner who'd scared her all those years ago. He looked old and ordinary.

Twenty minutes later Kurt had narrowed his choices down to three different items: the antique statue of the Virgin of Guadalupe, a silver icon of Saint Luke done in the *repujado* punched metal technique, and a delicate clay tree of life depicting the life of Saint Francis with his animals surrounding him. Tifani had placed them all on the low glass counter and Emilia and Kurt sat down on the velvet chairs to decide.

"The Virgin is very nice, from a very old church in Guadalajara," Tifani said encouragingly.

"It's nice," Kurt said. "But ubiquitous."

Tifani smiled uncertainly. "A very special piece," she said.

Kurt picked up the *repujado* icon. "What do you think,

Em?"

"It's beautiful, but I think it's too fancy," Emilia said. The silver was inlaid with seed pearls and what she hoped were crystals and not real jewels. It was stunning but she could hardly see it in their plain little house.

"You sure?" Kurt asked.

"Yes," Emilia said honestly. "Don't get that one. Word would get out that they had it and the house would become a magnet for burglars."

"All right," Kurt said and laid the work of *repujado* aside.

Emilia touched the tree of life. "I like this, too. But it's so fragile and Ernesto isn't the most careful person." She visualized the knife grinder's work-worn hands and the way he sat, elbows out, in his chair at the kitchen table waiting for Sophia to serve up his breakfast. "Maybe the Virgin is the safe choice."

"Look, Em, I don't want to sound godless," Kurt said. "But everybody has a Virgin of Guadalupe in the house. It would hardly be special."

With a jolt, Emilia realized that Kurt was nervous. She'd been so worried about others' reactions that it hadn't occurred to her that meeting her family and making a good impression were important to him. The thought made her feel happy and queasy at the same time.

"Wasn't there an icon of Saint Jude?" she asked, turning around in her chair to peer at the shelves across the room. "He's the patron saint of impossible causes. It would be fitting."

"Em," Kurt reproved her.

Tifani smiled desperately as if starting to see her sale slip away. "You like the saints, no?" she asked. "Saint Jude is very special, but we have some even more special items. Perhaps you'd like to see them."

"For a wedding gift," Kurt reiterated. "Something simple but elegant."

Tifani slid over to her colleague. Emilia watched out of the corner of her eye as the two girls had an urgent conversation in low voices. Lupita disappeared through a doorway behind the cash register. She came back a moment later with a box decorated in the traditional *rayada* carved lacquer technique. It was the size of a loaf of bread and the bottom was fitted with a small drawer with a tiny gold knob.

"This is a most special and precious item," Tifani said as she moved the other items aside and spread a velvet cloth over the glass-topped counter. Lupita placed the box reverently on the fabric. "A relic of the most holy martyr Padre Pro."

Emilia's breath caught in her throat. "Really? Padre Pro?"

"Who's that?" Kurt asked.

"Padre Pro," Emilia said, as her heart thumped. She was glad she was already sitting down. The *rayada* box was lacquered in blue and black with an etched design of crosses rather than the usual animal motifs. "He was a priest. A martyr of the Cristero War."

Kurt frowned. "The what?"

"You've never heard of the Cristero War?" Emilia was surprised. Kurt had lived in Mexico for nearly three years and although she knew he wasn't Catholic, it seemed inconceivable he had never heard of the religious upheaval that had taken place in the country during the late 1920s and early 1930s.

"No," Kurt said.

Emilia got her heart rate under control as she considered how to explain it to him. "In the 1920s, the Church was deemed to have too much power," she began. "The government tried to shut it down. Made it illegal for priests to wear their vestments. Placed quotas on the number of priests in each state. Eventually made it illegal for priests to even say Mass. Convents and churches were closed and the property confiscated."

"Here?" Kurt sounded incredulous. "This is the most Catholic country I've ever been in. Are you sure?"

Emilia nodded. "We studied it in school. It went on for a long time. Priests and Catholics who wouldn't renounce the church were arrested and executed. At first the protests were peaceful, but when the army started killing people there was an armed rebellion. Really tore the country apart."

"And this Padre Pro was caught up in it?" Kurt lifted his chin at the enamel box.

"He was a Jesuit priest who defied the government ban on priests giving the sacraments and saying Mass," Emilia explained. "He wore disguises. Used safe houses. Was a good actor, apparently, and had a lot of narrow escapes. He actually got famous as the priest the government couldn't catch."

"Until," Kurt said leadingly.

Emilia nodded. "They trumped up charges and blamed him for an assassination attempt on a famous general. Someone turned him in. He was executed by a firing squad after forgiving the soldiers. Right before he was shot he spread his arms and shouted *Viva Cristo Rey*. He didn't die immediately so a sergeant shot him point-blank in the head. The government publicized pictures of his execution. It was pretty gruesome."

"They wanted to make an example out of him," Kurt said.

"Exactly." Emilia glanced at the lacquer box and at Lupita and Tifani hovering protectively around it. "But it backfired. *Viva Cristo Rey* became the Catholic rallying cry and the Cristero War really blew up after that."

"So this Padre Pro is a saint?" Kurt said.

"I don't think he's officially a saint yet," Emilia said. "But he's famous to Mexican Catholics."

Kurt looked up at Tifani. "Well, let's see this relic of the famous Padre Pro."

Tifani and Lupita exchanged glances, then Tifani carefully opened the shallow drawer set into the bottom of the box. "These are the letters verifying the authenticity of the relic," she explained. "Please do not touch."

She took out four letters, each encased in a glassine archival protector, and laid them on the velvet next to the box. Through the cloudy glassine, Emilia could see that two were folds of paper nearly crumbling with age. The other two were envelopes; one with a broken wax seal on the flap and the other relatively new with foxing on the corners.

"The relic of Padre Pro is genuine," Lupita said softly. "The bodies of saints do not, how do you say, corrupt after death. The relic is proof of his true sainthood."

Tifani slid the drawer closed and opened the lid of the box. She took out two pieces of styrofoam and set them aside. She reached back inside the box and drew out a small rectangular display case. Lupita whisked aside the now-empty enamel box and Tifani set the glass case on the velvet pad and turned it so that the front faced Emilia and Kurt.

The sides and top of the display case were made of clear glass. The wooden base was stained a dark mahogany and bore a small brass plaque with an inscription that read *A Relic of the Most Holy Martyr Blessed Padre Miguel Pro Juarez, S.J. 1891-1927.*

The back was decorated with a color picture of a priest in a bloody cassock lying with arms outstretched at the feet of an officer holding a sword and wearing a garish Napoleon-style uniform.

But it was the object inside the display case that took Emilia's breath away. A long-lost relic of Padre Pro. Her life had come full circle.

Was she actually in the presence of something so holy? Was it proof he was a true saint? She started to make the sign of the cross.

"Damn," Kurt said, his voice stinging like a bucket of cold water. "I don't know much about saints and their bodies staying intact after death, but this is somebody's finger, Em. And they didn't lose it all that long ago."

Chapter 2

The body was folded up and partially hidden by the animal carcasses hanging from ceiling hooks in the big commercial freezer. Emilia snapped on a pair of latex gloves as her partner Franco Silvio shoved aside half a cow.

"Male," Silvio said. "Maybe 30 years old."

Emilia squatted down to look. The place smelled like a butcher store. She had on a canvas motorcycle jacket, jeans, and black loafers with heavy lug soles. Her gun was tucked into its shoulder holster and her hair was pulled back into its usual ponytail. The door to the freezer was propped open but her ears were already tingling from the chill. "I count two small caliber rounds to the head," she said. "One exit wound, the other round is probably stuck in what's left of his brain."

"Execution." Silvio shifted his weight to keep the animal carcass off the dead body. "What do you think? About 24 hours ago?"

Emilia turned the dead man's head to the side and it fell forward. The two round black gouges in the side of his head were close together, between his eye and ear. The eye closest to the holes was closed, the other only partly so, as if the bullet's path had severed one optic nerve but not the other.

The stainless steel wall of the refrigerator where the head had rested was smeared with dried blood. There was no dent that an exiting bullet might have made.

"Looks about right, but the medical examiner can give us a better estimate," Emilia said. "Looks like he was shot somewhere else and dumped here."

"Or else he crawled in trying to hide and the shooter found him." The side of beef was starting to glisten with condensation. Silvio's latex-gloved hand slipped and the beef carcass swung free. It bumped into the body, which skittered awkwardly toward Emilia.

"Shit, Franco!" She hitched herself backwards to avoid being knocked over.

"Make friends, Cruz."

"Get the meat out of the way so I can check for identification."

Silvio wore his usual outfit of jeans, white tee, worn leather jacket, and grim expression. Now Acapulco's senior detective, years ago he'd been a champion heavyweight boxer and retained both the bulk and the menace. He pushed against the beef carcass again and Emilia scooted forward to rifle through the dead man's pockets. She came away with 800 pesos, some cigarette rolling papers, and a sprinkle of white powder on her gloved fingertip.

She held up her finger to Silvio. He got an evidence bag and she pulled off the glove and dropped it in.

The body was clad in gray cotton pants and an expensive-looking alligator belt. The blue button-down shirt and navy zippered jacket looked cheap but new. The man wore no watch or ring and his hair was long and slick with grease. His high-top sneakers were a big name brand. A professional *norteamericano* basketball player's signature was embroidered into the leather.

Emilia managed to turn over one of the stiff hands. The lines of the palms were etched with dirt. The fingernails were ragged and there was a rime of black under each one. "Doesn't look like he was a paying passenger," she reported. "Maybe he came here for work, never had time to change his address."

Footsteps rang on the metal floor outside the meat locker. "You need a little help, there, Silvio?"

The crime scene techs stood in the doorway to the meat locker, cases of gear piled at their feet. The two detectives exchanged greetings with the techs; after more than two years as a detective Emilia knew all of the techs and had a lot of respect for their role. She stood up, Silvio let the side of beef swing back into place, and the two detectives edged their way to the door. Emilia felt cold dampness against her hair as she brushed by a carcass. The meat was starting to defrost.

Hector Bonilla stood next to the techs, seemingly annoyed by their big toolboxes. "Is this going to take a long time?" he asked.

Bonilla was the ship's purser and seemed to regard it as his duty to play host to the visiting detectives. He'd met them at the head of the gangplank, a polished man with prematurely silver hair and liquid eyes who looked like a Latino film star in his crisp white uniform with its braided epaulets. He'd introduced himself in Spanish heavily tinged with an accent that suggested that he spent a lot of time north of the border.

Bonilla had taken Emilia's hand in the way that patronizing men sometimes did, by pressing his fingers against hers, instead of offering a palm-to-palm handshake. It rankled even more when he'd vigorously pumped Silvio's hand and said of course they were concerned about this unprecedented death aboard ship.

"It'll take as long as it needs to," Silvio replied.

"While the techs go over the scene, can you verify if this person was a member of the crew or a passenger?" Emilia asked. They all knew the answer but had to eliminate the obvious. "Have you checked if anyone is missing?"

"We did, but I'll verify our findings." Edgar Ramos, head of the ship's security team, scribbled something in a small notebook. Emilia assumed that he and Bonilla had been assigned as liaison to the police because of their Spanish language skills. The *Pacific Grandeur's* common language was English, as they'd been told by the captain in a brief meeting before they were taken into the hold where the body had been found. Emilia's high school English skills had been polished by weekends at the Palacio Réal, where she was more apt to hear English being spoken than Spanish. She would have managed to get by, but it was a relief to be able to conduct the investigation in Spanish.

The corridor outside the meat locker was crammed with more people than Emilia would have liked. Silvio wiped sweat off his upper lip and she wondered if he was feeling claustrophobic.

The *Pacific Grandeur* was a Norwegian-flagged cruise ship that made a regular run from Los Angeles to the Panama Canal, with three days in Acapulco along the way. Full occupancy was 5000 passengers, Bonilla had explained as he had led them down a series of narrow metal stairs. Just as Emilia was beginning to think they'd walked across the Pacific, they arrived in the hold used as storerooms for the various kitchens that served the ship. The corridor he led them down was wide enough for two to walk side by side. Every few feet a sturdy metal door was labeled with the contents and which kitchen section of the ship it was for.

Ramos said something to Bonilla, and left. Emilia moved through the knot of people clustered near the open meat locker door, gathering up names and their positions aboard ship. Most belonged to the kitchen staff, including the head chef who made little clicking noises with his tongue as he watched his meat defrost. Two others were Ramos's colleagues on the security team. All looked to Bonilla before answering her questions; the purser was clearly in charge.

"We're not going to get any prints out of here," the senor tech said to Silvio. He gestured to the interior of the meat locker. "Too wet. Probably wasn't shot in here, anyway."

"Okay." Silvio shrugged. "Get him out."

The techs pulled their cases away from the entrance and made room for the morgue body handlers to come in with their body bag and stretcher. Rigor mortis had set in and the body had to be wrestled into a bag with the knees still drawn up against the chest. The smell was a combination of cloying body rot, feces, and fresh butcher shop. One of the female chefs began to sob quietly and Bonilla said something to her.

The team from the morgue started cracking jokes as the zipper of the body bag caught on the dead man's hand. The techs got more equipment out of their cases and started moving around the corridor, obviously chagrined at the crush of people in the way.

"I think it would be better if you sent your staff into another part of the ship where we can talk to them in a more private setting," Emilia said to Bonilla. "The techs will have to look in this area as well."

Ramos reappeared. "I can take everyone who needs to make a statement into the wardroom."

"We'll talk to Señor Blom first, the chef who found the

body," Emilia said. She'd taken only a brief statement from the head chef as they'd made their way through the ship. "And all the other members of the kitchen staff who were down here in the last 24 hours."

"The wardroom will be fine," Bonilla said. "I'll bring the detectives when they are done down here."

Emilia opened her mouth to thank him but Bonilla turned away, pulled Ramos further down the hallway, and bent his head to speak quietly to the shorter man. Emilia watched as they conferred, after which Ramos left with the members of the kitchen staff. The two security officers stayed with Bonilla.

"Silvio, Cruz," the head tech called out. "You'll want to see this."

The tech flicked on an ultraviolet light and played it over the shadows created by the stair risers. A fine smear of blood decorated the wall under the stairway leading up to the next deck. "Somebody tried to clean it up," he said. "But blood sticks, you know? Check out the angle."

"He was standing there," Silvio said. "Under those stairs?"

"Probably like this." The tech guided Emilia to stand with her back to the wall and adjusted her chin so that she was looking down the corridor toward the meat locker. "Judging from the head wounds, I'd say the shooter wasn't far away. Bang, bang. Like that." He mimed shooting Emilia in the head.

Emilia shoved the tech's arm aside and stepped away from the space under the stairs. Bonilla had been watching very intently but turned away as soon as she'd moved.

"Looks like he was hiding. Or maybe he planned to meet somebody." Silvio indicated the pristine, well lit corridor beyond the stairwell. "Whatever happened, he got shot twice at relatively close range. Shooter or a friend dumped our boy in the freezer and cleaned up."

"Time of death?" Emilia asked.

"I'm guessing midnight, early morning," the tech said.

The rest of the walls were clean. No gouges, scratches or anything to suggest there had been a fight. The clean lines and spotless white walls made it easy.

Emilia motioned to Silvio with a jerk of her shoulder and they moved a few steps away from Bonilla and the two *Pacific Grandeur* security goons. "Murder weapon," she said, keeping her voice low. "I think we need some warm bodies to help search the ship."

"Who do you think is left to call?"

"*Madre de Dios*," Emilia swore softly. Every uniform was pulling extra duty this week. Not only were thousands of passengers from the *Pacific Grandeur* in town, but there was also a two-day rock festival out at Punta Huarache. But the main event in Acapulco that week was a visit by a "pre-assessment" team from the International Olympic Committee. Only the dead in Acapulco didn't know that the mayor, Carlota Montoya Perez, was determined that the city would one day host a summer Olympics.

Silvio pulled out his cell phone. "Ten to one we get told to get fucked."

Bonilla crowded in next to Emilia as Silvio started speaking into his phone. "Is there anything you need from the crew, Detective?"

Emilia gave him a hard look and stepped forward, forcing Bonilla to move away from Silvio. "Not right now," she said.

Bonilla gave her a tight-lipped smile. "We're ready to give the Acapulco police force every assistance."

"Good to know." If Emilia wasn't mistaken, Bonilla was actually straining to hear Silvio's phone conversation. "We'll need a list of everyone who left the ship today and what time they come back. We'll need to know as soon as possible anyone who doesn't return to the ship."

"Of course," Bonilla said.

"We appreciate the cooperation," Emilia said. They were evenly matched in a battle of fake sincerity, but there was something in Bonilla's tone Emilia couldn't quite identify. Disdain, perhaps. Or incredulity. Not at the body bag being wrangled by a team of body collectors from the morgue, but at her and Silvio. "I'm sure you're worried about the reputation of your ship."

Bonilla gave her that brittle smile again. "The *Pacific Grandeur*--."

"We'll need to tape off this entire corridor," the senior tech announced. He unfurled a length of yellow PROHIBIDO EL PASO tape and cordoned off the end of the hallway near the freezer.

Bonilla broke off eye contact with Emilia and practically ran to the freezer door, the two security officers at his heels. "No," he exclaimed. "That's not possible."

"It's a murder scene," Emilia said, not moving.

Bonilla swung his gaze between Emilia near the stairs and the techs by the freezer. They had plastered the door with tape. "We have to have access to this space," he said impatiently. "Ship's stores have to be loaded before departure on Wednesday. These are longstanding arrangements. Contracts."

Silvio ended the phone conversation and joined Emilia. "Señor Bonilla, can you please inform your security team that the Acapulco police will be searching the ship. A support team will be arriving shortly to assist."

The techs unfurled more yellow tape, effectively closing off the end of the corridor.

"We've already searched the ship," Bonilla said.

"Your captain called the police," Silvio said. "We want to be as thorough as possible."

"You will not be allowed to violate passenger quarters," Bonilla argued, his face tight with anger as he looked at the ribbons of crime scene tape.

"Please notify your laundry not to touch clothing or rags with possible bloodstains." Silvio rolled. "We'll be questioning your crew while we wait for backup to start the search."

Before Bonilla could protest, the crime scene techs shoved by on their way out. "We'll take a look at what we got," the senior tech said to Silvio. He checked his watch. "Need a couple of hours." Emilia knew they'd probably do the same thing at a dozen more crime scenes throughout the city that day and there'd be a dozen more scenes that weren't high enough priority to send out the overworked techs. This one was only a high priority because of the connection to the tourism industry.

The techs left, grappling their bulky equipment boxes and escorted by one of the ship's security officers, as the morgue guys finally strapped the body onto a stretcher.

"We're not going to wrestle him up those stairs," one of the morgue workers said. "You got another way out of this ship?"

Bonilla's anger had boiled off and his brittle cruise ship smile was back in place. "The loading hatch opens right onto the dock," he said. "It's how the ship's stores for this deck come in."

"That should work," Silvio said.

Bonilla murmured something into a radio clipped to his shirt. Several crew members in white shirts and denim pants appeared a minute later and went through an elaborate procedure to open a vast loading hatch and lay a second gangplank onto the dock. Emilia saw Silvio watching carefully. The loading hatch was wide enough to accept bulk deliveries, which made sense. No one loaded that amount of food on board a ship of this size by carrying boxes of vegetables and ice cream and flour down the narrow stairs. Not to mention the contents of a butcher shop.

She tried the handle of the door closest to the blood on the wall. An enamel sign on the door read "Dry Goods. Kitchen 4. Inventory Control:" A hand lettered placard reading "Whitley" had been inserted into a label holder. The door was locked.

"The storerooms stay locked." Bonilla was suddenly next to her. "The chefs and their assistants have the keys to the areas that are stocked specifically for their kitchens. The signs show who is in charge of that storeroom."

"What about the cold storage units?" Silvio asked. "Locked as well?"

Bonilla shook his head. "No. That is so no one ever gets trapped inside. There are telephones in the storerooms, but not inside a refrigerator."

Still radiating anger, Bonilla made a show of producing a key and unlocking the storeroom doors. There were ten storerooms for dry goods. The layout of each was the same;

boxes and big plastic containers, all clearly labeled, rested on wire shelves. Clipboards attached to each shelving run listed the inventory. Every time an item was taken out of the storeroom it was noted on the inventory clipboard, with someone initializing the transaction and marking the date.

"We'll need copies of the lists to see who has been down here," Emilia told Bonilla.

Silvio threw her a disgusted look and she knew why. The inventory lists were a long shot, as if the killer would have neatly recorded taking a kilo of sugar from the appropriate storeroom before shooting a stowaway in the shadows under a narrow metal staircase.

The storage spaces were clean, well-lit, and an efficient air handling system kept them smelling fresh. But somehow the stink of the meat hanging in the refrigeration unit clung to Emilia's clothes and hair. Or maybe it was the image of the folded body, stuffed in with the animal carcasses, that made her think she smelled like dead meat.

The discovery of the body had been around 8:00 am. Chef Werner Blom, who had worked more than two dozen cruises aboard the *Pacific Grandeur*, went down to take inventory before the ship restocked in Acapulco. Heading off a rant about how the meat currently on the ship was now tainted and would have to be disposed of, Emilia walked him through the morning's events as she scribbled a timeline in her notebook.

Blom had used the phone in the corridor to call the security team and got the man on duty, who in turn called Ramos. He and another security officer named Porter, who did not speak Spanish, met up with Blom and verified that there was indeed a dead body in the meat locker. Ramos notified the captain. After a search of the ship, in case the murderer was still on board, the captain had made the decision to inform the Acapulco police.

By 4:00 pm, Emilia felt that the *Pacific Grandeur* was sucking the life out of her. She had another cup of excellent coffee and silently vowed never to go on a cruise.

The assistance they'd received consisted of two uniformed cops who were on the second half of a double shift. Both looked shot to hell and acted like zombies. The ship's captain refused to give the police access to passenger cabins, just as Bonilla had predicted, and so the zombie brothers sleep-walked through the crew's quarters. They searched about half of the cabins and found nothing.

The crew interviews were equally useless. Bonilla insisted that both he and Ramos be present as Emilia and Silvio questioned members of the kitchen and security staffs. Emilia felt Silvio grow progressively more angry as each questioning session slowly turned into a farce. Starting with the head chef, it was clear that someone--almost certainly Ramos--had coached each person. No, they hadn't been down to the stockroom area the previous evening. No, they hadn't seen the man in question on the ship. No, they hadn't known anything about a body in the meat locker until the head chef had told Ramos. No, they had never seen anyone with a gun aboard ship.

None of the security team had anything to add. Each opined that the man was a stowaway. No one would hazard a guess as to how the man would have gotten on the ship or who could have killed him.

After the interviews, Ramos showed Emilia and Silvio where the ship's weapons were kept. Only members of the security detail had the keys to the lockers. A notice was sent to the ship's computer whenever a locker was opened. He showed them the records; none of the lockers had been opened since the ship left Los Angeles five days ago. Emilia wondered how easy it would be to hack into the program and erase an entry.

Bonilla joined them for a tour of the weapons lockers. A cabinet on the bridge deck held 9mm automatic handguns with the ammunition clips stored separately. Other gun lockers were located in crew areas, but camouflaged so as not to worry passengers. Those contained long guns and were only to be used in the case of pirate attacks.

"Lot of pirates here in Acapulco," Silvio said.

"A standard precaution," Ramos said.

"None of these weapons appear to be the same small caliber that killed our victim," Emilia said. "Of course we'll know better after the autopsy."

Emilia and Silvio were the last cops to leave the ship, as Bonilla and Ramos wound up the tour of the weapons locker at the head of the gangplank leading to the city docks.

"Perhaps this was a suicide," Ramos suggested.

Emilia stopped in surprise. "You realize--," she started.

"The ship will be detained in port until further notice," Silvio interrupted with a deadpan look.

Bonilla drew himself up. "I will notify the captain," he said. "But the ship has a timetable. Any delay will result in a demarche to the Acapulco authorities."

"We are the authorities," Silvio said. "And we'll be back tomorrow."

Emilia nearly snorted. "Man wanders onto cruise ship, shoots himself twice in the head, crawls ten meters to a freezer, goes inside and tries to hide behind a side of beef. Yes, excellent theory."

"Ramos mostly played it cool," Silvio said. He leaned against the side of the car and stared across the parking lot at the massive white ship. "But he couldn't keep it up."

"You think he did it?"

"Him or Bonilla," Silvio said. "The other one knows it and is trying to protect him. Both are fucking amateurs."

Emilia popped the top on a soda from the vendor on the corner and watched the tourists stream back to the ship. Most were laden with bags and bundles from Acapulco's markets. "So who was this guy?" she mused. "Stowaway? Dealer looking to sell a little weed or coke to the passengers? Or a thief who came on planning to rob a couple of staterooms?"

"Either way, Ramos or Bonilla finds him." Silvio picked up the thread after a long pull at his own can of soda. "Gets a little overexcited, shoots him with a personal weapon he's not supposed to have on board."

"Tells his best buddy," Emilia continued. "If the captain finds out about the personal weapon he'll get fired. So they shove the guy into the meat locker and dump the murder weapon overboard."

"Why the meat locker?" Silvio often played the devil's advocate during their brainstorming sessions.

"Easier than trying to carry him up those stairs," Emilia reasoned. "And opening that hatch is a big deal. They'd need help."

"Okay," Silvio said and burped. "Sounds like we got a working theory but it's mostly based on the fact that Bonilla and Ramos acted like stooges. Say it's them. Now they've had some time to regroup. Make sure the crew stories are consistent."

Emilia finished her soda. "Maybe we'll get some prints. We find out who the victim was. Find his friends. Family. Keep asking questions until we find somebody who saw him come on board."

"Get enough on him to make Bonilla and Ramos break." Silvio crushed his empty can in one hand.

"Maybe the crew won't give us anything, but the docks are always crawling with people." Emilia waved at the infrastructure supporting the cruise ship docks. "Customs, street vendors, hookers. No matter what time this guy was wandering around, there would be somebody here."

Silvio's cell phone rang. As he answered, Emilia walked to a metal trash can affixed to a stanchion reading *Keep Acapulco Clean!* and threw away her empty can. The call was brief. "Loyola needs us back at the station," he said.

Emilia slid into the passenger seat, Silvio started the car, and they left the lot in front of the docks.

"You're Catholic," Emilia said as the car turned onto the Costera Miguel Alemán boulevard. The coastal route was generally referred to as the Costera. "Do you believe that a saint's body doesn't decay after death?"

Silvio glanced at her in exasperation "We've been partners

for how long, Cruz?"

It had been about six months. "Too long," Emilia replied.

"Yet I'm still surprised when you talk shit."

"Answer the question, *pendejo*," Emilia said. She cranked down the car window. The wind off the water was salty and crisp, cutting through the butcher shop reek of their clothes. "Do you believe that saints are so holy that their dead bodies don't decay?"

"That stiff on the ship is no saint."

"I'm not talking about him," Emilia said. "I think I found one yesterday."

"A saint?"

"Yes."

Silvio signaled a left turn. "Hollywood's that good, is he?"

"Don't call him Hollywood," Emilia said automatically. Silvio and Kurt had met a few months ago, and to Emilia's surprise, got along well. She knew that Silvio only referred to Kurt as Hollywood to needle her, the same way she couldn't resist annoying Silvio by using his first name. But despite their often adversarial relationship, Silvio had been the first person she'd told that she was staying at the Palacio Réal on the weekends. After all, they were partners. "I'm asking because we ran across a relic that's supposed to be a finger of Padre Pro, the Cristero War martyr."

"A real finger?"

"A relic of the martyr Padre Pro," Emilia repeated.

"I got that part," Silvio said. "Where'd you find it?"

"Villa de Refugio," Emilia said. "That fancy Catholic store in El Centro. They had it in a special case with letters of authentication."

"You think they're dealing body parts?" Silvio's scowl deepened as he turned north onto a narrow street flanked by mid-rise buildings and palm trees that would take them up to Avenida Cuauhtémoc.

"Do you ever listen to me?" Emilia said with a flash of exasperation. "It's the relic of a famous Catholic martyr."

"Sure it is," Silvio snorted. "If Padre Pro's finger was floating around, it would have floated right over to the

Vatican. Take it over to Prade at the morgue and get it tested."

"That's what Kurt wants me to do," Emilia admitted.

Kurt had paid an enormous amount of money for the relic, not as a gift for her mother and Ernesto, but on the condition that Emilia take it to Acapulco's medical examiner. Back at the penthouse last night they'd looked through the letters and then argued fiercely over the relic's authenticity. She'd left that morning after a quick cup of coffee and a terse goodbye, with the relic in a hotel cooler.

"Never said Hollywood was stupid," Silvio said. "Just too pretty."

"Why don't you believe it?" Emilia asked, nettled by the thought that both Kurt and Silvio were skeptical that the relic was genuine. "Everybody knows that saints never decompose like real people. Why can't this finger be like that? Evidence that Padre Pro is a saint?"

Silvio looked over at Emilia in disgust. "You're not seriously going to whine like a woman that this could be some Church miracle crap. If Pro's body never decomposed, where is the rest of it?"

"He was executed by the government," Emilia countered. "The letters that came with the relic say that the finger was amputated and hidden by his mother before he was buried. It got passed on to churches, but never talked about because people were afraid the government would confiscate it."

"So if this is his finger, that proves he's a saint?" Silvio asked, his voice larded with skepticism. "You could dig him up and there'd he'd be, bullets and all, still nice and fresh."

Emilia knew it was a long shot, but she couldn't deny she wanted the relic to be real. Padre Pro's finger could be the miracle they needed in order to survive the cartel drugs and violence that had become all too common in Acapulco. It could be her miracle, her sign of forgiveness. "In theory, yes," she said.

Silvio guffawed. "Tell you what, Cruz. Get the finger tested over at the morgue. If it turns out to be the priest's I'll help you dig him up."

Chapter 3

There was a handsome young man wearing a faultlessly tailored gray suit sitting at Silvio's desk when the two detectives walked into the squadroom. A cord ran from a pair of hi-tech earphones into the breast pocket of his jacket. The young man's eyes were closed, his mouth wore a slack smile, and his heels were propped on the desk top dangerously close to Silvio's favorite coffee mug.

"Who the hell are you?" Silvio thundered. He swatted the polished shoes off the desk, causing the young man to spill out of the chair.

"I'm waiting for Detectives Cruz and Silvio," the young man said breathlessly, recovering his balance.

"Get your ass the hell away from my desk." Silvio shoved the chair, sending it careening into the side of a nearby filing cabinet.

The young man removed his headphones, folded them flat and slipped them into the pocket along with the rest of the cord. "I was told that it could be my desk if I wanted it," he said.

Silvio stepped forward until the young man was pinned and their noses nearly touched. "What the fuck did you say?"

Emilia elbowed Silvio backwards. "I'm Detective Cruz," she said to the young man. With his curly hair and expensive clothes he looked like a high school kid with too much money. "Detective Silvio's my partner. Why were you looking for us?"

The young man smiled confidently at her and extended his hand. "Detective Orlando Flores Almaprieto."

Silvio folded his arms and scowled as Emilia took the proffered hand. Flores extended his hand to Silvio but withdrew it when it was clear the big man wasn't going to respond.

"You're from Vice?" Emilia asked hastily. "Tech Ops?"

"I'm assigned here," Flores said. "First day."

"What the fuck," Silvio exclaimed. "Did you know about this, Cruz?"

"No," Emilia said. They'd been shorthanded for months but generally there was an announcement as to the patrol cops who'd achieved the highest scores on the detective exam and had thus qualified to apply for squadroom vacancies. Emilia nodded at the shabby, crowded squadroom with its metal desks and green filing cabinets. The bulletin boards, punctured with a thousand tack holes, dripped with pictures and notes from the most significant investigations. Only the copier and coffeemaker were relatively new. "Welcome. You took us by surprise. What unit were you with?"

Flores's smile was replaced with an expression of caution. "You mean, police unit?"

Silvio shifted to stand next to Emilia. "Yeah, kid, where was your beat?"

It made a difference. If Flores had spent a couple of years in the administration building he wouldn't have the street smarts of someone who'd survived as a uniformed cop in the violence-torn neighborhoods of El Roble or Arroyo Seco.

"I just graduated from university," Flores said. "That's why I'm supposed to ride with you two. On the job training."

Silvio made a noise like a goat caught in a wire fence.

"Really?" Emilia frowned. No one walked off the street and into a detective billet. Every detective in the squadroom had spent at least five years as a beat cop. She'd spent ten. "What's your degree in? Criminology? Psychology? Computers? We could really use somebody with cyber skills."

"Music theory and composition," Flores said.

There was a rushing sound as Silvio barreled across the squadroom. He banged once on the door to the lieutenant's office, slammed it open, and charged across the threshold.

"Excuse me," Emilia said.

"What the fuck," Silvio repeated.

"Chief Salazar called me this morning and the courier

dropped off the file." Loyola slumped in his chair and the overhead fluorescent light accentuated the shadows under his eyes. The deep creases running from his nose to the edges of his mouth hadn't been there six weeks ago. "He said it's a new program to integrate university graduates. Flores is the first."

Emilia picked up the file from the corner of the cluttered desk. There was little in it: standard identification picture, fingerprint card, and a personnel action notification that said Flores had been hired by the city of Acapulco. His starting salary was more than what Emilia made after 12 years with the police force. But she didn't have a college degree.

She handed the open file to Silvio whose face twisted in anger as he read. A moment later he slapped the file closed in front of Loyola, causing the papers strewn across the messy desk to flutter onto the floor. "There's no new program," the big detective snarled as Loyola dove to catch the mess. "This is *por dedazo*, pure and simple."

Emilia had to agree. *Por dedazo* literally meant *by the finger*, as in a finger pointing to a job for a friend. Someone with power wanted Flores to be a detective and had pointed to the most direct way possible. Her mind lit on a bad pun about the Padre Pro relic and as quickly dismissed it.

"I only know what Chief Salazar told me," Loyola said defensively as he piled the fallen papers back on the desk top.

For the past three months, ever since Lieutenant Rufino had been shot and left the force, Loyola had been acting lieutenant. Emilia hadn't any strong feelings about Loyola one way or the other before his appointment, but under the bespectacled former schoolteacher, the squadroom had slowed to a crawl. She didn't know if Loyola was unsure of his authority or had been ordered to do so, but every decision now had to be vetted through the office of Acapulco Chief of Police Enrique Salazar Robelo.

The appointment as acting lieutenant had been a surprise to everyone in the squadroom, including Loyola who'd been notified by text message. Silvio was the senior detective as well as the squadroom's dominant personality and natural leader. But Silvio had a checkered past that included a temporary suspension resulting from unproven charges of murdering his own partner, charges that Emilia knew to be false. Moreover, there was bad blood between Silvio and Vincent Obregon Sosa, the head of the police union for the state of Guerrero.

Emilia pressed a hand to her temple and rubbed at a burgeoning headache. In the confines of the small office, the meat locker aroma clinging to her hair and clothes was especially raw. Silvio didn't smell like a garden, either. "He's actually expecting us to train him? A kid with a degree in music?"

Silvio paced in front of Loyola's desk. "Tell Salazar to put him through the academy with uniformed recruits."

"Chief Salazar was very specific," Loyola said. "Flores comes directly into the squadroom and we're to give him on the job training. He'll ride with you two for a couple of weeks. You'll have to get him qualified on the shooting range, get him trained on the intranet and evidence procedures, walk him around so he can figure out who's who and find case files."

"No." Silvio stopped pacing. "Either tell Salazar to send him to the academy or give the fucker to somebody else."

"There isn't anybody else," Loyola said.

"I don't give a fuck." Silvio leaned over the desk and shook his finger at Loyola. "Cruz and I got work coming out of our asses and we don't have time for this."

Loyola planted his hands on the desk as if to steady himself and rose to face the irate senior detective. "Ibarra's flying solo and I'm not putting some rookie with him who is going to get him shot," he said. "Macias and Sandor are in Mexico City starting next week at that training course. It's either you or Gomez and Castro."

Silvio huffed out a breath, rubbed a hand across his bristly gray crew cut, and turned his back on Loyola. Emilia gave an inward groan. Gomez and Castro were the squadroom's troublemakers. She'd had run-ins with both of them and knew that they'd pilfered evidence from an important money laundering case against a casino. As a result, the case had collapsed and the casino had reopened. At least Castro's brother, who'd turned up with some of the stolen evidence, was now in jail.

"*Madre de Dios.*" Silvio swore and smacked the wall. He spun around, always agile despite his heavy musculature. "We're now babysitting somebody's precious baby boy. What the fuck's his name? Flores?"

"Whose baby boy is he, anyway?" Emilia asked. Who had pointed on behalf of Flores? Chief Salazar or someone else?

Loyola raised his hands in surrender and sat down again. "I only know what's in his file."

"*Madre de Dios,*" Silvio swore again. "Between Cruz's fucking finger, that ship of fools, and now this kid, it's been a hell of a day."

"What's the matter with you?" Loyola looked at Emilia's hands.

"I bought a finger yesterday," Emilia said.

"Tell me it was chicken or fish," Loyola said.

"Supposedly a finger of the Cristero martyr Padre Pro," Silvio said as he dropped into one of the chairs by the desk. Plastic and metal squeaked in protest.

Loyola's mouth opened in surprise.

"Found it at the Villa de Refugio store downtown," Emilia said. She leaned against the wall by the office door. "Fancy place, all religious items. Came with letters saying it's the priest's finger."

"How fresh does it look?" Loyola asked.

"Hard to tell," Emilia said. Why was she always surrounded by skeptics? "It's in a glass box."

"Take it over to Prade," Loyola said. "Call some of the private security companies, too. See if anybody's dealing with a chopper."

Emilia slid into the other chair in front of Loyola's desk, suddenly tired. She'd been so focused on the chance that the finger was truly that of Padre Pro that she hadn't considered more obvious possibilities.

The number of kidnappings in Acapulco had climbed steadily during the years Emilia had been a cop, as the drug cartels turned to creative extortion to fund their bloody wars with each other, as well as the lifestyles that kept the ranks of the young and unemployed flocking to join up as lookouts, mules, and assassins. "Choppers" were kidnappers who cut off the kidnapping victim's body parts in order to pressure families into paying a hefty ransom. In cases where it took the families a significant amount of time to scrape up the money, victims lost multiple body parts.

Local police were rarely part of the effort to rescue a kidnaping victim. Families invariably either used a relatively trusted federal unit or a private security firm to guide them through the negotiations and eventual ransom payment. Corruption was endemic throughout local police forces and most families were rightly afraid that the police were either part of the kidnapping ring or would insert themselves into the situation in order to make off with some or all of the ransom. Emilia had first-hand experience of how a kidnapping could go awry when a previous lieutenant had offered to deliver ransom money and switched the cash for counterfeit bills. The young victim had lost both thumbs.

"Open a case file." Loyola began to swivel his desk chair from side to side, a nervous habit he'd acquired lately.

"Don't we need to clear it with Chief Salazar's office first?" Silvio asked.

He'd made no effort to hide his sarcasm and Emilia shot him a warning look.

But Loyola hadn't noticed. "I'll call," he said, looking under piles of folders and loose pieces of paper until he found a well-thumbed spiral-topped notebook. He flipped to a clean page and began to write. "It's a good case for Flores to cut his teeth on. No violence, just some phone calls. He can make some contacts right off."

"Sure," Emilia said unhappily.

Loyola looked up from his notebook. "Is that it?"

Silvio looked disgusted. "Well, there was the little matter of the body on the cruise ship. But hell, if you're not interested--."

"That's right," Loyola said. "What have you got?"

"Unidentified male, late twenties or early thirties," Emilia said. "Shot in the head under a service stairwell on a deck used principally for kitchen storage and loading cargo. Killer tried to wipe off blood stains and then stuffed the body into their meat freezer."

Silvio stood up as if restless. "Probably a dealer, thief, or stowaway."

"So basically, nobody important," Loyola said. He rubbed his eyes and resumed scribbling in his notebook. "Regrettable incident but not the high priority it would be if the victim had been a passenger from *El Norte*. Murder weapon?"

"Small caliber," Emilia answered. "The two sleepwalkers you scraped up did a search of crew quarters only. We'll finish tomorrow, for what's it's worth. The captain refused to let us into passenger areas and we'd need an army to do that, anyway."

"Suspects?"

"Two. Both crew members," Silvio said. "Working theory is crew member caught him, killed him. Panicked and tried to hide the body. Tomorrow we'll follow up with Customs, dock employees, local vendors. Find out who might have seen him come on board."

He went to the door and yanked it open. From where she was sitting, Emilia could see straight into the squadroom. Flores was now standing next to her desk. He was talking to Castro and Gomez, both of whom were rangy men with ponytails, scraggly beards, rock band tee shirts and slouchy jeans. Neither was trying very hard to hide his amusement.

"Fine." Loyola kept writing. "Well, keep me apprised."

Silvio snatched the pen out of Loyola's hand. "Let's get one thing straight. Taking on this Flores kid was your decision. Whatever fucking happens to him is your responsibility."

Loyola bolted to his feet and thrust a finger at Silvio. "This is an order from Chief Salazar, Franco. Show a little loyalty."

"You really need to grow a pair," Silvio said, in a surprisingly quiet voice. "If you had any guts at all, you wouldn't be dumping some clueless kid on the street. He's not going to last."

As Emilia watched through the open door, Castro said something in his usual jittery way and Flores looked down at the fly of his pants. When the young man's gaze came back up to the two detectives, Gomez slapped him on the back hard enough for the folded earphones to fall out of his jacket pocket. They tumbled the length of the cord. Flores stuffed them back in as Castro and Gomez jinked around him like two drug addicts who'd found a lost tourist.

Emilia closed her eyes and said a little prayer.

Chapter 4

It wasn't too late, only about 7:00 pm, when Emilia drove the clanky white Suburban into the courtyard of the house. A cartel mule's wagon that had been confiscated by the police, the Suburban had seen its share of Mexico's drug war. The rear window--which had been shot out and replaced--leaked in the rain. The doors jammed in hot weather because of the way they'd been rigged to carry bricks of cocaine. But having an official vehicle was one of the perks of being a detective and the Suburban had served Emilia well.

The lights over the front door were on, revealing the tidy yard and the pots of red geraniums that Sophia loved. Emilia sat in the car with the engine off and rolled her shoulders. It was her Monday night ritual, a way to cushion herself against the culture shock of returning to her mother and Ernesto after weekends with Kurt.

Emilia closed her eyes, counted to ten and opened her car door. She pulled out the Palacio Réal cooler in which the relic of Padre Pro had resided all day and carried it past Ernesto Cruz's grinding wheel and the wooden sign with his prices for sharpening knives and scissors and machetes.

Ernesto was watching television in the living room. He was about 50, with skin tanned to leather from hours sitting in the sun and working his wheel. He wore a simple cotton shirt and trousers, but they were clean and neatly pressed.

She said hello and put down the cooler. Ernesto nodded at Emilia and his gaze went back to the screen. It was their usual interaction. He'd come into their lives almost a year ago, a sad broken man from Mexico City whom Sophia had found wandering in the *mercado*. His name was the same as her long-dead husband and so she'd simply declared that her man had come back to her. Ernesto had slid almost seamlessly into the role. In a few weeks they'd make it official.

Emilia followed the sounds of pots and pans through the small living room into the kitchen.

"*Buena noche*, Mama," she said tiredly and gave her mother a kiss.

Sophia returned her kiss on the cheek and gave Emilia a gentle squeeze before letting go.

"I was worried about you, *niña*," Sophia said.

Mother and daughter shared the same generous mouth, high cheekbones, chocolate eyes, and arched brows but Sophia's guileless expression and floral clothing often made her look younger than Emilia. She wore a cotton dress and flowered apron and her hair was plaited into a single thick dark braid.

"It's not late," Emilia said. She got a beer out of the small refrigerator, twisted off the top, and drifted over to the stove.

"Where were you yesterday?" Sophia looked worried as she unwrapped waxed paper from a stack of fresh corn tortillas.

"Yesterday was Sunday, Mama." Emilia sniffed appreciatively at a pan of shredded pork. "I was with Kurt. If you were worried you should have called."

The schedule of when she was at the Palacio Réal and when she slept at home was taped to the kitchen wall above the tile countertop, along with emergency telephone numbers: her cell phone, Kurt's cell and office numbers, plus the number that rang in the hotel penthouse.

"That boy again?" Sophia frowned, then elbowed Emilia away from the stove so she could warm the tortillas on the flat round *comal* griddle.

"Kurt," Emilia reminded her. "His name is Kurt."

"What kind of a name is Kurt? Are you sure it's not Carlos?"

"I'm sure, Mama."

"Go sit down," Sophia said.

The scent of pork and tortillas was rich and reassuring. Emilia felt hunger and fatigue rush in to claim her as she took off her jacket and unbuckled her shoulder holster. The late day encounter with the new detective had been a momentary diversion but now she realized how upsetting it had been to handle the rigid cadaver amid the swaying carcasses aboard the cruise ship. Hopefully, given that they had two suspects, the case could wrap up quickly. But she never liked to predict. As a detective, she'd learned long ago that some weeks were an exercise in sleep deprivation. A week would start slow, like this one, with only one new case—if she didn't count Padre Pro—but speed up until the days stretched to 12, 14, or 16 hours. And still the case would be retired to the files as more crime rushed in.

Sophia put a plate on the table in front of her and Emilia gave a start, realizing that she'd all but fallen asleep as she sat there. The plate of *carnitas* looked enticing; warm corn tortillas wrapped around pork that had been slow cooked and then fried until hot and crisp.

"Thank you, Mama," Emilia said. The first bite was heaven and made even better by the bowl of *bayos blancos* that Sophia set next to the plate. The salsa was already on the table. Emilia ladled a spoonful onto the beans and proceeded to inhale the food.

Sophia sat down across from her. For several minutes neither spoke as Emilia ate.

"I think I should speak to this boy's parents, Emilia," Sophia said at length.

Emilia nearly choked on a bite. "Mama, we've been over this before," she said after getting the food down. "Kurt is not a boy from school. He's grown. I'm grown. We like to spend time together on the weekends when we're not working. If you ever need me, I'm only a phone call away."

"What about your homework?" Sophia looked disapprovingly at her daughter.

"Mama, you're not listening to me. Again." Emilia threw down her fork and it rang against the thick pottery plate. "I'm not in school. I have a job."

"I'm a mother worried about her daughter," Sophia said. Her eyes filled. "You missed church."

Emilia mentally counted to ten. Some days Sophia remembered everything Emilia told her. Other days, like today, her mother was stuck in the past and arguing only led to tears.

"You're right, Mama." Emilia took her plate to the sink. Experience told her to surrender to the inevitable. "I'll go talk to Padre Ricardo. Right now."

"That's my good girl," Sophia said with a watery smile.

"You don't need to worry, Mama." Emilia came back to her mother at the table. She'd known it was going to be difficult to balance life with Kurt with her mother's needs, and days like this were a painful reminder. Emilia leaned down to give Sophia an awkward hug and kissed the top of her mother's head. "We're all fine."

☼

Padre Ricardo took off his reading glasses and replaced the last letter in its glassine envelope. It was written on heavy linen stationary, foxed with age at the edges.

"What do you think?" Emilia asked. There was a cup of his famously tasteless chamomile tea in front of her on the kitchen table in the rectory.

Over the years, the church of San Pedro de los Pinos had become her second home and Padre Ricardo Suarez the closest thing to a father that she'd ever had. More than once she'd consulted him on an ethical dilemma relating to an investigation. Seemingly ageless, he wore faded *guayabera* shirts and dark cotton pants as he organized neighborhood social events, children's religious instructions, holy day pageants, women's groups, and fatherhood lessons, all with the energy level of a teen.

A few months ago he'd asked her to look for a girl missing from their neighborhood. It was a case that Emilia wished could have had a better ending. Any ending, actually. But her efforts had been an inconclusive disaster and the 16-year-old girl, Lila Jimenez Lata, was now just another name and picture in a big binder of missing women Emilia kept in the bottom of her desk drawer at work.

"I don't think it's as simple as the letters would have us believe, Emilia." The priest passed the four envelopes back to her.

"But it's all there." Emilia put them back in the drawer of the enameled box. "It's why Padre Pro's finger never decayed."

The glass-encased relic sat next to its protective box in the bright circle on the tabletop thrown down by the kitchen's pendant light. The index finger pointed up, mounted like a trophy to the wooden base. The skin around the knuckle was wrinkled, the nail was short and blunt, and the general effect was of a small sculpture made out of sweet brown *piloncillo* sugar.

"The soldiers' uniforms are all wrong in the picture, you know," Padre Ricardo said. He turned the glass box so that the dramatic print affixed to the back panel was angled toward them.

"Probably for effect," Emilia reasoned.

The priest got up and peered in Emilia's cup. "Don't you need more tea?"

"No, this is enough for me, thanks." Emilia sipped at the vaguely flavored warm water.

Padre Ricardo moved out of range of the light over the table. "The uniforms in the picture aren't the uniforms the army wore in the 1920's." His face was lit for a moment by the bright blue flame of the gas stove but fell into shadow again as he placed the kettle on the hob. "Padre Pro didn't die wearing a cassock, either. He had on a suit and a checkered vest. Practicing the Sacraments was illegal. Anyone wearing a roman collar or a cassock would be arrested as a matter of course."

"A fanciful drawing doesn't mean it isn't his real finger," Emilia said.

Padre Ricardo made himself a mug of tea with the same used teabag that had flavored Emilia's mug. He put the mug on the table and left the kitchen. A light went on in the living room and Emilia heard him muttering to himself. He returned carrying a thick leather scrapbook.

He put it on the table and opened it. Emilia caught a glimpse of some faded newspaper articles glued to the thick pages.

"*Il Papa* Juan Pablo II came to Mexico City in September 1988," he said. "You're too young to remember, but that's when the Vatican beatified Padre Pro as a martyr of the Catholic Church."

"The first step to becoming a saint," Emilia said.

"I was a seminarian in Mexico City then." Padre Ricardo flipped a page and ran his finger across an article with a picture of people standing in front of a blocky tomb. "It was quite unforgettable. As part of the beatification procedure, the body was exhumed."

"As in, dug up?" Emilia asked, remembering Silvio's mocking promise.

Padre Ricardo nodded. "Padre Pro was executed in 1927 along with his brother Humberto. His body was taken by ambulance to the hospital and then to the Pro home where the two brothers were laid out. People came to the Pro home throughout the night. The next day, thousands attended the funeral. Five hundred cars in the processional. Thousands and thousands walking with the bodies to the cemetery. The brothers were buried in Mexico City."

Emilia opened her mouth but Padre Ricardo held up his hand and continued. "When the body was exhumed, no one said anything about missing body parts. His remains are now in a reliquary in the church of the Holy Family in Mexico City."

He flipped another page and shifted the scrapbook so that Emilia could see a newspaper photograph. Two slender marble columns flanked a portrait of a serious young man with an oval face and big eyes. Below it, a large silver coffer, topped by a cross, sat on a marble altar. The silver box looked solid and heavy . . . and small.

"That's where his remains are? Emilia asked. "It's not big enough."

"It's a reliquary, Emilia. Not a coffin."

Emilia kept staring at the picture, trying to make the scene fit her hopes. "That means his body wasn't intact when they exhumed it. Otherwise they would have put it on display. Or at least kept it in a coffin."

"The only thing we can say for sure is that the reliquary contains his remains," Padre Ricardo said. "The Vatican beatification process is very thorough."

"That doesn't mean that the letter is wrong," Emilia insisted. She opened the drawer and took out the letters again. The oldest one supposedly verified how the finger had been preserved. "You said that his body was taken home after the execution. That's how his mother was able to save the finger. It's right here in the letter."

"It's a little known fact," Padre Ricardo said sadly. "Padre Pro's mother passed away while he was a seminarian in Belgium."

Emilia left the letters on the table. She got up and brought her mug to the sink, where the light wasn't so bright. Tears pricked the back of her eyes as she slowly poured out what was left of the tepid grass-flavored water. "So Kurt was right," she said at length. "Silvio was right. It's a fake."

"Isn't there some way to tell?" Padre Ricardo asked. "DNA testing? Can they find out how old it might be? Perhaps, if it's the right age, you could petition to have the reliquary opened and do comparison testing."

"Yes." Emilia came back to the table. She didn't look at the priest as she packed the relic and letters into the blue enamel box. "There are tests."

Chapter 5

"We got a problem," Silvio announced as Emilia slung her shoulder bag on top of her desk Tuesday morning.

"Besides . . .?" Emilia cut her eyes to Flores.

The young man was sitting at the desk she'd directed him to last night before leaving. The screen was lit and he was following the prompts to gain access to the police intranet. He had on another expensive suit, this time with a navy shirt, striped tie, and a heavy gold tie pin. The combination made him look like an advertisement for an Italian clothing designer. She made a mental note to ask if he had a pair of jeans.

Silvio snapped his fingers to get Emilia's attention again. "Customs is giving me the run-around."

"Like you expected bureaucratic excellence from them?" Emilia unlocked her desk's deep file drawer and dropped her shoulder bag on top of the binder full of records of missing women. She called them *Las Perdidas*—the Lost Ones. Lila Jimenez Lata had been the 43rd entry in the binder. Emilia had only ever found one of the missing women.

"I called Customs for their work schedule," Silvio said. "We'll need to talk to everybody on duty Sunday night. Got referred to"—he checked a scrap of paper on his desk—"Irma Gonzalez Perot."

"So?"

"She's the head of Human Resources for the region. Secretary said I had to make a fucking appointment."

"Give it to me. I'll follow up." Emilia dug out her notebook and scribbled down the information he gave her. "Think we can get a few more uniforms today?"

"I called," Silvio said. "A team will be there midmorning."

He could be a major pain, but Silvio was an excellent investigator. He knew the right people to call, and never wasted time. Emilia flipped her notebook closed and leaned over her desk. "We're going to have to take Flores with us," she whispered. "We can't leave him here. Castro and Gomez will steal his wallet and lock him in a closet."

"*Rayos*," Silvio muttered. He darted a glance at Flores, whose head was bobbing gently to whatever tune was playing in his headphones. "You can introduce Flores to the wonders of the morgue, see what Prade has on our victim. I'll go over to the ship, finish the search, start asking questions around the dock."

"Take the kid to the morgue on his first day?" Tougher-looking men than Flores had slumped to the tiles the first time they saw an autopsied body.

"Take smelling salts or whatever they use now when girls faint."

"Why can't Flores go with you?" Emilia whispered. "If the zombie brothers are all the help we're going to get on this case, you can use another pair of hands."

"He doesn't know procedures," Silvio growled.

Emilia wheeled her chair around the side of the two desks. "You can't shove him off on me because you're mad at Loyola."

"Careful, Cruz, your drama is showing." Silvio stood up, grabbed his coffee mug, and pounded over to the coffeemaker in the corner of the squadroom.

"*Pendejo*," Emilia hissed.

Of course she'd be saddled with the new kid. Probably for days, until they arrested Bonilla or Ramos or both, and Silvio was in a marginally better mood.

Emilia went over to Flores and gave him a quick briefing on the essentials: the daily 9:00 meeting of all detectives, the rota system for assigning new cases, a few words on the cruise ship case. The kid smiled easily, seemingly pleased to be in the squadroom, but didn't ask any questions or take any notes.

The regular morning meeting went the same way all the meetings had gone since Loyola became acting lieutenant. Major cases were reviewed. Loyola interrupted to ask questions, always with an edge of worry in his voice that the detectives were moving ahead before obtaining the requisite permission. He introduced Flores with the caveat that the new detective would be riding with Emilia and Silvio. Castro and Gomez cracked a few jokes about Flores getting lucky that was obviously a play on words. Ibarra, Loyola's one-time chain-smoking partner, looked relieved, as did Macias and Sandor, a quiet team with a strong arrest record.

Silvio briefed the cruise ship case, outlining what the techs had said at the scene, and their concerns about Bonilla and Ramos. The squadroom discussion about the case was brief; the victim with fake identification was obviously a small-time thief or dealer who'd managed to get on board and was surprised by a member of the crew who for obvious reasons, didn't want to admit to the crime.

"When does the ship leave?" Loyola asked.

"Tomorrow late afternoon," Emilia said. As always when starting any investigation she'd made a timeline. In more than one case, the linear display of facts had helped distill information and reach a conclusion.

"Plenty of time," Loyola said. "It hasn't hit the news yet and I've had word from on high to keep it that way."

"And if we don't have an arrest before it sails?" Emilia asked. "Can we detain the ship?"

"It's a low priority case, Cruz," Loyola said pointedly.

"So we let a murderer sail off," Emilia said under her breath, although she knew the reasoning behind his decision. Acapulco enjoyed an average of three murders a day and at least half the bodies that transited the morgue or city hospitals were unidentified. The problem was so bad that the morgue wanted to put up a website with pictures of the dead, in hopes that friends and families could identify them. The mayor's office opposed the idea, claiming it would be detrimental to the city's all-important tourism industry. The issue still simmered but Emilia had yet to see a battle that the city's enigmatic mayor, Carlota Montoya Perez, hadn't won.

"Unless we've got something solid, like a signed confession." Loyola spread his hands as if to say *whatever* and the discussion moved on to a case that Macias and Sandor were handling and would have to offload before they went off to their training course in Mexico City. Emilia took notes; the case almost certainly would come to her and Silvio.

Castro started shuffling a deck of cards and Flores turned to watch.

☼

"Detectives Cruz and Flores. Here for the report on the body found on the *Pacific Grandeur* cruise ship." Emilia lifted the Palacio Réal cooler so the young man in his scrubs could see what she carried. "I've also got a secondary case to discuss with him."

"Doctor Prade's in the holding room," the attendant said. "I'll take you back there."

Emilia hated the morgue, hated that she was there so often. The overflow of unidentified bodies meant that two chiller vaults had been reconfigured so that older bodies could be stacked like sardines rather than held in individual drawers. Of course, whenever Emilia needed to see a particular body, it was at the bottom. Morgue workers would pull out the bodies like so many frozen fish before finding the right one.

When there was a big accident or a mass cartel grave uncovered, body bags lined the halls. Prade would prioritize them and abbreviate the autopsy to a handful of procedures. Gurneys with their cargos of naked bodies would form a queue waiting for their turn in the small operating theater while the cleaning crew--six older women who seemed immune to the death around them--continuously mopped the floor.

Today the place was relatively empty but the air was still thick with the morgue's trademark smell; a mixture of cloying sweetness and eye-watering antiseptic. The attendant led them into the main holding room. Flores's boyish face tightened as he took in the rows of drawers built into the walls, the way the floor sloped down on all sides toward a central drain, the worktable cluttered with labelled bags full of personal effects of the dead.

Doctor Antonio Prade was perched on a stool at the long

counter built into the one wall without drawers. He wore a surgical mask around his neck, reading glasses perched on his nose, and a wrinkled lab coat misbuttoned over a plaid shirt and brown corduroy trousers. The once-white coat had some smears on it, which Emilia prayed were soap. He raised his pen in a *just-a-moment* signal, then continued scribbling on a form.

"I hope that's your report on the body found on the cruise ship yesterday." Emilia put down the cooler and dug out her notebook.

"Introductions, Detective Cruz?" Prade didn't look up but his voice rang out against the tiled walls.

"Sorry," Emilia said. "Doctor Antonio Prade, meet Orlando Flores, our newest detective."

Prade finally put down his pen and peered at Flores over his spectacles. "Welcome to the *charro*, boy," he said, taking in Flores' expensive suit. "How long have you been on the job?"

"Since yesterday," Flores replied

Prade turned to Emilia, eyebrows raised.

"Second day as a cop," Emilia said and tapped her forefinger against the cover of her notebook. "First day on the street as a detective."

Flores looked as if he didn't get why Prade had called their occupation a rodeo, but Emilia knew that Prade would immediately understand the *por dedazo* gesture. The medical examiner had been in his position for several years and knew the politics of the Acapulco police force better than most cops. He often joked to her that he saw a lot of bare assholes and more were attached to the living than the dead.

"Where's Silvio?" Prade asked. "There hasn't been a reshuffle, has there?"

Emilia shook her head. "He's at the docks, following up on the same case."

Prade got off the stool. "That's too bad. I wanted to hear what Silvio had to say about this." He consulted the form he'd been completing, crossed the room, and tugged at the handle of a numbered stainless steel drawer. There was a slight sucking sound as the rubber seal parted. Cool air escaped with a sigh as the drawer rolled open.

The body was no longer folded up, the way Emilia had seen it on the ship, but flaccid, naked, and straight. Both eyes were closed. The bullet holes in the temple were less glaring, less final, if only because they were overshadowed by the fact that the crown of the head had been sawn off.

Behind Emilia, Flores made a gagging noise that tapered into a cough.

"Died between midnight and 2:00 am on Sunday night," Prade said. He pointed to the disfigured head. "Two shots to the brain. Twenty-two caliber."

"Seven hours after the ship docked in Acapulco, more or less." Emilia didn't turn to look at Flores.

"Not a passenger?"

Emilia wished she'd taken a mask from the worktable before looking at the body. "What did you want Silvio to see?"

"I thought maybe it had something to do with boxing clubs," Prade said. He turned the cadaver's left arm to expose the inside of the forearm.

Emilia bent to look. The arm bore a large green tattoo of two crossed fists in front of the tines of a devil's pitchfork. The words *Salva Diablo* were printed over the point at which the wrists intersected. "Save the devil," she murmured. She dug out her phone and snapped a picture of the tattoo.

"Have you seen it before?" Prade asked.

"Only in pictures." She took a picture of the man's face. "Briefings. Alert memos."

"I'm almost afraid to ask," Prade said.

"It's just a tattoo, right?" Flores sounded bewildered. His boyish face was tinged with green and Emilia wondered if he was going to pass out.

"Salva Diablo is a gang from Honduras," Emilia said. "Known *tumbadores*. Rip crews. They steal other people's drug shipments and sell it for what they can. So far they've stayed out of Acapulco."

Flores flinched backwards as if the body had made a

motion and startled him.

"Detective Flores, go sit down." Prade jerked his head at the worktable. The younger man crossed the room and settled onto a stool.

"This isn't the best surprise I've ever had," Emilia said as she texted the picture of the tattoo to Silvio. "What about prints?"

"He's not in the system." Prade pointed at the body. "Got enough pictures?"

Emilia nodded and he rolled the drawer shut, its dead gray cargo disappearing into the wall. The medical examiner went over to the worktable where Flores was sitting and Emilia followed.

"Another item of interest." Prade shuffled through the forms he'd been completing and pulled out a printed test result. "The lab found traces of heroin and a hallucinogenic chemical in the pocket of his jacket and on the glove submitted with the body."

Emilia quickly scanned the printout. "Ora Ciega."

"What's Ora Ciega?" Flores asked.

"Ora Ciega. Blind Gold." Emilia dropped the test result in front of Flores and rapidly tapped out another text to Silvio. *Madre de Dios*, but this low priority case just became a major drug investigation. Honduran gang member, who'd been handling Ora Ciega, murdered on a ship with a giant loading hatch that would eventually end its cruise in *El Norte*. Loyola would have to be an idiot not to see the connections.

"Colombian variety of heroin laced with a synthetic drug similar to meth," she said as she texted it all to Silvio. "Name comes from users who say they go blind from longing for it so hard."

"Oh." Flores sounded bewildered.

"Ora Ciega," Prade said. "That's a new one."

Silvio texted her back almost immediately. They'd need to bring in dogs, see if there was Ora Ciega aboard ship. But they'd need a sample.

"Can I have his clothes?" Emilia asked Prade.

Prade looked through the labeled bags on the work counter

and picked one out. "Sign for it and it's all yours."

She would bring the clothes, Emilia texted back to Silvio. Two swift texts and they'd planned out the next few hours, both gripped by a fresh sense of urgency. Ora Ciega was rarely seen in Acapulco. Despite the demand, it was difficult to blend and the Mexican cartels had largely stayed away from it. Emilia couldn't help thinking that if the Honduran Salva Diablo gang was looking to move into Acapulco, it wasn't big enough to operate on their own. They'd try to align with an established gang or cartel network. Was Ora Ciega from Colombia their price of entry?

"What would we do without modern technology?" Prade asked as he stripped off his latex gloves and mask before pointedly gathering up his handwritten forms.

Emilia was ready to rush out of the holding room but the cooler was still there, like a giant stone. She picked it up and set it on the worktable. "Can you give me another two minutes?" she asked Prade.

"For you, Emilia," Prade said. "Five."

He set the paperwork to one side of the table.

Emilia opened the cooler, removed the enamel box, and lifted out the glass relic case. She set it in front of the medical examiner. Flores gave a muffled gasp.

Prade adjusted his reading glasses and read the inscription aloud. His eyes narrowed behind the lenses. "Where did you get this?"

Emilia opened the little drawer and took out the letters. "The Villa de Refugio. It's a very high end Catholic store in El Centro. These are letters attesting to its authenticity as Padre Pro's finger."

Prade took off his reading glasses and held up the glass box. "I dimly remember the legend of Padre Pro. How old is this thing supposed to be?"

"Padre Pro died in 1927," Flores said faintly.

Emilia glanced at him.

"I went to Catholic school," Flores explained.

Prade switched on a large adjustable lamp. He angled the shade to illuminate the box. For a minute he said nothing as he turned the relic carefully so as to view the finger from all sides. Emilia waited without speaking. When Prade turned the box upside down and shook it, the finger stayed rigidly in place.

"I think it's stuck onto a big nail," Prade said.

Flores made a funny sound, pressed a hand to his mouth, and hopped off the stool. He walked out rapidly. Emilia hoped he made it outside before he threw up.

Prade put down the relic box. "Somebody has taken pains to preserve it," he said. "The skin has some sort of sealant on it."

"Do you think it could be genuine?" Emilia asked. Now that the relic was here in the morgue, under a glaring light with Prade's dispassionate eye on it, she felt all hope ooze away. Maybe it had been wrong to give in to Kurt. She should have left the relic in Villa de Refugio. Some true believer, untroubled by harsh realities, would have bought it and venerated the memory of Padre Pro.

Prade held up one of the letters in its glassine envelopes. "Did you test these? Are they authentic?"

"I know that at least one of them is factually incorrect," Emilia admitted. "But . . . I thought . . . maybe."

Prade took off his glasses and pinched the bridge of his nose. "I'll run a few tests on the finger, see if I can at least assess the age. Who knows, we might even be able to get a print. But once I break this glass, it's broken. The morgue isn't going to be responsible for putting this thing back together."

Emilia packed up the enamel box and letters in the cooler, leaving the relic with Prade, and tucked the Salva Diablo gang member's bag of clothes under her arm.

Prade walked her to the exit. "I'm not sure if you've heard," he said. "But we've just gotten approval to do a beta version of the victim identification website. It won't be an open website, the way we initially wanted, but a site that requires a login and profile before a user can look through the pictures."

Emilia stopped walking. "But even a limited site is good news," she exclaimed. "I mean, it's a start, right?"

"We'll start with the most recent unidentifieds from the morgue," Prade went on. "Unless you have something else about his identity, we can include the Salva Diablo."

"Might help us get a lead on the case," Emilia agreed.

"I'll let you know when the site is up. Shouldn't be long."

"What about expanding beyond the bodies in the morgue?" Emilia asked, thinking of Lila Jimenez Lata. "Any chance we could include photos of missing people from the local area? Instead of relying on posters outside the mortuary when the bodies get sent there?"

"One step at a time, Emilia," Prade admonished her, with a shake of his head at her impatience.

"That's the problem," Emilia said. "We take one step at a time. And the cartels take two."

☼

Flores was waiting by the Suburban. Emilia beeped open the locks and slid behind the wheel. Her watch said 11:00 am. For the second time in two weeks she smelled bad.

"Sorry I walked out," Flores said.

"You lose your breakfast back there?"

"Yes, but I found the men's room first so I'm calling it even."

She looked at Flores, surprised that he was managing to keep a sense of humor. "A cop's first body is always bad," she said. "And this one was missing half his head. Always adds a certain something to the experience."

"I was ready for the body," Flores said. "Not a finger belonging to Padre Pro."

"It might not be his," Emilia warned as she started the engine. "Nobody thinks so."

"It would be wonderful if it was, wouldn't it?" Flores said.

Emilia blinked. Flores was the first person who'd echoed her own thoughts. "Padre Pro is a saint," she said. "Or will be one day. Yes, I'd like to think I'd once been that close to him."

"Could you not tell Silvio I got sick in the morgue?" Flores asked as he buckled his seatbelt.

"Sure." Emilia headed for the gate enclosing the morgue lot. "We'll keep it between the two of us for now."

"It's not that I'm scared of him or anything," Flores said.

Emilia showed her identification, the gate rolled open and she drove over the forward-facing spikes. Once out of the lot she turned right and headed for the docks.

"Silvio's a hell of a detective," she said. "You'll be learning from the best. Just don't confuse his manners with his brains, okay?"

"Okay." Flores nodded.

"The next couple of weeks are going to be tough, like drinking from a water cannon," Emilia went on. "Lose the suit and wear shoes you can walk in all day."

"I really appreciate your advice, Detective Cruz," Flores said.

"Sure," Emilia said. "Call me Emilia."

Flores grinned. He was really quite good-looking, with his curly hair and big eyes, in a soft young pup kind of way. "I'd like that, Emilia. And I'm Orlando."

"This is a tough job, Orlando," Emilia warned.

"I always knew I was going to be a cop," he replied, taking out his headphones and music player.

"Why the degree in music?" *And why didn't you take any notes this morning?* Emilia slowed the car; the midday traffic was heavy.

"Music is my life," Flores said. He thrust the headphones at her, like a toddler excited to share a toy. "Here. It's Bach's Toccata and Fugue in D minor."

"Maybe later," Emilia said. *Or never.* "I'm driving."

Silvio was going to eat this kid for lunch.

Two hours later, Emilia was alone in the small office of Irma Gonzalez Perot, regional head of Human Resources for the federal Department of Customs, known as Aduanas. Irma was a small, fine-boned woman with wavy blown hair and a severe business suit who'd said, yes, the secretary had remembered the call from Detective Franco Silvio. Irma hoped to be able to help.

The woman had consulted her computer, then excused herself after taking a phone call. Something in the way the woman's back stiffened during the call made Emilia fairly sure that it had been Irma's boss.

Emilia did a few arm stretches as she sat in an upholstered chair by Irma's desk. It was nice to have a few minutes to herself and let her thoughts slow down. Silvio and a uniformed team had finished the cursory search of the ship, and as expected, had found nothing. The K-9 team was on its way from the airport. Silvio said he'd even babysit Flores for a chance to see the look on Bonilla's face when the dogs tracked the scent of Ora Ciega back to the man's cabin.

Irma's office was impressive, with a blonde wood desk, four blue and green print upholstered chairs around a matching blonde wood table, and a large window framed in slubbed silk blue draperies. Two Frida Kahlo framed prints on the wall by the door and a blonde wood credenza laden with framed pictures of what Emilia assumed were Irma's family completed the decor. The centerpiece of the credenza tableau was a posed family portrait of Irma, a fairly good-looking man who was evidently her husband, and a little boy of about four or five. Several other pictures were of the boy wearing a school uniform complete with navy shorts and matching blazer.

Above the wall were Irma's college diploma and several certificates she'd earned from the Customs service. Irma had done well, they all suggested, their crests and bolded script proclaiming her proficiency in team building, mediation skills, and human resource dynamics.

Emilia's phone chirped. She dug it out of her shoulder bag to see a text from Kurt. *Hi.*

One little word. It braced Emilia like a fresh latte. *Hi,* she typed back.

Kurt replied a second later. *Sorry we argued* :(

Irma bustled back into the office with a folder in her hands.

Emilia shoved the phone back in her bag as the human resources executive sat behind her desk, leaving the office door open. "I'm sorry about that, Detective. We've had a systems crash. We're so dependent on technology these days that everyone goes crazy when there's a problem."

"Of course," Emilia said. "I realize how busy you must be. If you could print out that duty roster, I'll get out of your hair."

Irma had small hands, half the size of Emilia's, and they skittered over the computer keyboard to the accompaniment of clicking keys. "That's the problem. I can't access the information."

"I can wait."

Irma stopped typing and met Emilia's eyes. "We're going to need a systems administrator to look into the problem," she said. She seemed nervous, but it was an honest emotion, as if the problem was far bigger than Emilia's request. "The whole database has crashed. I don't know how long it's going to take. The whole back end is magic to me."

"Bad timing," Emilia said with a rueful smile.

"I'm so sorry," Irma apologized. "If you'll give me your number I'll call when we're back online."

Emilia dug out one of her cards. To preserve a detective's much-needed anonymity, it was only printed with her cell phone number. She wrote in her first name with a pen. "I really appreciate your help," she said.

"Hopefully, this is only a matter of a few hours," Irma said.

Chapter 6

Emilia navigated around the downtown tourist crowds by swinging west from the bay. It was high season in Acapulco, although the crush of wandering tourists, buses, and cars would be worse in a few weeks, when the *norteamericano* college crowd came down for spring break. She bulled her way through the messy intersection where Jose Valdez Arevalo and Calle 5 de Mayo collided with La Noria and Xochitl, and finally turned south on La Costura.

Playa Dominguillo was on her left, a stretch of the bay's shoreline that for her was the real Acapulco. It wasn't the best swimming beach; there were too many rocks. Instead, it was a good place to fish from a small boat. Several skiffs bobbed out in the bay like white birds skimming on dark blue water. More boats were pulled up on the pebbly beach. Their traditional turquoise painted interiors were a sudden reminder of the door at Villa de Refugio.

But everything was dwarfed by the sight of the *Pacific Grandeur* berthed at the city docks. Once again Emilia was struck by the sheer size of the thing. The ship could swallow up entire neighborhoods, houses, schools, streets and all. Cruise ships had been coming to Acapulco for as long as she could remember, and as their size grew, so did the feeling that soon they wouldn't fit into the bay at all. Someday, a ship would be so big that it would get stuck like a cork in the neck of a bottle between Isla la Roqueta on the west side, and Punta Bruja on the east. Its bottom would batter the ocean floor and the iconic white skyscrapers that ringed the bay would be swept away in a tsunami.

It was a foolish thought and Emilia grinned to herself. It had been a fairly good day so far, what with Prade's news about the trial website and Irma Gonzalez Perot's helpful attitude. She wasn't sure what to think about Flores, however.

The Costera curved to the west, slicing between the small Parque de la Reina on her left and the massive walls of the ancient Fuerte de San Diego on her right. The *Pacific Grandeur* loomed ahead.

But it wasn't until Emilia parked the car in the lot next to the docks that she realized what was wrong with the scene in front of her.

The big hatch of the cruise ship was open and five trucks from a company called Fiesta Verde were parked in the loading zone. A steady stream of crew appeared to be offloading pallets of supplies from the trucks and trundling it aboard using hand trucks. And that meant that someone had taken down the crime scene tape closing off the kitchen supply deck.

She found Silvio and Flores next to the trucks. Flores was sitting on a bench, headphones on. He gave her a little wave.

Silvio was pacing, phone in hand.

"What's going on?" Emilia asked with a nod at the purposeful activity surrounding the trucks and the ship.

"Exactly what you think is going on." Silvio was livid. He shook his phone in her face. "The fucking food trucks arrived an hour ago. The ship's crew had already taken down the crime scene tape and disinfected the entire deck by the time I got inside. I called for backup, got nothing. Too late to do anything about it now."

"What about the dogs?"

"We've been waiting for the dogs since you left. Now the delay is because of the fucking Olympic people. They're at the airport and the dogs are on fucking parade for them."

"Wait a minute." Emilia felt her blood pressure match his. "No dogs? Nobody came? Did you tell Loyola about the Ora Ciega?"

"I talked to Loyola." Disgust was evident in every word Silvio spat out. "Didn't want me to do anything to get in the ship's way. Said to let the loading go on. Like he thought I was going to start shooting dock workers."

"That's all he said?" Although it wasn't inconceivable that Silvio would have done just that.

"Loyola said he'd call the K-9 unit, the uniformed dispatch office, and Chief Salazar's office. He called me back ten minutes ago. Get this. Chief Salazar and every one of his toadies are at the fucking airport with the mayor and the fucking Olympics. And the fucking dogs!"

"*Madre de Dios*." Emilia got out her phone but there was no one else to call.

"Bonilla's in there laughing," Silvio went on angrily. "Watching me and the music man here do jack shit about them taking down the tape."

It was noisy by the trucks, what with the continual rumble of hand trucks being wheeled down the gangplanks, crew shouting directions to each other, trucks driving in and out of the loading area, and the cries of gulls and pelicans sensing easy pickings around the food. Emilia pulled Silvio over to the fence around the parking lot. "Did you talk to Bonilla or Ramos? They say anything?"

"I had a five minute conversation with Ramos earlier. Told him that we'd be coming on board with a K-9 unit," Silvio said. "Didn't say anything about drugs but my guess is that he knows. Wouldn't make eye contact after that."

"What about Bonilla?"

"Nice conversation about the delivery. Said what he said yesterday. The cruise line has contracts with Acapulco vendors that can't be broken. The ship will be leaving tomorrow."

Silvio's phone rang and he punched open the connection. The conversation was brief. He hung up and nodded at Emilia. "Finally. Two dog teams on their way."

Afternoon stretched into evening. The Fiesta Verde trucks departed and a dairy delivered gallons of milk and ice cream. Both Silvio and Emilia worked their phones, getting a mix of assurances and notices of delays in regard to uniformed backup and the dog units. Flores strolled around the parking lot, listening to whatever the hell a Toccata and Fugue in D minor was.

At 8:00 pm, as Emilia was seriously worried that Silvio was going to have a stroke, three men in white waistcoats and black pants proceeded down the Pacific Grandeur's gangplank. They each carried a tray topped with a silver lid.

"What the fuck is this?" Silvio muttered as the three waiters came directly toward them.

"Compliments of Mr. Bonilla," one of the waiters said in English. The trays were carefully deposited on a bench and the three men headed back to the ship.

Flores lifted one of the lids to reveal filet mignon, a lobster tail, and an assortment of roasted vegetables. "Wow, look at this--."

Silvio wrenched the lid out of the younger man's hand. "Don't you fucking touch that food, boy," he said furiously.

"What's the matter?" Flores asked in amazement.

"Bonilla is a fucking murder suspect," Silvio thundered.

"But I'm hungry," Flores said.

Emilia stepped between them. "You never accept gifts from a suspect," she said to Flores, knowing full well that Silvio would have swallowed that steak in two bites if the food hadn't been a such obvious attempt at mockery by Bonilla. "Doesn't matter if you're hungry or not."

Her phone beeped with a text and she got Silvio's attention. They moved away from Flores but Emilia's heart sank as she read the screen. The dog units weren't coming after all. According to the union, they had already worked more than the allowable number of hours per day for dogs and handlers.

"I think we're screwed for today, Franco," she said. "Well and truly screwed. We can try for the dogs again tomorrow."

"No, tomorrow morning bright and early, we question both Bonilla and Ramos at the station," Silvio said. "We'll get some uniforms here to bring them in. Put them each in a separate room and act like we know all about their Ora Ciega smuggling ring."

"Look, I like the strategy," Emilia said. "But all we've got to go on is some bad smack in a no-name dead guy's pocket."

"Maybe," Silvio said. "Maybe the guy strolled onto the ship looking to get lucky. Maybe he was fucking lost and wearing a friend's jacket. But it fits together too well. I say we use everything we've got to build a story. Crank up the pressure on Bonilla and Ramos, accuse them of dealing. See who cracks first."

Emilia nodded. "Okay. Maybe if we have them in for questioning, Loyola will go up the chain and ask to hold the ship. Maybe we can keep it here another day. Or at least detain Bonilla and Ramos, not let them depart with the ship."

"I like it. Let's get the fuck out of here." Silvio marched back to the bench, tossed aside all of the food lids, grabbed Flores by the arm, and marched the younger man to the car.

Within seconds, the benches were blotted out by a storm of screaming gulls tearing at the food and each other.

Chapter 7

As the detectives assembled for the morning meeting on Wednesday, Emilia realized that Flores was dressed exactly like Silvio. The newest detective was clad in faded jeans, a white tee shirt, a short brown leather motorcycle jacket, and scuffed work boots.

A titter started in the back and ran around the squadroom as Loyola came out of the lieutenant's office. That's when Silvio noticed Flores. Emilia watched her partner's face slowly redden as he pretended to drink his coffee.

The week had picked up pace, with the discovery of three bodies in a house in the hilly Colonia Libertad, the deliberate sabotage of a water main in Colonia San Miguel up in the northwest, and the death of a squadroom alumni who'd gone to work in Internal Affairs before Emilia had become a detective. Apart from the late detective, who'd severed all ties when he transferred, no one in the squadroom knew who worked in the shadowy Internal Affairs unit, which was routinely referred to as Alma. No one knew how it had gotten the nickname, which meant *soul*. The joke was that once a cop came under the scrutiny of Internal Affairs, their soul was as good as lost.

A couple of robberies rounded out the day's new assignments. Briefings on existing cases were brisk. Silvio reported the previous day's utter failure and Loyola nodded mournfully, reminding Emilia uncomfortably of Ernesto Cruz at home. Loyola promised to lodge a protest about the canine unit with Chief Salazar's office, which they all knew would be a feckless exercise given that the chief himself had been at the airport with the dogs and the departing Olympic committee. Silvio went on to say that a couple of uniforms had already brought in their two chief suspects for questioning. Loyola nodded his agreement.

When the meeting broke up Emilia showed Flores how to resume his intranet training. Once he understood the process, she gathered up the recently augmented *Pacific Grandeur* murder file. Silvio joined her and they headed for the new interrogation rooms on the other side of the station.

"Looks like you've got a Mini Me, Franco," Emilia said as they passed the holding cells. She shot the guard with her thumb and forefinger and she shot her back.

"I blame you," Silvio sputtered. "What the fuck did you say to him?"

"I told him to lose the suit." Emilia grinned. "Take it as a compliment."

"He calls me Franco and I'll beat the shit out of him," Silvio warned.

Each of the new interrogation rooms had an audio feed, one way mirrors, a single table, and three chairs, plus cameras in the ceiling and a hidden squawk button in case a cop needed emergency help. There was a narrow anteroom outside where watchers could hear the audio and watch the interrogations. Space age techniques compared to the solid cinderblock walls of the grubby interrogation cells down the hall from the squadroom, although from personal experience Emilia knew those vastly more private rooms had their uses, too.

Bonilla was in one interrogation room, Ramos in the other. Both men were seated. Ramos was jiggling his knee up and down. Bonilla's arms were folded and his eyes were closed.

"Is he asleep?" Emilia asked the cop by the viewing window into Bonilla's room. He was a young uniform named Calles.

Calles shook his head. "Asked for some coffee. Wants his cell phone and keys back, too."

Silvio snorted. "Ramos?"

"Hasn't said a word."

Emilia checked her watch. Both men had been stewing in their separate rooms for almost an hour by now. "Anything from the tech team yet?" she asked. Bonilla's cell phone had been turned over to the small technical unit with orders to trace any questionable numbers. Ramos had been smart enough not to bring a cell phone.

Calles shook his head. "Not yet."

"I saw we start now, anyway," Emilia said.

"You ready?" Silvio asked. "Thirty minutes. Wind him up, see what we get."

"I'm ready," Emilia said.

She flounced into the room where Ramos sat impatiently, the thick file under her arm. Most of the content was paper from the recycling bin by the copier in the squadroom, but some useful pages had been lifted out of the squadroom's collection of cold cases.

Ramos looked up as she closed the door, slapped the heavy file onto the table, and sat across from him. "Good morning, Señor Ramos," she said. "If you recall, we met Monday morning. I'm Detective Cruz Encinos."

"Yes," Ramos said with an annoyed spin on the word. "You took my statement. I really have nothing to add."

"Some new evidence has come to our attention since Monday," Emilia said.

"I don't see how that's possible," Ramos said dismissively. "Your investigation technique appears to be limited to sitting on a bench staring at cruise ships."

Emilia gave him a brief, pained smile, and turned her attention to the thick file on the table. She opened it, ran her finger down the page, flipped it over, studied the next page. As the silence thickened in the room, Emilia could hear a rubbery pinging from Ramos's shoe as it vibrated on the floor.

"Señor Ramos," Emilia said in a bored voice. "Were you aware that the murder victim found aboard the *Pacific Grandeur* was a Honduran gang member?"

"As I said on Monday," Ramos said. "I know nothing about him."

"Were you aware that this Honduran national was engaged in smuggling a relatively rare form of Colombian heroin known as Ora Ciega?"

"As I said," Ramos repeated forcefully. "I never saw him before."

"How long have you known Señor Bonilla?"

Ramos looked startled at the unexpected tack.

"First cruise together?" Emilia asked. "Third? Fourth?"

"You can check with Noble Pacific Cruise Lines," Ramos said. "If that's relevant to your case, which I doubt it is."

"Ahh." Emilia nodded her understanding. She flipped through a few more pages of the file. She made a note in the margin. "Although if you and Señor Bonilla were business partners, that would be a factor."

"I'm head of security on the *Pacific Grandeur*, Detective," Ramos said testily. "I'm not selling the tickets."

Emilia suddenly slammed the file closed. "Frankly, given your position, it's surprising that you would be unaware that your shipmate Hector Bonilla has been smuggling Ora Ciega aboard the *Pacific Grandeur*."

Ramos stilled his knee. "You have no proof of any such thing," he said.

"What are your qualifications for your position, Señor Ramos?" Emilia asked softly. "Did Señor Bonilla hire you for your position? Perhaps he needed another Spanish speaker in a position of authority for these specific cruises?"

Ramos didn't answer. The rubber pinging of his shoe was audible.

Emilia opened the file again with exaggerated effort and found a large glossy photograph of a .22 Ruger automatic handgun. A case file number was printed on the photo. She turned the picture and shoved it in front of Ramos. "Did you ever see this gun in Señor Bonilla's possession?"

Ramos's mouth twitched but he didn't speak.

Emilia rapped sharply on the table. "Señor Ramos. I asked you a question. Have you ever seen this weapon in Señor Bonilla's possession?"

Ramos looked sick. "Am I under arrest?"

"Perhaps you are unfamiliar with Mexico's legal system, Señor Ramos." Emilia stared at him. "An arrest isn't necessary to hold a suspect. I'm sure you'd greatly prefer to answer the question."

"I'd like to call the American Embassy in Mexico City," Ramos said. "I'm an American citizen."

There was a tap at the door. Emilia gathered up the file and walked out.

Silvio was in the anteroom. He thrust a printout at her. "Bonilla made two calls Monday morning at about 1:00 am. First was less than a minute. Second was seven minutes. Tech unit tried to trace the number. It was a throwaway cell."

"Fits the time of death exactly," Emilia said. "I can't believe he actually brought the phone with him."

"Like I said. A couple of amateurs."

Emilia tucked the printout into the file. "Bonilla obviously has a partner here in Mexico."

"Not in this smuggling game alone," Silvio said.

"What do you think about Ramos?" Emilia asked.

"He's scared," Silvio said. "Asking for the *norteamericanos* like a kid who wants to run home to his mother. Doesn't want to rat on Bonilla, but doesn't want to stick around either."

"The picture of the gun really rattled him," Emilia said. Using the picture of a weapon from an old case had been Silvio's idea and it had worked. "He's in there now thinking we scraped it up from the water around the ship."

"Let's let him stew a bit more," Silvio said. "Sit there and panic all by himself."

"Okay." Emilia handed Silvio the thick file. "Good cop, bad cop," she said. "I'll go get him a cup of coffee."

"Well," Bonilla drawled. "*Los Dos Chiflados.* Aren't you missing one?"

If nothing else, Emilia had to admire the man's nerve. He'd been sitting alone for 90 minutes in a police interrogation room in a foreign country, yet was cracking Three Stooges jokes with the confidence of a seasoned comic.

"Your coffee," Emilia said and handed him a paper cup.

"To your health." Bonilla took off the lid and blew on the hot beverage.

"Glad you're in a good mood, Bonilla," Silvio dropped the thick file on the table with a thud. "This could take awhile."

Bonilla saluted Silvio with the coffee cup. "Sorry you

didn't enjoy your dinner last night," he said. "Probably don't get top grade surf and turf very often on a cop's salary, do you?"

Silvio's only reaction was the tiny pulse of a muscle in his jaw. "Let's review the events of Sunday evening after the *Pacific Grandeur* docked here in Acapulco."

Emilia sat back to watch the show. Silvio was good as he led Bonilla down one line of questioning, then abruptly changed to another, waiting for Bonilla to stumble. But the ship's purser stuck to his story while peppering his responses with snide comments about low police salaries and poor quality coffee.

"So you were busy with duties related to the ship's arrival until 10:00 pm that evening," Silvio went back over the story again. "And were unaware that an intruder had boarded the ship and been murdered until the following morning."

"Again, yes." Bonilla sipped at his cup.

"Were you aware that the murder victim found aboard the Pacific Grandeur was a Honduran gang member?"

Bonilla clicked his tongue. "Gang member. Dangerous occupation."

"Were you aware that this Honduran national was engaged in smuggling a relatively rare form of Colombian heroin known as Ora Ciega?"

"Didn't know him," Bonilla said. He put the now-empty paper cup on the table and slouched in his chair. "If he hadn't decided to find himself dead on my ship, I'd be on the beach enjoying a couple of cold *cervezas* and a little Mexican *chiquita* right now."

"With money from Ora Ciega," Silvio said. "You, Ramos, and the Hondurans were bringing Ora Ciega on board. But as happens to so many partnerships in the drug business, you had an altercation."

Bonilla pinched his fingertips together to form a talking hand. "Great imagination. Just like television."

Emilia had to sit on her own hands before she punched him in the head. She knew that the only thing keeping Silvio from throwing Bonilla around like a wet sock was the fact that the interrogation was being heard and watched. The old rooms were better, she decided. Confessions came much more quickly.

Silvio took out the cold case file picture of the handgun and turned it to face Bonilla. "Your shipmate Edgar Ramos indicated that this weapon belongs to you."

Bonilla shrugged. "He's mistaken."

"How could that be?"

Emilia admired Silvio's restraint as Bonilla shrugged. "Low blood sugar. We're Americans. We need to eat at regular intervals. Not like you Mex. Go for days without eating to cross our border and get to the land of plenty."

Silvio took the picture back. "This is the weapon used to kill the Salva Diablo gang member aboard your ship."

"How clever of you to find it." Bonilla leaned over the table, his face close to Silvio's. "Tell me, Detective Silvio. How much money do you make a month? Two hundred? Three hundred dollars? Got something going on the side? I hear all cops in Mexico do."

Emilia had run into murderers with iron guts before. They either were sick enough to rationalize away their crime or they were convinced something—or someone—protected them. Bonilla seemed to be a little of each.

"Who did you call early Monday morning?" Silvio asked, without moving. "About 1:00 am. Right after the gang member was shot on your ship."

Bonilla settled back into his seat. "My girlfriend."

"Why so late?"

"Time difference," Bonilla said. "She's in New York."

"You called a Mexican cell phone," Silvio said.

"Hey." Bonilla's condescension showed its first crack. He'd made a mistake and he knew it. "You've had my cell phone for two hours now. Probably loaded it with all sorts of fake data."

"A call for help?" Emilia took over, her voice loaded with sympathy. "The Salva Diablo was a troublemaker, wasn't he? Got himself aboard ship and confronted you. Probably had a gun, too, didn't he?"

Bonilla didn't answer.

"It was him or you, wasn't it?"

Bonilla stared at her.

"It was him or you," Emilia repeated. "The whole thing was supposed to be smooth as glass. Load up the Ora Ciega in Acapulco. Sit on it until the ship docked in Miami. But he showed up."

Bonilla folded his arms. "Go on."

"It went down all wrong," Emilia continued. He was on the brink, rattled by the phone call blunder, and all she had to do was guide him to the right offer. "You panicked. Anyone would. This wasn't supposed to happen but you were prepared, weren't you? Had a contact number but he said to take care of your own mess. You managed to dump both guns overboard but couldn't get the body out. Ship buttoned up too tight. So you hid it in the freezer."

"Unless I confess, you can't prove anything," Bonilla said.

"Don't care about proving it," Silvio said, sliding in behind Emilia's narrative and going for the sting. "You're right about shitty cop salaries. That's why we want to know where the Ora Ciega is."

"Now I get it," Bonilla said. "A trade. You take the Ora Ciega and I walk away from a murder charge."

There was a tap on the door. Before either Silvio or Emilia could rise, the door opened and Loyola, Ibarra, and Flores walked in. Loyola was carrying one of the plastic trays they used in the holding area for the contents of suspects' pockets. It held Bonilla's cell phone, wallet, and keys.

"Señor Bonilla, you're free to go," Loyola said. "We're sorry if you've been inconvenienced in any way. The uniformed officer will escort you and Señor Ramos back to the *Pacific Grandeur*."

Bonilla's mask of condescension was back. He pulled out a wad of dollar bills from the wallet and dropped a handful on the table. "Glad to know I was right about shitty cop salaries," he said mockingly. "Get yourselves some decent coffee, Detectives."

No one spoke a word as Calles led Bonilla and Ramos out

of the interrogation area.

The next few minutes were like the aftermath of a nuclear explosion; oxygen fled the room, the silence was shattering, a vacuum rose, and Emilia found herself holding her breath.

Suddenly the mushroom cloud, in the form of Silvio's wrath, billowed out, encompassing everyone and everything. Loyola fought back, Ibarra defended the acting lieutenant, Flores looked scared, and the room turned into a sea of red anger.

Emilia pushed herself past the argument, stepped into the anteroom, and switched off the audio. The argument had come through loud and clear and a small crowd composed of uniforms from the holding cells, the secretaries from the Records department, and the sergeants who manned the dispatch desk had materialized. Emilia shot them all with her thumb and forefinger, then jammed her hand on the button which caused the one-way glass to shimmer into an opaque screen, effectively ending the day's entertainment.

She went back into the interrogation room and slammed the door. The almost visible buffet of air made each of the four men swivel their heads toward her. "Okay," she exclaimed. "We were this close to getting him to admit to the murder. Two more minutes. There better be a good reason for why you let him go. Like he's going to lead us to the biggest fucking dealer in Acapulco."

"Hold the bitch act, Cruz." Loyola held up a hand. "Orders from on high. The case has been transferred to Organized Crime because of the Salva Diablo tie-in."

"Where the hell is Organized Crime?" Silvio raged. "Cruz is right. Two more minutes and it would have all been on tape."

"We'll send a copy of the audio over to Perez," Loyola said, naming the unit's liaison officer. Organized Crime worked the major narcotics cases with deep undercover operations. "If they think they have a confession, they'll run with it."

"And if they don't, what happens?" Emilia cut in. She checked her watch. "The ship leaves in a couple of hours--."

"With a couple of killers on board." Silvio finished.

Loyola yanked open the door. "Organized Crime wanted the case. Fine, they're welcome to it."

"This can't keep going on." Silvio grabbed Loyola by the shoulder and spun him around. "Every other police unit in this city is scraping its boots on you."

"Take the rest of the day off, Silvio," Loyola snarled. "That's an order."

Silvio shoved Loyola aside and stormed out of the room. Loyola and Ibarra looked at each other and moved off.

Emilia pocketed the dollar bills scattered over the table. Flores followed her out.

With Flores in tow, Emilia found Silvio leaning against his car at the dock parking lot at 3:00 pm as the *Pacific Grandeur* slipped away from her berth at the docks. The white monolith began a slow glide that would take it around the tip of the peninsula that pointed like the thumb of a left hand into the mouth of the bay. Beachgoers on the east side of the thumb would see it pass Punta Grifo and leave Acapulco behind as it met the crystal waters of the Pacific past Isla la Roqueta.

The decks of the ship were lined with passengers. Some jazzy music played and a throng on shore waved frantically. Sail boats bobbed in its wake as the ship churned through the bay. The *Pacific Grandeur's* horn blew twice, long brays that delighted the crowd on the dock.

Emilia had to admit that it was a majestic sight. An entire floating city, dazzling white in the afternoon sunshine, with every luxury conceivable for its citizens. Two weeks of purposeless playing, eating, and drinking.

She'd be *loco*.

Silvio showed his badge to the guard at the gate and walked to the loading zone by the ship's now empty berth. Emilia followed suit with Flores. The three detectives watched without speaking until the ship rounded Punta Grifo and passed out of sight.

"This isn't over," Silvio said.

"You're mad because that *pendejo* was right." Emilia stood next to him.

Flores looked uncomfortable. He slipped on his headphones and stepped away.

Emilia stared at the water rippling across the bay. "No cop makes enough to put up with the kind of shit we do."

Maybe Bonilla was guessing, but he'd come close to the truth when he'd mocked their salaries. Emilia had made 3000 pesos a month as a uniform and she made just over double that as a detective.

"You take the cash he threw down?" Silvio asked. "How much was it?"

"I bought Flores a cup of coffee," Emilia said.

Silvio snorted. "Organized Crime only wanted the case because of the status thing," he said. "Must think Salva Diablo's the new player in town."

"Yet they let Bonilla and Ramos go."

"They don't care who killed the damn kid." Silvio looked at her as if she was stupid. "Adding Salva Diablo to their hunt list makes them look good to Chief Salazar."

"So Bonilla sails off because Mexican cops are too incompetent and busy fighting each other to catch him." Emilia slumped onto the same bench where they'd roosted the previous day. Flores wandered along the waterfront, headphones on, head bobbing.

"You're not giving up on me, Cruz?" Silvio jammed one foot on the seat of the bench next to her knee. Gulls wheeled through the air behind him.

Emilia squinted up at him. "What are you talking about?"

"We're going to nail Bonilla," Silvio said. "Either get an extradition order from *El Norte* or arrest him when the ship comes through next time."

"You mean stay on the case?" Emilia asked in surprise. "What if we bump into Organized Crime? Loyola will have a stroke."

"Loyola doesn't have to know."

Emilia stared at the bay; at the sailboats tacking with the

breeze and the dots on the far eastern side that were colored beach. Over the past six months, she'd come to respect Silvio as a good detective, probably the best in Acapulco, but she'd never completely stopped fearing him.

Silvio wasn't simply trying to catch a murderer. No, he was testing her loyalty. Testing her as a partner. He'd probably done that with Garcia, too, the partner who'd gotten himself killed a few years before Emilia became a detective.

If she passed the test this time, there would be another one. With higher stakes. How long would it take before she completely threw away her integrity?

Yet, trust was in short supply among cops these days. No one knew who was being paid to look the other way, who was being blackmailed, or who was willing to betray a fellow cop in return for cartel cash. Acapulco lost a handful of cops every year, betrayed to the cartels for irresistible sums of money. Nothing was airtight. Drug money bought loyalty and information. Holes through which blood poured through like water.

Franco Silvio and her cousin Alvaro Cruz were the only other cops Emilia truly trusted.

"I'll check again with Prade tomorrow," she said. "Make sure the Salva Diablo mug shot gets on his website of unidentified. Follow up with Customs to get that roster of who was working here."

Silvio nodded and she had the impression he'd let his breath out. "I'll ask around here again tonight," he said. "Vendors, hookers, the usual types. Somebody must have seen the guy lurking around."

"What about Flores?" Emilia asked.

"He'll do whatever we tell him to do."

Flores came toward them, as if he'd heard his name. "Are we done here?" he asked. "Just talking doesn't seem like detective work to me."

With a hand as fast as a knockout punch, Silvio snatched off the younger man's headphones and palmed the music player as it dangled at the end of the cord. He wadded the equipment into a ball and sent it flying out into the bay. The shiny little music player spiraled away from the headphones, bounced on a wave, and then everything was swallowed by the water.

Flores blanched and emitted a little shriek before turning to Silvio. "Are you going to pay for that?" Face-to-face and dressed alike, Flores was Silvio's slender and upset twin.

"You want to be a cop, kid," Silvio growled. He shoved Flores in the chest. "You start paying attention to what is going on around you. You're not on holiday. You're not a tourist. You're a cop and that means somebody is trying to kill you. Every fucking day." He stepped closer and Flores struggled not to move. "So you either start paying attention or you can sit in the fucking office all day long. Cruz and I aren't going to be collateral damage because you did something stupid and got yourself dead. As for real detective work, I'll let you know when you're doing real work or not."

Silvio pointed at Emilia, turned it into a sort of salute, and left.

"He hit me," Flores said dazedly when they were back in the Suburban. "He actually hit me."

"He gave you a shove, Orlando." Emilia watched the setting sun blaze itself into streaks of pink and gold. She had an overwhelming urge to go to the Palacio Réal instead of the little house where Sophia would ask her how school had been and Ernesto would occupy the television all night. At the hotel she'd curl up next to Kurt, sleep without dreaming, and tomorrow be ready to be a cop again.

"It was to make a point," she went on. "He's right. You need to start paying attention. This isn't a game. And lose the white tee shirt. Silvio has that market cornered."

Flores stared out the passenger side window and for a horrible moment Emilia wondered if he was going to cry.

"Look," she said hastily. "You heard Loyola say that Organized Crime was going to take the *Pacific Grandeur* murder case. That's fine and all. We'll wrap up our end before we turn it over. You know, tie up loose ends."

"Okay," Flores said to the window. "I understand."

"Loyola might not see it that way," Emilia pressed. "I'd

appreciate if you didn't talk about it in the squadroom."

Flores turned back to her. "Are you asking me to lie for you, Emilia?"

Emilia hesitated. "I'm asking for some discretion, Orlando."

"Because I would," Flores said. "Lie for you. If you needed me to."

The strange scene at the docks played itself over and over in Emilia's mind as she lay in her narrow bed, listening to the creak of mattress springs coming from her mother's room. Ernesto had gradually moved from the sofa into her mother's bed. Emilia wasn't even sure when he'd stopped being the man Sophia had found wandering in the market and when he'd slid into the role of husband. Sophia's insistence that he was Emilia's father helped blur the line.

Silvio had asked Emilia to help him nail Bonilla for the murder of the Salva Diablo gang member aboard the *Pacific Grandeur*, despite the fact that Loyola had given the case to Organized Crime. Emilia, in turn, had asked Flores not to talk about it. Yet somehow the conversation had ended with a declaration of loyalty. Flores would lie for her, he'd said. Maybe he'd seen too many *norteamericano* cop shows and was too immature to know the difference between television and real life. Or maybe he assumed that's what partners did for each other.

But they weren't partners. Her partner was still Silvio.

Emilia turned on her side, trying to get comfortable. She never realized how hard her mattress was until she started sleeping at the Palacio Réal on the weekends. As sleep blotted out the day, Emilia realized that she hadn't talked to Kurt since Monday morning.

Chapter 8

"What's going on?" Emilia asked Prade as they walked down the hall. The morgue was full of uniforms, or so it seemed.

"We're missing a body," the medical examiner replied.

"You mean you lost one?" Flores asked, making no effort to hide the surprise in his voice.

Prade didn't answer as he led them past the main holding room and into his office. It wasn't large, and made to feel even smaller by the teetering stacks of file folders and x-ray envelopes rising up from the cluttered desk. Books on anatomy, surgical techniques, and trauma procedures were jumbled together next to the computer, on top of a filing cabinet, arrayed over the seat of the single visitor's chair, and towered precariously against the wall by the door. A folder was open in the center of the desk, with pictures of a website. Emilia leaned closer. The pictures were mockups for the website with pictures of the unidentified.

"Your case, as a matter of fact," Prade said. "The victim from Honduras, if I remember correctly. With the boxing tattoo."

"That's not our case anymore," Flores announced. He smiled proudly at Emilia.

"Our night guard saw nothing," Prade continued. He sat behind the desk. "The staff on duty saw nothing, of course. But the back entrance was forced after the midnight shift change and one body is missing."

Emilia's thoughts reeled. Out of all the bodies to steal, why this one. Why now? Did it have anything to do with the ship leaving yesterday? For a wild moment she wondered if the body had been taken and put aboard the *Pacific Grandeur*, so that Bonilla could have his victim with him. But the ship sailed early, long before the morgue shift change.

Prade perched his reading glasses on his nose and looked up at Emilia standing by the desk. "Not your case?"

"Gang tattoo, remember," she said. "It's been reassigned to Organized Crime. You should let them know the body's gone missing."

"Perhaps they'd want the entire report," Prade remarked casually.

Emilia got his meaning. Organized Crime hadn't requested the report and probably had done nothing on the case. Of course, perhaps Loyola had sent it over himself. Either that or Silvio was right and Organized Crime only wanted the case to boost their hunt list and look good to Chief Salazar.

"Here we go." Prade opened a file and resettled his reading glasses. His lab coat bore the same stains from Monday. "Your finger couldn't have belonged to Padre Pro. It's a woman's forefinger from the right hand."

Emilia had never expected this. "A woman's finger? Are you sure?"

"Lots of DNA in that finger," Prade said. "All of it female."

"*Madre de Dios*," Emilia swore. She gave herself a second to mourn the loss of Padre Pro as reality sank in. They were dealing with a chopper after all.

The daughters of rich families were sometimes snatched up, victims of express kidnappings in which the kidnappers used the victim's own ATM cards to empty a bank account or called the family using the victim's phone to demand a ransom of a few thousand pesos that the family could pay relatively quickly. In those cases, the victim was invariably returned within a day or two, as soon as the kidnappers had the money, and were generally shaken but unharmed. It was the serious kidnappers, demanding millions of *norteamericano* dollars from families with large holdings, who chopped off body parts. Those victims tended to be male businessmen or politicians. But some female politicians were snatched as well.

Prade pulled on a fresh pair of disposable latex gloves, opened a small refrigerator, took out a stainless steel pan covered with a cloth, and set it on the desk. He pulled off the cloth to reveal the short brown stick that had once been attached to someone's hand.

Prade picked up the finger. He held it upside down so that Emilia and Flores could see the stump end; like a stiffened paper tube holding a loose collection of chicken bones and fibers. "It was severed from the hand with a snipping tool, probably something like a bolt cutter. Both sides are cut at the same angle and they broke the bone at the knuckle."

Flores coughed.

Prade grinned. "Still got a glass stomach, Detective?"

"I'll be all right," Flores said.

Emilia crossed her arms in front of herself, an unconscious defensive posture as if to protect herself from whatever evil had befallen the owner of the finger. "Was she alive when the finger was cut off?"

"I don't know," Prade said. "It hasn't been professionally preserved and there's significant decay."

"I'll take your best guess."

Prade probed the stump with the tweezers and Emilia's stomach did a flip.

"I'd say the woman was between 25 and 35 years old," Prade said. "Worked with her hands. The fingertips are calloused and the cuticle wasn't trimmed with any special care. No nail polish residue under the varnish. Not extreme callouses, but a definite thickening of the skin at the fingertips. Whoever she was, or is, she was accustomed to manual labor."

Emilia swallowed hard. Up close, without the distance that the glass box had created, the finger was too intimate, too immediately painful. She had seen many dead bodies, but severing a finger had a deliberateness about it that made Emilia sweat. "Can you tell how long since the finger was, uh, detached?"

"I'd put it at between two and three weeks ago," Prade said. "The varnish on top stopped some of the corruption."

He picked up a tweezers and started to pull back the skin. Flores coughed again.

"We don't have to see," Emilia said hastily. She got out her notebook and began rapidly writing a list. Flores could start making calls, as Loyola had suggested. Put him onto the files, too, now that he had intranet access. See if they could match this up with previous kidnapping cases; who else cut off fingers, used a bolt cutter, had religious affiliations. She and Silvio would go back to Villa de Refugio. He could vent some of his bad temper on the owner, find out where the relic had come from.

Prade put the finger back into the steel pan. "As I thought, it was mounted on a construction nail."

The remains of the display case, a wooden block covered in red velvet impaled by a nail as long as the finger, was amid the jumble of books on the floor. "This was hardly the way to treat a sainted relic," Prade observed, setting the block on the desk next to the pan. "Somebody simply shoved the finger onto the nail. There was enough loose skin for them to do it and not break any of the bones. They varnished the finger after it was mounted. Some of the varnish spilled onto the velvet."

"Any fingerprints?" Emilia asked.

"No," he said. "The varnish filled in too many of the ridges."

Emilia felt sweat trickle down her neck. The air in the office felt cloying and warm. "So basically we have the finger from a woman who did some sort of manual work, which was cut off her hand two or three weeks ago. It was mounted like a trophy, varnished, labelled as Padre Pro's finger, and sold in a very nice store with false documents saying it was a sainted relic."

Prade shrugged. "I'm sorry I can't give you more than that," he said. "More time and a better lab might get you something else. But you know more now than you did before."

"This is the strangest thing I've run into in twelve years as a cop," Emilia confessed. "Can you write up a formal report so that Loyola knows we're not kidding?"

"Of course," Prade said. "More importantly, can you take all this with you now?"

Emilia had a mental image of Castro and Gomez tossing the finger around the squadroom in a morbid game of monkey-in-the-middle. Flores, of course, in the middle. "I'll come back for it," she assured Prade.

"Bury it, pickle it, donate it to a church," Prade said. "Just make sure you pick it up this week. We don't have room for odds and ends."

He replaced it in the refrigerator, started to take off his latex gloves, then stopped. "Before you go, another one of your *perdidas* came in yesterday."

"*Perdidas*?" Flores asked.

"Unidentified women," Emilia said.

They followed Prade to the holding room where they'd viewed the Salva Diablo body. He consulted a clipboard, scanned the numbered drawers, and rolled one out. As the refrigerated unit released the section with a slight hiss, Emilia steeled herself. Too many of these nameless women in the morgue weren't a pretty sight. Generally they'd been raped, beaten, mutilated with a knife by some insane hand.

The drawer slid all the way open, the body was revealed. Emilia felt the shock like a blow to the back of her knees and she dropped her notebook. Without thinking she grabbed Flores's arm to steady herself.

Even with the gray skin of death and all makeup wiped away, Emilia recognized the woman's slightly Asian features, china doll haircut, and voluptuous figure. Except for the bruises, she looked exactly like the magazine photograph Emilia had of her, a relic of the hunt for missing teen Lila Jimenez Lata.

Yolanda Lata. Estranged mother. Professional hooker.

"Cause of death?" Emilia heard herself ask.

"Take your pick," Prade said and pointed out the recent needle tracks on the left arm. "Drug overdose or internal bleeding. She was badly beaten."

"Her name is Yolanda Lata," Emilia said.

"One of your missing?"

"Yes. When did she come in?" Sadness washed over Emilia as she let go of Flores and picked up her notebook. When Lila Jimenez Lata went missing, she'd been hunting for her mother Yolanda. Emilia had looked for Yolanda as well, as a possible lead to Lila, and had come up empty-handed. Emilia's last hope to find the teen had been a man who'd had a brief fling with Lila; he'd been murdered. It was hard to think that Yolanda must have been working the streets right here in Acapulco and that Emilia had missed her.

Prade consulted the toe tag. "Found dead on the street yesterday. Avenida Galeana. Beaten, robbed. Nothing on the body except a dress. Dead for 48 hours before she arrived here."

Emilia copied down the information on the tag, sick at heart. The woman had been dead in an alley for two days.

"Do you know if there's anyone to notify?" Prade asked. "Someone who'll claim the body?"

"She has a son," Emilia said. She'd met Yolanda's son once. He'd parted ways with his mother long ago and now had a new name and identity. "I'll notify him but I'm not sure he'll claim the body."

"If he won't, let us know and the city will take care of her," Prade said matter-of-factly. "There won't be a full autopsy, just the routine blood work and report. There's no time and we need the space."

Emilia opened her desk drawer and took out the thick binder of *Las Perdidas*. The squadroom was quiet. Silvio was probably eating a double order of fish tacos somewhere, Ibarra had grabbed his jacket and announced to his computer that he was out of cigarettes, and Flores had gone to find a vending machine. The other detectives were all out on cases. Loyola's door was closed.

She flipped to the report she'd written about Yolanda Lata. The woman had married Lila's father, bringing into the marriage a 10-year-old son from a previous relationship. When Lila's father died, Yolanda left with the son, but leaving her daughter in the care of Berta, the paternal grandmother. As Lila grew, Berta told her that Yolanda was dead. Yet somehow, Lila had connected with her half-brother, who periodically received money orders from their mother. When Lila ran away from Berta on her quest to find Yolanda, she'd had ample cash from those money orders. What little else

Emilia uncovered suggested that Lila had experimented with being a hooker, too. The girl was as striking as her mother and looked older than her 16 years. The brother had the same looks. Emilia copied down his contact information.

When she looked up, Flores was sitting quietly on the edge of her desk. He held out a cold can of cola. "Thought you could use this."

"Thanks," Emilia said gratefully. "I owe you."

She closed her eyes and drank, willing the caffeine and sugar to do their job quickly. Seeing Yolanda Lata in the morgue had been more unsettling than she wanted to admit. The case had obsessed her a few months ago and Yolanda had stayed in the back of her mind as an unresolved lead. She'd always thought that with enough time, she'd be able to track down Yolanda, and through her, find Lila. That hope had been shut away in a refrigerated drawer.

"Are you all right?" Flores asked.

Emilia nodded. "I'm fine." She exchanged the binder for a slim folder from the bottom of the drawer and handed it to him. "This is a list of the major private security companies in Mexico," she said. "They all handle kidnappings for private families. These are my personal contacts."

She went down the list, giving him some details about each of the contacts, then wound up by saying, "Call each one, explain who you are and ask if they have handled any kidnappings that has involved a loss of the victim's arm, hand, or finger within the last year. If they have, ask to set up a meeting."

"Arm, hand, or . . ." Flores trailed off as he understood her implication.

Emilia handed over a second file. "Here's the number for the *federale* anti-kidnapping unit to call as well. Over there you want to talk to Captain Genaro. He'll give you a yes or no answer and if it is yes, we'll have to follow up in official channels."

"Okay."

"Do you remember how to access case files online from the training the other day?"

"Yes."

"Good. You'll want to read through any old kidnapping files."

"I'm looking for similarities," Flores interrupted. "Same tool, same part. Church things."

"Exactly."

"This is real detective work, isn't it, Emilia?" Flores asked. Once again he reminded her of an eager young pup, looking for her approval and wanting to be petted.

She regretted the vertigo that had caused her to hold his arm so tightly in the morgue.

Silvio parked in front of the Villa de Refugio in almost the same place where Kurt had parked on Sunday, reminding Emilia that yet again almost another day had rushed by and she hadn't even had the time to text him. She'd apologize Friday night when she got to the hotel. Let him know he was right about Padre Pro's finger, too.

"The Salva Diablo body's really missing?" Silvio asked. He'd been uncharacteristically quiet since she'd told him about developments at the morgue. "Any others?"

"According to Prade, just the one. Nobody saw anything, of course."

"Fuck sakes." He cut the engine. "Coincidence?"

"Hard not to think so," Emilia agreed. "But it happened on the midnight shift, after the *Pacific Grandeur* left."

"Bonilla's mystery cell phone contact?" Silvio threw out. "Covering his boy's mistake?"

"Another couple of days and the morgue website would be up," Emilia said. "The Salva Diablo picture would be on it. Now, without a body, they probably won't include him."

Silvio punched her in the shoulder. "Good thinking, Cruz. Who else knows about the website coming online?"

A rare compliment and a new bruise. Silvio always managed to keep things even. "Prade," Emilia said. "Morgue staff. Chief Salazar's office. Mayor's office. Site developer. A bunch of cops whose cases are going to be on that site."

"Conspiracy theory time," Silvio said.

"Let's get this over with first."

The guard in front of the turquoise door didn't recognize Emilia in her cop clothes: jeans, black denim jacket, loafers, ponytail, badge. Silvio held out his own badge as he brushed past, his always effective combination of menace and bulk on full display.

"You the owner?" Silvio barked at the dapper man behind the long glass counter.

"Yes." The man adjusted his half-moon reading glasses and smiled nervously. He wasn't the owner from Emilia's childhood but looked enough like him to be the son; same protruding eyes, moustache, and slicked hair above a stiffly starched white shirt and conservative gray tie. "Señor Fernando Gustavo at your service. Perhaps you are looking for something special? A gift, perhaps."

"Señora!" Tifani, the attentive salesgirl who'd waited on Emilia and Kurt on Saturday, hustled over to her boss's elbow and beamed at Emilia. "Another wedding gift, señora?"

"You sold a relic," Silvio said. He raised a wooden statue of the Virgin of Guadalupe and grimaced at the price tag stuck to the bottom. "Finger of Padre Pro, the Cristero martyr."

"Ah." Gustavo took off his reading glasses in a gesture of respect and rolled his eyes to the ceiling. "The sainted Padre Pro. It was a blessing to have such an artifact in our store."

"I'm sure it was," Emilia said dryly.

"I'm sorry, but it has sold," Gustavo said. "It came and went so quickly. Even before the official unveiling."

Before Tifani could get a word in, Emilia showed Gustavo her badge. "I know. I bought it. And it's a fake."

Silvio put both hands on the glass and leaned forward so that his badge was likewise visible as it dangled from its lanyard. "That means, señor, you're about to be arrested for dealing in human body parts."

Tifani gasped and covered her mouth.

Gustavo replaced his glasses with an indignant jab at his nose. "Officer, I assure you, the Villa de Refugio does not sell

fake articles. Doing so would be a defilement of the Church."
He glanced sharply at the salesgirl. "Tifani! Go get the
inventory list." The girl darted into the back room.

Silvio gestured to the guard to close the turquoise door.

Tifani rushed back to Gustavo with a large ledger. The
store owner took the book and flipped through the handwritten
pages, his face pinched with indignation. "Let me assure you
both, the Villa de Refugio only sells genuine articles and our
reputation as Acapulco's most authoritative dealer in religious
antiquities and relics has been firmly established for more than
100 years."

"Until the day you put that finger up for sale," Silvio said.

"The Villa de Refugio only sells genuine articles," Gustavo
insisted, his voice growing shrill and his face mottled with
emotion. "You should have received the letters of provenance,
proving and verifying that the relic was in fact from the most
holy body of the blessed Padre Pro." He turned to Tifani,
nearly frantic. "Where are the copies? What did you do with
the letters?"

"I have the letters." Emilia held up her hand to keep the
girl from scurrying off. "They are fake. The Acapulco medical
examiner has determined that the finger is actually a woman's
forefinger."

"This is police harassment," Gustavo shrilled. "You want
protection money. So that thieves don't break into my store? Is
that it?" He looked from Emilia to Silvio as if he'd trumped
them.

"This is trafficking in body parts." Silvio snatched up
Gustavo by his shirt collar and hauled him over the counter.
"It's the same as if you'd sold a kid's liver to some
norteamericano who drank his own to pieces."

"Señor Gustavo," Emilia said, putting on her good cop
role. "This is really about the relic."

"Enough of this crap," Silvio scowled and let go. "Where
did you get it?"

Gustavo slid back to his side of the counter. "One of my
best suppliers. It's all right here," he said breathlessly.

Silvio swung the ledger around. "How much did you pay

for it?"

"Eight thousand pesos." Gustavo sniffed.

"The finger of a saint is only worth 8000 pesos?" Silvio exclaimed.

"That's more than I usually pay," Gustavo was still trying to reassemble his dignity. "But for such a remarkable item, I was willing to make an exception."

"Fuck, Cruz." Silvio cut his eyes to Emilia. "How much did Hollywood pay for the thing?"

"You don't want to know." Guilt swept over Emilia at the thought of how much Kurt had lost because of her.

Gustavo looked from one detective to the other while Tifani hovered next to him, wiping her eyes. "My supplier assured me that it had been in the Church of San Sebastián in the Distrito Federal for years. The relic had been in the chapel of the school and the church was clearing out the building before it was sold."

Emilia gave Silvio a shrug. "That's what one of the letters said."

"What did you do to verify the letters?" Silvio asked.

"I read them," Gustavo said.

"You didn't do anything else to verify if they were real or forgeries?" Silvio thundered. "This was an entire finger in a glass box, supposedly 100 years old. You just took it on faith?"

"Faith is the foundation of the Holy Mother Church," Gustavo ventured. "Villa de Refugio is a symbol of that faith."

"*Rayos*," Silvio exclaimed. "How did you know this supplier wasn't cheating you?"

"I've been dealing with this supplier for years. He brings in religious antiques from all over Mexico. Central America. Brazil and Argentina. Paintings from Peru." Gustavo ran a shaky finger down the entries on the ledger, still obviously not believing that the relic was a fake. There were numerous entries of purchases from the same vendor, each with a detailed description noting condition, age, and provenance.

Emilia realized that Tifani was holding out a business card. "Señor Ignacio Blandón Hernandez," the salesgirl said softly.

"He comes every few weeks with things to show Señor Gustavo. Always rare things. Expensive."

The card was embossed with the man's name and the legend *Antiques and Rare Books*. There was an address in the upscale Colonia Costa Azul neighborhood.

"There's no phone number," Emilia said. "How do you get in touch?"

"Always by email," Gustavo said.

"How many times did you buy a finger from him?" Silvio asked.

"Only the Padre Pro relic."

Emilia noticed how the store owner refused to acknowledge the finger. No, it was always *the holy relic*.

"What else do you have from him?" Silvio asked.

Gustavo came out from behind the counter cradling the open ledger in his arms. He moved in a wide arc to avoid Silvio. "Tifani. Take down the statue. The tall one."

Tifani crossed the room to the wall of cabinets Kurt had studied so assiduously on Sunday. She carefully lifted down an antique wooden statue of Saint Francis. The chipped hands were outstretched, a bird sat on his shoulder, eyes stared forward. The saint wore a long vestment clinched by a frayed belt made of real leather.

"Did this come with letters as well?" Silvio asked.

"Yes," Gustavo read something in his ledger. "Two."

With the help of the ledger, Gustavo identified four other items purchased from Blandón. All were purported rare antiques, with letters of authentication.

"Go get all the letters," Silvio said shortly.

Tifani replaced the statue in the cabinet, darted into the back room again, and returned with a collection of letters.

Like the Padre Pro letters, they were encased in glassine protectors. Gustavo separated them by item. "You see. There is a mistake. We have meticulous documentation. This is why my customers have complete faith in Villa de Refugio."

Gustavo trailed off as Silvio leaned against the counter and watched Emilia examine each letter.

It wasn't until she was about halfway through the pile that

she found the match. The letter was written on heavy linen stationary, foxed with age at the edges. The handwriting was the same as well, thin spidery lines supposedly written in 1935. The letter referred to the Cristero conflict, nearly whispering an intense message about hiding religious relics and praying in secret even after the armistice between Church and government had supposedly been struck.

"This one," Emilia said. It was the last nail in Padre Pro's coffin. "It's the same paper, the same handwriting, almost the same wording as one of the relic letters."

"Your supplier is selling you false items," Silvio said in disgust and threw down a card with his cell phone number on it. "Saint Francis was probably made in someone's barn last week. If he gets in touch, you call and let us know. Otherwise we'll be back to confiscate all of your inventory and arrest you for collusion, selling body parts, and anything else I think of in the meantime."

"How long have you owned this store?" Emilia asked Gustavo as Silvio went to unlock the door.

"Ten years," Gustavo said.

"Do you have problems with hooligans?" Emilia wanted to run out of the store, find this Blandón and throttle him, but she couldn't help asking. "With kids who come in and make trouble?"

"This is a religious store," Gustavo said. "There is nothing here of interest to troublemakers."

Emilia tightened her hold on her shoulder bag and followed Silvio out of the store.

Emilia's phone rang as Silvio started the car. The display showed a name from the past.

"*Bueno?*"

"Detective Cruz, do you know who this is?"

"Yes." It was the recognizably bad accent of Alan Denton, a Pinkerton agent whose name had been on the list she'd given Flores.

Silvio looked questioningly at Emilia as he gunned the engine. She gave him a thumb's up.

"A colleague of yours called me this morning," Denton said. "I gather that you gave him my number."

"Did he explain the circumstances?" Emilia asked.

"He was asking about kidnapping cases the Pinkerton Agency may be handling," Denton said. "He should know that we don't give out that sort of information."

Despite the bad accent it was clear that Denton was angry. He'd been almost manic about not being connected with the Acapulco police in any way when she'd first met him six months ago and apparently nothing about his attitude had changed. Of course, she could hardly blame him, given the frequent number of times it turned out that police across Mexico were complicit in kidnapping, murder, hiding evidence, money laundering, and extortion.

"We've found a finger," Emilia said. "A woman's finger. Two or three weeks old and clipped from the hand with a bolt cutter."

There was a long pause. Emilia heard a sound in the background like running water.

"Maybe we should speak in person," Denton said.

Chapter 9

Emilia watched from the sofa in the dance studio's tiny office as Mercedes Sandoval made them each a cup of tea. The dancer wore one of her usual outfits of leggings and colorful tunic. Mercedes was ten years older than Emilia, yet had the grace and flexibility of a teenager. She'd been a ballroom dance champion in her heyday, along with her late husband, and now struggled to make ends meet running a dance studio in Emilia's neighborhood. She'd taught Lila Jimenez Lata and tried to help Emilia look for the girl.

"The recital was great," Emilia said, and tried to suppress a yawn.

"How much did you actually see?" Mercedes handed Emilia a mug of tea.

"Just Lila's class," Emilia confessed and blew on the surface of the hot liquid. "Maria is doing really well."

"Thanks to you." Mercedes settled on the other end of the sofa. "How long are you going to keep paying her tuition?"

"As long as she keeps coming." Emilia had met Maria, a teenager who worked as a maid, during an investigation several months ago. The girl dreamed of being a dancer and had some promise. Mercedes gave her a discount and Emilia had been paying for the lessons ever since.

Mercedes frowned. "You look tired."

Emilia took a comforting swallow of tea before she answer. "I found out this morning that Lila's mother is dead."

Mercedes gave a start and spilled a little tea.

"Drug overdose. Her body was found in an alley between the Fuerte San Diego and the city docks. She'd been dead awhile before they found her."

"*La pobrecita*," Mercedes mourned.

Emilia drank more tea. "Poor thing is right. She'd been robbed and beaten as well. No wallet, cell phone, jewelry, or money found on the body."

"Are you going to tell Berta?" Mercedes asked, naming

Lila's grandmother.

"*Madre de Dios.*" A severe woman who'd tightly controlled her granddaughter's life, Berta had gone to Padre Ricardo when Lila went missing and the priest had turned to Emilia for help. "I never even thought about Berta. She'll probably want to know where Yolanda is buried so she can spit on her grave."

"What about the brother?" Mercedes asked. "Pedro, wasn't that his name? Or did he change it?"

"He's Pedro Montealegre now," Emilia said. "Works at the water park. I'll have to go down there and talk to him. It's not news you can deliver over the phone."

"Isn't there someone else who can do it?" Mercedes asked. "Why do you always have to do things like that?"

"We all do," Emilia said. For all his brusqueness, Silvio was surprisingly adept at handling the onerous job of giving bad news, probably because he came at it straight as an arrow. No fooling around or drawing it out, and ready in case anyone fainted or threw up. "Except for the new guy."

"Really? You're working with someone new?"

"Flores." Emilia took another sip of tea. "He's right out of college and they dumped him in the squadroom. We're supposed to be training him. It's like having a confused puppy around all the time. Makes Franco nuts."

"I have to meet Franco one of these days."

"He's married."

"I didn't say I was romantically interested," Mercedes admonished her. "He just seems like such a character."

"He is." Emilia had a perverse sense of pleasure in gossiping about Silvio, who would be appalled if he knew she was talking about him.

"Speaking of romance, how is Kurt?"

"He's--." Emilia stopped in mid-sentence.

"What's the matter?"

"*Madre de Dios,*" Emilia groaned. She handed Mercedes her mug and dug her phone out of her shoulder bag. "We had an argument the last time I was at the hotel. He sent me a text about it. I meant to text him back but I forgot."

But she had responded, in a way. As Emilia stared in horror at the outgoing messages in her phone's mailbox, she thought back to the moment she'd read his last text. She'd been sitting in Irma Gonzalez's office in the Customs building. When Irma returned, Emilia had stuck her phone back in her bag. Her finger must have slipped.

"Was it a serious argument?" Mercedes asked, her voice full of concern.

"Sort of," Emilia confessed. "It's a long story, it was about one of my cases . . . Kurt texted that he was sorry we'd argued . . . and I . . . *Madre de Dios*, that was two whole days ago. He probably thinks I don't care."

"Do you?"

"Of course I care." Emilia wanted to howl in frustration. How could she have been such an *estupida*? "Kurt's great. Amazingly great."

"So what's wrong?" Mercedes pressed.

"There's nothing wrong." Emilia had been worried that meeting her family would end things with Kurt. But no, she could take care of destroying the relationship all on her own. "No, if I'm honest, I'm not sure things are working out."

Mercedes sipped her tea with a questioning look on her face.

"Being at the hotel feels strange." Emilia retrieved her tea. It had cooled but she drank it anyway as she struggled to put into words what she'd been feeling for weeks. "It's not like being in my own neighborhood where people know me. Apart from the staff, it's full of tourists and rich people. That's fine for him but I never have on the right clothes or say the right things."

"If Kurt's important enough, you can fix the rest of it," Mercedes pointed out. "Get different clothes. Make friends with the staff. Talk about the news."

"I can't fix this." Emilia tossed the phone onto the sofa so Mercedes could see.

The reply to Kurt's conciliatory message had been simple: *RRRRRRRRrrrrrrrrr.*

Chapter 10

The office of Señor Ignacio Blandón Hernandez, purveyor of antiquities and rare books, was located in an industrial warehouse complex. The guard at the security perimeter looked suspiciously at their badges, but eventually gave them directions to the third building in the complex and raised the barrier so that Silvio could drive through. Emilia could sense that Flores was restless by himself in the back seat, but that was his problem.

At least the new detective hadn't shown up in the squadroom that Friday morning looking like Silvio's Mini Me. Flores wore black jeans with a gray tee topped by a trendy black cotton jacket with a drawstring waist. It was a daring choice for a squadroom that ran to worn leather and threadbare denim, but Emilia had to admit he looked good.

Four long warehouse buildings made of white painted cinder block with corrugated tin roofs fanned across the tarmac of the huge parking lot like the fingers of a hand. A green circle of grass served as the palm. Silvio drove three quarters of the way around the circle to the third building.

They spilled out of the car. Silvio yanked open the door to the building and passed through, showing his badge to the security guard sitting at a desk inside. Emilia followed as Flores darted forward to hold the door for her. The move took her by surprise; only Kurt ever held doors for her. When she was with other cops it didn't feel right, as if it mocked the equality she'd fought so hard to achieve. He followed close enough for her to hear him breathing, as if using her as a buffer to protect himself from Silvio. Flores wasn't the first youngster the senior detective had scared and he wouldn't be the last.

The inside of the warehouse was fairly sterile, with the same whitewashed cement block walls inside as out. A large board attached to one wall listed all the occupants of the building. On the opposite wall big promotional signs introduced the larger companies occupying spaces there, including an airline catering company, a sign maker, and a company providing instruments to the maritime industry. Construction noises filtered in from the far end of the warehouse; the buzzing of machinery and the muffled thumps of a hammer.

The security guard verified that Blandón Hernandez's office was on the second floor. Flores stayed on Emilia's heels in the dim stairwell.

A small sign in the middle of the second floor corridor indicated even numbered suites on one side and those with odd numbers on the other. Blandón Hernandez was located in Suite 209.

They passed other offices as they headed down the hall. Only one door was open, revealing a girl frowning in front of a computer. The sign by the side of the door read *Estrella de Acapulco, Charter Tours.* "There's a little of everything here," Flores observed.

Blandón Hernandez's office was next. Silvio tried the knob; it was locked. He rapped on the door. After a couple of moments of silence, the senior detective flicked his eyes to Emilia. She pressed her ear to the door, listened to the silence.

"You think he's got any more fingers in there?" Silvio asked.

"Go ahead and open the door, Franco," Emilia said.

"Isn't it locked?" Flores frowned.

"Shut up, kid." Silvio pulled a small tool out of his pocket and used it to fiddle around with the keyhole in the knob. He turned the knob at the same time, easing on the pressure. The door opened as the tool turned in the keyhole.

"Can you teach me how to do that?" Flores asked.

Ignoring the younger man, Silvio walked into the office and found a light switch.

It was a simple, two room set-up. The front room was an office, with a desk, filing cabinets, some comfortable chairs in a corner. The white cement block walls were undecorated. A doorless opening led into a room lined with industrial gray metal shelves on one side and glass-fronted barrister shelving on the other. There were about two dozen packages on the shelves. From the shape of the wrapped bundles, Emilia could guess at what the object inside was. Most appeared to be crucifixes, small framed pictures, or statuettes.

A bale of new bubble wrap and a big strapping tape gun lay on the last shelf, along with a box of cards pre-printed with the office address.

The barrister cases were about half filled with old books, many of which were in foreign languages. Flores came to stand next to her and as Emilia lifted one out. It was covered with worn blue leather. "It's a Bible," he said, taking it from her. "In Italian."

Emilia took out anther book. It was a encyclopedia-sized edition in Cyrillic. It appeared to be a picture book of religious icons, the glossy pages full of large photographs.

"Greek," Flores said. "I took a class in art history. Greek icons are marvelous. Some even say they're more beautiful than Russian ones."

"There's no computer in here," Silvio called from the office.

Emilia replaced the icon book in the bookcase and Flores followed suit with the Bible. She went into the other room with again Flores at her heels.

"He probably uses a laptop," Emilia said. "Let's look through these files, see if there's anything useful."

After an hour, Emilia was ready to admit defeat. They'd found nothing related to the relic of Padre Pro. No copies of the letters, no evidence of where they came from, nothing of the relic's antecedents or where he got it.

"He must keep everything on the laptop." Emilia slid the last folders they'd examined back in the filing cabinet. "Or in his head."

Silvio look around to make sure everything looked the way it did when they'd arrived. "You think Gustavo called him and Blandón Hernandez has done a runner?"

"Maybe," Emilia said as Silvio carefully relocked the door behind them. "Gustavo's got a reputation to protect. He might have been angry enough to call and accuse Blandón of selling fakes."

"That's what police work is about isn't it, Emilia?" Flores mused. "Figuring out what motivates people."

Silvio scowled.

"Yes," Emilia said. "Although if you guess it's about money, you'll be right almost every time."

As they went down the hall, Silvio jerked his head toward the open door to the Estrella de Acapulco charter service and they went in. The girl looked thrilled to have visitors. "Can I help you?" she said.

"We're looking for Señor Blandón Hernandez," Emilia said. "The antiques dealer from 209. Do you know where he usually is this time of day?"

The girl smiled at Flores. "No. He only comes in now and then," the girl said. "Usually when he's expecting a delivery."

"Do you know where he is when he's not in the office?"

"Well." The girl kept her eyes on Flores. "I know that he travels."

Emilia edged Silvio to the side. Flores bobbed his head at the girl.

"All the time," the girl went on. "He's not here very often. But when he does, he always has such interesting things."

"What sort of things?" Emilia asked, willing Flores to open his mouth and say something smart.

The girl considered, cocking her head to the side. "Books. Sometimes little statues. Once he even showed me a gold chalice from a church in Brazil."

"What sort of deliveries does he get?" Emilia asked when Flores didn't say anything.

"Mostly paperwork," the girl said. "His insurance company delivers a lot of paperwork. Senor Blandón says you have to have a lot of insurance for priceless antiques."

"Do you know the name of the insurance company?" Emilia felt that she was grasping at straws. Beside her, Silvio folded his arms, evidently amused at Flores's lack of perception.

"No." The receptionist simpered a little at Flores and scribbled something on a piece of paper. "The courier is nice, he always waves."

"Do you know his name?"

"No, but he's very handsome. Very thin. Like a supermodel." The girl folded the piece of paper and slid it across the desk to Flores. "But not as cute as you."

"Thanks," he said.

They left the building and got into the car. From the backseat Emilia heard the rustle of paper.

"She gave me her cell phone number," Flores said, seemingly surprised.

Silvio backed the car out of the parking space.

Emilia looked over her shoulder at Flores as they drove past the guard shack and got back on the main road. Flores was attractive, in his young pup sort of way. The black jacket made him look like a slightly dangerous young pup. "Lucky day," Emilia said.

"I wonder why she did that," Flores said. "She had to know I was with you."

Chapter 11

They talked to Loyola, who immediately put in a call to Chief Salazar's office. Emilia wrote up the details while Flores continued to look through the files for kidnapping patterns and Silvio left to prowl the docks and call Irma Gonzalez at Customs. Emilia hit the Send button to submit the report, then grabbed her shoulder bag. She had two conversations scheduled for the afternoon and neither would be easy.

"Maybe we can get together for dinner tonight, Emilia," Flores said when she stopped by his desk on her way out. "Celebrate my first week as a detective."

"Another time," Emilia said vaguely, her thoughts already running ahead. "You have a good weekend, Orlando."

She checked her watch as she drove along Avenida Cuauhtémoc, cutting south to get onto the Costera. Fifteen minutes later, she was walking through the administrative offices at the popular CICI Water Park, breathing in fishy air from the dolphin tanks and hearing delighted screams from patrons hurtling down the water slide. The last time she'd talked to Lila's brother, he'd been one of the dolphin handlers, looking like a model in his wetsuit and tossing fish to the dolphins like bones to dogs.

Before that he'd been a young boy named Pedro Lata, set adrift by his mother. Emilia had tracked him down during the hunt for his half-sister Lila and he had been the one to give Emilia what little information there was to be had about Yolanda Lata.

He'd impressed her when they'd met, with his combination of brains, street smarts, and the striking looks he'd inherited from his mother. Emilia didn't know the full story of how the abandoned boy named Pedro Lata had remade himself into Pedro Montealegre from Monterrey, rising star of Acapulco's premier tourist attraction. She suspected she never would.

According to the plaque on the door, Pedro Montealegre

was now the Director of Guest Visits. Before she even had a chance to knock, Pedro jumped up and came around the side of his desk.

"Emilia!" He was still fit, handsome, and polished. His pronounced cheekbones and sultry good looks topped a CICI Water Park polo shirt and crisply creased khaki pants. "I was so surprised when you called."

"Congratulations on your promotion." Emilia looked around the office. "What does the Director of Guest Visits do?"

The space was bigger than the lieutenant's office at work, with a window that overlooked Playa de Ioacos. Blonde wood desk, streamlined sofa, modern metal guest chairs, expensive view. Yet even this office couldn't avoid smelling like a can of sardines.

"In charge of scheduling private visits to swim with the dolphins." Pedro had a precise and educated manner of speech. Emilia guessed he'd practiced it long and hard.

Emilia's eye was drawn to two big posters of dolphin shows. "Is that you?" she asked, pointing at a dark head bobbing in the water in each photo.

"Yes," Pedro said. He gestured for her to sit on the sofa. "I still substitute when one of the swimmers can't make a shift."

They both sat. Emilia looked around the office again. "I'm really happy for you. I know you've worked hard for this."

"You could have said all that on the phone." Pedro clenched his hands together. "This is about Lila, isn't it? Is she dead?"

"I don't have anything new on Lila," Emilia said slowly. "I wish I did, but I don't. We're still where we were."

"Okay."

Emilia took a deep breath of fishy air. "Your mother was found dead Wednesday morning."

"Where?"

There was a world of meaning behind the question. Emilia knew that since parting ways with his mother about ten years ago Pedro had never known her whereabouts. The money orders she'd sent him never had a return address.

"Here in Acapulco." There was no way to make this sound better. "Behind a store dumpster a couple of blocks away from the Fuerte de San Diego."

"Drug overdose?" Pedro's question was without emotion.

Emilia nodded.

Pedro suddenly got up, walked to the door and checked that it was firmly closed.

"I'm sorry," Emilia said.

Pedro leaned against the door and closed his eyes. He was five or six years younger than Emilia but in that pose, with his lips compressed into a line against his teeth, he looked as old and hard as Silvio. "Did she have a phone?" he asked. "A wallet? Anything that could be a lead to Lila?"

"No," Emilia said. "By the time the body was found, she'd probably been dead at least a day. If she'd had a phone or a purse, they were stolen. When the morgue team picked her up, there was nothing on the body except a dress."

Pedro opened his eyes. "Maybe it isn't Yolanda."

"I recognized her from the picture," Emilia said. "She was still a striking woman. You and Lila look just like her."

Pedro didn't reply. With the door closed, the scent of bait was spreading like a storm cloud through warm air. Emilia wasn't sure she'd ever be able to eat fried fish again.

He crossed the room and stood in front of the window, hands spread apart on the sill.

"She's in the morgue," Emilia said softly. "Can you claim the body? Give her a decent burial. Say goodbye once and for all?"

Pedro continued to stare out the window, his sculptured face like stone. The silence stretched out.

Finally Pedro turned around. "Do you think Lila ever met her?"

"There's no way to know." Emilia gave a slight shrug.

"Was she still a hooker?"

"Possibly." Emilia had been dreading exposing the details but he had a right to know, although she could put it more delicately than Prade. "Wear and tear on the body . . . was . . . consistent with that line of work."

"Only the best for Yolanda," Pedro said savagely and turned back to the window.

Emilia waited for him to come to grips with his feelings. The minutes stretched out and the air thickened into *caldo de mariscos* fish soup.

"I can take you down to the morgue now, if you want," Emilia prodded. She had time before she had to meet Alan Denton.

"I said my goodbyes to Yolanda Lata a long time ago," Pedro said without turning around. "I have no intention of claiming her body."

"If no one claims the body," Emilia said. She went to stand next to him at the window. "The next time the morgue has to clean house, she'll be buried with other unclaimed bodies in a city grave."

Pedro looked sideways at her but his glance took in the whole bright office. "I'm Pedro Montealegre from Monterrey," he said softly. "What would I be doing with the body of a hooker named Yolanda Lata?"

The Pinkerton Agency was the preeminent private security company in Mexico; the ultimate in personal security, the refuge for the country's rich when they had to deal with kidnappings, blackmail, or extortion. It was nice to be affiliated with an organization with the opposite reputation, Emilia thought wryly as she watched Denton from across the park. Twilight had fallen over the Vicente Suarez park. It was mostly locals this far away from the water, although a few tourists were there, too, milling about or lounging on the grass.

Like before, Denton didn't want to be seen openly with an Acapulco cop in any place where they might be recognized. And like before, he didn't want to meet in a restaurant where they'd be trapped into waiting for food or the check to be delivered. Emilia had only met Denton once before but it was enough to know that he prized anonymity and mobility even more than she did.

It had been six months since Emilia had seen the Pinkerton agent, but Alan Denton seemed much the same. He was a trim, swarthy man with sun-darkened skin and hooded eyes that gave him an Arab look.

He was already on the northeast corner of the park, paying a vendor for a cardboard cup of ceviche when Emilia strolled up. He didn't acknowledge her as he finished paying. She waited behind him as he got a napkin and a plastic fork. When he moved off Emilia bought a portion of the pickled fish and shrimp salad for herself.

She caught up with Denton as he sat on a bench forking up the food. She sat down and opened her container and inhaled the scent of fresh lime and cilantro.

"So, Detective," Denton said without looking at her. He kept his attention on the container of ceviche in his hand. "A grand Friday night in Acapulco. Do we have unpleasant things to discuss?"

"It would seem so," Emilia said. "I told you we have a finger. It was being sold as a religious relic at the Villa de Refugio Catholic shop."

"Selling body parts seems to be an odd sideline for a religious goods store." Denton finished his ceviche, left his fork in the empty cardboard container, and set it down on the bench between himself and Emilia as if to create a barrier.

"They were billing it as the finger of a martyred priest," Emilia went on. "Padre Pro, who died during the Cristero War."

"The Cristero War," Denton said dryly. "I'll have to look it up."

Emilia didn't like the way he seemed to be mocking the Church. "The store owner bought it from one of his regular suppliers. Antiques dealer named Ignacio Blandón Hernandez with an office in Colonia Costa Azul."

"Never heard of him," Denton said.

"He supplied letters of authentication for the items he sold to the store," Emilia said. "Some of them look alike. Probably done by the same person."

"I don't care about your letters, Detective," Denton said

testily. "Tell me about the finger."

Emilia pronged some shrimp. The ceviche wasn't as good as the ceviche at the Palacio Réal's Pasodoble Bar. "According to the medical examiner, it's a woman's right hand forefinger. Probably came off the hand two or three weeks ago. Snapped the bone, likely with a bolt cutters or pruning shears."

It was still light enough to read. Denton took his time studying the photos and letters Emilia passed over.

Emilia finished her ceviche. She stacked her empty container on top of his with both of the used forks in it. Denton looked up from the materials in his hands and she could tell he didn't like the fact that she'd touched something he'd used, as if by doing so she'd stolen his DNA.

"I've shared," Emilia said as twilight slid into darkness. "Your turn."

Denton put everything back in the envelope. "We have an ongoing case," he said. "Not in Acapulco but close enough."

Emilia waited for him to tell her where the kidnapping had occurred but he didn't. "I need a little more information." She held out her hand for the envelope.

Denton passed it over, hesitated, then started speaking. "She's the wife of a Russian businessman who has been buying up property in Mexico. She went to the same gym every day, always at the same time and they picked her up on the way home. They're asking for 10 million dollars and he doesn't have that much money liquid cash here. It's taking him awhile to get it together."

"How long has it been?" Emilia asked.

"Four months," Denton said. "I know what you're thinking. Right about now the kidnappers are getting antsy. They want to get rid of the woman and pick up their money. So they're upping the pressure with a body part left for the family to find or a video of them shooting her in a place that will wound but not kill."

"Tried and true methods of upping the pressure."

"In this case, that would probably make our client lose his mind. The wife is a former Miss Nigeria who competed in the

Miss Universe pageant. That's where they met, although I don't know what he was doing there. At any rate, she's his jewel in the crown."

Denton spoke dryly and Emilia inferred that he didn't like the unnamed Russian businessman. She could imagine the type, many of whom were using their newly minted Russian mob money to buy up condos in Acapulco. The Russians were easy to spot; they wore too much polyester and flashed stacks of cash in the city's nightclubs and casinos. The detectives had all been briefed on Russian mafia attempts to get into the Mexican drug business but so far it didn't seem likely that they'd cracked the local wholesale market.

"Does he have cartel ties?" she asked.

"Not that we can tell."

"Do you think she's dead?" Emilia asked. "That's why they never sent the finger to the husband? She died and either the kidnappers had this creative way to make money or the finger fell into the hands of somebody else who did."

"I'm not going to speculate, Detective," Denton said. "But I do think you need to be on the lookout for the rest of the hand. Might be a few more martyred priests coming to your attention."

Emilia froze. "What are you implying?"

"Only that Mexico is a very violent place and the sanctity of life is hardly what it used to be."

That was hardly new information. Emilia felt the same as the last time she'd spoken to Denton; she was dealing with someone who didn't like her, didn't like Mexico, but was making good money out of the country's drug war violence. "So how do we determine if my finger belongs to Miss Nigeria?" she asked. "Do you have the victim's DNA? Can you send it to Doctor Prade at the Acapulco morgue?"

"We'll send a courier service to pick up the finger," Denton said without hesitation. "We'll use our own resources to determine if it's a match."

"And make sure nothing related to Pinkerton falls into the hands of corrupt city employees," Emilia said.

"You know the game, Detective."

"Sure," Emilia said, for lack of anything else.

Denton tapped the envelope in Emilia's hand. "The testimonials," he said. "I suppose you plan to track down who made them."

"I plan to try," Emilia said.

Denton looked away. "There's a man called El Flaco who runs a business out of a taxi in the Universitaria neighborhood."

"A forger?"

Impatience passed over Denton's face. "You tell him what you need. He decides if you're legit. If you are, you get in the taxi and he takes you to his brother who does the work."

"You think these brothers did this?"

"I hear the brother is a hell of an artist but never goes out. He's known as El Gordo."

"El Flaco and El Gordo," Emilia murmured. The Skinny One and The Fat One. "Do you have any real names?"

"No."

"How will I know which guy is El Flaco? A lot of skinny guys drive taxis."

"He's very tall," Denton said. "And very thin. Supermodel thin."

Emilia caught her breath.

Denton stood up. "I've given you all the information I plan to, Detective. Might I remind you that when we spoke before, it was with the implicit understanding that it was a private conversation?"

Emilia stood up to face him.

Denton's lip curled as he went on. "So you can imagine my surprise when a voice calling itself Detective Orlando Flores Almaprieto blithely said he got my number from you."

Emilia bristled at Denton's lecturing tone. "We're talking a kidnapping case that your company may have fucked up and you're whining about Flores calling with information?"

"Flores," Denton interrupted her. "Is he related?"

"Related?" Emilia echoed. "What are you talking about? He's a new detective."

"This the second time, Detective," Denton said softly.

"That I have the feeling that you're either abysmally naïve or running one of the best bluffs I've ever seen."

Emilia took a step back.

Denton looked over his shoulder, assessing the crowds. "I'd appreciate it if you lost my number."

Emilia didn't reply.

Denton walked away. He almost immediately melted into a knot of tourists.

Drained. Spent. It was the week that wouldn't end. Emilia felt like a zombie as she pulled the car into the courtyard next to Ernesto's grinding wheel. He was in front of the television. They exchanged nods. Sophia had already gone to bed, he said.

Emilia got herself a beer and stared at the kitchen wall as she drank. Finding something to eat seemed like too much effort so when she finished the beer she plodded upstairs. It wasn't until she'd changed into a tee shirt and slid under the blanket that she realized she was in the wrong bed.

It was Friday.

She sat up and grabbed her cell phone from the bedside table. Kurt answered after the second ring.

"Em." Steel drums played in the background. "Where are you?"

"I'm on a case." Emilia was too tired to feel guilty about serving him up another lie. "I won't be able to come out to the hotel until tomorrow."

"You're kidding," he said.

The steel drum music made it difficult to hear him. "What's going on there?" Emilia asked. "Where are you?"

"It's the regatta weekend," Kurt said and Emilia nearly dropped the phone.

He'd been talking about it for weeks, yet she'd totally forgotten. The hotel chain was sponsoring an America's Cup yacht, Kurt's hotel was the flagship, and this weekend was the kickoff.

"I'm sorry," Emilia said. "I'll be there tomorrow morning as early as I can."

"Don't worry," Kurt said. "Christina is here. Everything's fine. Take care of things on your end."

Christina meant Christina Boudreau, the hotel's skinny blonde head concierge. The woman was from some European country where everybody's skin looked like alabaster. She spoke English to Kurt, touched his arm when she laughed, and always managed to make Emilia feel like an interloper. *Fuck. Fuck.*

"Hey," Emilia said hastily. "I didn't mean to send that weird text. I was in the middle of something for a case and got interrupted."

"It's okay, Em," Kurt said. "We'll talk about it tomorrow. I've got to go."

"Sure," Emilia said, and then the connection to Kurt was gone.

Chapter 12

Between breakfast with her mother and the need to do some laundry, Emilia didn't head for the Palacio Réal until after 10:00 am. Traffic was bad and she found herself winding through the Costa Azul neighborhood, not far from Blandón Hernandez's office, in an effort to avoid the worst of the traffic heading for weekend beach parties.

As she turned onto Castillo Bretón, one of the semicircular streets north of the CICI Water Park, she noticed a gray sedan. It was three cars back, but she was sure it was the same car that had been behind her as she had come off the busy Lomas del Mar road near the golf course.

Emilia wound her way through the mixed residential and commercial area. The gray sedan kept with her, occasionally disappearing from her rearview mirror, but always popped up again at an intersection two or three cars behind. Emilia abruptly turned left onto the narrow Niños de Veracruz, which led her into a hilly neighborhood where the streets spewed in all directions. After a dozen twists and turns, the gray sedan was nowhere to be seen. Emilia pulled to the side and switched on her phone's GPS. If the gray sedan had followed her, the driver was either extremely familiar with Acapulco or hopelessly lost.

She got herself out of the winding neighborhood and eventually made the turn onto the Costera near the Torre Metropolitano construction site. Only partially finished, the building's angular steel beams elbowed into the sky. Just past the construction site, a median split the Costera, which changed names to the Carretera Escénica.

This far from the popular water park, the traffic was much lighter. The Suburban picked up speed as it rumbled south. Emilia checked her mirrors.

There it was, two cars behind her. The gray sedan must have doubled back and waited, betting that she'd come out of the hilly neighborhood where she did.

"*Madre de Dios*," Emilia swore out loud. She tried to think straight, not let panic take over. If this was going to be a cartel hit, they would attack where the traffic was the lightest, on the cliff above Punta Bruja or closer to the turnoff to Punta Diamante where the road was a simple ribbon of tarmac carved from the mountain without guardrails or a safety net.

She took her foot off the accelerator and the Suburban slowed. The car in back changed lanes and passed on the left. The gray sedan braked to stay behind Emilia.

Only a driver was in the sedan. The lack of shadow on the passenger side was a good sign. One man in a sedan wasn't the usual assassination profile. If she was worth killing, there'd be a truck or an SUV full of *sicarios* with long guns.

Emilia eased the Suburban into the left lane and shoved her foot on the brake. The gray sedan slid by on her right, followed by a family minivan. Emilia sped up and kept pace with the van.

The gray sedan gradually pulled away and Emilia was able to see the plates. She read the *placa* number out loud to herself as a means of committing it to memory.

The gray sedan stayed ahead of her as the road unwound around the side of the mountain. Emilia focused on her driving rather than on the dramatic view of ocean far below as lines of white froth skimmed toward the shore. She passed the Las Brisas hotel on her left and considered turning in, but she was too curious to end the game now. Plus, she had the advantage of the heavier vehicle if it came to a duel on the highway.

If the driver knew her habits, they'd know she would need to get into the right lane for the turn onto the road leading down to Punta Diamante. As Emilia drove the familiar curves and the turnoff neared, she found herself holding her breath and waiting for the sedan to make its move.

But nothing happened. The sedan stayed a fair distance ahead of her and in the right lane. The minivan passed Emilia on the right, as did a truck loaded with chickens in cages. Emilia eased into the right lane behind the truck and immediately swore. The cages blocked her view of the vehicles ahead.

As she slowed in anticipation of the turn, the truck jolted into the left lane, the abrupt movement sending a gust of feathers across Emilia's windshield. Even so, she could see that the gray sedan was smack in front of the Suburban, nearly dead in the road. Emilia yanked the wheel to the right. The Suburban jumped the curb and bounced into the turnoff. As Emilia stood on the brake to prevent the vehicle from slamming into the scrolled iron *privada* gate that kept the unclean from the exclusive Punta Diamante area, the gray sedan continued along the Carretera Escénica.

Thanks to the Palacio Real sticker the Suburban had been wearing for the past few months, the guard swung open the gate and Emilia guided the SUV onto the steeply pitched cobbled road. It led down to the water, linking private villas, a luxury condominium building, and the Palacio Réal hotel complex.

As Emilia gave the Suburban over to the valet and grabbed her shoulder bag, her hands were shaking and damp. The lobby was crowded with people. She stopped by the elevators to get her breathing under control, then got out her notebook and scribbled down the *placa* number for the gray sedan. She'd find Kurt, let him know she was there. When she went up to the penthouse to change she could call dispatch to run a trace on the car.

She walked through the lobby and down a few steps into the vast central expanse of multi-level terraces open to the ocean. A white grand piano usually anchored the space but had been moved to the side so as to accommodate a scale model of the America's Cup racing yacht. The Pasodoble Bar was on the left side of the lowest level, a blue mosaic of its name fronting the long mahogany bar. Emilia recognized the bartender as he sliced limes from behind the counter. He returned her lifted eyebrows by tipping the point of his knife toward the beach. Emilia waved and passed through the bar, skirting the knots of people sipping tall drinks and having noisy conversations.

The beach below the bar was set up with a buffet. The steel drum band was keeping things lively. With his blonde hair, wide shoulders, and white Palacio Real polo, Kurt was easy to pick out. He was near one of the buffet tables talking to two waiters. Christine Boudreau, in a white bikini top and gauze pareo around her hips, was by his side.

Emilia wiped her palms on her pants, gripped her shoulder bag a little more tightly, and marched across the sand. She'd worn the clothes she'd need for Monday—loafers, skinny jeans, tee shirt, black cotton blazer, gun in a shoulder holster—and was sweating like a stevedore before she'd made it halfway across.

Christine saw her first and said something to Kurt, who turned to greet Emilia with a smile. "Hey, Em," he said. "You finally made it."

"Hi." Emilia stretched up to give him a quick kiss. "Let me go change and make a phone call. Then I want to hear how the regatta is going."

Kurt frowned and touched her cheek. "Everything all right?"

Emilia nodded. "I'm fine. Yesterday was crazy."

"This place would have been crazy yesterday, except for Kurt," Christine said. Her Spanish was good but bore the traces of her native language, whatever that was. "He's an exceptional organizer."

"I'll want to hear all about it," Emilia said sweetly.

Kurt winked at her. "Go change for lunch," he said to Emilia. "But let's plan for a swim later. I'll need to burn off some energy."

Emilia gave his hand a brief squeeze. *Energy* was their code word for *stress*. "Me, too," she said.

"I'll be around." Kurt lifted his chin at the buffet tables. "But if you can't find me, send a text."

"Okay." Emilia felt Christine's eyes on her as she plodded back across the sand to the bar.

Once in the penthouse, Emilia shucked off her jacket, holster, and shoes, got herself a mineral water from the refrigerator, and called dispatch. She gave the sergeant on duty the plate number from the gray sedan, along with the make and model of the car and asked for the registration information, including the owner's *cédula*. The *cédula* was the national identity card and the fastest way cops had to track someone via the national database. The sergeant promised to call her back quickly.

She sat down in front of Kurt's computer. It was sleek and new, as were all his electronics, and the connection was three times as fast as the one internet-capable computer in the squadroom. Kurt had a *norteamericano* keyboard, however, which meant there was no ñ key and Emilia never could remember how to find symbols like the @ sign.

The first search she typed was for Blandón Hernandez. The first few pages were worthless, but as she refined the search by adding terms like "antiques" and "religious" she got more hits that made sense. The dealer had donated a cross to a seminary, received an award from a Catholic newspaper, been an advisor to a museum Emilia had never heard of. He was listed in several online directories of antique dealers.

In short, he looked as legitimate as all the other companies Emilia had encountered over the years that masked illicit transactions behind real and very successful enterprises.

From that search, Emilia segued into companies that insured antiques. Although the insurance courier described by the receptionist at Blandón Hernandez's office complex could well be Denton's forger, it was hard to be sure.

She kept at it until her cell phone rang. It was the dispatch sergeant.

"Car is registered to Bandera Rentals," he said. "They're out at the airport."

"Who is the car rented to right now?"

"Juan Colón Sotelo. Mexico City address."

Emilia felt marginally better. The Knights Templar or Sinaloa cartels didn't send *sicarios* from Mexico City to rent sedans when they wanted to kill cops. Maybe this had been nothing more than a lost tourist. "Give me his address and *cédula* number."

"I got the address. You didn't say you wanted the *cédula* number."

Yes, I did. Emilia bit back a snarky comment about police

incompetence and scribbled down the address; she could look up the *cédula* information in the office on Monday.

She drank some mineral water and opened a new search. Time was forgotten as she found the website of Acapulco's unidentified dead. As Prade had said, she had to create an account before being shown the pictures. There were only six faces of men whose bodies were presently awaiting identification in the morgue. None were of the Salva Diablo gang member found dead on the *Pacific Grandeur*. Emilia didn't know any of them. At least Yolanda Lata's face wasn't there.

Somehow, one search led to another, and Emilia discovered the Flores family. No wonder Denton had asked if Flores was "related." *Madre de Dios*, he was related to half of Acapulco's real estate.

Flores had made the news a dozen times, all associated with musical performances. He played the oboe, of all things. Notices in society columns and music festival websites mentioned his appearances with youth orchestras in both Mexico and the *Estados Unidos*. In one account, Flores was mentioned in conjunction with his father, Rigoberto Flores, who had underwritten a concert tour.

A search for Rigoberto Flores returned scores of hits. Rigoberto Flores was a real estate speculator connected with several major buildings in Acapulco, including the new hotel and apartment complex at Playa Revolcadero on the beach beyond the Palacio Réal, the Torre Metropolitano skyscraper, and plans for a floating casino off Isla la Roqueta. All of the projects were high risk in terms of location and complexity of the architecture, not to mention getting approval from the city. But they were also big, dramatic projects that would change both the landscape and economy of Acapulco.

Emilia clicked through the articles until she simply couldn't stand it any more. She closed down the search program, confused and angry. If Flores had a rich father willing to support his love of music, why bother to become a cop?

Maybe it was different with money. She'd fought to get

where she was every step of the way, clawing her way up the police wage scale, driven by basic needs like food, shelter, and medical attention for her mother. She'd faced outright opposition, physical risk, and intentional career sabotage. She'd wept over the unfairness more times than she could count.

In contrast, Flores wanted to play out a childhood fantasy of cops and robbers and was rich enough to do it. His family had simply bought him the job he wanted. It didn't matter that Flores wouldn't be properly trained, that he endangered his colleagues by being clueless. Never mind that everyone else had had to work their asses off to get where he'd gotten. No, with enough money, anyone could buy anything. Even Chief Salazar's soul.

She was suddenly glad that Silvio had trashed the expensive music player and headphones.

With a start, Emilia realized she'd been sitting in front of the computer for five hours. She hastily changed into her bathing suit, the expensive red one that Kurt had given to her on their first date, grabbed her cell phone and a towel, and left the penthouse.

The buffet had been cleared away and the beach was nearly deserted. Emilia wandered around, inwardly fuming at herself. She considered going back into the hotel and checking Kurt's office but that would mean she'd tracked him down twice in one day, like a nagging wife. Christine might be there, too, and Emilia wasn't sure she could deal again with the sight of the concierge oozing charm at Kurt.

She sent him a text saying she was on the beach. When he didn't reply, she left her cell with the bartender in the Pasodoble Bar, dropped her towel on the sand, and headed for the water.

The hotel's floating dock was anchored about 500 meters offshore and Emilia made for it with deep strokes. She'd always been a good swimmer but tonight she churned through the water, not aiming for speed, but to release the anger and resentment that had been building all week and had been brought to a head by what she'd found out about Flores.

The water was gray this late in the day. The horizon was gray, too, as the sun hung low. Emilia stopped to tread water and get her bearings. The dock appeared just beyond her, its white edge rising and falling against the dirty sky. She kicked hard and shoved herself through the swell.

Emilia reached the dock and pulled herself up. There was no one else there, no jet skis tied up to the big platform. She sat near the edge and hugged her knees as the breeze cooled her wet skin. The week had been a catalogue of things she'd never wanted to happen. Padre Pro's finger was likely that of a woman being held for ransom. Yolanda Lata was dead and the last possible link to Lila Jimenez Lata was gone. A murder case they could have solved—and not many fell into that category—had been snatched away. Flores had appeared out of thin air to turn her and Silvio into professional babysitters.

Plus, she'd lied to Kurt last weekend when they were sitting in the car in front of Villa de Refugio. For no good reason except embarrassment and worry that he'd think less of her. They'd argued over the relic, only to have Prade's results show how wrong she'd been. To complete the litany of stupidity, she shouldn't have sent Kurt that awful text, forgotten to drive to the hotel last night, or stood him up for the regatta event today.

A few people crossed the beach, their shadows stretched across the sand by the setting sun. Torches marking the perimeter of the Pasodoble Bar were lit by a staffer in the hotel's trademark blue printed shirt and khaki pants. A tall figure with yellow hair, wearing a white shirt and board shorts, stopped to speak to the staffer. When the conversation was over, the man peeled off his shirt, dropped it on top of Emilia's towel, and waded into the water.

She watched as he swam directly to the dock, powerful arms thrusting the water away, his face barely visible. His kicks created a wake of spume. The dock rocked as he hauled himself over the edge.

"Hey there." Emilia tried a smile. "Did you get my text?"

Kurt shoved wet hair away from his forehead and squatted down next to her. "Where were you?"

"What?" she stalled.

"You said you were going to change and make a phone call," Kurt said. Water from his shorts dripped onto the dock next to her leg. "You missed lunch, the awards, the whole afternoon. Where were you?"

Emilia squinted up at him. "Upstairs. Work stuff. I had to get a trace. Do some research online."

"It couldn't have waited? You had to do it this afternoon?"

"Kurt, don't make a big deal out of it," Emilia groused. "I lost track of time. You were working, anyhow."

He dropped into a sitting position next to her and leaned back on his elbows. "You know, Em. These weekends of ours. They're important to me. I live in this hotel, which means I'm always at work. But when you're here with me, it's not so much like work." He waved a hand at the beach in the distance. The tiki torches were bright spots against the darkening sky and the glow from the bar illuminated movement and faint music. "This weekend was a big deal and I was really looking forward to sharing it with you. Showing you off a little, too. Banquet, dancing, concerts on the beach, a lot of interesting people. Stupid me, I actually thought you'd have fun."

"Sorry," Emilia said, torn between guilt and resentment. Other women handled relationships; why couldn't she? *Madre de Dios*, she didn't know there was anything wrong with herself until Kurt Rucker came along.

But there he was, the setting sun turning his wet body into molten gold, and Emilia wanted nothing so much as to throw herself at Kurt, beg him not to be angry with her, tell him she'd do anything to make things right between them. That she cared more than he knew and never wanted to let go.

"You were right," she said instead. "About the Padre Pro relic. According to the morgue it's a woman's finger. We're treating it like a kidnapping case."

Kurt jerked himself upright. "Don't change the subject. We

need to talk about us, Em. Not work. For five minutes."

Emilia squeezed her knees, scared of the way her heart clenched in her chest, scared of the commitment he was always seeking and that she ran away from every time. "Look, I said I'm sorry. It's been a bad week and time got away from me. End of story."

"That's all you have to say?"

"What do you want me to say?" Emilia demanded. "That I'm not good at being a girlfriend? It's not like that should be any big surprise. I stink at this. I stink at being a girlfriend."

Kurt stood up and the dock surged against the water. "Maybe if you practiced," he said tightly. "You'd get better at it."

Emilia looked at her toes.

Kurt jackknifed off the edge and disappeared underwater. When he resurfaced, he was already halfway back to the beach. Emilia watched as he swam rapidly back to shore, pulled himself out of the water, collected his shirt, and went into the hotel. He didn't look back once.

Chapter 13

Emilia's watch said 8:30 am. Prade would have been at work for almost an hour already. She punched in the number for the morgue and asked to be put through to him.

"Detective Cruz." His voice boomed over the line. "How are you this fine Monday morning?"

"Excellent," Emilia lied. She was sitting in the Suburban in the police station lot, hoping she didn't look as bad as she felt.

Yesterday morning, she and Kurt had smoothed things over, although she suspected they'd been able to put the week behind them only because he'd made a conscious decision not to press her. After Kurt had overseen the dismantling of the regatta exhibits, they'd gone to a movie and a new restaurant in Playa Guitarrón. Sunday night sex was as fantastic as it ever was, but later as Kurt slept, Emilia had stared at the ceiling, wondering if she was being fair to him. Kurt deserved more than distracted weekends and the lies that slid off her tongue so easily.

"Did a courier from the Pinkerton agency pick up the finger from the relic?" she asked.

"Yes," Prade said. "Fine work on your part, making that connection."

"They're trying to get a match for a kidnapping victim."

"I assumed as much," Prade said.

"One other thing," Emilia said. "It's about Yolanda Lata. The *perdida* I identified. Her son declines to claim the body. Sorry."

"Lata." Prade sounded surprised. "Hold on . . . let me check."

Phone to her ear, Emilia watched the ebb and flow of both uniformed and plainclothes cops in and out of the building. The day shifts were getting out on the street. The night shifts were coming in to report. Her life was falling apart but police business continued as usual, supported by drugs and thieves and killers.

Prade came back on the line. "You must have been mistaken," he said. "Her name wasn't Yolanda Lata, it was Yola de Trinidad. The body was claimed on Saturday by her husband."

"What?" Emilia scrabbled in her purse for her notebook and pen, nearly pulled out her rosary instead.

"Claimed by her husband," Prade repeated. He sniffed and she imagined him at his metal worktable, reading glasses perched on his nose, messy file in hand. "Saturday. Late in the day."

"Are you sure?" Emilia felt as if she'd been punched in the gut. The body had been that of Yolanda Lata, she was sure of it. The Asian cast to her face, the disturbing similarity to her daughter Lila.

"Yola de Trinidad," Prade repeated. "Wife of Vikram Trinidad."

Emilia tucked the phone between her ear and shoulder so she could write. *Yola. Yolanda.* "Do you have an address? A phone number?"

Prade clicked his tongue. "Of course."

Silvio wiped greasy fingers on a paper napkin before speaking. "You'll have to go in unarmed," he said. "If these forgers have been in business for more than a week, they're looking for cops."

"What about you, Orlando?" Emilia asked. "You feel okay about going in there with me? Are you comfortable with the story?"

After Prade's revelation about Yolanda Lata's husband, Monday morning had swung into hyper drive. Chief Salazar had decreed the finger to be a high priority kidnapping case, Loyola announced at the morning meeting. Emilia briefed on what she'd gleaned from Denton, as well as her research into Blandón Hernandez's business, and there was a lively debate over whether or not the antiques dealer was knowingly dealing fakes or was being duped by a secondary vendor. That led to the decision to follow up on the forged letters, with Loyola almost breathless with the need to show Chief Salazar some action on the case. The acting lieutenant actually authorized some folding money to use in the operation.

There had been no time for Emilia to check out the *cédula* from the driver of Saturday's gray sedan before she and Silvio, with Flores in tow, scouted the park where Denton claimed El Flaco, the taxi-driving half of the forgery duo, was to be found. They looked around, then retreated to a fast food place a block away to figure out how to play it. A pile of burgers and colas later, they had a plan.

Flores carefully folded the waxed paper wrapper his burger had come in. "I'm ready whenever you are."

The plan wasn't complicated and having Flores along was actually an asset. Flores had no street history, and none of Silvio's muscular street swagger that so many found intimidating. Flores appeared to be what he was; a naïve and nonthreatening young man. He'd give Emilia an extra layer of cover and they'd worked up a story that fit their profiles. If Denton's information was solid, they'd convince El Flaco of what they needed, get in the taxi, and meet El Gordo, the master craftsman. It would be up to Emilia to guide the conversation around to Blandón Hernandez and the so-called letters of authenticity. Silvio would tail the taxi, find a spot to wait near the final destination, and be ready to move in if Emilia called.

Flores headed off to the men's room with Silvio's backpack to take off his holster and gun. Silvio reached across the table and grabbed Emilia's wrist. "You break up with Hollywood?" he asked.

Emilia jerked her arm back. "No, I didn't break up with Kurt. Not that it's any of your business."

"Then what's the problem?" he snapped. "You look like shit."

"Thanks, Franco. You're a fashion statement today, too."

"You know what I'm talking about." Silvio ignored her jibe. "What the fuck's going on with you?"

Emilia wadded up her wrapper. "Nothing. I didn't get

much sleep last night. Had stuff on my mind."

Silvio frowned. "If you're not ready for this, we'll put it off."

"I'm fine," Emilia said sharply. Her personal life had never interfered with being a cop and it wasn't going to start now. "If this is a kidnapping, we're working against the clock."

Flores came back to the table, Emilia hit the ladies room to stash her gun and badge, and they left. Silvio separated from them to go to his car, taking the backpack of weapons. Emilia and Flores strolled down the street flanking the park, toward the corner where two taxis were pulled over to the curb. The drivers lounged against the hood of the second car, talking and smoking and evidently not in a rush to get a fare. Both men were ordinary looking, neither tall nor thin.

"We'll have to wait," Emilia said out of the corner of her mouth when Flores slowed down.

They crossed at the intersection and went into a café. Emilia sat at a table by the window. Flores took the chair opposite her. The waitress gave them two menus.

"We'll stay here for awhile," Emilia said. "See if El Flaco drives in. For all we know he could be home eating or taking a siesta."

"Or with a client."

"That, too," Emilia agreed. "We don't even know if he's here every day."

"So you're sure about this story?" Flores asked. "Silvio seemed to like it but I'm not so sure."

"It'll be fine," Emilia said. "I got fired. In order to get a new job I need a letter of recommendation."

"But I'm supposed to be your brother."

"It's a good cover story. What girl would go to a stranger's place alone to get a forgery? She'd be too stupid to live. Of course I'd bring my brother."

"Do you have a brother?"

"What, for real?"

"Yes."

"No."

"I don't either," Flores said. "I'll bet we have other things in common, too."

"You keep looking on that side of the park and I'll look this way," Emilia said. The park wasn't large and by sitting across from each other they could cover all the intersections.

The waitress took their orders for iced coffees and a chocolate *pastel* for Flores. Emilia kept watch on the square, willing El Flaco to show up

"—about yourself."

Emilia glanced at Flores. "Excuse me?"

The waitress set down two tall glasses loaded with caffeinated froth and a plate with a thick piece of chocolate cake.

Flores grinned as he stuck a straw into his iced coffee. "I said, I'm glad we have an opportunity to talk. You know, really talk. Tell me about yourself."

"I've been a cop for more than 12 years." Emilia didn't look at him as she found a packet of sugar, tore it open, and poured the contents into her glass. "A detective for almost three. I didn't go to college. I came up through the ranks. Was the junior man in the squadroom until you showed up."

"What about besides work?" With his lips pursed around the straw Flores looked even younger.

"I'm a pretty private person," Emilia replied.

When she didn't offer anything else Flores held out his fork. "Would you like to try some *pastel*?"

"No, thanks." Emilia stirred her coffee with a straw. There was something too intimate about sharing food with a man who'd already put the fork in his mouth.

Flores ate his cake in silence as each of them looked across the other's line of vision. There was some play equipment in the middle of the park being enjoyed by a preschool class and some teachers. Women with plastic bags of vegetables and bread strolled the shops along the flanking streets, school kids in their uniforms and backpacks darted into the candy store and the stationary place, the bank guard repeatedly held the door open for patrons. A few cars honked as they jostled at intersections.

Another taxi came around the corner and pulled in behind

the others on the corner, but not so close as to make it appear that it was in a line or unable to pull out easily. The driver angled himself out, unfolding like a blind man's cane into one long length.

"That's him," Emilia breathed.

El Flaco was tall, almost emaciated. His gauntness accentuated the planes of his face and threw his cheekbones into sharp relief. His hair was so short as to be nothing more than a shadow. The descriptions had been accurate; he was as thin as a female supermodel, with a startling beauty created by the hollows of his face and the smoothness of his head.

Flores snapped his fingers, the waitress materialized, and the younger man paid the bill before Emilia could grab her wallet.

They left the café, circled around the park and approached El Flaco's taxi from the rear.

He watched the street, as attentive as a cartel lookout. His fitted shirt, skinny jeans, and suede loafers did nothing to pad his skeletal frame. His clothes were better quality than that of the other two taxi drivers, whom had only given him a cursory nod before resuming their conversation. He wasn't part of the usual taxi driver network and it showed.

El Flaco's gaze gradually settled on Emilia and Flores as they strolled up the street toward his taxi. Emilia looked up and down the street, letting El Flaco see that she was nervous. El Flaco looked at her with undisguised interest and half a smile played on his narrow lips.

"How you doing, *mamacita*?" he asked as they came closer. His eyes stayed on Emilia, ignoring Flores.

"I'm looking for a ride," Emilia said. "A ride so I can get a letter."

"What kind of letter?" El Flaco asked Emilia with a slow wink. He knew his looks were striking and Emilia thought back to the young receptionist in her lonely office.

"Not so much a letter, as a certificate," Flores broke in, stepping in front of Emilia. "A marriage certificate."

Emilia froze.

"He's too young for you." El Flaco smiled knowingly at

Emilia.

"We want a marriage certificate," Flores said more forcefully. "We can't get the apartment without a marriage certificate and my parents won't approve."

Emilia knew her face was burning and hoped that El Flaco would take it for embarrassment rather than the fury it was. *What the hell was Flores doing?*

Flores pointed at El Flaco. "We heard you could help."

"Who said so?" the taxi driver asked.

"Señor Blandón Hernandez," Emilia managed.

El Flaco showed no signed that he recognized the name.

"Señor Blandón Hernandez," Flores repeated. "He's an antiques dealer. Sells things to my father. He's been kind to us."

"Is that so." El Flaco regarded Flores with amusement but again, the name Blandón Hernandez seemed to be meaningless.

"I hate my father," Flores said with heat.

Emilia had to admit that Flores wasn't a bad actor, but she didn't know where he was taking them. Damn him for departing from the script.

"So you want to be married, eh?" El Flaco asked. "Get your apartment and score off your *papi*?"

"That's right." Flores put his arm around Emilia.

"Marriage certificates are expensive," El Flaco said.

"That's not the issue," Flores said.

"A thousand pesos," El Flaco said. "Plus the cost of the trip."

"Will it look real?" Emilia had the presence of mind to ask. "City seals and all?"

"It will be identical to the real thing," El Flaco said.

"We can pay," Flores said.

El Flaco told them to wait and folded himself into the car again. Through the window of the taxi Emilia watched him take out a cell phone and make a call. It was brief. After a minute he rolled down the window and repeated the price.

Flores handed over the pesos and for a moment Emilia thought El Flaco was going to drive away with the money. But after slowly counting it, he told them to get into the back of the taxi.

Emilia tried to look excited and nervous as the taxi pulled away from the curb. Flores kept his arm around her shoulders as the vehicle swung into the street and was soon bumping down side streets north of the park. Silvio was behind them somewhere; keeping the taxi in sight, playing a better game than Juan Colón Sotelo and his gray sedan.

El Flaco glanced at them in the rearview mirror. Emilia managed a shaky smile and Flores kissed her on the cheek. She kept herself from jerking away or punching his head and instead began to mentally compile the howling lecture she was going to drive through his thick, self-centered, rich boy head when this was over.

At least she'd learned two things. First, El Flaco was just the conduit. He took his orders from someone else. Second, El Flaco wasn't all that bright. He was more interested in getting laid than in driving his taxi.

Twenty minutes later, after a series of maneuvers Emilia knew were designed to both spot a tail and confuse his passengers, El Flaco pulled into the drive of a walled house. El Flaco touched a remote control button and the gates opened. He pulled through as soon as the gates opened and parked on a brick driveway in front of a tidy house painted a soft melon color. They all got out of the car and El Flaco patted them down for weapons, his hands lingering on Emilia's torso longer than necessary. Next, he searched Emilia's purse, pulling out her water bottle, her wallet, her rosary. For a moment she thought he was going to pocket the beads but he merely dropped them back into their case and into the bag. He didn't look at any papers. Emilia took the bag back with relief.

The house was nicely furnished with a cotton rug over terracotta pavers, cushioned woven willow furniture, and bold pen and ink drawings on the far wall. An older woman, with El Flaco's cheekbones and gaunt frame, stepped into the hall from a doorway that likely led to a kitchen. Her short gray hair didn't match her jeans, white blouse, and floral apron similar to those Sophia always wore. The woman watched without reacting as they filed past her.

El Flaco led them out a back door, across a small courtyard, and to a small building. He knocked once and a voice yelled for them to enter.

The door opened into a small art studio crammed to bursting. Shelves stacked to the ceiling faced the door and a triple cabinet of drawers ran the length of the adjacent wall. In the middle of the space, a desk dominated by a jeweler's magnifying lamp was dwarfed by the fattest human being Emilia had ever seen. He was ten times as wide as El Flaco, with a huge moon face stuck on top of a tent-like blue shirt, rolls of fat spreading over the collar where a neck should have been. A smell like moldy peas rose from his body.

"They want a marriage license," El Flaco said.

El Gordo's fingers were long and slender as they adjusted the jeweler's loupe in one eye. "Who is getting married?" he demanded. His voice had a wheezing quality as if his lungs were perpetually constricted by the weight of all that fat. "Let's see your *cédulas*."

Flores turned a questioning face to Emilia and she wanted to throttle him. By throwing out this unrehearsed story, he'd placed them in a position of having to reveal personal identification. They hadn't planned for that and she didn't have a false identity to use. They'd discussed the identity issue over burgers and she knew she could play the fake employment letter without it. But by hooking the license to an apartment rental--a real transaction--he'd boxed them into a corner. Before Emilia could figure out how to create false names and *cédula* numbers on the spot, Flores had whipped out his *cédula* and put it on the desk in front of El Gordo.

El Gordo picked up the *cédula* and held it up to the light, turning it to see the authentic watermark. Satisfied that it was genuine, the big moon face looked at her expectantly, the loupe still in place.

She was stuck. Emilia opened her shoulder bag and slowly fumbled around as if looking for her wallet. She brought out the copies of the Padre Pro letters and put them on the desk.

"What the hell is this?" El Flaco asked.

"Did you make these letters?" she asked. "They're about a finger belonging to Padre Pro."

Like a mountainous cyclops, El Gordo swung his head to look at his brother.

"I only need to know who paid you to make them," Emilia said. "Was it Blandón Hernandez or somebody else?"

"What's she talking about?" El Gordo wheezed at his brother.

Emilia looked from one brother to the other. "I'm looking for whoever asked you to make these letters."

"Are you a cop?" El Flaco demanded, tension flooding his features.

"*Cristo Rey*," El Gordo swore. The loupe fell out of his eye and a gun appeared in his hand. It had either been in a desk drawer or hidden in the rolling folds of flesh. "A cop? You think you can hit us up for protection money?"

"No, no. I'm looking for the woman who once had that finger attached to her hand," Emilia said, putting a crack into her voice. She hesitated, offering up a mental prayer that Flores wouldn't fuck it up this time, then burst into noisy tears. "It might be my sister's finger."

El Flaco swore as Emilia cried as hard as a little girl setting up for Alvaro and Raul; gasping loudly around her sobs, real tears streaming down her face.

"We got an email," she sobbed. "Maria's husband is rich, but he isn't as rich as they think." Flores opened his mouth and she dug an elbow into his ribs.

"What the fuck's going on?" El Gordo demanded of his brother, as the gun wavered between Emilia and Flores. "Cops or con artists?"

El Flaco hauled Emilia toward him with surprising strength. "Let's find out which it is, *chica*."

"Please," Emilia gasped as El Flaco dragged her toward the door. "We need to find Maria, that's all."

"Leave her alone!" Flores launched himself at El Flaco, only to receive a backhand that sent the younger man to the floor. And then the cold muzzle of a gun was against Emilia's temple and the click of the safety echoed in her ears. Emilia's eyes watered as rank body odor clogged her nostrils.

El Gordo breathed heavily with the effort of having left his chair and pulling his mass past the desk. The gun rose and fell against Emilia's head in time with his breathing and the effort to keep his arm outstretched. "Who are you?" he rasped.

"My name's Emilia." It wasn't hard to sound scared. "He's my brother Orlando. We're trying to find our sister."

The door opened and the woman who'd watched them enter the house came into the art studio. She looked from El Gordo and Emilia, to El Flaco, then to Flores on the floor. "What's going on here?"

"My sister," Emilia blurted, knowing she had one shot to make this woman her ally. "My sister's been taken and these letters were sold with her finger."

"Shut up," El Flaco shouted.

"Please listen to me," Emilia begged. She couldn't see Flores and didn't dare turn her head.

The woman almost certainly was the mother of the two men. She smelled like garlic and tomatoes, like a comfortable kitchen should smell, and had a kitchen towel over her shoulder. She marched up to Emilia and gasped her chin, banging the side of Emilia's head against El Gordo's gun. Her work-roughed fingers dug into Emilia's jaw. "You lying to me, *chica*? You here to make trouble for my boys?"

"No," Emilia gasped and held up her hands, palms out. The woman's grip across her face was like iron. "I'm looking for my sister. No trouble, I promise."

The woman locked eyes with Emilia. "What about him?" She jerked her head at Flores.

"No trouble, I promise," Emilia repeated.

Finally the woman dropped her hand. "Talk," she said.

"There have been emails," Emilia said. She hoped the woman hadn't cracked her jaw. The pain in her face equaled the pain of the gun pressed against her temple, as if the fat man was leaning his weight against her. "They told us to go to a store and there it was. With these letters."

"Who told you to come here?" the woman asked.

"Señor Blandón Hernandez." Emilia had to walk carefully,

especially if Blandón had been the one to commission the letters. "I don't know if he is being honest with me or not."

"We don't ever ask questions," El Flaco said. "Never talk about jobs."

"I don't know what else to do." Emilia felt the tears stream down her face again. "Please. Please help me."

No one said anything.

The woman in the doorway pointed at El Gordo. "Do you know this Señor Blandón Hernandez?"

"Maybe."

The woman turned to El Flaco. "You?"

"Maybe."

"Tell her what you do know, then get them out." The woman looked at Emilia. "You don't come back here, *chica*. Understand?"

"I understand," Emilia managed.

El Gordo lowered the gun and Emilia swayed in relief. He made his ponderous way back to the desk and sat, breathing heavily from the effort. The gun rested on the desk near his hand. Flores stood up but stayed where he was.

The enormous forger picked up the copies of the letters with his incongruously nimble hands. "I remember this job," he said, sucking in air between every word. "It was a few weeks ago. I had to age the papers, make them different, recreate the vegetable inks that would have been used at the time. We don't do too many jobs that take a long time, but letters are easy. No official seals, no special forms. Just letters."

By the door, the woman played with the kitchen towel in a way that made Emilia think of a rope used to strangle. El Flaco's angry confusion thickened the tension in the room. Flores breathed in little panicky puffs.

"The buyer couldn't wait here, of course." El Gordo went on, spittle forming on his lips as he struggled to breathe and speak at the same time. "He paid us and when the letters were done we delivered them to the address he gave us. A business in a warehouse. Delivered there two, three times."

"Blandón Hernandez's office," Emilia supplied. "In the

Costa Azul neighborhood."

"That's right."

"But did he pay for the letters?" Emilia pressed. "Or they were simply delivered there?"

"The buyer is a regular," El Gordo said. "Sometimes the deliveries are to his stall at the Mercado Municipal. Other times to someone else like Blandón Hernandez."

Emilia wiped tears off her face with the back of her hand. "He runs a stall at the Mercado Municipal?"

"Juan Fabio," El Gordo huffed. "The junkman. Go ask him where your sister is."

"Thank you," Emilia breathed. El Flaco hustled her and Flores out the door, past his hulking brother and the gray-haired woman and the towel twisted tight in her hands.

"What the hell were you thinking of?" Emilia snarled.

"Don't walk so fast," Flores said.

"Shut up, shut up," Emilia muttered. The trip back to the park in El Flaco's taxi had been silent and excruciating, Emilia expecting any moment that he'd take a wrong turn and produce the twin of his brother's gun. But they were unceremoniously dumped out a few blocks from the park and it was taking every bit of Emilia's self control not to run all the way to the burger place, which Silvio had designated as the rendezvous spot. If she didn't kill Flores before they got there it would be a miracle. "What the fuck were you thinking of? Feeding him some story that meant we had to show him identification?"

"I was protecting you," Flores exclaimed. "I didn't like--."

"You never, ever, ever give your real ID to a known criminal," Emilia rolled on. "Unless there's a gun to your head. Do you realize the problem you created?"

"It was more convincing this way," Flores said. "Otherwise if it was just about you needing a letter to get a job, why did I need to be there? That would make them suspicious."

"We talked about this!" Emilia exclaimed. She pulled him

into an alley behind a small grocery store. Plastic bags of trash reeked of rot and rats rustled near a dumpster. "The story would have worked fine. Instead you made up something on the fly that nearly got us both killed."

"I was protecting you," Flores insisted. "That taxi driver looked at you--."

"That didn't matter," Emilia wanted to scream. "You stick to the plan. The agreed-upon plan. You don't make up shit because that leaves you vulnerable."

Flores blinked at her.

"Who the hell do you think they work for most of the time?" Emilia poked him in the chest. "Do you know who their friends are? How they make enough money for that nice house? No, you don't. You weren't even thinking like that!"

"What are you saying?"

"Maybe they do some work for one of the street gangs that don't like cops. Maybe El Flaco gives them your real name and address. After all, he didn't seem to like us very much, did he? Thought maybe we were cops. Those two brothers want to get in good with the gang, well, we're going to be the cops they give up."

Flores flinched. "What about your bit of play acting?"

"I was pulling our asses out of the fire," Emilia said. "And barely pulled it off."

"We got what we wanted," Flores pointed out. "I thought you'd be happy."

Emilia turned and headed for the burger place.

Silvio was in a corner booth. He slid a cold cola across the table to Emilia and she marveled at how the world had changed to the extent that she could be so pathetically grateful to see his ugly face. She gave him a quick rundown of what had happened, expecting her partner to blow up at Flores. Instead he'd shaken his head and said, "You're lucky Cruz isn't wiping the floor with you, kid."

No one spoke on the way back to the police station. Once they parked the car, Flores got out and marched into the building.

Emilia didn't open her door.

"You got a name," Silvio said. "We can follow up."

"We got a name," Emilia affirmed.

"This is your fault, you know," Silvio growled.

Emilia grabbed her shoulder bag from the car floor. "How's that?"

"His story was a marriage certificate? Because he didn't like the way the taxi driver was coming on to you." Silvio rubbed a hand over his crew cut. "*Rayos*, Cruz. Better warn Hollywood he's got competition."

"Okay, Flores has got a crush on me," Emilia acknowledged. "Not my fault. I haven't done anything to encourage him. And when I kill him, he'll get over it."

Silvio scowled. "This is why women detectives are such a fucking bad idea."

Emilia jabbed her hand on the button to unlock her door. "You know what's such a fucking bad idea, Franco?"

"What?"

Emilia was so angry words failed her. "Nothing, just fucking nothing." She threw herself out of the car but stuck her head back in before she slammed the door. "You get him tomorrow."

Chapter 14

Emilia walked into the squadroom Tuesday morning. Silvio reached across their two desks and snatched up her coffee mug. As she dumped her shoulder bag into the desk drawer on top of the binder of *Las Perdidas*, he filled both her mug and his own from the coffee maker in the corner, then left the squadroom.

"What the hell?" Emilia glanced around. Flores wasn't there yet. The door to the lieutenant's office was closed. Castro and Gomez were at their desks. When Castro saw Emilia looking around he smacked his lips together suggestively.

Emilia locked the drawer. She crossed the squadroom to the door and nearly collided with Ibarra and Loyola coming in together. They were deep in conversation and ignored Emilia as she slid by. Ibarra left the stale scent of cigarettes in his wake.

She headed for the rear exit of the building past the holding cells. She shot the guards with her thumb and forefinger, like always, and they whistled and shot her back.

Silvio was waiting for her outside. Emilia closed the door and he held out her mug like a peace offering. They walked a little ways around the corner without speaking. Emilia drank the hot coffee with eyebrows raised over the rim of the mug.

"I talked to Perez in Organized Crime," Silvio said. "Found him in the gym this morning."

Emilia gave him a *so what?* look.

"Nobody's been assigned to the *Pacific Grandeur* murder case. Same as I predicted."

Emilia lowered her mug. "They haven't listened to Bonilla's interrogation tape yet?"

"No." Silvio slurped some coffee. "Nobody's been assigned, either, to find the Salva Diablo body that disappeared from the morgue."

"I thought it had been assigned to a uniformed unit."

"Salva Diablo," Silvio reminded her. "Anything related goes to Organized Crime. Perez said it's being regarded as an internal morgue fuck up."

"Prade did not lose that particular body by accident," Emilia said.

"It gets better." Silvio finished his coffee. "I asked Perez about the Customs cameras at the docks. Haven't been turned on since November. Cost cutting."

"So no chance of any footage showing the Salva Diablo guy getting on board the cruise ship," Emilia conceded unhappily.

"Makes you think nobody gives a shit about this case, doesn't it?" Silvio folded his arms, empty mug dangling below forearms thick with muscle.

Emilia shook her head. "Or somebody's going to a lot of trouble to make sure Bonilla, Ramos, and the *Pacific Grandeur* aren't examined too closely. What did Perez say about the possibility of the *Pacific Grandeur* being used to smuggle Ora Ciega?"

"Not much," Silvio said. "Basically dismissed it as conjecture based on shit in a dead guy's pocket."

"How stupid would we be if we didn't make that connection?" Emilia exclaimed. "Ora Ciega, transport to *El Norte*, dead *tumbadore*. It's not a hard one."

Silvio squinted up at the sky. "If you were going to start running Colombian Ora Ciega through Mexico, using Honduras as your trampoline, who would you pay off first?"

"Local cops," Emilia said, still fuming at Organized Crime. "*Federales*. The usual. Why?"

"Customs, Cruz," Silvio said, as if she'd missed the point. "First Mexican authority a cruise ship encounters when it docks."

"Maybe," Emilia said. She finished her coffee. "But consider this. Bonilla and Ramos are two *norteamericanos*. If they're moving high-priced Ora Ciega through Acapulco, they aren't doing it on their own. Same for Salva Diablo. They might be big in Honduras but they're nobodies here. They'd need permission from a big player already operating here, at the very least."

"Agreed," Silvio said. "Salva Diablo doesn't have a foothold in Mexico. Bonilla and Ramos are two guys who'd be dead already if they were moving Ora Ciega on their own. More likely all of them are at the bottom of the pyramid and somebody big is calling the shots and making the local payoffs. Same network that Bonilla called after killing the Salva Diablo kid."

Emilia's coffee was beginning to kick in. "You think it's Customs."

"Interesting coincidence their database going down when it did."

"It actually seemed genuine," Emilia pointed out. Irma Gonzalez's sympathetic smile lodged in the back of her mind. "If there is something going on, the woman in charge of that employee database doesn't know."

"We can try her once again," Silvio said. "But we don't tell Flores. He'll run his mouth off and somebody will end up real dead. We just keep him on the kidnapping case."

"Regarding the kidnapping case," Emilia said. "I've got something to do before trying to find this Juan Fabio."

Silvio spewed out air. "Now what?"

"Do you remember Lila Jimenez Lata?"

"The lost girl." Silvio nodded.

"Her mother turned up dead in the morgue last week. At least it might be her mother." Emilia gave Silvio a swift rundown of encountering the body in the morgue, Pedro Montealegre's response, and Prade's startling news of a name change and husband. "I've got an address for the husband."

"You think he can lead to the daughter?"

"It's worth a shot."

"Fuck, Cruz." Silvio stamped his feet. "How long is this going to take?"

"I don't know," Emilia said. "Take Flores to the gym. Teach him how to handle himself. El Flaco put him on the floor with one slap."

Silvio's scowl shifted into a rare sideways grin.

"Make it look like an accident," Emilia said. She was

pretty sure she was kidding.

The sign over the pink-painted stucco building read *Academia de Belleza Trinidad.* It was located at an intersection in Colonia Bellavista, a working class neighborhood northwest of the docks. Like so many of the parts of the city hugging the base of the mountains, Colonia Bellavista was bereft of the glamour and money that ringed the bay. Here, Acapulco was just a city where people scrambled to stay away from the violence, make a living, go to church.

The windows of the beauty school were covered with scrolled white iron grilles but the door was open. Emilia slowed as she drove past, checking out the people lounging in front. It was a sociable corner, with a newsstand a few meters down the way on one side, and a small *abarrotes* shop selling snacks on the other. A couple of rusted vehicles were parked on the street but nothing looked immediately threatening. Emilia drove around the block. It was all the same; scuffed and sagging cement, tears of rust around downspouts, advertisements painted onto walls, thick dust courtesy of the dry season and the chronic water shortages of forgotten neighborhoods. The buildings were low here; one or two stories with flat roofs and tangled electrical wires overhead; a far cry from the shiny white towers a bus ride away.

Emilia parked and walked to the beauty school. The interior was cool and dim. She stood in the entrance for a moment, letting her eyes adjust. There wasn't much to see. Two white plastic chairs, the kind in every outdoor taco joint, were clustered to the right near a desk littered with an appointment book and well-thumbed beauty magazines. On the other side of the room, two salon work stations sported vinyl swiveling chairs on pedestals and mirrors scarred by age and hairline cracks. An old fashioned hair dryer with a big plastic hood was propped on a makeshift wooden ledge above a faded blue fabric office chair. A pink sink with a cutout in front hung on the wall next to the dryer. The plumbing pipes were exposed and shiny with green mold.

A woman of indeterminate age, enveloped in a dotted plastic poncho, sat in one of the swivel chairs in front of the mirrors. A young girl, with a wad of gum in her mouth and electric blue streaks in her own hair, was doing something with the woman's head that involved foil wrappers and toxic-smelling brown glop.

The girl looked at Emilia questioningly as she twisted another piece of foil into her customer's hair.

"I'm looking for Vikram," Emilia said.

"You got an appointment?" The girl champed her gum as she slathered glop on another unfortunate strand of hair.

"I need to talk to him about his wife," Emilia said.

The girl paused to wipe her nose on the back of her hand. Emilia realized that the customer in the salon chair had her eyes closed. She appeared to be sleeping. Or maybe the stink of the hair potion had asphyxiated her and no one had noticed.

"She's dead."

It took a moment for Emilia to realize the girl was talking about Vikram's wife, not her client. "I know," Emilia said.

"The funeral was yesterday." The gum circled the girl's mouth, slid over her lips and back.

"Is Vikram here?" Emilia asked.

The girl pasted more glop on the woman's head. "He's only talking to customers."

Emilia walked over to the desk and turned the appointment book so she could read the entries. There were entries for Vikram and Juana, who presumably was the blue-haired stylist. Emilia wrote her first name in Vikram's column. "Now he's got a customer."

Juana made a big show of putting down her bowl of glop, digging out a cell phone, and pressing buttons. "You got a customer," she said into the phone and broke the connection. She picked up the bowl again and turned to look at Emilia, as if remembering something difficult. "Have a seat. He'll be right down."

Emilia took a chair by the desk and idly flipped through

one of the beauty magazines. She rarely read fluff like that, even more rarely bought makeup. The hairstyles were all layered or colored or updos; styles worn by guests at the Palacio Réal. And Christina Boudreau.

A man came around the side of the partition, smiled vaguely at the three women in the room and went to the desk. He had caramel skin and ageless features that spoke of a blended heritage. His hair braids, woven with tiny beads that clattered by his shoulders, suggested the Caribbean, rather than Mexico, yet he wore a long white tunic that Emilia had seen men wear in news stories about India or Pakistan. Below the tunic he had on jeans and loafers that were shined but not new.

He looked at the appointment book, then raised his head. "Emilia?" he asked. "What would you like done today?"

His words flowed with an attractive Jamaican lilt. Emilia stood up. "Are you Vikram Trinidad? The husband of Yola de Trinidad?"

"Yes, of course." He suddenly looked to be on the verge of tears and hid it by crossing to the second salon station and rattling the combs in a glass cup of blue solution. "Thank you for your sympathies."

"I was sorry to hear of her passing," Emilia said. She didn't know why she should be so taken aback at the obvious display of emotion. Perhaps Pedro Montealegre's reaction to the news of his mother's death had led her assume everyone would have the same reaction. "I'd like to ask you a few questions about her."

"We shall style and talk, no?" As if to cover his tearful state, Trinidad plopped Emilia into the swivel chair, used the foot pedal to raise the seat, and draped a giant dotted plastic tarp around her neck, trapping her arms under its weight. "Maybe a perm today, no?"

"I'm not--." Emilia had barely started to speak when Juana's toxic potion got the better of her and she began to cough.

Trinidad took out her ponytail holder and fluffed her hair over her shoulders.

"I'm not really here for a new hair style," Emilia said, managing to swallow another cough. She tried to find the edge of the plastic tarp. The pink polka dots seemed to be everywhere. Her similarly swathed neighbor in the other chair was still asleep.

"Maybe some highlights, no?" Trinidad doused Emilia's head with cold water from a spray bottle and combed it out. "This is the Academia de Belleza Trinidad. You want the best style, you come to Vikram."

Emilia looked into the mirror through the strands of hair in front of her face. Trinidad's face was more composed, as if his work was a solace. "Maybe a quick trim," she conceded. "Like in the magazine."

Trinidad beamed, grabbed a magazine, found a page, and waved it in front of Emilia. "A beautiful look for you, no? Something a little fancy."

Before Emilia could answer he'd stowed the magazine and squirted enough water on her head to wash an elephant. Emilia waited while he examined his selection of scissors and razors, making a show of laying everything out on the shelf in front of the salon chair. When he began combing out her wet hair she started with an easy question. "How long were you married to Yola?"

"Two years."

"How did you meet?"

He hesitated. "A mutual friend."

Emilia wondered if it had been a pimp. "I knew her family," she said.

"Yola knew a lot of people," Trinidad said carefully. He began snipping Emilia's hair.

At the other workstation, Juana popped her gum a few times and set a timer. She took her bowl and applicator to the sink across the room, washed them out and left them on the rim. "Ten minutes," she said to Trinidad. She stepped into the street with cell phone, and a pack of cigarettes in hand.

Emilia glanced at the client whom Juana had left. The woman now had a full head of foil wrappers yet hadn't moved a muscle since Emilia had walked into the beauty school. The pink polka-dotted plastic covered her from neck to knees and every fold was exactly the same. The woman's eyes remained closed.

"Did you know Yola when she called herself Yolanda Lata?" Emilia asked.

Trinidad's snipping stopped. "Yes."

"Did you know she had children?"

"Yes." He sighed and began snipping again. "Two. Grownup children."

"I've been looking for the girl," Emilia said leadingly. She watched Trinidad's reaction in the mirror as he combed and snipped, combed and snipped. "Lila Jimenez Lata. She's gone missing and I wondered if Yolanda—I mean, Yola—had seen her recently."

"She didn't come to the funeral," Trinidad said. "She probably doesn't even know her mother is dead."

Emilia felt her heart race. "She was here before? When?"

"Maybe two months ago."

"Do you have her phone number? An address?"

Trinidad shook his head. "It was the first and only time Lila was ever here. They argued. Lila had a new boyfriend and she was going someplace with him. Yola didn't like him."

"Do you know where this boy was going to take Lila?"

"No. It was Yola's business, not mine," he said.

He made a funny noise in the back of his throat. When Emilia looked in the mottled mirror she could see his face working with the effort not to cry. "I know that Yola died of a drug overdose," she said. "Can you tell me what happened?"

"We were here," he said and jabbed his scissors at the ceiling to indicate the second floor. "Sunday evening. A little before 8:00 pm."

"Did she go out?"

Trinidad owned the cabinet under the mirror and took out two toothpaste-sized tubes. He got Juana's bowl from the sink and began mixing orange and black goo from the tubes into the bowl. "I went to my friend's house to watch the boxing, no? He has a big television and we sometimes go there. Yola didn't want to go. She said she didn't feel right. Sometimes when she said that I knew she missed the drugs. I shouldn't have gone but I did. She wasn't here when I came home."

"Had she ever done that before?" Emilia asked. "Go out without telling you?"

"I knew what Yola was when I married her," he said. "The whole time I wondered when she would leave. And she did, in the way I always feared." He began pasting dye onto Emilia's hair, using foil wrappers like the other stylist. "When she didn't come home, I called and called. When she didn't answer I started looking. Talked to everyone who knew her. Went to all the hospitals. Finally, to the morgue."

"I'm sorry," Emilia said.

Trinidad's hands moved rapidly, creating foil rolls over Emilia's head. He stepped back. "Good. Now we wait for the color." He discarded the empty tubes of dye. "If you want, you can look through Yola's things. See if there's anything about Lila."

Still swathed in her pink dotted tarp, Emilia followed Trinidad up a flight of stairs and into a small apartment. The building was old and the walls were faded stucco but the furniture was decent and a flat screen television dominated the living room. Trinidad led her into a bedroom with a double bed under a thick cotton spread, a rocking chair strewn with women's clothing, and a dresser topped with perfume bottles, makeup, and a capiz shell dish. Trinidad touched the dish. "This is where Yola always put her phone." He told Emilia to look around, then left.

There was so little in the room that it barely took five minutes to rifle through the dresser and check for hiding places. In the bottom dresser drawer Emilia found a sheaf of mementos: a wedding day photograph of Yolanda and Trinidad, their marriage license, a faded photo of a little boy who would one day call himself Pedro Montealegre, another of a toddler girl. A strip of photos taken in a booth, similar to a strip Emilia had once found of Lila and Pedro together, revealed four recent poses of Yolanda and Lila with their arms around each other.

Emilia sank onto the bed. In all the months she'd been

hunting for Lila, all she'd known was that the girl had wanted to find her mother. This was the first confirmation that Lila had found the mother who'd abandoned her as a toddler.

Mother and daughter looked like sisters, rather than mother and daughter, mostly due to the amount of makeup Lila wore. In two of the pictures Yolanda was holding a cell phone as if taking a selfie at the same time. Her phone case was bright pink and had a "Y" outlined in rhinestones on the back.

Emilia went into the living room and showed the photo strip to Trinidad. "This is Yolanda and Lila, isn't it?"

"Yes."

"Can I keep this?"

Trinidad agreed and they went back down to the salon where he busied himself taking out the foil from Emilia's hair, rinsing it in the sink, and then exclaiming over the improvement. Emilia could barely bring herself to look. When she did her mouth fell open. Her hair was streaked with a harsh ruby color. Red tentacles leached out of the center of her head.

She managed to smile weakly at Trinidad, who was obviously very pleased with the result. "Just what you needed," he beamed. "You're young. Have some fun with your looks."

It's just hair, Emilia reminded herself before she cried. "Can you tell me more about Yolanda—er, Yola's friends?" she asked.

"You know Alfonso?" Trinidad asked as he pummeled Emilia's hair with a blow dryer.

"He's a dealer?"

"A pimp. When Yola needed drugs he'd help her find a way to pay."

"You think Yola introduced Lila to Alfonso?"

Trinidad sighed. "Maybe. They were alike, you know. Even in those pictures you can see Yola in her daughter's eyes."

"Do you know where I can find Alfonso?"

"No, but I know that he's little." He held his hand at his hip. "Only this tall."

"*Madre de Dios,*" Emilia murmured. *Chavito. He was talking about Chavito.* All of the detectives knew the dwarf who pimped out most of the girls who worked the streets across from the Fuerte San Diego fortress. Not exactly glamor territory but a steady stream of tourists visiting the museum inside the fort made it worthwhile.

The timer rang, making them both jump. The woman in the other salon chair opened her eyes, saw Emilia's red streaks in the mirror, and screamed.

Chapter 15

By the time Emilia got to the Mercado Municipal it was late in the afternoon. She parked in a relatively safe street a few blocks west of the market and stopped inside the entrance where an older woman with scarred hands was grilling quesadillas on a flat steel *comal* griddle set on an open flame. A small child stoked the fire, which crackled inside half a steel barrel perched on homemade wrought iron legs. He giggled and pointed when he saw Emilia's hair.

The smell of tomatoes, cheese, and onions bubbling together over the open flame made Emilia's mouth water and she realized how much coffee she'd been drinking lately in lieu of food. She ate two quesadillas standing up by the grill. When she was done she asked the woman if she knew Juan Fabio, the junkman.

"Which one is he?" the women queried.

"The one named Juan Fabio," Emilia said.

"Which junkman?" The woman tossed another tortilla on the *comal*, her face damp with sweat. Two customers jostled for a spot near the small griddle. Emilia moved on.

The Mercado Municipal was a warren of corrugated iron stalls arranged in rows and divided by narrow pathways. The fearless shopper could find everything there from holy candles to skinned pigs to baby formula and everything in between. It was a high crime area and tourists were recommended to stay away but there were still booths that sold sea shells and tin ornaments and black *barro* figurines for the unwary to buy. Tourists were always calling the central police number to report being pickpocketed or having bags stolen. As far as Emilia knew, no one ever followed up on any of those calls.

There was more than one entrance into the market and she'd ended up by the food section. Vendors showcased their offerings by stringing up scrawny red carcasses that could be cats or jackrabbits or odd cuts of beef between the uprights of the booths. A bloody board invariably waited for the vendor to chop off as much meat as the customer could afford. The rest of the carcass would be put back on display and some unlucky late shopper would be left with just the head or feet.

Emilia stifled a retch as she plowed through, often having to turn sideways to pass through the narrow aisles full of dawdling shoppers and aggressive vendors. The meat section gave way to the fruit and vegetable stalls where the attar of rotting fruit was as cloying as the butcher smells.

She kept going, turning into a section devoted to containers: woven palm baskets, plastic tubs and buckets, melamine bowls and cups. In the aisle, two old ladies argued over plastic tumblers decorated with cat cartoons and Emilia had to practically shout "*Permiso!*" before they let her get by. The baby section was next, booths full of disposable diapers in clear plastic-wrapped bundles of 10 or 20 stacked next to cans of baby formula, cloth bibs, and boxes filled with assorted jars of baby food.

Dogs and cats in cages dominated the next aisle, along with bags of dry pet food. Emilia passed flowers and a shoe repair stand, a few men selling picture frames, and then she was in an aisle with candles on both sides, pillars of wax decorated with pictures of Our Lady of Guadalupe, San Juan Diego, and San Miguel el Arcángel. There were plain wax candles besides the religious ones, candles that smelled like apples or melon, candles that had strings and plastic coins wrapped around them to bring luck and wealth.

A turn down the next aisle and Emilia was in junk heaven. The booths were larger, each a second-hand store. Many had garish signs advertising their wares. A pig advertised *Everything For The Home*, while a pirate pointed to *Hidden Treasures*. The best sign incorporated a half-naked hula girl whose grass shirt spelled out *Chatarra*. Junk.

Emilia drifted up to the first stall on the right. Musical instruments in varying shades of tarnish hung from the ceiling joists alongside pots, pans, buckets, and handled washtubs. Bundles of fabric were piled on top of appliances, jostling for space with plastic crates of toys, Christmas ornaments, pocketbooks, hand tools, and plastic dishes.

"You need kitchenware, señora?" A greasy man in a dirty plaid shirt flashed a smile at Emilia, revealing a gap where two upper teeth had once been. The gum line was dark with disease. He shoved aside some crates and fingered some curtain fabric. "Drapery. Like new. Or maybe you're looking for sheets? What size bed?"

"Are you Juan Fabio?" Emilia asked.

"Juan Fabio," the man scoffed. He thrust a bundle at Emilia. "He has nothing new. This is the best *chatarra* stall in the entire *mercado*. You need something pretty for your bedroom? This is where all the ladies come."

The bundle was a bedspread made of some quilted material stiff enough to be sharkskin. Emilia set it back on top of what appeared to be an ancient washing machine. "No, thanks, not today."

The vendor unhooked a heavy iron pan from a hook in the ceiling. "See, French iron. Cast iron makes the best *guisados*. Good for catching a man." The vendor winked. "Or teaching a lesson if he looks around, no?"

"Maybe I'll need it for Juan Fabio," Emilia said archly.

The old man hooted with laughter. "Last on the right. The best corner."

Two stalls down on the left, the vendor had evidently seen the exchange with the cast iron pan because he held out the exact same pan as Emilia passed. "Five hundred pesos," he sang out as Emilia neared. "Best price for a pretty señora."

"Five hundred?" Emilia asked. She could buy it new for less. "I heard Juan Fabio has the best prices."

The vendor shook his head and frowned when he couldn't get Emilia to handle the pan. "He doesn't have the good stuff."

Emilia gave a little backwards wave as she kept going down the aisle. The stalls on either side were a blur of old and new, colors and scratches, chipped edges. Emilia could have bought an entire household, from pictures of the Virgin of Guadalupe to a drain stopper and everything in between. There was everything except marked prices. Negotiations determined final cost. The vendors were sharp and experienced; Emilia was sure no one came away from the market with a bargain.

The sign on the corner stall was simple: *Juan Fabio The Best For You.* The other vendor was right; the corner location got Juan Fabio foot traffic from the main aisle but also from the intersecting one. A café across the way was an added bonus.

The stall was full to bursting with the odds and ends of life: dishes, pots, pans, trays, flashlights, hammers, packages of nails and screws, knobs, cans of paint with color smeared on top so the customer would know what they were buying. Emilia picked her way through packages of hairpins and sewing notions, a collection of dog leashes, stacks of nearly new school notebooks, and a display of rolled up towels. Empty frames of all sizes hung on nails protruding from the back wall. The stall was more orderly than others, with items tucked into wooden shelves. An effort had been made to arrange things by household category.

A teenaged girl sat on a stool near the entrance to the stall. A corner of the wooden shelves functioned as a desk, and held a calculator and a pad of receipts. Pink plastic bags dangled from a hook on the wall. Like most of the vendors, the girl had a money belt strapped to her waist in lieu of a cash register. She was playing a game on the same sort of expensive tablet that Kurt had given Emilia for Christmas. The tablet was sleek and modern and out of place.

"Hi," Emilia said, forcing the girl to look up. "Is Juan Fabio around?"

"No." The girl appraised Emilia. "Cool hair. You look like Avenga."

"Who's that?"

The girl held up the tablet. "Avenga. You know. From the game."

Emilia nodded like, sure, she knew who Avenga was. Had always wanted hair like a cartoon character. "Is he going to be back soon?"

"No," the girl said. "You need to buy something or are you here for the petition?"

"What petition?"

The girl sighed, put down the tablet, and handed Emilia a brochure.

The cover proclaimed *Sainthood for Padre Pro!* It was decorated with a color drawing of a priest in a cassock with his arms outstretched being threatened by a soldier with a drawn sword. It was an exact copy of the picture on the back of the Padre Pro relic case.

Emilia skimmed the text. The brochure was from the Friends of Padre Pro, asking the faithful to sign a petition forcing the Vatican to canonize him as a saint. Details of Padre Pro's life, death, and reported miracles were given. Emilia recognized some of the language from the forged letters that had accompanied the relic. Contact information for the Friends of Padre Pro was an email address from a free service.

"If you sign the petition, you can have a novena dedicated to Padre Pro said for you." The girl rattled off the words as if he did it dozens of times a day. "Only 200 pesos."

Emilia pocketed the brochure. "Let me see the petition." Juan Fabio might be a junkman, but he was also either a religious zealot or a con artist scamming Padre Pro's legacy.

The girl thrust a grubby clipboard at Emilia. The first page repeated the message from the brochure. The rest of the pages were full of barely legible signatures. Emilia estimated that the total number of signatures on the clipboard was around 200.

As she studied the signatures, half-hoping to find something relevant, it occurred to Emilia that the Friends of Padre Pro might not be local to Acapulco. There could be national chapters hawking the petition, with other body parts floating around purporting to be that of the long-dead priest. The thought made Emilia's stomach churn.

"I need to talk to Juan Fabio before I sign anything." She handed back the clipboard. "When is he going to be around?"

"Saturday."

"I really need to speak to him now," Emilia said. She tucked 400 pesos under the receipt pad; 200 for the novena, 200 for the girl. "Where does he live?"

The girl eyed the money, obviously making the same

calculation. "I don't know."

"How about a cell phone number?" Emilia asked.

"He doesn't have one."

"What do you do when there's a problem here at the stall and you have to ask him a question?"

"I tell him on Saturday."

"What about the money at the end of the day?" Emilia pressed. "What do you do with it?"

"There's a safe."

Emilia slid the pesos back into her pocket, teeth gritted in exasperation.

"You don't look so much like Avenga after all," the girl said scornfully.

Sophia dropped a plate and screamed when Emilia walked into the kitchen. "Emilia, you're bleeding!"

Madre de Dios. Panic surged as Emilia felt her chest, her arms, her face.

Sophia screamed again and pointed to Emilia's head.

Emilia swayed with relief. "Mama, it's hair dye."

She pulled her mother close so that Sophia could more clearly see the red streaks.

"Hair dye?" Sophia cautiously touched the colored strands. "Why did you do such a thing? What was going on at school today?"

Emilia set down her shoulder bag, stripped off her jacket and holster, and picked up the shards of broken china. "It was an accident. I'll get Mercedes to help me dye it back to normal."

Ten minutes later, the kitchen floor was clean and Emilia tied an apron around her waist. It didn't happen often, but when Sophia was having a good day, it was nice to putter in the kitchen with her mother and talk of insignificant things; the price of onions, Padre Ricardo's Sunday sermon, how fast her cousin Alvaro's children were growing. Of late, the talk had turned to Sophia and Ernesto's upcoming wedding, as well as Ernesto's growing business. A sewing workshop a few blocks away continually brought him scissors to sharpen, and the courtyard saw a steady stream of gardeners with blunt-edged grass clippers, pruning shears, and machetes.

"Padre Ricardo said I should ask you if we want music for the wedding." Sophia poured oil into the bottom of her biggest pot.

"Sure." Emilia stuck a fork into a tomato, wrapped a cloth around the handle, and began the careful process of roasting off the tomato skin over the stove's gas burner. "We could get a mariachi. Everybody does. But it's up to you, Mama."

Sophia sniffed. "But this is a remarriage. Do people do that for remarriages?"

The tomato skin blackened and blistered and Emilia turned it carefully to get the other side. Ernesto bore the same name as Emilia's late father. Despite many conversations, Sophia frequently insisted that her intended was her original husband. "I think you can do what you want, Mama," Emilia said.

Sophia reached into her apron pocket and pulled out a handful of paper. Receipts from the market, a folded piece of lined school paper, and a business card fell onto the counter. She unfolded the lined paper. "This is what Padre Ricardo gave me."

Emilia's eye slid to the business card. The name *Lupita Navarro* was printed on it. "Mama, where did you get Señora Navarro's card?"

"Honestly, Emilia. I told you." Sophia shook her head at such a forgetful daughter. "Señora Navarro was here this morning asking to talk to you."

"No, you didn't tell me," Emilia said, trying to mask her irritation. Lupita Navarro was the owner of their house. Emilia had first rented from the woman eight years ago, when the monthly payment had felt exorbitant, and had always been the one to deal with her. Señora Navarro rarely dropped in unannounced. She almost always called first or sent an email asking if it was convenient for her to stop by.

"Yes, I did." Sophia looked at the crisping tomato. "Don't burn it."

Emilia plunged the blistered tomato into a bowl of cold water, rubbed away the scorched skin, then began the process again with a second tomato. "Did she say why she wanted to talk to me?"

"Something about insurance." Sophia began chopping a white onion.

"Did you give her my cell phone number?"

"Was I supposed to?" Sophia asked. "You didn't tell me to."

"I didn't know she was coming."

Sophia made a disapproving face as she minced the onion. "You should have told her to tell you."

Emilia counted to ten in her head. "Yes, that would have been good. I guess I'll have to call and see what she wanted."

Sophia stirred rice and onions into the hot oil while Emilia chopped the peeled tomatoes. When the rice changed from opaque to transparent, Emilia added the tomatoes, cilantro, and chicken broth. While the *arroz rojo* cooked, Sophia took out three small sea bass. Emilia was reminded of Pedro Montealegre's office.

The stink of sardines and sadness. A sense of things struggling to remain hidden.

Chapter 16

Wednesday morning, Emilia's police badge got her through the security at the entrance to the Customs building. Once inside, her name was still in the computer from the last time she'd been there and the security guard handed her a visitor tag to pin on her lapel. She remembered the way to the Human Resources department and Irma Gonzalez Perot's office.

She rode the elevator to the right floor. When they opened she saw the frosted green glass wall, plush carpeting, and the semicircular receptionist desk that sat like a guard post in front of doors leading into the Human Resources department. The doors were of the same frosted glass and their long chrome handles were the only way to tell they were doors and not a continuation of the wall. Again, in that setting, Emilia thought that Irma had done well career-wise. The place was certainly a big step up from a battered metal desk in the detectives squadroom.

The receptionist popped to attention as the elevator doors swished closed behind Emilia. "May I help you?"

"I'm here to see Irma Gonzalez Perot," Emilia said. She tapped the visitor chit. "I've been here before and she has something for me to pick up."

The young girl sucked in her breath as she blinked nervously at Emilia. "Was she expecting you?"

"Yes," Emilia said. "My colleague called yesterday."

The girl pointed to a row of chairs. "Could you please take a seat?"

"I don't have a lot of time," Emilia said. Either the red-streaked hair had unnerved the girl or there was another problem.

"Yes, of course," the girl assured her. "It will only take a minute."

Emilia walked over to the chairs. There was a small coffeemaker in the corner, the type that swallowed up capsules of goo and dribbled out plastic-smelling liquid. Magazines were artfully arranged into a fan. Emilia selected a thick fashion magazine featuring a well known Hollywood actress. Emilia flipped through the glossy pages. None of the clothes looked remotely practical, everything cost a fortune, the shoes had ridiculously tall heels, and for the first time Emilia wanted it all. Not for everyday life, of course, when jeans and a jacket to cover her gun were the most sensible things to wear. But when she was at the Palacio Réal or when she and Kurt went out.

The elevator doors swished open and an older man in an elegantly tailored brown suit got off. The receptionist indicated Emilia. He approached and Emilia stood up.

"Wilfredo Sarmiento," he introduced himself and held out his hand. "I understand you are here to see Irma."

"Yes." Emilia shook his hand and was pleased he didn't give the limp or partial hand grasp handshake so many men did. "Emilia Cruz Encinos."

"What was the nature of your appointment?" Sarmiento looked at her with concern. "A job application perhaps?"

"I'm a police detective," Emilia said. "Irma has some information for me that may be helpful in a murder investigation. But if she's not available, maybe one of her staff can help."

"What sort of information?" Sarmiento asked.

"A list of Customs employees who were working a particular shift at the cruise ship dock several weeks ago." Emilia watched Sarmiento as he wrung his hands in distress. He was close to retirement age, a grandfatherly man with thick gray hair and a moustache. He obviously held a very senior position from the way the receptionist regarded him with a mix of awe and fear.

Sarmiento gestured for Emilia to resume her seat and took the one next to her. "Were you close to Irma?" he asked.

Emilia noted the past tense. "Has something happened to her?"

Sarmiento pressed his lips together, closed his eyes as if in pain, and took a deep breath. He opened his eyes. "We lost

Irma yesterday. No one knew that she was depressed. She wiped the entire Human Resources employee database then drove her car off the road."

Emilia blinked. "Irma committed suicide?"

"We lost the data for the last two years," Sarmiento went on as if Emilia hadn't spoken.

His words rattled around in Emilia's head as if the walls of the handsome lobby had become an echoing canyon.

"You say Irma wiped the database?" Emilia verified, trying to keep her face from betraying her thoughts. "Why would she do that?"

Sarmiento shook his head sadly. "The database was her baby. She'd written the code for it. Nursed it into being. There were a few glitches. But no one blamed her."

The back end is all magic to me. Emilia felt her mouth start to tremble and put up a hand to cover her lips.

Sarmiento gestured to indicate the modern Customs building and all the compassionate employees it housed. "As I say, no one knew how depressed she must have been. Irma was very popular. A successful young mother. We are all still in shock."

"Of course," Emilia murmured from behind her fingers.

"I'm afraid we won't be able to provide you with your list, Detective."

Emilia stood up, desperate to get out of the building. "I understand. Thank you for letting me know." She managed a mournful expression, despite her wild heartbeat and the need to run, flee, get away *now now now*. "It wasn't that important. An afterthought, really."

"I'm sorry you had to come down here for nothing," Sarmiento said with feeling.

☼

Emilia's dumped her shoulder bag on the desk, slumped into her chair, and buried her face in her hands.

"*Rayos*, Cruz." Silvio's snicker filtered from across their desks. "Head get caught in one of those machines that paint stripes on the road?"

"Yolanda Lata's husband runs a beauty school," Emilia said from behind her hands.

"Must not have passed your finals," Silvio guffawed.

"She's dead," Emilia said, trying to get her breathing under control.

"I know, that's why you went there."

"Not Yolanda," Emilia said. "Irma. From Customs. The nice lady with the little kid and the handsome husband."

"She's dead?" Silvio demanded. "Since when? I talked to her yesterday."

"After talking to you, she supposedly destroyed their human resources database and committed suicide by driving off the road."

"Did you get the employee rosters?"

"What do you think?"

The only answer Emilia got was the furious clicking of Silvio's computer keys, followed by a string of muttered profanity. "Got the accident report," he said finally. "Uniforms responded. Went off the cliff east of Playa Revolcadero by the new construction."

Emilia dropped her hands. *"Madre de Dios,"* she breathed. "The same road."

"What about the road?"

"I think I was followed on that road on Saturday," Emilia said. "Rental car, but I have a name and address. I haven't had time to check out the *cédula.*" She told him what had happened with the gray sedan and produced the information that the dispatch sergeant had given her.

"Juan Colón Sotelo, Mexico City," Silvio muttered, typing furiously again.

Flores was across the squadroom at his desk, a pile of folders at his elbow. He didn't look up. Emilia assumed he was still plowing through past kidnapping cases, trying to find a link to the Padre Pro finger case.

"If this is your guy, he's a ghost," Silvio said quietly. Emilia walked around to look at his screen. Silvio pointed to the database entry.

The name was correct. The address was correct. But Juan Colón Sotelo had died two years ago.

The squadroom blurred and Emilia had to steady herself with both hands on Silvio's desk. Recycling old identities was a well-known cartel practice, as was using forged *cédulas*. Certain national police operations reportedly used *cédulas* from the deceased for undercover operations, but as far as Emilia knew the practice was limited and not used by municipal police forces. She hauled in air and the room steadied. "Now what?"

"What else besides the *Pacific Grandeur* case have you been working on that could get somebody real mad at you?" Silvio asked. "Somebody big."

They quickly reviewed the last dozen or so cases they'd handled. Several thefts, a string of car window smashes, two murders that looked like the result of domestic disputes. The investigations had gone the usual way, which meant that no witnesses had come forward with credible information and they hadn't even come close to an arrest. There hadn't been any security lapses or other odd episodes during the investigations that would call attention to her. "There's nothing here that would make me a target," Emilia said. "No more than you."

Silvio closed down his computer. "You got something to do the rest of the day that doesn't involve the *Pacific Grandeur* case?" he asked. "Or anything to do with Ora Ciega? What about your finger?"

"We're on hold until Saturday." Emilia gave him the short version of her trip to Juan Fabio's stall at the market. "But Trinidad gave me another possible lead to Lila. I need to look into it."

"Take Flores with you," Silvio said as he stood up and grabbed his jacket. "He's better than nothing."

"Where are you going?"

"Another little talk with Perez," Silvio said.

"I hear you had a friend named Yolanda Lata," Emilia said. "Some people called her Yola."

"Lata," Chavito corrected her. "That was her street name."

Chavito was definitely a dwarf, but he wasn't as small as Trinidad had indicated. He had a broad, flat face with a high forehead and a sheen of hair marcelled into ringlets. Given his custom fitted jeans, designer logo tee, and heavy gold neck chains, Emilia figured he was making decent money off his stable of girls.

She'd told Flores the story of Lila Jimenez Lata on the way over to the area by the Fuerte San Diego. Parking was hard to find, so she left the car at Sanborn's, one of her favorite stores, and they strolled toward the pedestrian walkway leading into the pentagon-shaped fort's maze of massive walls and museum displays. Flores listened attentively and asked a few questions. He'd lost Monday's tone of defensive bravado; Emilia figured his day with Silvio had done the young cop some good.

They'd found Chavito loitering about half a block from the entrance to the fort, by the intersection of Hornitos and Morelos, handing out flyers for "Acapulco's Top Models." The pimp had recognized Emilia and hooted at her hair. Flores had been discomfited when Chavito extended his hand, but shook it anyway.

"Okay, Lata," Emilia confirmed.

Chavito smirked and mimed opening a can of soda. "Lata. Because no matter what the customer wanted, she'd always pop her top."

Flores caught his breath.

"She's dead," Emilia said with ice in her voice.

Chavito nodded. "Overdose."

"How long did she work for you?" Flores asked. He had a faint bruise on his jaw and was wearing the black jacket again.

Chavito squinted up at Flores. "I don't have such a good memory any more, you know?"

"He wants money," Flores said to Emilia.

Of course he wants money, you idiot. Emilia knew her temper was balanced on the knife edge. She grabbed Chavito by the collar and swung him down the street. "Let's go for a walk."

"Hey, hey." Chavito clawed at her hand. "I'm remembering. Lata was around a long time. Six years, maybe more. Sometimes she found other gigs but she always came back."

Emilia shoved Chavito against a wall, then jammed Flores in front of the pimp, blocking his escape. For good measure she stepped on Chavito's foot. "Next question," she said. "Lata came to you about two weeks ago. A Sunday night. Said she needed a hit."

"You know I don't sell shit," Chavito said, his words punctuated with indignation. He held up the flyers. "I run an introduction service."

"Sure," Emilia said. "Who did you introduce Lata to?"

"If her husband gave her money from his panty-assed beauty school she wouldn't need to pull tricks." Chavito leaned forward, eyebrows raised, ringlets quivering around his ears. "But I'll tell you a secret. Lata loved the tricks. Never saw a girl who loved it more. I thought when she hitched up with Trinidad she'd disappear. But she always came back and I always set her up real good."

Emilia thought of Pedro. He'd known his mother well. "So tell me about her last set up. What happened?"

Chavito tried to squirm his foot out from under Emilia's. "I don't know. He paid, they went to the hotel. El Lago. Two streets over. I assumed Lata got her fix, went home to her husband. Next thing I hear, Lata's been found dead a block from the hotel. I put the word out but nobody's seen the guy."

"When you saw Lata," Emilia asked, stamping harder. "Did she have her phone with her?"

"Sure." Chavito nodded and stopped trying to free his foot. "Big pink thing with her initial on it. She probably fucked that phone, too, she loved it so much."

"I need to find it," Emilia said.

"Why?" Chavito looked at her with suspicion.

Emilia could follow the pimp's train of thought. If there was anything in Yolanda's phone liable to get someone from the street in trouble, Chavito would be blamed for helping. She dug out the photo strip of Yolanda and Lila and showed it to him. "I'm looking for Lata's daughter. Have you seen her?"

Chavito studied the picture. "No, but I'll run her if she needs a job."

"No, you won't," Flores said.

Chavito rolled his eyes.

"I need Lata's phone," Emilia said. "The girl's number is probably in it. Any idea who took it?"

The dwarf shrugged. "I figure her last john."

"Tell me about him."

"Plain. Young." Chavito pointed at Flores. "Older than him. Dark blue jacket with a zipper."

"Scars? Tattoos?"

"No."

"Tall? Short?"

Chavito shook his head. "You people all look the same height to me."

"Very funny. What else did he have on besides the jacket?"

"Nice shoes," Chavito said thoughtfully. "Basketball high tops, you know. LeBron or something like that. Expensive."

Emilia almost heard a click as things fell into place. "What else?"

"Backpack. Real possessive of it, too. I figured that's where he had his stash."

"He was a dealer? Local?"

"Not from around here," Chavito said. "I know all of them."

"What else?"

"He didn't argue over the price," Chavito said. "He paid cash for Lata and promised her a high, too. You know, in return for something special."

"You let her go to work high?" Flores asked.

Madre de Dios. Flores had incredulity all over his face. Emilia wondered if he realized that Yolanda's "work" would have been to take her customer to some dirty pay-by-the hour hotel and have whatever sexual encounter the man wanted. There would not have been any condom or way to check for disease.

Chavito smirked and Emilia knew the pimp could tell that Flores was a rookie.

"You said he wasn't local," she said. "Take a guess. Where was he from?"

"Out of town. Talked funny."

"What do you mean, funny?" Emilia pressed. "Speech impediment? Lisp? Cleft palate?"

"Hey, no." Chavito bristled at her barrage. "A funny accent. Like maybe he wasn't Mexican."

"You ever meet anybody from Honduras?" Emilia asked.

"No." Chavito eyed the sidewalk behind Flores. Two women in short skirts and high heels, obviously his girls, loitered halfway down the street. The pimp nodded and they disappeared around the corner.

Emilia snapped her fingers to get his attention back. "Did you get a name?"

Chavito clicked his tongue. "Who has names in this business?"

"Did anybody around here know him? How did he find you?"

"He was hanging around," Chavito recalled. "Said he was waiting for his friends. Said he might as well have a good time until they got there. Made it sound like they were all going to party later."

"Did the friends show up? Anybody looking for him since that night?"

"No." Chavito shook his head and Emilia knew he'd thought enough of Yolanda to ask around on her behalf. "I figured he was lying. Playing the big shot."

Dark blue jacket with a zipper. Nice shoes. Not Mexican. Had a stash.

Looking for friends.

Emilia dug out her phone and found the picture she'd taken of the Salva Diablo gang member lying in the morgue. "Is that him?"

"Maybe." Chavito looked from the cell phone to Emilia. "But that guy is dead, right?"

She gave Chavito 200 pesos and they walked away.

Emilia drove toward the center of the city, until she found a place to park close enough to smell the clean air breezing off the bay. Flores looked at her curiously as she found a number in her cell phone.

"This is Emilia," she said when Prade came on the line. "Did you keep any blood samples from Yolanda Lata? Yola de Trinidad, I mean. Can you test them for Ora Ciega?"

Chapter 17

"Doing a little personnel reshuffling," Loyola said, staring at a point between Emilia and Silvio as they sat in the chairs fronting his desk.

"What kind of reshuffling?" Silvio asked suspiciously.

Thursday after the morning meeting, Loyola had asked both detectives to come into his office. The acting lieutenant made a show out of looking through the papers on his desk, mumbled something about best use of resources. "We got too many cases," he said. "Need to spread out more. So, Silvio, you'll be riding with Ibarra. Cruz can handle Flores and his training on her own."

"No," Emilia said. It was an automatic, reflexive reaction.

"Why not put Flores with Ibarra?" Silvio asked at the same time.

"Flores would prefer it this way," Loyola said primly.

"Since when does a rookie get to decide shit?" the senior detective demanded.

Loyola continued to stare at nothing. "It's my decision. Flores needs to take his time settling in."

"*Jesu Cristo*," Silvio exploded. "That kid needs to get his ass chewed at the police academy. Then spend a couple of years on the streets, learning about real life."

"He's catching on," Loyola said. "I've been watching him."

"You haven't been on the street with him," Emilia jumped in. "Flores doesn't have any idea how things work in real life. He must have grown up in a bubble."

"He seems smart enough." Loyola fooled again with some papers on his desk. "Maybe he doesn't know how things work because you haven't done a good enough job of showing him."

"Are you really going to let some kid make decisions for you?" Silvio leaned forward and planted his hands on the desk.

Loyola took off his glasses and rubbed his eyes. He'd aged in the few months he'd been acting lieutenant; his skin had taken on a gray tinge and his eyes were perpetually bloodshot. Even his hair seemed to lie limp against his head. If it had been Silvio behind the desk he would have reveled in the authority, popping with muscular energy, barking out directions. The vibe would have been contagious and the squadroom would have been bubbling. Instead, the pall created by Loyola's nervousness in the job seemed to grow thicker every day.

"Lay off, Silvio," Loyola said. "This is from Chief Salazar's office."

"So not your decision." Silvio's voice was thick with contempt.

"You should be happy," Loyola countered. "You didn't want to ride with Flores in the first place."

"That's not the point." Silvio stood up, looming over the desk. "I'm talking about the integrity of the squadroom. Tell Salazar no. You're acting lieutenant, you make the personnel decisions around here."

"Don't you talk to me about integrity, Franco!" Loyola exclaimed. His desk chair shot out as he got to his feet.

"What do you mean by that?" Silvio's fists clenched so tightly his knuckles turned white.

"You got a problem, take it to Alma," Loyola snapped.

"Hey, hey." Emilia stood up, too, and smacked her hand on the desk top to break the angry electricity humming between the two men. Talking about an Internal Affairs investigation was going too far; no career ever survived. "Let's figure out what to do that's best for Flores. We're stuck with him and somebody expects us to turn him into a cop."

"Cruz and Flores keep the kidnapping case," Loyola said to Silvio, as if Emilia hadn't spoken. "You'll work Ibarra's cases and whatever would have been assigned to Macias and Sandor."

"No," Emilia objected. She needed Silvio on the *Pacific Grandeur* murder case, or the Irma case, or the Ora Ciega smuggling case. Whatever it was now. Plus, they always had a backlog of loose ends, unsolved cases, reports to write. "Silvio can't just walk off the rest of our cases. Flores is no help."

"Cruz is right. What about the rest of our work?" Silvio was still furious. "You expect me to dump it all on that kid?"

"You'll have to retire a couple of things. Won't be the first time we couldn't work a case." Loyola sat down again, his anger spent. "If we don't reshuffle we're all out of a job."

"Who says so?" Silvio asked skeptically.

"Chief Salazar."

"You misheard," Emilia protested.

"Exact words," Loyola said. "Called me at home last night."

"We'll go to the union," Emilia said.

Neither man replied.

"So who's the kid's patron?" Silvio asked the ceiling at length. "Chief Salazar or Obregon?"

Victor Obregon Sosa, the union chief for the state of Guerrero was an enigmatic man named. All three detectives knew he played whichever side was most advantageous to him. And he kept score.

Obregon's relationship to Chief Salazar was a mystery. They might be allies or they might be enemies and Emilia had no way of knowing. But she did know that Obregon and Silvio were enemies, to the point where Obregon had once tried to frame Silvio for a dirty cop's murder.

"Doesn't matter." Loyola looked like he'd had enough. "Cruz, you'll ride with Flores. Silvio, you're with Ibarra. I've already briefed him."

"If this kid is getting to call the shots," Silvio said tightly. "We are all seriously fucked."

He stormed out, leaving the door swinging on its hinges.

Loyola passed a hand over his face. "So what's wrong with the kid?"

Emilia closed the door and returned to her chair. "Flores is," she said. "He's . . . he's . . . immature."

Loyola shrugged. "He's young. Time and experience will take care of it."

"He's having a hard time understanding the concept of

professional relationships," Emilia said carefully. She didn't want to say that Flores had a crush on her; Loyola could well have the same first reaction as Silvio. But she had to convince Loyola that the kid wasn't ready for street work. "Also he has trouble with the concept of a plan. He's not reliable. He could really get himself in trouble."

"Cruz, just deal with the kid, okay?"

"This isn't something you can snap your fingers and fix," Emilia said with heat. "He doesn't understand what it's like on the streets. Frankly, I don't think he understands danger. For himself or anybody else. He's incredibly immature. I didn't want to say anything in the morning meeting, but he messed up big time when we met with the forgers."

"He couldn't have bungled it too bad. You got a name." Loyola turned to his computer, hit some keys.

The printer next to his computer chugged into life.

Emilia stood up, shoved her hand on the printer button, and turned it off. The paper jammed and the machine let out an electronic death rattle.

"What the fuck, Cruz?" Loyola swore.

"This is not going to end well," Emilia said. "He's got no experience or natural instincts. He's a rich kid who managed to buy his way into the job because when he was five it sounded cool to be a cop."

"We all have to suck it up sometimes, Cruz," Loyola said.

"Let Ibarra suck it up," Emilia said. "You said sticking him with the new kid meant nobody would have his back, but you don't seem so worried on my behalf. Let Cruz take a fall, is that it? Protect your partner but not me."

Loyola turned the printer back on and it flashed a red warning light. He jabbed ineffectually at the machine's array of buttons. "Salazar said he wants the kid to be happy and happy means riding with you."

"So he buys his way into the squadroom and gets to say who his partner is, too?" Emilia felt her blood pressure rise as she paced in front of the desk. "Silvio is right. We're all fucked."

"Maybe he's in love." Loyola stood to remove the printer's

cover. He tried to work the paper out of the feeder. "You're still driving that Suburban. It's bigger than some people's houses. Give the kid a blow job in the back seat now and then. Everybody stays happy and nobody gets fired."

"What the hell, Loyola!" Emilia exclaimed. She stopped pacing.

"Give me a break, Cruz." Loyola looked up from the internal workings of the printer. The light still pulsed a red warning. "You owe this squadroom. Here's your chance to pay everybody back."

"I owe the squadroom," Emilia repeated.

"We both know you're a looker," Loyola said. "You could have had a lot more of us making life tough for you than just Gomez and Castro being *estupidos.*"

Emilia took an involuntary step backwards. "So I blow Flores to thank you all for keeping it in your pants?"

Loyola shrugged. "If it works out with him, you can thank the rest of us personal-like, too."

Blood thundered in her head. "Let me help you with that printer," Emilia heard herself say. She came around the side of the desk. Loyola stepped back to give her room and she nailed him in the groin with her knee.

Loyola doubled up. Emilia left him on the floor behind the desk, gasping into the linoleum.

Emilia spent the afternoon in the comparative safety of the central police administration building, grimly marching Flores around to every department she could think of. He got the Records orientation briefing and a walk through the crime labs. For their last stop, she took him down to the police evidence locker run by her cousin Alvaro.

It was clear that Flores had never been anywhere with the gritty impact of the locker. His expression was a mix of awe and uneasiness as Emilia saw the immense windowless vault in the building's basement through his eyes.

A tall counter ran the width of the apparently endless space and a thick shield of bulletproof glass ran between the counter and the ceiling. The immediate impression was of denial of access; the glass was so thick that a diagonal glance distorted the view. The next impression was that the space was so long that a person seeking the end could be lost in the gray vastness, swallowed up by the color of bureaucracy.

Beyond the counter and bulletproof glass, there was space for three desks. In back of the desks, an enormous wire cage held a shopping mall's worth of automatic weapons, technical gadgets, and a million other items seized by the Acapulco police. Everything was packaged in plastic bags or steel bins and shelved according to some unique filing system known only to the wizard of the evidence locker--her cousin Sergeant Alvaro Cruz Ochoa--and his minions.

She'd called ahead. Alvaro buzzed them both through a steel door that led past the counter and into the staff area. Emilia introduced Alvaro to the squadroom's newest: Detective Orlando Flores.

Her cousin gave a much-practiced spiel about how the evidence locker worked, how many items passed through it every year, and it's role in fighting crime in Acapulco. Flores was agog.

Emilia had to admit that Alvaro was impressive. He was a highly decorated uniformed sergeant who knew his job well and was a good spokesman. Her mentor when she'd first joined the police force, he'd always had jobs inside the central police administration building. Over the years, he'd built up an impressive network of friends and contacts, yet made surprisingly few enemies. Alvaro was smart, but even more important, he was discreet.

When Alvaro was finished one of his uniformed staff took Flores through the chain link enclosure to show him some of the locker's holdings.

"*Madre de Dios,*" Emilia muttered when Flores had disappeared beyond the fencing. She dropped into the chair next to Alvaro's desk. "He's training with me for six weeks. At least. I wouldn't be surprised if it dragged on longer than that."

"Where's Silvio?" Alvaro asked. "And what happened to your hair?"

"The hair is what happened while questioning a witness who runs a beauty school." Emilia ignored her cousin's guffaw. "As for Silvio, he's been reassigned. The kid's got someone looking out for him, know what I mean?"

"A rabbi."

"You wouldn't know who, by any chance?" Emilia asked. Alvaro always had the inside story.

Alvaro shook his head. "No. Sorry, never heard of the kid before."

"Start asking," Emilia said. "Kid's got a rich daddy. Rigoberto Flores. A real estate mogul. The Torre Metropolitano. The new construction at Playa Revolcadero. Guess Papi bought him a cop job. No academy, no detective test. Nothing."

Alvaro nodded and Emilia knew his curiosity had been piqued. His network would be notified later.

Emilia looked at the clean surface of her cousin's desk. "Got any new pictures?"

"Of course." Alvaro pulled a small leather photo album from a drawer and flipped it open. He had two children; a 3-year-old son and a daughter who was five months old. "Daysi wants to enter the baby in a contest," he said. "But I said it would be too much publicity."

Emilia flipped through the album. The children were adorable. Before she'd started staying with Kurt on weekends Emilia had always seen the family at church on Sundays. "I haven't see them in months," Emilia said sadly. "They're getting so big."

"Spending your Sundays in sin, I expect?" Alvaro said.

"Pretty much," Emilia admitted. Alvaro knew a little about Kurt, but they'd never met. She grinned ruefully. "Speaking of sin, I'm bringing Kurt to Mama's wedding."

"It's that serious, is it?"

Emilia tried to downplay it. "Don't make a big deal out of him being there."

"Does your mother know he's coming?"

"I'm a little afraid she's going to ask him what school he goes to. What's his favorite subject."

Alvaro frowned at her. "Maybe you should, you know. Prepare him."

"He knows," Emilia said. "I told him. But you know how Mama can be."

"Okay." Alvaro grinned. "We'll treat him good."

"Thanks." Emilia grinned back. She still knew it would all be a disaster, but having Alvaro on her side would help a lot. "Speaking of the wedding, Kurt and I ended up at Villa de Refugio looking for a gift. Do you remember it?"

Alvaro thought for a moment. "The fancy Catholic store?"

"Yes, the one with the gold coins."

"*Por Dios*," he laughed. "I haven't thought of that place in years."

Emilia closed the album. "You wouldn't believe what we found. A relic of Padre Pro. More specifically, his finger."

Alvaro's mouth fell open. Emilia had known that he'd be shocked. Because he would remember. Alvaro always remembered everything. But in all the years that he'd known what she'd done, he'd never talked about it.

"It wasn't his finger, as it turned out," Emilia hastened to add. "It's the finger of a woman, according to the morgue. We're treating it as a kidnapping case."

Alvaro shook his head; shock had turned to disgust. "Do you have any leads?"

"One," Emilia said. "Have you ever heard of a group called Friends of Padre Pro?"

"No," Alvaro said. "But it's no surprise that there would be one. Sainthood, et cetera."

"About right," Emilia said. "But in this case, I wonder if they are making more of these fake Padre Pro relics."

"You need any help figuring this out." Alvaro gestured vaguely at the evidence enclosure. "Let me know what you need."

Head of the evidence locker was one of the most rewarding jobs in the police force; it gave the incumbent unparalleled ability to right wrongs and grant favors. Lose or replace questionable items and make sure official records were adjusted as needed. Any rewards received for a job well done were handled with discretion, of course.

Like Alvaro with her secret, Emilia never asked and he never told.

"Sure," Emilia said.

☼

"Would you like to get some dinner, Emilia?" Flores asked. They were back at the police station but he'd made no move to get out of the Suburban.

"I have somewhere I have to go," Emilia answered.

She was done for the day and certainly wasn't going into the building. The last thing she needed was to run into Loyola. If she did, she'd either punch him or apologize; she didn't know which. Better to put more space between what had happened in his office and the next time they met.

"Where?"

"I like to keep things private," Emilia said.

Flores pushed his lips out in a pout. "I thought that now that we're partners--."

"We're not partners," Emilia interrupted. "I'm training you. Silvio and I are partners. He'll working with Ibarra until your training is done and things get back to normal."

"All right." Flores sighed and fiddled with the zipper of his jacket. "What are we doing tomorrow? Following any more clues about this drug smuggling stuff? You know, the stuff with the funny name?"

"No." The word flew out of Emilia's mouth. She needed to talk to Silvio before doing anything else. "We should get you down to the range. Make sure you know how to shoot your gun."

Flores brightened. "Cool."

Emilia looked at his door. "Good night, Orlando."

He smiled. "Good night, Emilia."

Flores didn't open the door. The silence stretched like the awkward end to a first date. Emilia dug out her phone and started thumbing buttons.

"Okay, then." Flores fumbled for the door handle. "Good night."

"Bye," Emilia said, without looking up.

When he finally left, Emilia dialed Mercedes. When the dancer's phone clicked over to voice mail, Emilia knew she was giving a class. It would be over in an hour, ample time for Emilia to buy a box of hair dye and drive to the dance studio. As she drove out of the parking lot, she left Mercedes a message about hair that sounded totally stupid, but that was the way things were going lately. She'd explain when she got to the studio.

As soon she turned onto the Costera on the way to Sanborn's, her phone rang. The screen showed an unidentified number.

"*Bueno?*"

"Detective Cruz, do you know who this is?"

"How many phones do you have, Señor Denton?" Emilia transferred the phone to her left hand and kept her right on the wheel.

"Spare me your attempt to prove how clever you are, Detective." The voice on the other end was the familiar combination of bad accent and testy attitude. "I have some news for you."

"I was wondering how you were getting on with my relic."

"Your finger is not that of our kidnapping victim."

"I guess that's a good thing," Emilia said. The nagging urgency of a kidnapping faded, along with her own chagrin at having to wait until Saturday to find the next link in the chain. "Or not?"

"We were unable to make a positive identification of the owner of the finger, if that's what you are asking," Denton went on. The crackle of a poor connection vibrated against Emilia's ear. "Victim was female, Latina, likely under 35 years of age."

"Basically what we'd already found out," Emilia pointed out. So much for Denton's patronizing attitude.

"Well, Detective," Denton said. "I'll send over the full

report but you might be interested in knowing that we found trace elements of an unusual mix of illicit substances ground into the skin under the nail. Our experts say it's a Colombian mix of heroin and meth called--."

"Ora Ciega," Emilia said and almost hit the curb.

Emilia called Mercedes to cancel, too shaken by Denton's news to do anything but head to the house to think. Sophia and Ernesto were watching television. Emilia waved off her mother's offer to cook. A cup of tea and a box of crackers would be enough.

Sitting crossed-legged on her bed, the tea cooling on the nightstand, Emilia paged through her notebook. There had to be connections she had missed.

The murdered Salva Diablo gang member was from Honduras. Killed aboard the *Pacific Grandeur*, his body stolen out of the morgue and never recovered. He'd been looking for friends. They'd never shown up.

The Salva Diablo had stopped looking for his friends long enough to pay for a hooker. He'd been dealing Ora Ciega with his stash in a backpack and had almost certainly been the one to give Yolanda Lata her fatal hit. Had he also beaten her? Or left her to her Ora Ciega high and someone else had finished her off and stolen her phone?

Emilia drank some tea. Maybe the friends he'd been waiting for were Bonilla and Ramos. Maybe one of them had used Yolanda while she was high and beat her afterwards. Bonilla would do that, Emilia thought grimly, along with killing the Salva Diablo and stealing the backpack. She made a note to ask Silvio if he'd seen a backpack when he'd searched the ship cabins belonging to Bonilla and Ramos.

Thinking about the two cruise ship officers brought Emilia back to her original theory about the *Pacific Grandeur*. It still made perfect sense that the ship was being used to transport Ora Ciega to *El Norte*, but they still had no evidence to prove it. Organized Crime didn't even believe the theory.

She drank more tea and looked at her notes. Nothing connected to the finger of a kidnapping victim with Ora Ciega embedded in the skin under the nail. Emilia wanted to scream with frustration when she thought about how little she really knew about the finger's journey from its owner's hand to the Villa de Refugio store.

It was past midnight and Sophia and Ernesto had gone to bed by the time Emilia tossed aside the notebook and closed her eyes. Denton's news had done nothing but trip her up, make her less sure of everything they had so far.

Nothing connected, nothing made sense. She'd been so sure that the *Pacific Grandeur* was carrying a cargo of Ora Ciega to *El Norte*. But when the facts were laid bare, she had no proof of anything.

But investigations seldom ran on proof, she'd come to realize. Hunches were sometimes just as valuable.

Chapter 18

Loyola wasn't in the squadroom on Friday, which was a relief. Ibarra, as if having been Loyola's partner meant that he was now deputy acting lieutenant, took it upon himself to run the morning meeting. Emilia briefed on next steps in the finger case, including Flores's attempts to find a similar kidnapping case in the archives. She didn't mention Denton's findings, which he'd emailed to her, sure that if she did the case would get sent to Organized Crime.

After the meeting, she kept an eye on Silvio. After four cups of coffee, he went down the hall. Emilia silently counted to 30, then followed him into the detectives bathroom.

The space was long and narrow with three toilet stalls along one wall. The stall doors were enameled metal panels. On the opposite wall a row of urinals hung below a mirror running the width of the space. A single sink was located between the last urinal and the door. The cement floor was cracked but the walls had been painted white not long ago and were still miraculously graffiti-free.

"What the fuck, Cruz?" Silvio hastily pulled up his zipper and stepped away from the middle urinal.

"I figured this was as private a place to talk as any." Emilia said. She folded her arms and leaned against the first stall's blue partition. "What happened when you took Flores to the gym?"

Silvio turned on the sink faucet and shoved his hands under the water. "Nothing. A little sparring. He held his own."

"You put him in safety gear?" Emilia pressed. "He had a bruise on his jaw."

"Had him in safety gear the whole time," Silvio said scornfully. "Had to. The kid's made of fucking glass. Said he'd never been in a fight in his life."

"He's been too busy playing the oboe," Emilia offered.

Silvio turned off the water and got a paper towel. "What the fuck's an oboe?"

"Like a clarinet."

"Well, Señor Oboe got knocked around a little. Dumped on his ass a few times. Same as the rest of us when we were starting out. He didn't cry." Silvio wadded up the towel and pitched it into the can.

Emilia threw up her hands. "No, he ran home and complained to his rich father who made a call to Chief Salazar. Now you're pulled away right when there might be a break in the case."

"What case?"

"The *Pacific Grandeur* murder."

"What are you talking about?"

"Did you see a backpack in either Bonilla's or Ramos's cabin when you were searching the *Pacific Grandeur*?" Emilia asked.

"Maybe," Silvio said. "I think they both had backpacks and suitcases in their cabins. Why?"

"The Salva Diablo gang banger hired Yolanda Lata, according to Chavito."

"Chavito from the Fuerte?" Silvio asked in surprise. He leaned against the sink. "He was her pimp?"

"Looks like it." Emilia knew he understood her frustration in not having found Yolanda Lata earlier. "Chavito described him almost perfectly. Identified him from a picture on my phone. The Salva Diablo was looking for friends. Had a backpack with a stash in it. Promised some to Yolanda. He was her last john."

"That's a big break? All you know now is who gave Yolanda Lata her overdose."

"Don't you see?" Emilia demanded. "All along we kept thinking that the Salva Diablo came on board the *Pacific Grandeur* and was shot there. But he was looking for his friends, was going to party with them. Those friends were Bonilla and Ramos."

"Okay," Silvio acknowledged. "If he had a backpack with enough Ora Ciega in it to share with a hooker, maybe the ship hasn't been used to transport anything. Maybe their meeting was to set something up."

Emilia walked the length of the room, her brain humming. At the end of the room, the sole window gave a grainy view of the parking lot. For added security, the glass had steel netting embedded in it and iron bars were bolted into the wall on the outside. "Say they found him," Emilia thought out loud. "Argued. Killed him, took his stash, but were afraid to leave the body. So they took it back to the ship and stuffed it in the meat locker until they could come up with something else. But the cook found it first."

"What about the blood on the wall?"

"Carried the body down those stairs," Emilia said. "Head wounds bleed a lot."

"Okay, let's keep going with this," Silvio said thoughtfully. "It explains why nobody I talked to on the docks saw the guy. He was never there. Alive, anyway."

"We should have been asking if people saw Bonilla and Ramos coming and going off the ship."

Silvio nodded. "That's where Customs comes in. They would have seen Bonilla and Ramos. Maybe somebody from Customs helped them."

"That's what got Irma killed. Someone who was working that night saw them with the body."

"Okay," Silvio said again. "I'll buy that. But once the body was found, why would anyone risk stealing it out of the morgue?"

"So he wouldn't be included in Prade's website of unidentified dead," Emilia said.

The bathroom door swung open. Gomez stepped in, lean and lanky in ripped jeans, rock band tee shirt, and straggly goatee. He snickered when he saw both Emilia and Silvio. "Now that you two aren't partners, kinda hard to find someplace to do it, eh?"

"Get out," Silvio said.

Emilia stood her ground. She and Gomez had gone three rounds in this very bathroom less than a year ago. He'd attacked her and she'd defended herself with one of the metal stall doors that he'd removed as a punishment for not wanting to date him. Gomez had ended up in the hospital.

"I got no objection to a three-way, Silvio." Gomez licked his lips at Emilia. His eyes were hard and assessing.

"Go find a couple of dogs, Gomez," Emilia said.

Gomez's expression didn't change. "Your call, Silvio."

Silvio pivoted around Emilia, pressed a hand into Gomez's face, kicked opened the door, and shoved the weedy detective through it. "Piss on my car and I'll rip your dick off," he warned.

Emilia heard rapidly retreating footsteps as the door swung shut. "You really think he'd do that?"

"Gomez has style," Silvio said. He went to the sink and washed his hands again.

Emilia pulled a paper towel out of the dispenser and handed it to him. "I've got more," she said. "Report on the Padre Pro finger came back from the Pinkerton Agency. There was Ora Ciega ground into the skin under the nail."

"*Rayos*," Silvio exclaimed and wadded up the paper towel. "Just how much of this shit is floating around?"

"Enough for a turf war?" Emilia wasn't sure if she was asking a rhetorical question or not.

"Did we check to make sure that both the guy in the meat locker and Yolanda Lata had all their fingers?" Silvio asked.

"Yes, they both had all their fingers."

"I got a bad feeling about this." Silvio squeezed the damp paper towel into pulp with one big fist. "I don't like you running the case alone but Loyola's got me and Ibarra jumping around like a bag of assholes with all of Ibarra's cases, plus Macias and Sandor's leftovers." He threw the towel away. "Any more cars with dead drivers on your tail?"

"Haven't seen the car again." Emilia said. She stepped to the sink and washed her hands, too. "You never told me what Perez said the last time you talked to him."

"Organized Crime is another bag of assholes," Silvio said. "Perez said they still aren't doing shit on the *Pacific Grandeur*."

"Typical," Emilia sniffed.

Silvio gave the third stall door a random shove and the panel battered itself against the latch. "I don't like you being out there alone on this case. Like Irma."

Emilia shrugged, although her stomach tensed at his implication. "I've got Flores."

Silvio flashed that rare grin. "How's he liking the viper queen hair, Cruz?"

"Shut up, Franco," Emilia said.

They walked out of the bathroom. The words *Like Irma* spun inside Emilia's head. When Silvio turned to go into the squadroom Emilia kept on going, past the holding cells, and outside. The air was clean and she stood with her back against the wall for a few minutes, until the image of Irma's smile faded.

Chapter 19

Emilia let herself into the penthouse, tossed her jacket onto the sofa, and heard her phone chime. It was a text from Kurt, saying that he would be stuck in the office waiting for a conference call for at least another hour. He'd meet her in the bar later. They could go for a swim, then have a quiet dinner.

Friday night bliss. Emilia texted back that it sounded like the perfect plan.

An hour would give her time to shed the week. She got herself a glass of wine from the kitchen, carried it into the bedroom. The en suite bathroom was huge, with a tiled shower stall the size of Acapulco bay and a separate soaking tub. The tub had a whirlpool feature and it was pure heaven to sit in the water, letting the jets pummel her body, and sip cool white wine. She closed her eyes and tried to relax.

But there were too many incomplete timelines and unanswered questions. How did the Ora Ciego on the Padre Pro finger fit into the story? Were there suddenly several dealers in town with Ora Ciega? Given the way the substance had been found embedded so deeply, had the kidnapping victim been forced to work in a meth lab?

Emilia knew they couldn't discount a sudden influx of the rare stuff and a bitter fight to control distribution. Was Acapulco looking at a coming gang war over Ora Ciega? She swallowed the last of the wine. A gang war over Ora Ciega didn't mesh with the Friends of Padre Pro and their sainthood petition and she didn't know if the two were connected or not. The timing worked, but nothing else.

She set her empty glass on the tub rim. Tomorrow was Saturday. She'd go back to the *mercado*, find this Juan Fabio and shake the truth out of him. If he was a dead end, she didn't know what to do next. There were so many loose threads, so many things that she should be able to connect, but couldn't.

For a long time, she sat in the tub and listened to the drone of the whirlpool. Each thread was examined in turn and discarded, to be picked up again later, until only one thing stayed with her.

Kurt.

She wasn't going to make the same mistake she had last weekend.

The hotel wasn't such a foreign place. She knew much of the staff. There were a lot of nice people there. Not Christine, of course. But everybody else. For Kurt's sake, she had to try harder.

Wearing the right clothes would help. It would be like speaking the same language. Maybe she would even wear nail polish once in awhile. Right after she bought some.

She put on her red bathing suit, tied the matching pareo around her hips, and left the penthouse with just her keycard and phone. Tonight she was off duty.

The hotel's huge tiled lobby, with its check-in counter and concierge desk cooled by softly turning ceiling fans, had once seemed so grand and forbidding. Now it felt normal. She crossed the floor and avoided looking to see if Christine was on duty. The lobby segued into an immense tiled terrace open to the ocean on the far side, with a picture postcard view of the beach and waves licking up to the shore. The piano was centered on the tiles again, after having been moved for last weekend's regatta event, and she exchanged smiles with Raul, the pianist, as his fingers danced over the keys.

The Pasodoble Bar was busy. Tables and chairs were dotted about but somehow none obscured the view of the bay for the people soaking up the salty breeze and laughing over mojitos and margaritas. The barstools were all occupied. Half a dozen *gringo* businessmen in golf slacks and polo shirts, with conference badges around their necks, were enjoying themselves at a table on the far side of the bar while other tables were occupied by couples who looked like second honeymooners. All the women wore cotton caftans and chunky necklaces of semi-precious stones.

Emilia slid into a chair facing the ocean, glad for the stylish bathing suit and pareo. She didn't have the jewelry that so many women wore at the hotel with swimsuits, as if they expected a fashion photographer to take their picture at any moment, but she was also in better shape than any other woman there and the suit showed it off.

A waiter materialized and lit the lantern on the table. "Nice to see you again, Señorita Cruz," he said. "The usual mojito?"

Emilia smiled and pretended to consider the idea. "We're supposed to go swimming later."

The waiter winked. "A very light one."

He brought the drink quickly, without asking her to sign for it. As Emilia sipped, she let her mind clear, thinking of nothing more taxing than the hypnotic way the waves rolled again and again onto the sand. It was gravity and nature and a pull at her heart. Acapulco would always be the biggest part of who she was.

"My darling Emilia," a heavily accented voice said.

Emilia looked up. "Hello, Jacques."

Kurt's best friend was Jacques Anatole, the French chef who ran the hotel's famous restaurant which jutted into the bay like a Spanish galleon breasting the waves. The roof was made of soaring canvas sails, the floor was teak decking, and artfully strung antique signal flags crossed overhead. A piece of fish at the restaurant cost about as much as a treasure chest of gold doubloons. Emilia consciously avoided looking at the prices on the menu when she and Kurt ate there, despite the fact that they always ate for free.

Balancing two trays, Jacques bent to exchange kisses. "Wait here," he said. "I shall bring you a portion of heaven. A new appetizer."

She watched him go to the bar and set down the trays. Jacques didn't look like Emilia imagined the typical French chef; plump, red-cheeked, given to flowery expressions about food and wine. Instead, Jacques was a runner and swimmer like Kurt. He had jet-black hair, a large nose, and a sharp, almost pointed chin that gave his face mobility and character. The white chef's jacket and loose checkered pants disguised his lean frame.

He came back to her table with a small blue-edged plate and two forks. Grilled shrimp were arranged into a pinwheel on the plate.

"Try it, try it," Jacques urged as he sat next to her. "You will be first with a verdict."

"They're too pretty," Emilia protested.

Jacques happily stabbed a shrimp. "Beautiful food feeds the soul as well as the body. You torture me in that red suit, *non*? So you will eat my shrimp, the spell will be cast, and you will leave Kurt for me."

"You've always been my one true love, Jacques," Emilia said dramatically and ate a shrimp.

She'd had shrimp all her life. Fried, pickled in lime, drenched in salsa, stuffed into tortillas. This was totally different. It was exquisite.

"Shrimp bathed in Calvados, then grilled with garlic and brown sugar," Jacques said, helping himself to another. "Good, *non*?"

"*Madre de Dios*, it's wonderful." Emilia closed her eyes in rapture. "What's Calvados?"

"*Mon dieu*," Jacques said in feigned exasperation. "In this place I am teaching all the time."

"Yes, you are," Emilia agreed, loading up her fork again. "What is it?"

"A traditional and very famous French liquor made from apples."

Emilia shook her head. "I've never heard of it."

"Of course you have not," Jacques agreed amiably. "I am to be famous for introducing it to Mexico."

They talked for another minute, until Jacques announced he had to get back to his kitchen, kissed her on both cheeks, and loped up the steps to the lobby level.

Emilia finished the shrimp, the waiter brought her a second mojito without being asked, and her phone chimed with another text from Kurt saying he'd be there in 15 minutes. Not to worry, she texted back. She was watching the ocean and relaxing.

The colors of the sunset spread slowly toward the horizon. The sky darkened like fabric soaking up liquid.

Emilia swirled the straw around in her new mojito, took a

sip, and watched the sunset. The sky turning pink and orange and scarlet over the ocean was always a miracle. Lights switched by the bar, changing all the silhouettes. More people came through the lobby, past the piano. Most were first-time hotel guests. She could always tell because they stopped on the step and gazed wide-eyed at Punta Diamante's incredible view of sky and ocean. By the time the first-timers got to the massive bar with its blue mosaic spelling out *Pasodoble*, they'd collected themselves.

A man slipped into the chair Jacques had vacated. "Good evening, señorita," he said. "You look lonely."

"I'm waiting for someone," Emilia said. She gave him a pointed smile.

"I'm someone." He leered at her, a middle aged Mexican in gray pants and a white guayabera shirt who'd had a few too many.

Besides a very famous *norteamericano* rock star a few weeks ago, the man at the table was the first drunk she'd encountered at the Palacio Réal. It was too posh a place for drunks and people who made scenes. "Sorry." Emilia dropped the smile. "He'll be here any moment and I'd like to be alone until he comes."

"One, maybe two, high end clients a weekend, eh?" His voice was this side of slurred and his eyes slid from her striped hair to the red bathing suit top.

Made de Dios, she was Avenga the Hooker. "Señor, I am truly waiting for someone to join me," Emilia said coldly.

He leaned closer. "Do a couple of the hotel staff, like that cook, too, so it all stays quiet. Looking like that in a place like this, you probably pull in 50,000 pesos a weekend. A lot more than you make during the week."

Before Emilia could react, he reached across the table to cup her breast. Suddenly Kurt was there, dragging the man backwards with an arm around his neck. The man's chair skidded over the terrace flagstones, and his legs bicycled, seeking a purchase that wasn't there as Kurt twisted him into a painful head lock. The man's choking gasps were drowned out by the slap of the surf and the sounds of the bar—soft music, subdued chatter, the clink of glasses.

It wasn't a fight, not even a scuffle. An outsider would have said the blonde *gringo* in polo shirt and board shorts had unfair advantages of surprise, height, weight, and fury. The smaller Mexican never really had a chance, he'd been too busy licking his chops over the girl with the ponytail and red bathing suit.

Emilia watched as two burly hotel employees, dressed in the hotel's signature blue floral shirts and khaki pants, raced across the lobby and wrested the man from Kurt. As the man repeatedly apologized, they marched him rapidly across the broad space and disappeared down the corridor behind the concierge desk that Emilia knew led to the security chief's office. A waiter cleaned up the remains of her mojito. In seconds, the whole episode had never happened.

Kurt came back to the table where Emilia stood. She was still dumbfounded. "Are you all right?" he asked. From across the bar the bartender caught his eye and raised a glass in a silent query. Kurt shook his head but gave the bartender a thumb's up. The bartender put down the glass and returned his attention to the customers at the bar.

"Remind me to pick you to be on my side in a bar fight," Emilia said.

"I'm always on your side, Em." Kurt ran a hand through his hair and took a deep breath as if trying to tame his anger. "I thought he'd hurt you. That your head was bleeding."

"He was drunk," Emilia said. "Thought I was a hooker. You might have overreacted a little."

Kurt wrapped his arm around her shoulders. They left the bar and slowly headed for the elevators. "You sure?" he asked. "That's all it was?"

Emilia nodded. "Yes, some drunk."

"You don't want to arrest him?"

"If I tried to arrest everybody who was drunk in Acapulco on a Friday night . . ." Emilia let her voice trail off with a little laugh.

Kurt kissed her forehead. "You want to tell me about your hair?"

"No." Emilia leaned into him. "But I will. Over dinner."

They had her favorite kind of night; a swim in the large pool with the waterfall and dinner in the apartment in front of a funny movie. But as Emilia drifted off to sleep in the warmth of Kurt's arms, she wondered if the drunk drove a gray sedan.

Chapter 20

"You're going to attract a lot of attention, you know," Emilia warned. "Hardly any *gringos* go to the Mercado Municipal."

"I'm invested in this thing, Em." Kurt poured her a second cup of coffee. "I'm coming with you."

In the daylight, with the bay gleaming under the Saturday noon sun outside the penthouse window, Emilia felt as if the ridiculous conversation with the drunk last night had never happened. The morning had passed in a glow of lovemaking, laughter, and eventually a discussion of the Padre Pro case. Before Emilia could say that she needed to take time out of their weekend to go to the market and find the elusive Juan Fabio, Kurt had suggested it himself.

Emilia navigated them to the *mercado* and through the winding aisles to the junkman's stall. As predicted, Kurt attracted attention, with vendors vying for his attention with shouted offers of everything from a Rolex watch to a washing machine. Emilia cringed at the commotion it would cause if the stall owners knew how much money Kurt usually carried.

A compact man in his late thirties was on the stool behind the makeshift desk in the stall. His shirt sleeves were rolled to his elbows, revealing sinewy forearms. His hands were the big-knuckled, veined hands of someone who did manual labor. One thumbnail was black.

The hands were hardly the first giveaway, however. A thick piece of cloth, sewn into pockets to hold woodworking tools, was spread on the desk. He was busy sanding a small wooden pedestal.

"Are you Juan Fabio?" Emilia asked.

He smiled at her, revealing straight white teeth as the corners of his eyes crinkled. For some reason he reminded Emilia of a younger Padre Ricardo. The two men had the same earnest air about them, the same genuine smile. "Yes," he replied. "Just like the sign says. Juan Fabio. Best for you.

Everything for the house."

"I'd like to ask you some questions about a Padre Pro relic."

The genuine smile widened as Kurt studied the stall merchandise. "Would you like to sign the petition?" he asked.

"Maybe," Emilia said. "First I have some questions for you about a relic we found in Villa de Refugio, the Catholic store."

Juan Fabio put down the sandpaper and pedestal. "A very different store, as you can see, señorita."

Emilia stepped closer and touched the rough wood of the pedestal. "I think you can," she said. "You see, we bought a relic there. A relic of the martyr Padre Pro."

"You are very lucky to have found such a wonderful item," Juan Fabio said. "Padre Pro is my *patrón* and soon he will be a saint. You will have a blessed house."

"A laboratory tested the finger," Emilia went on. "It isn't Padre Pro's. It's the finger of a woman."

Juan Fabio blinked in astonishment, but the reaction was a bit too theatrical. "Truly?"

"You made the relic." Emilia didn't raise her voice. She gestured to the woodworking tools. "Asked some friends to create four fake letters that said the relic was the finger of the martyr Padre Pro."

"You are mistaken, señorita," Juan Fabio said.

Kurt stopped browsing and positioned himself to catch Juan Fabio if the man tried to run out of the stall.

"You even said what should be in the letters," Emilia continued. "Used the same words as in the brochure from the Friends of Padre Pro. When the relic and letters were finished, you sold it to an art dealer, Señor Blandón Hernandez. He's bought several of your creations, all with letters from a couple of forgers named El Gordo and El Flaco."

Juan Fabio slid off the stool and retreated into the recesses of the junk stall. Emilia kept on him while Kurt maintained position near the front of the stall by the stool and makeshift desk.

"If you tell me where you got the finger, I swear nothing bad will happen to you," Emilia said. With her back to the aisle, she showed the junkman her badge. "If you don't, I can arrest you for trafficking in body parts. You'll go to prison and certain inmates will know why you are there. Selling a woman's body parts, especially if this turns out to be a kidnapping victim, is a crime other prisoners don't like. You know what I mean?"

"Señorita." This time the man's voice was strained. "I swear on the head of the Holy Mother, that what you say is not true."

Emilia glanced at Kurt. Without a word, he began taking the woodworking tools out of their flannel pockets.

"Rasp," Kurt said and held up the tool. "Could be used for filing bones." He set it on the counter and selected another. "Coping saw. Useful to get the bones small enough to fit inside glass cases. Wire cutters. Organ harvesting tools, if you ask me." His voice was deliberately loud enough to rise above the usual patter of shoppers and vendors. His blonde hair and height made him stand out, as Emilia had opined that morning. Heads swiveled.

"Stop it, stop it," Juan Fabio whispered urgently. "Those tools are my fortune."

"And for display purposes." Kurt held up a big nail, as big as the one that Prade had shown Emilia in his office.

One of the stall owners, whom Emilia had seen before, sidled up to the stall. "You need tools, señor?" he asked Kurt. "If Juan Fabio doesn't have what you need, you come find Jorge."

Kurt slid a small pliers out of its flannel pocket. "I think Juan Fabio has everything I want."

As Jorge ambled back across the aisle, Juan Fabio rushed back to the desk, snatched up the tools and began replacing them in their flannel pockets. "I make crosses. Display cases," he whispered furiously. "I don't sell body parts."

"Sounds to me like you do," Kurt said and swiftly twisted a fist into the man's shirt, raising the smaller man to his toes.

The rasp fell with a clang onto the concrete floor. "No," Juan Fabio sputtered.

"How many Padre Pro relics have you sold?" Kurt asked.

Juan Fabio looked at Emilia for help; a fly pinned by a spider. "Just the one finger. Once."

"Sure," Emilia said sarcastically.

"I swear." Juan Fabio gave a desperate look over Kurt's shoulder at the busy aisle. "Gloria brought it to me. I made the relic and got the letters. Señor Blandón Hernandez bought it."

"I already know about the relic and Señor Blandon Hernandez," Emilia warned. "Tell me about the finger."

"I got it from Gloria," Juan Fabio said. "Gloria Sandino Rosas. She also venerates Padre Pro. She was the one who said it could be a sainted relic."

Kurt gave him a shake. "Where do we find her? Where does she live?

Juan Fabio tried to reach one of the tools on the desk and Kurt yanked him away. "I don't know where she lives." The junkman swallowed hard. "I only know she runs a food stall during the week. Near the construction site a few blocks away. On the weekends she goes home. To her mother. Somewhere in the mountains. Not Acapulco. That's all I know. She's always at her stall again on Tuesdays."

"Where did she get it?"

"She said she bought it. She came to me on a Tuesday, the day she's always back."

Emilia nodded. Kurt let go. Juan Fabio sagged against the desk.

"Why you?" Emilia pressed. "Why did Gloria come to you with the finger? Because you've done this before?"

"No." Juan Fabio kept a wary eye on Kurt. "Gloria only thought of me because I buy things and make them into other things. And because of Padre Pro."

"Leave Padre Pro out of this," Emilia snapped. The junkman and his friend had used Padre Pro simply to make money off the finger. What they'd done was both a sin and a sacrilege. "You bought it from her? How much did you pay her for it?"

"I paid her 50 pesos and a grill."

"*Madre de Dios*," Emilia breathed. Fifty pesos for a human finger. Fifty pesos was nothing.

"How much did you get from Blandón Hernandez for the relic?" Kurt demanded.

Juan Fabio shrank back and Emilia suddenly saw Kurt through the smaller man's eyes. An angry and muscular *gringo* in a black tee shirt. The confidence that Kurt so easily projected was now accompanied by physical anger and the promise of volatility.

"I made the case," Juan Fabio said. "Arranged for the letters. He paid me made 700 pesos."

They left the market. The car felt like a refuge. Emilia and Kurt were almost back to Punta Diamante when she emerged from her fog of thought and put her hand on Kurt's leg. "Thanks for helping back there," she said. "Between last night and today, I guess you're not just another pretty face."

"Thanks." Kurt took his right hand off the wheel and laced his fingers with hers. "How much do you think that crook Blandón Hernandez made off that so-called relic when he sold it to Villa de Refugio?"

"I don't know. A lot." Emilia sighed. "I'd still like to know if the store owner warned him off."

Instead of agreeing, Kurt grinned. "Not feeling so bad about stealing those chocolate coins now, are we?"

Emilia wondered if she'd ever tell him the truth.

Chapter 21

The whole day was going to be like this, Emilia thought on Monday afternoon as she waited for the police intranet to load. Blandón Hernandez's office was still closed. Nothing new had happened related to Customs or any aspect of the Ora Ciega case. The Salva Diablo body was still missing from the morgue, Yolanda Lata's phone was still missing, too, and Organized Crime hadn't shared a peso's worth of information. She had to wait another day before finding Gloria, the woman who'd sold the finger to Juan Fabio.

To make matters worse, whoever was pedaling the generator that ran the system was tired, and everything was running at half speed. That wasn't good, because Emilia planned to tackle the load of old case reports that were due. Normally, Silvio would have done half. Now she had to do them all and she wanted to put a dent in the pile before trying to find Gloria tomorrow.

The squadroom was quiet, almost as if it had surrendered. Macias and Sandor were still in training, Castro and Gomez had taken the day's assignments, and Silvio and Ibarra were over at the central administration building. She had texted Silvio the crux of what she'd found out Saturday, but there had been no time to talk.

Loyola had left right after the morning meeting.

That left her and Flores alone in the squadroom. He was working on another online class. This one was online computer security training. It was mandatory every year but virtually worthless, given that the squadroom had only one computer with an internet connection yet every cop could access social networks on their phone.

The intranet finally blinked and loaded. Emilia logged in and navigated to the national *cédula* database. She entered the name on the business card. A little circle started spinning to let her know that the database was searching.

The card was printed with the blue logo of a well-known

national insurance company and their catchy bilingual slogan. *Su casa protected es mi casa protected.* The company website and a national toll free telephone number were listed below the slogan.

The man's name was printed in the center of the card, but there was no personal phone number or email address.

Periliano Roa Fuentes.

According to Emilia's landlady, Señora Navarro, Roa Fuentes had come to her office to verify the insurance coverage on all the houses that the woman owned and leased out. He was a new representative from the company, he'd said, and wanted to confirm facts. He asked her questions like how many people lived in each house. He'd insisted that three people, not two, lived in the house rented by Emilia. Señora Navarro came to see for herself.

The circle spun faster and the database screen winked out, to be replaced by a "Page Not found" message. Emilia gritted her teeth, knowing the database had timed out due to the intranet's slow speed. She started the process all over again.

The dark screen reflected her face back at her. Her hair was back to normal, thanks to a visit on Sunday to the salon in the Palacio Réal.

Her meeting that morning to see Señora Navarro had gone about as well as the database search. The woman had been infuriatingly slow to grasp that Emilia was more interested in who had been asking about her than she was in Señora Navarro's concern that there were now three people living in the house. Neither had Señora Navarro been able to remember what color car the man had driven. In the end, Emilia got the man's name but her rent went up by 300 pesos a month.

The circle spun again, the database flickered, and a list of hits came up.

There was only one *cédula* registered to a Periliano Roa Fuentes.

He'd died in Guadalajara three years ago.

Chapter 22

Gloria was the sort of woman Emilia had seen a thousand times, and was nearly a twin of Lila Jimenez Lata's grandmother, Berta. She was stocky and ample and work-hardened; any age between 30 and 60. She wore a navy skirt and a faded tee shirt that fit snugly over her midsection's rolls. Both items of clothing were partially hidden by a smock-like floral apron on which she frequently wiped her hands.

Her food stall was on the edge of a parking lot serving a strip of stores on one side and a construction site promising a new run of shops on the other. Pretty soon Acapulco would just be stores and hotels, Emilia thought as she parked the Suburban. Gloria had rigged up a blue and white beach umbrella to protect herself from the sun and attract customers' attention. Under the umbrella was a small grill, two coolers, and a small metal folding table.

Emilia nodded to Flores and they both got out of the vehicle. Gloria had two customers from the nearby construction site. Emilia watched as the woman deftly shoveled chopped meat from the smoking *comal* into two irregularly shaped tortillas. She gave each a squirt of cream sauce from a plastic bottle, then wrapped them in foil for the two construction workers who gave her some coins in return.

The men left. Gloria reached into one of the coolers, drew out a bag of masa dough, pinched off a fistful and began slapping it flat. She looked up when the two detectives approached.

"Hungry this morning, *chica*?" she asked.

"Sure," Emilia said.

"Two?"

"Yes." Emilia jingled the coins in her jeans pocket. "Juan Fabio from the *mercado* says you have the best tacos in Acapulco."

Gloria gave a brief smile, revealing a significant gap in her upper row of teeth. It was an automatic smile at a customer, not one of recognition.

"Juan Fabio," Emilia repeated. "The junkman from the Mercado Municipal."

Gloria went on slapping her piece of masa dough. "Yes, he loves Gloria's tacos." She flipped the flattened dough onto the *comal* and the sweet charcoal scent of cooking corn rose in the air.

"He prays to Padre Pro," Emilia said leadingly.

"Ah, Padre Pro." Gloria flipped the tortilla using the well calloused tips of her thumb and forefinger. A wooden spatula was produced from her apron pocket to stir the shredded meat sizzling next to the tortilla. Emilia wasn't sure if the meat was pork or chicken.

"I bought a very special relic of Padre Pro," she said.

Gloria looked up. "You are a blessed woman, then." She made the first taco, twisted it inside foil and handed it to Emilia. "Padre Pro will protect you always."

"The relic is supposed to be Padre Pro's finger," Emilia said. "But it's somebody's else's finger. The finger you sold to Juan Fabio."

The practiced movements over the *comal* continued. Gloria scooped up the meat and dumped it into the second tortilla. Emilia had a horrifying thought that the unidentified meat could be the rest of some fingerless woman's body.

"I don't understand you, señora," Gloria said. She handed Flores his taco with one hand and thrust out the other for payment. Her face was blank; the friendly smile was gone.

"You sold a finger to Juan Fabio," Emilia said. She jingled the coins in her pocket but didn't yet pay for the taco. "He made it into a false relic of Padre Pro that ended up in a fancy store in El Centro."

"No," Gloria looked past Emilia and frown lines appeared between her eyes. "I don't know anything about places like that."

"You know Juan Fabio from the Friends of Padre Pro."

"Padre Pro makes miracles," Gloria said as if to steer the conversation back to safer ground.

"I'm not asking about Padre Pro," Emilia said. "I'm asking

where you got the finger."

Gloria shook her head, opened the second cooler and made a show of rummaging around in it.

Still holding his taco, Flores suddenly kicked over the *comal* in a shower of sparks and sizzling meat. "Where did you get the finger, old woman?" he shouted "Or do you want to go to jail for selling body parts?"

Gloria stumbled backwards and came up against the post of the beach umbrella. She stared at Flores. "Police," she said, her voice full of resentment.

"We don't want to arrest you," Emilia said quietly, her hand on Flores's arm. The young detective was red-faced and over-excited and unsure what to do next. "Just tell us where you got the finger."

"There's a man who lives by my mother in Gallo Pinto," Gloria said. Her voice registered nothing but disgust.

Flores looked blankly at Emilia but she knew where Gallo Pinto was. It was one of a clutch of small villages in the Costa Chica region south of Acapulco, where the coast now slammed up against the mountains courtesy of Hurricane Miguel. There was no room for beaches but plenty for the poverty that hemorrhaged people to Acapulco to find work. There was little civil authority in some areas and the state government of Guerrero had recently "partnered" with local vigilante groups in order to push the murderous Knights Templar drug cartel out of the area.

The vigilantes were called "community police" now, and their allegiance to state and federal law enforcement was tenuous. So far, however, Costa Chica hadn't seen the murder rates and extreme violence of the neighboring state of Michoacán, where federal troops had tried to disarm large vigilante groups arrayed against the Knights Templar. When the disarmament failed, the *federales* had organized a truce and a so-called "contract" to align the vigilante groups with state and federal authority. No one was really sure how it would all work out and bets had been taken in the squadroom that the Michoacán vigilantes would become a government-backed organized crime syndicate. And a role model for

Guerrero.

Gloria's eyes darted to the fallen griddle but she didn't attempt to pick it up. The hot coals shriveled the grass at the edge of the parking lot.

"This man in Gallo Pinto," Emilia prompted. "How did he get the finger?"

"He's not right in the head but my mother is nice to him." Gloria stared at the meat in the grass. "He walks all day. Sometimes he brings her things he's found. Glass from the beach. Sparkly candy wrappers. Things like that." She trailed off and wiped her hands on her apron as if wiping away the image of the man.

"Go on," Emilia said.

"He brought the finger to show her." Gloria looked around the parking lot, at anything except the two detectives. "I was there. It was the weekend."

"Where did he get it?"

"He said he found it growing on a hill."

"Growing?" Emilia shook her head. "Did he know it was a finger?"

"Maybe. Maybe not. He's not right in the head. When he came to show my mother what he found, I checked to make sure it wasn't one of his."

"What's his name?"

Gloria finally looked at Emilia. "Pepe.

"Do you know where he lives?"

"In Gallo Pinto. Near my mother. Off a dirt road. Now pay me for the tacos and the meat and leave me alone."

Emilia turned to Flores. "Pick up her grill."

Flores gaped at her.

"You heard me." Emilia took the taco he was holding and jerked her chin at a rag by the cooler.

Flores used the rag as a potholder to right the base of the grill and replace the *comal* on top, his face tight with embarrassment and anger. Gloria pulled the rag out of his hand and made a show of cleaning the greasy surface of the griddle.

Emilia didn't like the way the construction workers

continued to stare at the odd little group they made under Gloria's umbrella. "How much did you pay for it?" she asked.

"Ten pesos."

"Why?" Flores burst out. "Why would you buy a finger from him?"

Gloria looked sideways at him. "You can make money from everything, *muchacho*, if you're smart."

Emilia wanted to cry. A human finger for 10 pesos. Out of all the people who had passed along the woman's finger, Gloria seemed the most dispassionate; the most detached from the humanity involved in the transaction, the one most able to see the small rubbery object as something separate from a human life. The finger was nothing more than a commodity to buy and sell.

"So you gave him 10 pesos for it," Emilia said. "Because you knew you could sell it to Juan Fabio?"

"Sure." Gloria rubbed her thumb and fingers together. "Juan Fabio is a good businessman. He knows how to make one peso into two."

"He paid you 50 pesos and that grill," Emilia said.

Gloria nodded. "That was a good deal," she said. "I did well on that one."

Flores caught his breath.

"This Pepe. The man who found the finger," Emilia said to Gloria. "How much to take us to see him?"

Gloria sniffed. "Gallo Pinto is far. Three buses. That's why I only go on weekends."

"We have a car," Emilia said. "We'll take you."

"Three buses to get back." Gloria gave Emilia a sly sideways glance.

"We'll bring you back."

"I have food to sell."

They'd paid El Flaco 1000 pesos for no more than a name. Gloria's inventory was probably worth less than 200. "We're hungry," Emilia said.

☼

They loaded Gloria and all her gear into the Suburban. Flores looked downcast as Emilia said that Gloria had to sit in the front seat in order to navigate them to Gallo Pinto. As Emilia started the car she could feel the waves of hurt emanating from the younger detective.

But Gloria would need to trust one of them enough to get to Gallo Pinto and it was clear that Flores had closed that door when he kicked over the woman's livelihood. Emilia didn't know why he'd done that, maybe to show off some notion of *machismo*; or maybe because again, he couldn't handle the adrenaline of a high pressure situation. Out of earshot of Gloria, Emilia had explained about the vigilante groups to him but the conversation had been quick and she wasn't entirely sure he understood the situation.

Following Gloria's directions, Emilia drove east, around the lip of the bay. But instead of taking the familiar road southeast to Puerta Marques and the Palacio Réal, they headed due east on the road to San Marco and into the no-man's land of Costa Chica.

"Do you have a family, Gloria?" Emilia asked.

Gloria sat huddled in the corner of her seat, her shoulder pressed against the car window. "Three boys."

"Are they in Acapulco with you?" Emilia wondered how much time they had or if Gloria had to be back in the city before school let out.

"Two are with me," she said. "The oldest is in Gallo Pinto."

"With your mother?"

"He married a girl from the town," Gloria said. "They live with her family."

"Does he work?" There weren't many real jobs in small towns like Gallo Pinto, which is why people like Gloria earned their money in Acapulco. The few jobs that were available in the small mountain towns didn't pay much. In contrast, being a lookout or a courier for the Sinaloa cartel or the Knights Templar meant money, girls, a fancy truck. Guns. Respect. Power over your neighbors.

"At the vegetable cannery," Gloria said. "Everybody works

there."

"That must be a good job." Emilia's direction for the conversation was a straight path to what they would find in Gallo Pinto.

Gloria shrugged. "If you can get it."

"What about your husband?"

"Dead," Gloria sniffed. "Had the wrong friends."

Emilia took that to mean he'd aligned with the wrong cartel, whichever that one was today. It changed in small towns with alarming frequency.

They continued east. Emilia asked Gloria to verify the way at each road sign.

"You're really police?" Gloria asked after a few more kilometers.

"Yes," Emilia said. "I showed you my badge."

"And him?" Gloria didn't turn, just pointed over her shoulder at Flores in the backseat.

Emilia glanced in the rearview mirror before answering. Flores hummed and his head bounced gently as he stared out the car window. "Yes, he's a police detective, too."

"Why?"

"Why is he a cop?"

"Why are you?"

Emilia considered. *Because my cousins were cops first. Because I'm not afraid to fight. Because someone has to find the missing.* "I'm good at solving problems," she said.

Gloria sniffed. "The police only create problems. They're good at hiding the truth and taking money from people like me."

"I'm looking for the truth," Emilia said. "That finger could belong to someone important."

"Then how could Pepe have found it?" Gloria's tone implied that Emilia was an *estupida*.

"I don't know," Emilia admitted. "I hope he can tell me."

"I keep telling you," Gloria said. "He's simple. Simple-minded."

Emilia had a sharp, intense longing to see Silvio in the passenger seat instead of Gloria, gray crew cut imperious to wind or rain, scowl in place, tall cup of coffee in his hand. A growling noise and *"Shut up, Cruz"* coming out of his mouth when she said anything mildly funny.

After two hours, they left the highway for a narrow country road, past the silent cactus standing like surrendering soldiers. Eventually the tarmac deteriorated into gravel and the Suburban's suspension bounced its passengers like a trampoline. They began to pass animal pens and cement shanties. Farm fields, like irregular patches strewn over the hills, wore the broken and dried stalks of an old harvest. They would be planted again with corn and beans closer to the rainy season. It was a rough way to make a living, Emilia thought as the Suburban topped a rise. She braked as a couple of goats skittered past. Two old trucks were parked sideways across the road just beyond.

"Los Martillos de Cristo," Gloria muttered. *The Hammers of Christ.*

"Are they always here?" Emilia asked.

"Sometimes." Gloria looked pleased with herself. "When they expect trouble."

Red and white flags fluttered from the antenna of each truck. As the breeze snapped the red-bordered fabric taut, Emilia saw a crown of thorns centered on the white background above the silhouette of a hammer.

She counted eight men lounging against the trucks. They watched the Suburban approach. All wore bright white tee shirts with the hammer and thorns design, wide-brimmed hats or ball caps, and automatic rifles slung across their chests.

"Emilia?" Flores asked from the backseat. "What's going on?"

"These are the community police," Emilia said. She didn't know how well the cooperation between Los Martillos and officialdom was going, but it stood to reason that even if things were going badly the vigilantes would have little to gain by murdering two Acapulco cops.

"They don't look like police." Flores's voice was sharp and high.

Emilia caught his eye in the rearview mirror and kept her

voice steady. "Do what I say, Orlando, and we'll be fine."

A man stepped into the road and pointed his weapon. Emilia eased the Suburban to a stop. As his compatriots aimed their rifles at the car, the man approached the driver's side. Emilia rolled down her window and rested her arm on the opening. Relaxed. Nothing to hide.

"What's your business in Gallo Pinto?" he asked. Between his wide brimmed cowboy hat and aviator sunglasses, there was little of his face to be seen besides a poorly shaven chin and a stubby cigar clenched between gray teeth.

"Bringing Gloria to see her mother," Emilia said.

"I haven't seen this car before," he said suspiciously. "Cut your engine."

Emilia compiled. "From Acapulco," she said.

He stuck his head in the window and the cigar came dangerously close to Emilia's elbow. "Gloria." There was recognition in his voice. "It's not the weekend."

"They're police," Gloria said from the other side of the console.

"Bringing Gloria to see her mother," Emilia repeated.

"Why?" He came around to Gloria's side of the car. They obviously knew each other and the man had the same wary, yet sly, eyes as Gloria. Gallo Pinto was a hard place. "You in trouble?"

Gloria snorted. "She wanted to come here. Some crazy idea that someone found something of hers here."

The man leaned against the car door as if settling in for a chat. "In Gallo Pinto?" He chewed the end of the cigar, then spit into the road

"She wants to meet Pepe. The crazy one who lives on the hill." Gloria looked sideways at Emilia. "She's *estupida*, you know?"

He raised his eyes. "Show me your identification," he said to Emilia.

Emilia wore her badge on its lanyard under her shirt. She pulled it out and held it so that he could see the number on the shield and the words *Detective* and *Acapulco*.

"Anybody can buy one of those," he said.

He went to grab the badge but Emilia didn't let go. To cover, he leaned further into the car and stared at Flores. "Who's that?"

"Her friend," Gloria answered.

The man withdrew his head and marched over to the other men still aiming their weapons at the Suburban. They had a lengthy conversation before the cigar chewing vigilante came back to Gloria's window.

"I'm your guide," he said. "Understand? Follow the truck."

One of the trucks bounced off the shoulder of the road and swerved in front of the Suburban.

Flores leaned forward and grabbed Emilia's shoulder. "What is going on?"

"I don't know," Emilia said honestly. "They must be worried about Templar activity. Maybe something happened recently. Be honest, but don't say anything unless you're asked."

They didn't have a choice. Half of the vigilantes had climbed into the bed of the truck and sat facing the rear. Their blinding white tees were a nice contrast to the weapons pointing at the Suburban.

"I should sell bleach here," Gloria said.

☼

The road widened and the smattering of shanties turned into a small town. There were a few cars parked on the street in front of outdoor restaurants. As they slowly followed the truck bristling with men and guns, Emilia took in the few shops, the open food market, the vendors on the street selling pay-as-you-go phone cards and lottery tickets. The center square was dominated by a whitewashed church and a small playground with a painted metal jungle gym.

A few young men in more Los Martillos tee shirts lounged in front of place called The Movie Shack, a place where a man in a dirty shirt sold snacks and what appeared to be bootleg DVDs. A women and a little boy stood hand in hand by a bus stop. The child wore a school uniform.

The truck ahead of them pulled to the side. A few shouts told Emilia to do the same.

They were herded out of the Suburban and into a small restaurant where Emilia and Flores were searched for weapons. Both of their handguns were confiscated and the man who'd proclaimed himself their guide took Emilia's badge as well.

The place was empty. There were four plastic tables with matching chairs, all of which showed black scuffs and red drips from too many rough mannered eaters and too little hot water and soap. A glass counter was backlit with a naked fluorescent bulb, both illuminating and warming greasy empanadas, *chupata* rolls stuffed with ham, and some tired pieces of egg and spinach pie. Emilia and Flores were shoved into plastic chairs at one of the four tables in the place. Gloria stood by the wall.

"You want a cola?" the guide asked.

It wasn't spoken as an option. "Sure," Emilia said.

"One hundred pesos." Laughter rippled around the white shirts.

A curtain behind the glass counter parted and two men walked into the seating area. The guide went to the tallest, who was obviously the local *jefe*.

Emilia watched the tall man. He was twice her age, yet still carried muscle on his frame. He wore the white tee of Los Martillos, jeans, and a large belt buckle. His face was puffy, from either fighting or heavy drinking. Or both. As his eyes swept over Emilia and Flores, his eyes were appraising and dark under thick brows.

He left the guide standing by the glass case and came to the table. "Detective Cruz from the Acapulco police, no?"

"You have the advantage, señor," Emilia said. "You know my name and your men have my gun and my badge."

He gave a false little bow, one hand on his heart. "My apologies," he said. "I am Bernardo Valentino Pinto and Los Martillos are my men. With all the trouble we have had in my city we must be very cautious."

"I can understand that," Emilia said. "But I'm not here as a police detective. I am here to simply talk to a friend of Gloria's and she was kind enough to guide me to your lovely city." Gallo Pinto was hardly a city but Emilia was taking her cues from Valentino.

"Then why did you bring a gun?"

Emilia spread her hands in a gesture of supplication. "It is our regulations. An Acapulco detective must always carry their gun, even when visiting a friend. Even in a city secured by friends."

"Who is this friend you are here to visit?"

"Pepe," Gloria broke in. "Pepe the simple-minded who lives on the hill. This one"—she pointed to Emilia—"thinks he has something of hers. I say she's as simple as him. But she's paying me to show her."

Valentino finally looked at Flores. "Who is this? The man who sits in the backseat and lets a woman drive him around?"

Flores half rose in his seat and Emilia yanked him back down. "This is his town, Orlando," she said.

Someone chambered a round as Flores put both his *cédula* and badge on the table.

Valentino swept the identification off the table. Emilia held her breath and waited.

"Your name is Flores Almaprieto?" Valentino asked.

"Yes."

"This one drives the car?" Valentino still had Flores's *cédula* in his hand and he waved it at Emilia.

"Yes," Flores repeated.

"She is your driver, no?"

Flores frowned at the unexpected line of questioning. "Yes, she drives the car. But she's more than a chauffeur."

His response brought a volley of guffaws from both Gloria and the white shirts. Valentino tossed a red-faced Flores his identification and gestured to the guide to return Emilia's badge and their weapons.

☼

Gloria directed Emilia to turn left and they headed uphill

again. The vehicle jounced over a ridge and banged onto cobblestones, which soon turned into a gravel track. Flores made an annoyed sound from the back seat.

Sugar cane grew on one side of the track. On the other side they passed low cement houses, many with corrugated metal roofs. As the Suburban protested its way, the houses grew fewer and farther in between. They turned again, onto a dirt track and Gloria pointed to a small blue house surrounded by pots of plants. "That's my mother's house." It didn't have windows; instead the window openings were filled with cement blocks perforated in a flower pattern. Ventilation but no view.

"Is Pepe your mother's neighbor?" Emilia said.

"He lives beyond the road."

They continued to bounce along the dirt track. The cane gave way to scrubby pine and debris from long-since razed cement structures.

"The cannery had a place here once," Gloria said. "Then they built the big place closer to the road to San Marco."

The Suburban's clanks of protest competed with the roar of the engine as the heavy vehicle clambered over the uneven terrain and Emilia felt her teeth clatter together. The track dwindled down to a barely worn footpath and Emilia stopped the car, unable to drive any further.

They climbed out and Flores looked around in surprise. "You were right about the shoes, Emilia," he said.

It took ten minutes of uphill walking on the path before they saw a small shack of unpainted gray cement. Like the home of Gloria's mother, the windows were made of perforated blocks. The door was a canvas curtain. The place was surrounded by a makeshift fence; a conglomeration of driftwood, rusted pieces of corrugated metal, part of a shipping crate with huge stenciled letters, and pieces of plastic that once might have been a trash barrel.

Gloria clapped her hands loudly as they approached the crazy-quilt fence. "Pepe!" she shouted. "A pretty lady wants to talk to you."

Emilia was sweating in the heat but she wasn't winded.

Behind her she could hear Flores laboring to catch his breath.

The curtain was pulled aside and a man stood in the doorway. Even from a distance, Emilia could see there was something wrong with him. One shoulder was held higher and thrust forward and his head was inclined toward that side as if his nose and armpit were trying to touch. A shock of lank hair fell across his forehead. He had on a tee shirt and jeans, with sneakers that had once been white but were now stained the color of the brown dirt that swirled around Emilia's feet.

"*Hola*," Emilia called when she got to the rickety fence. The stench was strong and she was sure the place had neither running water nor indoor plumbing. A pack of dogs of indeterminate breed rose to its collective feet and began barking wildly. The pack sorted itself out into five dogs, all with short hair and large teeth. One sprang against the fence, paws against rickety metal, the dog's jaws level with Emilia's face. She retreated.

"Pepe," Gloria shouted again. She kept her distance from the fence. "Tell the dogs to shut up. This lady came all the way from Acapulco to talk to you."

The hunched man named Pepe stepped away from the canvas-covered doorway. The ground between the house and the fence was loose dirt kicked up by the pack of dogs. Dust puffed around his feet at every step. It was probably a sea of mud in the rainy season.

An older man came out of the house behind Pepe. Emilia guessed it was his father.

"What do you want, Gloria?" the older man asked.

"She's got business with Pepe," Gloria called back, with a nod of her chin at Emilia.

The old man fixed eyes on Emilia. "How do you know my boy?"

"He found something that belongs to a friend of mine," Emilia said. She had to raise her voice to be heard over the continual barking of the dogs.

"I find a lot of things," Pepe said. His voice was high for that of a full-grown man and the twist in his torso made it seem as if he was speaking to his side.

"You found a finger," Emilia said. Flores stepped up to stand next to her. He wasn't Silvio, yet she was glad that she wasn't doing this alone.

The father shouted at the dogs. The pack yelped one last time and then subsided into a silent, sinister presence, pacing between the older man at the door and the younger one near the fence.

"A finger," Emilia repeated into the sudden silence.

The rank smell of men and dogs filled her mouth with a gummy taste. Emilia fought the urge to run back down the rutted track, fling herself into the Suburban and drive without stopping until she was back in Acapulco; back where she belonged with the wind blowing the tang of salt and fish and suntan oil in her face.

Both father and son looked at her dully. Emilia tried again. "I want to know where you found the finger."

"Which one?" Pepe asked.

It wasn't a question Emilia had expected. Flores made a squeaky noise and Emilia put a hand on his arm. She turned to Gloria. "You didn't tell me he had more."

The woman shrugged, her eyes still on the older man by the doorway. The dogs were clustered by his bare feet. "He showed the one I paid for," Gloria said in a voice that suggested she would have bought more if they had been available.

"I need to see where he found them," Emilia said. "All of them."

"Pepe," Gloria called. "You need to come show the lady where you found the fingers."

"My boy don't need to do nothing." The old man waded through the dogs and stood by the fence. The dogs barking resumed, the dogs running back and forth with excitement.

"I'll pay you," Emilia said above the din. "I'll pay Pepe to be our guide."

"How much?"

The whole house wasn't worth the price of a pair of shoes. "Two hundred pesos," Emilia said.

"Four hundred pesos," the old man countered.

"Do you trust them?" Flores breathed.

Emilia glanced at him. He already had the money in his hand.

"Four hundred," Emilia called. "A hundred now. The rest after Pepe has shown us where he found the fingers."

"All right," the old man said. He gave his son a shove. "Go."

Pepe shuffled along the makeshift fence and pulled aside a heavy piece of corrugated metal. The dogs bolted through the opening and charged at the three people standing on the other side. The largest dog rushed up to Emilia. She froze as the dog barked wildly and stropped its front paws in the dirt. Its jaws were inches away from the crotch of her jeans.

"Emilia," she heard Flores whisper.

"Don't move," Emilia said out of the corner of her mouth.

Pepe ignored them as he shuffled across the dirt. The dog left Emilia and loped after him. The other four dogs retreated to the father.

Gloria crossed her arms with an expression of resignation and made it clear she wasn't walking any further.

"Come on," Emilia said to Flores. She forced her feet to follow Pepe and his mongrel. Flores fell in behind her.

Despite his shuffling gait, Pepe moved easily over the track. He led them through a path cut through the sugar cane fields, the dog alternately walking by his side and dancing back to snap at Emilia and Flores.

The sugar cane was as tall as Emilia's head. The path was little more than a car's width and rutted with tire tracks. Emilia felt her feet grow heavier with every step and her tee shirt was soaked with sweat. Even so, she was loath to take off her jacket and expose her gun. Flores panted heavily behind her but also kept his jacket on.

The cane field ended at the base of a rocky hill dotted with scrub pines. They were closer to the ocean, now, and Emilia could smell the change in the air.

Pepe found tire tracks again and the going got worse, the land uneven and unforgiving. Emilia wondered at the vehicles which had made the tracks; driving the Suburban up the road would have been a nightmare. The ruts weren't deep and Emilia guessed they'd been made in the dry season, so within the last few months. They would have been deeper if they'd been made in the last rainy season. After rains, tires sank into the mud and left deep prints that hardened into waves of clay. These tracks were less pronounced.

"How did you find this place, Pepe?" Emilia asked, trying not to sound out of breath.

"I like to walk," he answered. "I walk all over to find things."

"What sort of things?" Emilia walked faster to get closer but dropped back again when the dog lunged at her.

Flores gave a nervous gasp.

"Things other people leave behind," Pepe answered, oblivious to the dog's threatening behavior.

He kept up a mumbling prattle, most of which Emilia didn't understand, as they continued to trudge through the rocky landscape, his voice competing with the constant whine of cicadas and the dog's hoarse panting. The solitude and desolation were heavy and complete. They could have been alone on the moon if it wasn't for the hard cobalt blue sky and the sun blazing down from a golden halo. Despite the whiff of salt, the air was full of particulate and Emilia sneezed again and again, the sound reverberating off the rocks around her. Flores fell behind as they climbed. Emilia pushed herself, unwilling to lose sight of Pepe.

At the top of a small hill, the tire tracks dissolved into a swirl of dirt where vehicles had turned around. Emilia thought she heard the crash of waves below.

The rise sloped away into a patchy field of rocks, stumpy pines and overturned earth, probably one of the few flat pieces of land this close to the coast. Pepe looked around happily, as if this was a familiar place. Quivering with excitement, the dog raced from spot to spot where the ground had been disturbed.

"Is this where you found the finger?" Emilia asked.

"This is the finger field. I found all of them here," Pepe said proudly.

"You have to show me exactly where you found the fingers," Emilia said. She felt lightheaded from the sun yet weighted by dread of what she guessed was hidden in the stark landscape.

Pepe shuffled into the field as the dog continued its frenzied exploration of the site, scrabbling at dirt with its front paws or barking and darting at Pepe before rushing off to examine another bit of overturned earth and loose rocks.

Emilia kept her distance so as not to alarm the already hyper dog. Pepe stopped and pointed down. "Here's one of them," he said. The dog sniffed the ground by his feet and started digging.

Emilia came forward. Sticking out of the dry dusty earth was part of a human hand. The thumb and palm, minus four fingers, was covered in dirt. If she hadn't looked closely, she would never have realized what it was. The mangled hand swam in front of her eyes as the dog's mouth closed over it.

Emilia looked away and willed her stomach not to heave. "Did you take the fingers?" she asked.

Pepe kicked at the dog and it shot away, leaving the hand where it was. The boy shuffled further away from the swirl of tire tracks. "Here's another," he called a moment later.

Emilia followed to see another hand sticking out of the ground in the same condition. "Did you take all the fingers?"

"Gloria bought one," Pepe said.

"Who else bought one?"

He didn't answer, just kept walking, following the dog's excited howls. Emilia followed, passing a shoe, a baseball cap, part of a foot. Black hair half buried and coated with dirt.

Emilia stopped walking, acutely aware that she was standing in a sea of hasty graves. A place where bodies had been defiled and flung indiscriminately into even less than a pauper's grave. A killing field.

She dug her phone out of her hip pocket, hands shaking badly. There was no signal and she managed to stuff it back in the pocket before the dog came bounding over to her, tongue lolling, muzzle coated in dirt from all of the sniffing, digging, and chewing.

"Did you hear them?" Emilia asked Pepe. Her throat was dry and constricted and the words had to force themselves out.

Pepe gestured at the ground. "They don't talk."

"No." Emilia clenched her fists to keep herself from shaking apart. "The people who made the tire tracks."

"They had trucks," Pepe said.

"How many?"

He wandered away and the dog trotted with him.

"When?" Emilia felt close to the breaking point. "When did you take the fingers?"

Pepe pantomimed cutting with two fingers. "I did it like this."

The dog dug up something a few feet away and locked its jaws into it. A few tugs, the animal's entire body braced, and the dog pulled out a lump of dirty meat. The dog settled onto its haunches and began to gnaw.

Emilia felt hysteria rising, coming up from her gut, pushing through her core until she knew it was going to burst out of her like a primal scream. She wanted to run away from this place, run away from the broken earth and the rot of death and the lingering ghosts. Forget that she'd ever been there, ever followed this trail, ever heard of Padre Pro.

But she stayed, unable to take a step in any direction. Emilia didn't know how long she stood there, listening to the dog's slobbering grunts of satisfaction, afraid of what she might step on if she moved. She kept her chin tilted up towards the sky, trying to find fresh air, refusing to give in to the nausea that choked her. The bodies in their hastily shoveled graves had died violently. Emilia felt their panic, their fear, and the restlessness of their souls and she had no way to prevent all of it from overwhelming her like a storm surge eating up the shore.

"Emilia." The voice was soft, almost lost in the wind.

She forced herself to turn around, realizing that she'd all but forgotten Flores. He was a few feet away, streaked with dust and sweat. He had a cell phone in one hand and a thick stick in the other, presumably to keep the dog away.

"There's no phone service," Flores said, his voice choked

with tears.

His face contorted and he abruptly threw up. His retching went on for a long time, punctuated by sobs.

Emilia wanted to say something to him, but it was all she could do not to break down herself.

"You have to pay my *papi* now," Pepe said.

Chapter 23

Almost of its own accord the Suburban turned east on La Costura. Emilia knew she was driving too fast but it didn't matter. It was nearly midnight on a weeknight. The streets were relatively quiet. The few cars on the road stayed to the right as she barreled past in the left lane.

Emilia drove on automatic the entire way and it wasn't until she handed the vehicle to the valet parking attendant at the hotel entrance that she consciously realized where she was.

She never came to the Palacio Réal during the week and the place felt different than on weekends. Quieter. She could see that the big Pasodoble Bar was still open and background music carried through to the hotel lobby, but otherwise the luxury hotel felt asleep.

The only person on duty in the lobby was behind the long concierge counter. Emilia couldn't recall ever seeing him before.

"May I help you?" he asked. Emilia had to give Kurt credit, the young man's face curved in a hotel-worthy smile, never betraying the alarm he must have felt at seeing a distraught woman in filthy clothes and a bulge in her denim jacket under the left arm.

Emilia produced her key card. "I'm Emilia," she said over her shoulder as she made her way to the elevators. "Going up to Señor Rucker's apartment."

"Shall I call and announce you, señora?" the young man called.

"Do whatever the hell you want," Emilia said to the elevator door. She jabbed at the button. Her hand shook and she wondered if it had been shaking ever since the call to Silvio.

It seemed like a lifetime ago when she'd steered a still-sobbing Flores back down the track, away from the killing field and the dog and the simple-minded Pepe. By the time they got back to the car her cell phone showed one feeble bar of service. It had been enough.

She had no memory of what she'd actually said on the phone as Flores tried to collect himself and Gloria looked on stonily. But Emilia's directions and sense of urgency had been sufficient to bring out both Silvio and Ibarra. Two hours later, an entire technical crew was there, with lights and cameras and radios. The *federales*—national police, as well as an army unit—arrived shortly after that.

The elevator doors slid open. Emilia charged inside and came face to face with Christine Boudreau.

The blonde woman pressed a hand to keep the elevator doors open and stepped over the threshold. "An unexpected visit, Detective?" Christine asked as she pointedly took in Emilia's disheveled appearance. The blonde hotel concierge wasn't wearing her usual hotel uniform but a short white sheath dress and high heeled sandals. She carried nothing more than a tiny wristlet.

"Is that a problem?" Emilia asked. Her voice came out a little too loud and with a belligerence she hadn't intended.

She swiped her key card at the sensor and punched P for the penthouse. She had the satisfaction of seeing Christine's startled look as the elevator doors closed in her face.

The carriage rose smoothly. Emilia again fought rising hysteria as images of the killing field competed with Christine's smug attitude. It occurred to her that coming to the hotel on a Tuesday night might have been a huge mistake.

Her hands shook so badly that it took two tries to get her key card to open the penthouse door. The living room was dim as she walked in, the room illuminated only by the moonlight shining in from the uncurtained sliding doors. The expanse of glass looked out over the bay and reflected the moonlight rippling over the moving water.

The only other light was a thin glow from under the bedroom door.

Emilia let the door slam and dumped her shoulder bag on the floor.

"Hello?" Kurt's voice came from the bedroom. "Is someone there?"

"It's me." Emilia shucked off her jacket and left it on top of the bag by the door.

"Em?" The bedroom door opened and Kurt came out, clad only in long neoprene swim trunks and flip flops. He had a tee shirt in one hand and a towel in the other.

"What are you doing dressed like that?" An invisible hand squeezed Emilia's heart.

"Going for a swim." He tossed shirt and towel on the back of the sofa, took her by the shoulders and kissed her. "This is an unexpected pleasure. Why didn't you call and let me know you were coming?"

"No one goes for a swim at this hour." Emilia ducked out of his grasp. "Were those just the first pants you could find?"

Kurt dropped his hands. "I had a 16 hour day and need to work off some energy." He looked at her filthy pants. "What happened to you?"

"Never mind me." Emilia felt her blood pressure rise like a rocket. Part of her was still in that field; fighting for control, fighting against the scream threatening to burst out of her. "You really want me to believe you're going swimming at this hour of the night?"

"Yes, I expect you to believe what I tell you." Kurt gave a step back as if he sensed she needed space. "What's going on, Em? What are you doing here?"

"Apparently finding out what really happens in this hotel when I'm not here."

Kurt folded his arms. Backlit by the moonlight, he was something out of a magazine. Golden hair, golden skin, a body made of power and promise. And she'd thought it had all belonged to her.

"Really?" he asked. "What do you think happens when you're not here?"

"This . . . this . . . this," Emilia sputtered as she waved a hand at his bare chest. Her voice was too shrill, too loud. "The little boy at the desk wants to call up here. Warn you, right? The elevator takes forever to come and when it does, who gets off? Christine. With her teeny dress and smirky expression, looking like she just rolled out of bed."

Kurt's eyebrows shot up. "Are you seriously——."

"When I get here, you're half naked," Emilia finished, interrupting him.

To her utter surprise, Kurt laughed. "Em, you're had a pretty bad day if you think there's something going on between me and Christine."

"Don't you dare laugh at me!" Emilia shouted. She charged down the hall and into the bedroom. She stood in the doorway.

The bed was neatly made. A pair of khaki pants and a white dress shirt were on the end and a pair of loafers were kicked over by the dresser. Nothing else was out of place.

Of course, maybe they'd done it on the sofa.

She marched back to the living room. Kurt held up his hands, palms out. "Em, what's going on?"

"I guess this is my fault for coming on a Tuesday." It was as if Emilia had absorbed the fear and panic she'd felt from the restless souls at the killing field. Reason had fled, chased by adrenaline. "You keep saying that this is my home now. But obviously only on the weekends when Christine is otherwise occupied."

Kurt's face tightened. He turned around and headed for the kitchen, his flipflops making soft slapping sounds. "Tea or wine?"

"What?"

He didn't turn around. "Hot tea or a glass of red wine?"

"Tea," Emilia said. "No. Wait. Wine." She grabbed up her jacket and shoulder bag. "No, nothing. I should go."

This was all wrong. The penthouse wasn't home. She didn't live with this arrogant, cheating *gringo*.

Kurt stopped in the dining area. He poured something from one of the bottles on top of the buffet into a tumbler and added a little water from one of the snotty imported brands he liked. "Here." He held the tumbler out to Emilia as she stood in front of the door. "You look like you need this."

Emilia shook her head.

Kurt set the glass down, came to Emilia, put an arm around her shoulders, and steered her into a chair at the dining table. She let her jacket and bag tumble to the floor as Kurt pressed the glass into her unresisting hand. He took the chair next to her.

"What is it?" Emilia asked, eyeing the glass.

"Scotch," Kurt said. "You look like you've seen a ghost, then had a wrestling match with it."

"I didn't win," Emilia said.

Kurt mimed drinking. "Slow sips," he said.

The mellow flavor numbed her tongue and the cool fluid turned into warm fumes as it slipped down her throat. Emilia closed her eyes and took another swallow, then another.

"What happened, Em?" Kurt asked again.

Another swallow of amber fire and the words came, slowly at first. After a few more sips, the whole story flowed out.

She told him about finding Gloria, the trip to Gallo Pinto, the trek to find Pepe. How the man with the simple mind had led them through the hills to a cliff above the coast where they found the killing field. About the dog and Flores.

"The *federales* have taken over." Emilia closed both hands around the tumbler of Scotch as she wound up. "They want me to come back tomorrow to talk to Pepe again."

"Will you go?" Kurt asked. He'd been mostly silent as she talked, yet somehow had managed to coax it all out of her.

Emilia stared at him. "I have to. He might have seen something. Whoever did this. After all, how did he know to walk up there in the first place?" She gave a bitter laugh. "I didn't even think to ask him tonight. I didn't say anything useful."

"You found the place, Em." Kurt made a *drink up* motion again. "If you hadn't kept looking for everyone who'd bought and sold that finger, probably no one would have found the bodies. You can ask all the smart questions tomorrow."

"Maybe." Emilia took a final sip of Scotch.

Kurt refilled her glass, poured some Scotch for himself, and came back to the table. "What about Gloria and Juan Fabio? Are you going to arrest them?"

"I doubt it. Everybody's got bigger cases. Maybe we can get Blandón Hernandez for fraud but nobody has even suggested we try. I don't even know where he is." The Scotch had taken the edge off her hysteria but the adrenaline was still there, clanging an alarm through her veins. Emilia felt herself start to shake. "Plus, it's not likely any of them will do it again, is it?"

"No, I guess not."

"I'll see those mangled hands forever," Emilia said. "That thumb coming up out of the dirt. Hair. A foot. Hear that dog in my head every time I close my eyes."

"Em--."

"All those pieces that had once been people. *Madre de Dios*, it was as if they were all clawing at me, asking for help. And the smell." She pressed her hands to her eyes. "There were birds, too. Did I tell you about the birds? They'd pecked out eyes. Lips. All the soft tissue. Someone's eyes that could have been mine."

"You can't think like that, Em."

"I can't do this anymore. I've had enough." Emilia wanted to be quit of everything. Of being a cop. The dead bodies and the dregs of humanity who cut off the fingers of the dead.

"I know," Kurt said. He downed his Scotch.

"I'm going to have nightmares forever. Wake up screaming for the rest of my life." Her whole body was shaking now, icy cold, her teeth clattering together. The strength and control that had gotten her through the afternoon and evening fell away, routed by exhaustion. Emilia dropped her hands and looked around the room, unable to remember where the thermostat was. "It's freezing in here. Why is it always so cold in here? Why do you have the air conditioning set to frozen all the time?"

Without a word, Kurt pulled Emilia out of her chair and propelled her down the hall, through the bedroom, and into the en suite bathroom. As she stood shaking on the mat, he stripped off her shoulder holster, jeans, socks, shoes, and tee shirt. A moment later she was standing under a hot shower in her bra and panties. Still in his swim shorts, Kurt stepped into the tiled stall with her.

Hot water cascaded down and warmth seeped into her skin. Kurt pulled her against his chest. Emilia slid her arms around his waist, pressed her face into his bare skin, and wept for the dead.

"Listen to me, Em," Kurt said softly when she ran down. "This place is your safe zone."

Emilia gulped moist air, grateful for the steam curling off the tiles and the way his arms held her upright.

"Your safe zone," Kurt repeated. His voice was as clean as the falling water. It penetrated her fear and adrenaline-fueled reaction. "The place where you rest and get strong enough to face whatever you have to. It's tough out there. I know. I've been there, too."

His body was strong and solid. A bulwark standing between her and the horror she'd seen.

Kurt pushed wet hair off her forehead. "I'll never let you walk out before you're ready."

They stayed under the hot water for a long time. Emilia clung to Kurt's strength as her body defrosted, listening to him quietly tell her all the things she very desperately wanted to be true.

An hour later, having finally eaten some dinner and dressed in one of his old tee shirts, Emilia curled up against Kurt and pulled the covers up to her chin. She'd asked him to leave the bathroom light on, so that the bedroom wasn't completely dark. Kurt had left the curtains open as well, so that they could see the moonlight shining on the ocean far below.

She closed her eyes and slept deeply, without dreaming.

Chapter 24

The *federale* in charge of the killing field excavation was a Captain Espinosa. The place looked totally different than it had 15 hours ago.

The path Emilia had followed on foot yesterday was now a dirt road scooped out of the ground by machinery. Half a dozen distinctive navy and white *federale* trucks were parked in the scrub on either side.

Yellow crime scene tape blocked off an area the size of a *fútbol* field. Two large tents, erected at right angles to each other, dominated one corner of the field. At least 25 people in uniform were at the site with another half dozen in civilian clothes. Teams were scattered around the field, using various tools to dig up the remains and a system of plastic markers and neon spray paint to mark their findings.

Espinosa was a hard-faced man in his early fifties who gave her a brief rundown as he handed her a cup of coffee from a makeshift coffee bar in the tent. "Can't give you an actual body count yet," he said and raised his own paper cup to indicate the workers in the field. "They're still finding parts."

Emilia stared out the tent flap at the teams of excavators. Dismembered bodies were once a hallmark of the Los Zetas cartel. The intimidation practice, however, had spread to other cartels and associated gangs. "Somebody was out to make a statement."

Espinosa nodded. "Exactly," he said. "We've already got a team looking to see if a video was posted. That's become the message channel of choice. If there is a video, it will help identify not only the victims but whoever is responsible."

"How can I help?" Emilia asked.

Espinosa crumpled his paper cup. "I want to go over what happened yesterday and then we'll go talk to the kid who brought you up here."

Emilia finished her coffee. Without her nose buried in its

aroma, the smell of death and decomposition assaulted her. Like yesterday, Emilia felt the restlessness and terror of the souls trapped in that place.

Espinosa wasn't given to small talk as he took her statement as they sat at a small table in the tent. Emilia gave a brief account of how she'd tracked down Pepe, omitting details about the forgers, and what the strange young man had told her yesterday. Espinosa typed it into a small laptop as she talked. Her cell phone didn't have service but his gear appeared to be connected to some central server. *Federales* might have the worst reputation but they always had the best equipment.

The troubled national police force was routinely blamed for aiding drug lords, hiding or tampering with evidence, taking kickbacks, and conducting kidnappings and extortions. Even murder. There was little evidence to refute the charges and journalists who reported the abuses often went missing or had to flee to safety north of the border. She could only hope that Espinosa was an exception.

Emilia watched as two uniformed *federales*, both wearing surgical masks and gloves, brought a canvas stretcher over to one of the excavation teams. They loaded it with a leg, identifiable by dirty denim and a once-white sneaker, and carried it to the second tent about 50 meters from where Emilia sat.

"What about Los Martillos?" Espinosa asked. "The community police? Were they with you yesterday?"

"When we drove in they were almost paranoid about a private vehicle," Emilia said. "But once the head, a man named Valentino Pinto, let us in, no one bothered us. None of them came up here with us."

"Did they respect the badge?"

"It was a strange dynamic. I actually think they let us in because Valentino Pinto thought it was funny that a woman was driving." Emilia paused, wondering how forthcoming Espinosa would be. "Do you think they're responsible?"

"Let's first figure out when this happened, Detective," he said and pulled out disposable masks and gloves from boxes near the coffee maker. "But I'm not ruling out anything."

Espinosa led Emilia into the other tent. He introduced her to two forensic experts who would do the initial examination of the findings. Doctors Vargas and Furtado were both acquainted with Prade and seemed to be as serious about their work as the Acapulco medical examiner. Like Emilia and Espinosa, they wore surgical masks and gloves.

The floor of the tent was mostly covered with a thick black plastic tarp. Body parts were arranged on the tarp by type.

Albeit streaked with dirt and remnants of clothing, the pieces of flesh were pale, as if the blood had drained out long ago. The body parts were lifeless, impersonal, simply so many pieces of meat. If it wasn't for the recognizable shapes, the lumps might have been Serrano hams selling in a gourmet store for 300 pesos a pound.

Emilia breathed shallowly behind her mask. She'd eaten a light breakfast that morning, at Kurt's insistence, and hoped it wouldn't make a return engagement.

"Last one. Female." The two uniforms Emilia had seen before trundled in with their stretcher and awkwardly rolled a woman's torso onto the tarp.

The remains wore a stained blue bra and denim shorts. Both legs had been cut off at the knee and the arms severed at the shoulder.

"It's as if a mad man swept through here," Emilia said.

"We've seen this sort of thing before," Vargas said. "Chopping houses in Colombia, killing fields in Sinaloa and Michoacán. Lots of specialists in mutilation out there. It's usually to send a message."

"This brings the tally to 11 total. Nine men and two women." Furtado stood at the edge of the tarp and pulled on a fresh pair of latex gloves before touching an obviously male arm. "All but one have been in the ground six or eight weeks at least. One set of parts looks distinctively fresher as if buried relatively recently. All dismembered the same way, however, regardless of length of time in the field. Each was executed by shots to the brain. Bodies were cut up and scattered after death. Hatchet, if I had to make an immediate guess."

"Any identifying marks?" Emilia asked, forcing herself to stay composed.

"Yes." Furtado nodded, eyes serious above the surgical mask. "Despite the decomposition, there are still some distinctive body markings. All the men have the same tattoo."

He directed Emilia's attention to a male arm lying on the tarp. It bore a tattoo on the inside of the forearm. Green dye stood out on the bloodless flesh. Two crossed fists in front of a devil's pitchfork and the words "Salva Diablo" printed across the wrists.

"Salva Diablo," Espinosa said. "Honduran gang."

"I've seen that tattoo before," Emilia said.

"Where?" There was a sharp edge to Espinosa's voice.

"A shooting victim found on a cruise ship a couple of weeks ago," Emilia said. She wasn't sure she had permission to share an Organized Crime case with a *federale*; but it was clear now that the cases were linked. "Aboard the *Pacific Grandeur*, one of the largest ships that come through Acapulco. Male, shot twice in the head execution style just like these. Stuffed into a meat freezer and found about 12 hours after the time of death."

Espinosa ushered her out outside the tent, out of earshot of the two doctors. "Are we looking at a range war?" he asked urgently. "Somebody going after the Salva Diablo gang in Mexico?"

"Maybe," Emilia admitted. "There's a good reason for thinking that. We think the Salva Diablo from the cruise ship was dealing Colombian Ora Ciega, maybe looking to move it on the ship. He'd been with a hooker who died of an overdose. We're testing her for it."

"A range war over Ora Ciega. This field might be the tip of the iceberg." Espinosa pulled a pack of cigarettes out of his back pocket and offered it to Emilia. When she shook her head he lit one for himself and replaced the packet. "What else can you tell me about your cruise ship victim?"

"Not much," Emilia said. "We never got an ID on him. His prints weren't in the system. Before we could add him to the morgue's new website his body went missing."

"Now he's probably the fresher set of parts." Espinosa waved his cigarette at the entrance to the doctors' tent.

As Emilia stared at the field in front of them, she realized that the friends Chavito talked about had never been Bonilla and Ramos. The Salva Diablo gang member had been waiting for these other gang members from Honduras. But they'd been long dead.

Espinosa blew cigarette smoke upwards and breathed it in. "Go back to Ora Ciega. Did you trace it? We don't see that much of it."

"Test these bodies for it," Emilia said. "The finger that led us here had Ora Ciega embedded in the skin under the nail. It was tested in a private lab so I trust the results."

"Under the nail is consistent with someone who handled it a lot," Espinosa said. "Mixing, measuring. Packaging. If we find the same presentation here we can draw the obvious conclusion."

"These people were either mules or they stole a stash from someone else," she said. "Could the same people have killed our cruise ship victim as well as all these people?"

Espinosa drew hard on his cigarette. "I take it you didn't get an arrest?"

"No," she said. "We had two suspects, both members of the crew. The purser all but confessed. We were in the interrogation room, when we learned that the case was being reassigned and they were both free to go. The ship sailed the same day."

"Could the crew have done this as well?"

"I don't know," Emilia said doubtfully. "They were prissy *norteamericanos*. It seems a long shot." Without knowing Espinosa's allegiances, Emilia wondered if she'd said too much. For all she knew, he'd gotten himself placed in charge of this investigation in order to hide evidence or deflect blame.

One of the uniformed officers walking the perimeter of the yellow tape marched up to Espinosa. The senior officer turned his back to Emilia and had a conversation with his subordinate. Emilia gathered that the press had heard of the killing field and a news team was on the way.

As Espinosa talked and smoked, Emilia shivered despite the heat. She felt those restless whispers again, stories from the souls of those who'd been chopped up and discarded like trash. Mexico was full of untold stories of people who disappeared or died violently and left little behind except sorrow and questions. Someday, someone like Emilia might find out what had happened. But even if she did, who could she tell?

☼

Ten minutes later, after a bumpy drive over the new dirt road, Espinosa parked in front of the crazy quilt fence. The dogs howled an angry welcome.

Emilia got out of the vehicle. "Pepe," she yelled.

Father and son emerged from the curtained doorway. The old man beat the dogs into silence with a stick as Pepe shuffled over to the makeshift gate.

"You didn't say goodbye yesterday," he said to Emilia.

"I know." Emilia nodded. "That's why I came back."

She and Espinosa had stopped by the equipment tent to grab some sweet rolls from the coffee mess. Emilia held out the box, conscious of offering the food as if to an animal. "I brought you a treat."

Pepe cautiously passed through the gate. To Emilia's relief he closed it behind him without letting any of the dogs through. "What's in there?"

"*Conchas*," Emilia said.

Espinosa got out of the car but stayed on the other side of the vehicle.

Pepe grabbed the box, opened it, and took out a shell-shaped roll. He squeezed it, mashing the fluffy pastry, and jammed half of it into his mouth.

"I want to talk to you about the finger field," Emilia said.

Pepe stuffed in the rest of the roll. He chewed with his mouth open, beige bits of dough swirling between rubbery lips.

"How did you know it was there?"

Pepe shook his head. He reminded Emilia today of a cow. Dull, slow-moving, cud-chewing.

"It's far to walk all the way up there," Emilia tried again. "A long walk from here."

Pepe swallowed. "I like to walk."

"How did you know to go there?"

"I followed the trucks."

"You told me about seeing trucks yesterday," Emilia said encouragingly. "Whose trucks were they?"

"The men who planted the finger field." Pepe stuffed another pastry into his mouth. "I wanted to watch the people grow. But nobody came to water them."

Emilia felt her stomach flip again. She forced a smile. "Who were the men who planted the field, Pepe? Were they friends of yours?"

"There were trucks," Pepe said around his mouthful.

Before Emilia could speak again she had to turn her head to find a breath that didn't smell of either sewage or body odor. "How many trucks?"

"He doesn't know his numbers." The old man behind the fence spoke up for the first time.

Emilia took a roll out of the box in Pepe's hand and went over to the fence. "Did you see who was in the trucks?" She handed the roll to the old man, keeping her arm high to avoid the dogs' snapping jaws.

The old man turned the roll over in his hands. "They came at night. In the dark."

"When was the last time they came?"

The old man bit into the roll. "One truck came six or seven days ago. Not like the feast day of the Virgin of Guadalupe when there were lots."

Emilia looked at Espinosa. The feast day was 12 December. That made the timing right, based on what the forensic experts at the field had said. The *federale* nodded in silent agreement.

"Did you tell anyone about the trucks?" Emilia asked.

The old man turned.

"Did you tell Los Martillos?" Emilia called. "Or did the

trucks belong to them?"

He went into the house.

Pepe dropped the box and edged toward the fence. Emilia blocked his path. "Did you tell Los Martillos? The men in the white tee shirts."

"His dog's dead," Pepe said.

Emilia took a step back, disconcerted by the abrupt change in direction. She looked around. The dogs were still on the other side of the rattletrap fence, stropping their paws in the dirt and nosing at unseen debris. "What do you mean?" she asked.

"I forgot," Pepe said. "We're not supposed to talk to you." He disappeared through the gate and into the house. Left alone, the dogs began to bark and howl as they ran along the inside perimeter of the fence.

"Over here," Espinosa said.

The *federale* was standing in the tall grass several meters away. Emilia clambered over the ruts in the hard-packed dirt and waded into the grass. Espinosa held up a hand to stop her progress.

There was a dead dog at his feet.

It was a short-haired mongrel like the dogs in Pepe's yard. It had been shot several times and flies buzzed around the bloody wounds. From the sight and smell, Emilia guessed that the dog had been dead less than 24 hours.

She stumbled back to the path and counted the dogs behind the fence. There were four. One less than yesterday.

"A warning from Los Martillos," Emilia gulped. "We have to check on Gloria's mother. She's a friend of Pepe's. They might think Gloria took me to see her mother, too."

Espinosa looked grim as he dug out his keys. "You're a decent cop," he said, to Emilia's surprise.

By the time Emilia was ready to leave Gallo Pinto, the television news trucks from Acapulco had begun to arrive. Emilia drove slowly down the main road toward the roadblock still guarding the route to the highway and the turnoff to Acapulco at San Marco. She saw men in brilliant white Los Martillos tee shirts, including Valentino Pinto, surrounding two vans. The Televisa logo on the vans was outlined against the setting sun. Journalists were showing their credentials. One had his cell phone pressed to his ear and was speaking excitedly. A couple of *federale* cops in dark uniforms watched, long guns hanging off their shoulders by safety straps, their hands on the stocks of the weapons.

Emilia slowed the Suburban. She'd driven in that morning in a convoy with the *federales,* but this time she was alone. She fully expected to be stopped.

Valentino turned away from the vans to watch the Suburban. His eyes met hers.

Emilia knew he'd recognized her. His stony expression shifted imperceptibly.

One of the Los Martillos moved to halt the Suburban. Keeping his eyes locked with Emilia's, Valentino used the flat of his hand to stop him.

Emilia rode the brake and the Suburban inched through the roadblock. Valentino's gaze followed and she felt the release like the snap of an elastic band when she was clear of Gallo Pinto.

Chapter 25

Loyola wasn't in the squadroom Thursday morning, and the morning meeting was cancelled again. Which was just as well, because the first thing Emilia saw when she opened her email inbox was a notice that Loyola had filed a grievance with the union.

She read the message through twice, furious with herself, both for dropping her guard and for responding with such a show of anger. The message directed her to appear at a preliminary union hearing on Monday regarding the charge of sexual assault. She should be prepared to answer questions related to a reported incident on the date in question. A lawyer was not advised at this time.

Emilia looked around the squadroom, Besides herself and Flores, only Castro and Gomez were there. Ibarra and Silvio had left already, taking the day's dispatches with them, and Macias and Sandor were still at that training course in Mexico City. Without Loyola radiating waves of uncertainty, the place felt calm.

Gomez sang something vulgar as he filled his mug from the coffeemaker and Emilia felt another flush of anger. Emilia had never filed a grievance against either Castro or Gomez for their attacks on her in the detectives bathroom, knowing that any complaint would have been turned into a career-killing farce.

Apparently Loyola had no such qualms.

One by one, she'd called it a draw with the detectives who'd openly opposed her, even Castro, although not with Gomez. She'd gotten used to the mix of open taunting and silent resentment, but also grudging acceptance, that had developed in the squadroom over the years. But Loyola had shown her how tenuous it all was. She'd fallen into a trap of her own making with her rash response.

Castro and Gomez left, noisily shoving at each other like a couple of teenaged idiots, and Emilia and Flores were alone in the squadroom. The young detective had called in sick on Wednesday while she'd been in Gallo Pinto. Today he was pale and subdued.

"You want some coffee?" she asked as she got up with her mug.

"No, thank you, Emilia." Flores sat hunched in front of his computer, as if he'd been recently filleted with a boning knife.

"Let's go over some case files in ten minutes, okay?"

"All right." His voice was nearly inaudible.

She got herself a cup of coffee and read through the rest of her inbox. Nothing was of real consequence until she found a note from Prade, confirming that a test of the blood sample taken from the body of Yolanda Lata, alias Yola de Trinidad, indicated the presence of drugs. Of interest, the substance in the blood sample matched the substance taken from the unidentified finger. Prade helpfully quoted the report provided by Señor Denton of the Pinkerton Agency.

Emilia stared at the message. Three violent crimes: the killing field, Yolanda's overdose, and the murder victim aboard the *Pacific Grandeur*. All connected by two threads: the Salva Diablo tattoos and the Ora Ciega deadly heroin mix.

Bonilla and Ramos might be the chief suspects for the *Pacific Grandeur* murder but that was based on proximity and their own nervousness. There was nothing to link them to the death of a drugged-up hooker or a killing field 30 miles outside of Acapulco. Except the fact that the victim's body had been stolen from the morgue, cut into chunks and dumped along with the pieces of other Salva Diablo gang members in the middle of nowhere.

She uploaded the tattoo pictures she'd taken at the killing field, found her notebook, and copied all her disjointed notes into a master timeline encompassing the events of all three cases, going back as far as the feast day of the Virgin of Guadalupe, 12 December, when Pepe and his father had first heard the trucks. The feast day was always celebrated with fireworks, which would have been loud enough to cover the executions and melee of body chopping afterwards. Pepe had harvested the fingers about two weeks later.

The timeline grew as she filled in the approximate dates when the Padre Pro finger was sold each time. Those dates were all prior to the day the *Pacific Grandeur* docked in Acapulco. Which coincidentally was the same day a man with a Salva Diablo tattoo went looking for a hooker, filled her full of Ora Ciega heroin from Colombia, and wound up dead of execution-style gunshots to the head. By the time he appeared on the scene, his fellow Salva Diablo gang members had been dead in their shallow graves for six weeks.

Had he been part of the group but had somehow escaped the slaughter? Stayed in Mexico to look for whoever had killed his fellow gang members in that lonely field? Or had he been expecting the return of gang members who'd been muling drugs north, and came looking for them when they didn't return to Honduras? Emilia didn't have the answers to those questions and didn't know if they mattered or not.

The timeline wasn't telling her anything. She flipped to a fresh page and started listing linkages. Customs and the cruise ship docks. Bonilla and Ramos. The Salva Diablo gang and Perez's Organized Crime unit. Valentino and Los Martillos and Pepe's dead dog. Espinosa and *federales*. Ora Ciega.

She put down her pen, remembering the look on Valentino's face as she'd driven through the roadblock on her way out of Gallo Pinto yesterday. Emilia wondered what his reaction would be if he knew that a box of sweet rolls had had a greater impact than his gun. Valentino and Los Martillos almost certainly had killed the dog belonging to Pepe's father. Had they also murdered and dismembered the people in the killing field? But why?

A second cup of coffee and her nerves were on fire. Emilia pulled out the schedule of all the dates the *Pacific Grandeur* had visited Acapulco. She'd have to requisition immigration records to see if Bonilla and Ramos had been on the ship every time. But even if the ship's schedule said the timing was right, and Bonilla and Ramos had a reason to kill the Salva Diablo gang member, how did the two officers connect to Los Martillos?

That was the problem. The players didn't connect in any

reasonable fashion. A gang from Honduras, two cruise ship officers, and the ragtag community police from some obscure Costa Chica village known only for poverty and a vegetable cannery.

"Fuck," Emilia blurted out loud.

She shoved back her chair and nearly ran across the squadroom to the one computer that had an open link to the web. The machine took forever to boot up but then she was in, typing *Fiesta Verde cannery* into the search engine.

The first 5 pages of results listed recipes for *salsa verde*. Emilia searched again: *cannery Gallo Pinto*, but that, too, yielded only recipes. Eventually she came to a directory of agricultural industries in the state of Guerrero. On the third page of the directory website she found a one paragraph listing for the Fiesta Verde cannery:

Fiesta Verde Holdings. 30 employees. Specializing in canned tomatoes, beets, and beans for Acapulco food service firms. Major customers: Noble Pacific Cruise Lines, Sea Salt Restaurants.

A phone number was listed, along with a post office box address.

Emilia forced herself to breathe. She had it. The cannery was the cornerstone of the whole mess.

It was why Bonilla and Ramos were so worried about the kitchen holds being taped off. She replayed the scene at the ship the first time she and Silvio were there. The way they'd insisted that the food deliveries had to be made, even to the extent of taking down the crime scene tape.

Somehow the Salva Diablo gang had figured out that someone was running an Ora Ciega pipeline from Colombia, through the Fiesta Verde cannery, and onto the cruise ship from *El Norte*. The known *tumbadores* had followed the route and tried to intercept and steal the drugs at the cannery. Whoever ran the pipeline killed them and chopped them up to send a message. As Espinosa had opined, the executions must have been videotaped; a very effective way to get a brutal point across.

The video had found its way to the lone Salva Diablo

who'd ended up in the *Pacific Grandeur's* meat locker. The "friends" he'd been looking for weren't either the people in the field, nor were they Bonilla and Ramos. No, he'd been looking for killers, but only had information about the *Pacific Grandeur's* schedule.

"Are you all right?" Flores asked.

Emilia started and realized he was over by the coffee machine looking at her quizzically. She refreshed the screen in front of her. "Orlando, come look at this."

"All right," he said.

Flores wheeled his chair over to the internet machine and sat down. His eyes were red.

"When we were at the docks," Emilia said, trying to sound brisk and hoping that he'd pull himself together. "The *Pacific Grandeur* was loading supplies. Some of the trucks were from a company called Fiesta Verde--."

Without any warning, Flores began to cry. He covered his face with both hands and the quiet squadroom echoed with his gasping sobs.

"Look, Orlando," Emilia said uncomfortably, after a minute of unrestrained weeping. "This is part of police work."

"Those poor people." Flores sucked in his breath and wiped his eyes with the back of his hand. "It doesn't matter who they were. No one deserves to die like that."

"No, they didn't."

"All cut up like cows in a slaughterhouse." Flores began to cry all over again.

If she didn't get him to stop, Emilia knew that she'd be sobbing, too, right in the middle of the squadroom. And with her luck, it would be right when Castro and Gomez decided to come back. Not that she wanted them to catch Flores crying, either. They'd never let him live it down.

The problem was that Flores was so unprepared for this job. Too young, too immature. *Madre de Dios*, but he was in the wrong line of work.

Emilia swiveled her chair, and put her hands on the younger man's shoulders. "Orlando, look at me."

"I'm sorry, Emilia." Flores gulped.

"It's okay," Emilia said. She gave him a gentle shake, then dropped her hands. "This was a really bad thing. But if you're going to be a cop you have to learn to deal with stuff like this."

Flores shook his head. His eyes were swimming. "I didn't know this job was going to be so hard."

"It is a hard job," Emilia agreed. "But after a while you get used to it." *Or you quit.*

"Like you."

"It's still hard for me," Emilia admitted, thinking of Tuesday night. She didn't know how she would have coped without Kurt. She'd probably still be crying two days later, too.

"How do you cope?"

"Family. Friends," Emilia said vaguely. "I work out. Kickboxing helps get a lot of the anger out."

Flores shook his head. "I'm terrible at boxing."

It was like consoling a sad puppy. Despite everything, Emilia felt a protective rush for this kid. She'd had her cousins to take care of her, explain things, and prepare her for what she'd have to face as a cop. But Flores, despite his *por dedazo* appointment, seemed to have no one. Except her.

Emilia gave half a smile. "Everybody does something. Runs or lifts weights or martial arts." She paused. "But if this job isn't for you, there's no shame in that, either."

"I have to be a cop," he said, seemingly startled at her implication.

Emilia didn't really want to deal with Flores's life choices right now. "Just give it some time," she said.

"Thanks, Emilia." Flores sniffed again.

"Sure--."

Before she could take the conversation back to her theory about the Fiesta Verde cannery, Flores enveloped her in a hug with his arms around her waist. He nestled his head on Emilia's shoulder.

Emilia didn't move. It was an embrace a child would give to a teacher. Her body was pinned awkwardly to her chair by his weight. She desperately hoped no one was anywhere near the open squadroom door.

After a count of three, she twisted her weight to one side. Flores immediately let go. But to her surprise, he brushed his lips against her cheek before settling back in his chair. His eyes were still watery and he gave no indication that he'd done anything peculiar.

"Maybe you should go home, Orlando," Emilia heard herself suggest. "Take a little more time to get past this. Nothing is going to happen today."

Flores unconsciously turned to look at the open doorway. "Are you sure that will be okay?"

"I'm sure."

Flores stood and looked down gratefully. "I'm really lucky, Emilia," he said. "So lucky to have you as a partner."

"On the job training," Emilia corrected him. "Mentor, not partner."

Flores closed down his computer and left. He hadn't heard her. Probably hadn't even realized that he'd kissed her.

With the Fiesta Verde information still on the computer screen, Emilia slumped in the chair, trying to process exactly what had just happened with Flores. His crush wasn't going away. Sooner or later she was going to have to deal with it.

Her cell phone rang, giving her a start as it buzzed angrily against her desktop across the room. Emilia got to the phone and leaned against the desk as she answered the call.

Ronaldo Olivas Camacho, head of security for the Palacio Réal, was on the other end. He was a former cop from Monterrey, humorless and discreet. They'd spoken before and exchanged greetings when she was at the hotel. But he'd never called her. Emilia braced herself to hear that something bad had happened to Kurt.

"I'm calling about an incident in the bar a week or so ago," Olivas said. "A drunk accosted you."

"It was hardly even an incident," Emilia said, both relieved and surprised. "To tell the truth, I'd almost forgotten the whole thing."

"Our staff takes such things seriously," Olivas said. "Not because you're associated with the Señor Rucker, you understand. The Palacio Réal has certain standards."

"Of course." Emilia relaxed. She hitched herself up onto the desk and let her feet dangle off the side.

"The man who accosted you carried a *cédula* in the name of Efraim Vilez Garcia," Olivas said.

Carried a cédula in the name of. Not *was named.* Emilia tensed again. "Go on," she said.

"I still have some contacts," Olivas said. "They ran his *cédula.* Efraim Vilez Garcia died six months ago in Puerta Vallarta."

Emilia found a pen. She scribbled the name in the margin of a robbery report. "Anything else?"

"His business card listed him as a rep for a medical supply company in Mexico City." Olivas paused and Emilia heard the rattle of papers. "Acuna Technologies."

"It doesn't exist," Emilia said.

"You knew all this already?" Olivas asked sharply.

"No. I'm guessing." Emilia wrote down the details he read off from the business card. "One other thing. Was he driving a rental car? From Banderas Rentals at the airport?"

"Yes." Olivas cleared his throat. "Is there something we here at the Palacio Réal should be aware of, Detective?"

"Nothing that involves the hotel," Emilia said.

"What about Señor Rucker?" Olivas asked.

"He's not involved, either."

Olivas cleared his throat again. "I'll be passing on this information to him. This was a courtesy call, given that you were involved in the incident. And of course, your position in law enforcement. In case there was additional information we needed to be aware of."

Emilia felt a grudging respect for the man. Olivas was fishing for information, the way any good investigator would do. He was well connected and loyal to both the hotel and his boss. But if Kurt was going to find out that Emilia was in trouble, he wasn't going to find out from his security chief.

When the call ended Emilia went back to the internet computer and tried to concentrate again on her discovery. The excitement over the Fiesta Verde cannery was still there, but now it was tempered by fear.

The gray sedan on the cliff above the Palacio Réal, Señora Navarro's insurance agent, and the drunk at the hotel. Three encounters, three dead men.

She could guess who they were and why they were circling around. But it would be better to know.

Before a fourth showed up.

Chapter 26

"Don't you see?" Emilia pressed Silvio. "They're using the cannery in Gallo Pinto to package up the Ora Ciega. It's probably loaded onto the ship labelled as canned tomatoes or green beans."

To her surprise he didn't respond. He turned his beer glass around on the coaster.

Emilia leaned over the table. The music in the Counter Club was too loud and she wondered why he'd picked the trendy tourist bar as a meeting spot. Especially on a Friday night, when the place would be even more crowded than usual. She'd been surprised when he suggested meeting there, but it was on the way to the Palacio Réal so she'd agreed. "Did you understand what I said?" she asked.

"I heard you fine, Cruz." Silvio took a deep swallow of beer. He'd taken off his jacket to reveal his usual white tee shirt but not his shoulder holster. Emilia assumed his gun was strapped to his ankle. She still had on her work uniform of jeans, black tee and khaki blazer, and felt underdressed amid the night club denizens with their flashy clothes and overdone makeup.

"So?"

A techno light show flashed, bathing Silvio's grim expression in purple and blue sparks. His white tee shirt glowed. Again, Emilia wondered why he'd picked the club; he was at least 20 years older than the average patron, hated this type of synthesized music, and the beer cost double what it would be anywhere else.

Silvio squinted as the lights flashed. "This isn't your case any more."

"So? We take the information to Loyola. Perez. Somebody."

"No. We don't do anything."

"Are you kidding?" Emilia exclaimed.

Silvio slapped his hand on the table. "You got bigger

trouble than this case, Cruz. I overheard Loyola and Ibarra talking. Loyola's got it in for you. Said if it wasn't for the fact that you were keeping Flores busy, he'd can your ass tomorrow. Want to tell me why?"

Emilia swore under her breath. "We had a little argument and my knee accidentally . . . Okay, to be honest, I nailed him in the balls."

Silvio sputtered beer. "What the fuck, Cruz?"

"He suggested that I give Flores a blow job or two. Then perform, uh, similar services for the rest of the squadroom."

"*Rayos*." Silvio shook his head like a bull about to charge.

"He filed a grievance with the union accusing me of sexual assault. There's a hearing on Monday."

"That's it," Silvio announced. "Forget the fucking Ora Ciega. You keep your head down. Babysit Flores. Say whatever you have to say to the union and get it over with."

"I'm not dropping the case," Emilia exclaimed.

"You have to," Silvio said. "Think about it. You know a hell of a lot more than Irma Gonzalez and have run into three dead men. Somebody's got to be wondering when you're going to get the message to lay off."

Emilia drank some beer, ignoring her suddenly shaking hand. She remembered the moment Loyola had come into the interrogation room, and let Bonilla go, just as the ship's officer had been about to incriminate himself. "Is that somebody Loyola?" she asked.

"I don't have anything solid," Silvio said, barely audible above the music. "My guess is that Loyola's following somebody's directions. He's too scared to be in charge of whatever is going on."

Emilia looked around at the jolting lights, the twentysomething tourists, and the bartenders juggling rum bottles. No wonder Silvio had picked this place to meet. Nobody they knew would come here. She thought of the lines she'd drawn in her notebook yesterday. Lines connecting the players. Maybe she needed to add a few more players.

"I gave him a great excuse to get rid of me, didn't I?" Emilia asked.

"That's right. You reacted like a fucking girl." Silvio glared at her. "At least a union grievance is better than him taking it to Alma."

Emilia clenched her fists on the table. "I can't believe this. I've got the key to the whole Ora Ciega mess and you're telling me I can't use it?"

Silvio's face tightened. "Listen to me, Cruz," he growled. "Loyola's more scared of whoever is calling the shots than he is of you. If you continue with the case, Loyola will have to take you out."

His words were scaring her but Emilia wasn't ready to give up. "What about Irma Gonzalez? Yolanda Lata? Where's the justice for them?"

"Somebody else will make the same connection," Silvio insisted. "This Espinosa sounds all right for a *federale*."

"He didn't see the Fiesta Verde trucks loading up the ship," Emilia pointed out.

Silvio shrugged. "The ship will come back. Bonilla's cocky enough to try again."

"Staying on the case was your idea, remember?" Emilia pressed. "You were so pissed when Bonilla walked. We both knew Organized Crime wasn't going to do shit and they haven't."

"We're not going to win this one, Cruz," Silvio said. "Live to fight another day, okay?"

Emilia didn't reply. They sat without speaking. The music changed tempo and at random intervals the DJ shouted out words like "Booty" and "Hustle." Emilia wiped all the condensation off her glass with a still shaky hand, then pressed her palm onto the table top. When she took it away a perfect watery handprint remained.

"Give me your word, Cruz," Silvio said finally. "You'll drop it."

The techno light show ended. In its place, a purple spotlight roamed the room. As it passed over their table, Silvio looked strangely deflated; a boxer who knew that his best days were behind him.

"Ibarra must be rubbing off on you," Emilia remarked.

"Minimal effort, maximum smell. You a chain-smoker yet?"

Silvio stood up, shrugged on his jacket, and threw down some peso bills. "If you keep after it, Cruz, you're on your own," he warned. "I been down this road before and I'm not doing it again. You get yourself killed, I won't be at the funeral."

"Thanks for the beer," Emilia said.

Silvio stalked out, leaving Emilia alone with her warm beer and sticky handprint.

Chapter 27

Juan Fabio was not pleased to see Emilia and Kurt at the entrance to his stall at the Mercado Municipal early Saturday morning.

The place looked much the same as before. Kurt browsed the stall as Emilia cornered the junkman.

"I already talked to you," Juan Fabio said to Emilia.

"Let's talk again," Emilia said. "Different question this time. Easier."

Juan Fabio shook his head and pretended to be busy with his receipt book. "I got nothing to say to you. Gloria is real mad. Bad things are happening up in her mother's village because of you."

The discovery of the killing field was all over the national news. Kurt had put away the morning newspaper when he saw Emilia blanch at the pictures.

"So far nobody's mentioned the finger that came from the field," Emilia said slowly. "Or the junkman who passed off the finger as a relic of Padre Pro."

Juan Fabio looked up from the receipts. "You're a bad woman," he said. "You don't deserve to say the name of Padre Pro."

Emilia found herself inexplicably on the brink of tears. She took a step back, clutching her shoulder bag. "You're a middleman," she said harshly. "You know a lot of people who buy and sell things."

He waved a hand at the aisle full of people haggling over prices. "It's a *mercado*. What did you expect?"

"Who's been buying and selling *cédulas* of the dead?"

It was clear that Juan Fabio hadn't seen her question coming. He blinked and rapidly glanced around.

His reaction gave Emilia a moment in which to pull herself together. She leaned in close. "Not fake *cédulas*. Not forgeries. Real *cédulas* from people who have died. But the *cédulas* haven't expired yet."

Juan Fabio clutched his receipt book as if she was trying to take it. "How should I know? I sell real things, not bits of paper."

"You hear things," Emilia said. "From friends in the *mercado*. Or your business associates like El Flaco."

"Never heard anything like that." The words came out a little too fast.

"Juan Colón Sotelo. Periliano Roa Fuentes. Efraim Vilez Garcia," Emilia said. She showed him a piece of paper with the three names written on it. "Vilez Garcia hasn't even been dead six months. Whoever is buying the *cédulas* is moving pretty quickly."

"Never heard of any of those people."

"I need the name of the buyer," Emilia said. "That's all. Just the name of whoever is dealing *cédulas*."

"I don't know anything about *cédulas*," Juan Fabio declared with false bravado, pointedly not looking at the paper. "You should go. If you aren't buying anything, you should go."

"Maybe if I called Televisa and told a reporter about the finger, it would help you remember."

"Can't remember what I don't know," Juan Fabio said.

The junkman's knuckles were white. Just like Loyola. Juan Fabio was more afraid of whoever was calling the shots than he was of her. She put the paper next to the receipt book. Juan Fabio didn't touch it.

Emilia and Kurt walked out of the stall. She felt eyes on their backs as they made their way out of the market.

"You gave him three names," Kurt said as they got into the car. "How many drunks have you run into lately?"

"Silvio. Every day." Emilia pretended to be busy with her seat belt.

Kurt frowned. "Olivas told me that Vilez Garcia, the drunk in the hotel last weekend, had false identification. But you gave Juan Fabio three names. You're looking for three fake *cédulas*."

Emilia gave him a tired smile. "Macias and Sandor have had a couple of cases where unexpired *cédulas* have shown up. We think there's someone local dealing in fake identities. We're all asking our contacts."

It came out naturally, her best lie to date.

Kurt's gaze didn't lighten. Emilia reached across the console and kissed him. "Don't get all crazy on me, *gringo*," she said with her lips against his.

"My girlfriend's a cop," Kurt said and kissed her back. "Crazy is the norm."

He drove out of the parking lot and started talking about a new restaurant they should try for lunch.

Emilia hadn't planned on lying to Kurt again, but something in the back of her mind said that the less he knew, the safer he'd be.

Chapter 28

By Monday morning, Emilia's equilibrium had returned. If the union hearing went badly, and her job was in jeopardy, she'd use the Fiesta Verde information as a lever with Espinosa. Not every job with the federal police stank of shit; maybe he could help her find something that protected her from dead men and didn't involve selling her soul.

At 10:00 am, dressed in her gray suit, Emilia was ushered into a conference room in the union building. As instructed, she took the chair in the middle of one long side of the table. It meant that her back was to the door, which made her uncomfortable. Every cop needed to be able to see when danger entered the room. No doubt the seating was intentional and intended to keep the accused off balance.

The secretary told Emilia to help herself to the water and cookies on a tray in the center of the table, then left.

Emilia poured herself some water. She was ready with a statement. Hopefully, this preliminary hearing would be brief. Afterwards she'd go shopping with Mercedes. No matter which way the hearing went, she wouldn't want to be in the squadroom this afternoon.

Too jittery to stay seated, Emilia got up and made a circuit around the conference table. The room was fairly forgettable. The conference table dominated as if intended for a bigger space and crammed in this room by accident. The chairs were nice; navy leather over a wooden base on casters. One wall was covered with heavy draperies. Emilia pushed a panel aside to find iron bars protecting the window from a view of the parking lot.

She sat down again. No one came in.

After 10 minutes, Emilia got up, circled around the table and sat in the chair directly facing the door. There was a small control panel set into the table at that place.

Two more glasses of water and Emilia left the conference room and went down the hall to a restroom she'd seen on the way in. The hallway was deserted both coming and going.

She'd been in the conference room almost an hour when the door opened and Victor Obregon Sosa marched in. The union chief for the state of Guerrero was followed by three minions. The two women and one man were all well dressed and carried a variety of recording equipment.

As his staff began setting up, Obregon came around the side of the table. "Detective Cruz," he said slowly, as if savoring the words on his tongue. "You're sitting in my place."

As every other time Emilia had seen him, Obregon was dressed entirely in black. His suit was an immaculate silk weave, his shirt was starched cotton, and his tie was a tone-on-tone stripe. Black suited Obregon's ebony hair and the high cheekbones which betrayed a strong *indio* bloodline.

"Señor," Emilia said in acknowledgment. She took her glass of water and slid over one chair.

Obregon gave her the appraising stare she remembered. It was the look of a hawk assessing how fast a mouse could run. When Emilia met his eyes the look changed to faint amusement. He sat down in the chair she'd vacated.

Their last encounter had been months ago, a chance meeting in the gym in the central police administration building. She'd called in a marker, as he called it, and asked for a favor which would balance the books between them. Obregon had come through, to her surprise, and saved a man's life in the process. The act had reversed her opinion of him only a little; Obregon almost certainly had his finger in a number of dirty enterprises including money laundering and drug smuggling. Emilia had come close to his involvement once, but they both knew she'd never be able to prove it.

Even if Emilia had wanted to try, Obregon had better protection than most. He had a relationship with Acapulco's wildly popular mayor, Carlota Montoya Perez. Emilia wasn't sure exactly what that relationship was, but a few words came to mind. Lover. Advisor. Spy.

One of the minions signaled from behind the video camera that they were ready. Obregon pressed a button on the panel set into the table and a microphone lowered itself from a panel in the ceiling.

Obregon cleared his throat, gave the date, and announced that this was a recording of a preliminary hearing of charges against Acapulco police detective Emilia Cruz Encinos. He asked her to state her full name, date of birth, and badge number. Emilia rattled off the information.

"Detective Cruz, are you aware of the full extent of the charges filed against you?"

"No."

Obregon opened a thin file folder he'd brought into the room with him. He took out a piece of paper and slid it across to Emilia. "The union is making a copy of the grievance filed against Detective Cruz available to her," he said for the benefit of the recording equipment. "Detective Cruz is accused of making lewd advances to her superior officer and conducting a sexual assault upon his person for the purpose of sexual gratification."

Loyola's grievance sounded as if Emilia had raped him in his office. "This is a piece of crap," she said hotly.

Obregon read out each of four charges and asked her to confirm or deny each one. Emilia denied them all. *Madre de Dios*, but Loyola was a *pendejo*.

"You may now make a statement, Detective," Obregon said, again with that smile of faint amusement playing around his lips.

"Acting Lieutenant Loyola suggested that I give blow jobs to the newest detective, Orlando Flores Almaprieto, to keep him happy," she said, rolling out the script she'd rehearsed in front of the bedroom mirror at the Palacio Réal all weekend. "Flores was having some trouble fitting into the squadroom owing to his youth and inexperience. Acting Lieutenant Loyola also suggested that after making Flores happy I could give blow jobs to the rest of the squadroom. He said I owed it to all of them for not raping me. After that I helped Acting Lieutenant Loyola fix a printer jam. My knee might have accidentally touched him in an inappropriate place while we were working on the printer. If so, I deeply regret the incident."

Obregon grinned and shook his head. "Detective Cruz, is it your opinion that Acting Lieutenant Loyola mistook this inadvertent touch for a sexual advance?"

"I would have thought it unlikely," Emilia said. "But it's possible."

"Were there any witnesses to this event?"

"No, it was just myself and Loyola in his office."

"You alluded to Flores? Was this officer nearby?"

"No. Detective Franco Silvio had been in the office with us but he'd left by then."

"This hearing is suspended at this time," Obregon drawled. "Examination of the grievance charges will be resumed pending collection and examination of new information."

He punched the button to turn off the microphone. His staff was told to make a transcript and have it on his desk in two hours. "Detective Cruz," he said. "Please come with me."

Emilia followed Obregon out of the room and into the elevator. They rode down to the first floor in silence and continued down a corridor to the lobby. Everyone they passed either nodded, or if they were seated, bolted to their feet. Obregon ignored them all as he strode across the lobby, Emilia in his wake.

Five minutes later they were seated in an elegant restaurant a block away. Obregon perused the wine list and Emilia tried not to look disoriented as the waiter draped a linen napkin over her lap.

Obregon gave the waiter an order for what Emilia was sure was a very expensive bottle of wine. The waiter thanked the union chief by name and reeled off a selection of appetizers. Obregon chose the *mariscos a la marinera* and the Yucatan-style *calabaza frita*. They'd decide their main courses later, he intoned, as if they had all the time in the world.

The waiter bowed and scraped his way out of earshot. Emilia leaned forward. "What is going on here?"

"Lunch." Obregon gave her that assessing smile again. "Your investigative skills need polishing, Detective."

Emilia wadded up her napkin and shoved it onto the table.

"I can't afford to eat here."

Obregon was an arresting man and once upon a time she'd felt weak-kneed around him. Every instinct told her she'd been a fool for following him, warned her not to become beholden to him for even as simple a thing as a meal.

The waiter came back before Obregon could reply. "Your choice of wine, Señor Obregon." The two men went through the elaborate uncorking and tasting ritual, Obregon pronounced the vintage acceptable, and Emilia's glass was filled. As Emilia sat stony-faced, a second waiter whisked onto the table two appetizer plates, additional forks, a fragrant platter of crisp fried pumpkin sticks, and a glass bowl of seafood salad.

"You'll find the food is excellent," Obregon said, helping himself to both appetizers.

Emilia looked around. The place hadn't seemed like much from the outside, and the first floor was the same; modern décor and half a dozen tables filled with people eating tacos and sandwiches. They'd climbed a narrow stairway to the second floor, which was a different story. Dark wood paneling and crystal chandeliers created exclusivity. Each private table was sheltered by an angled half wall. The diners that Emilia had seen were all men in business suits. The place was clearly some sort of exclusive men's club.

It was an odd place to bring her and Emilia couldn't help but be curious why he'd chosen it. Nothing was coincidence with Obregon.

He handed her the bowl of seafood salad.

"I'm not hungry," Emilia said.

Obregon tucked his tie between two buttons of his shirt and did the same with his napkin, making him look startlingly like a younger version of Ernesto waiting for Sophia to put his dinner on the kitchen table. "Sure you are," he said. "After reading Loyola's charges you were mad enough to chew nails and spit rust."

"That was anger, not hunger."

"Anger creates appetite." Obregon ate a piece of the fried pumpkin and closed his eyes for a moment in appreciation.

"You really should try this. Superb."

"Maybe you should tell me why we're here."

Obregon put down his fork. "Relax, Detective. Consider this the union's apology for Loyola's behavior." He sipped some wine. "Besides, I don't like to eat alone."

By now Emilia was ravenous. The tangy scent of the seafood mixed with tomato, onion, and avocado was enticing. But she still hesitated, knowing the danger of being in Obregon's debt. She looked around at the quietly opulent room. "Since when has the union apologized for anything?"

"I said for Loyola, not for the union. Man's an idiot." Obregon clicked his tongue. "Frankly, I'd always been impressed by your self control. Until now."

"So this is meant to be a lecture on my behavior?" Emilia demanded. "Go lecture him. Everything in his grievance was a total fabrication."

"I assumed as much." Obregon helped himself to more pumpkin. "He's far too old and worn out for you."

"If you knew he'd made it all up, why the whole farce of a hearing?" As much as Emilia hated to admit it, he was right about anger and appetite. She gave up, threw some food onto her plate, and began to eat. The pumpkin was fried into light puffs of flavor, the perfect counterpoint to the acidic bite of the seafood. She'd have to tell Jacques about this meal.

"Loyola is entitled to union services, same as you," Obregon said. He swirled the wine around in his glass. "Did he actually falsify his grievance charges? In a legal sense, hard to know. His word against yours. It works both ways. You could have filed a grievance for his blow job suggestion and he would have said you misunderstood his comments."

"Which is why I didn't." Emilia pronged a cube of avocado out of her salad.

"You're catching on."

"So where exactly does this leave the grievance process?"

"Loyola will hear that we had lunch together, after which he'll get the official notification that the grievance is on hold pending additional information. The paperwork will go into a desk drawer. You and he will learn to live with ambiguity.

Which is hardly anything new in a detective squadroom."

"I see," Emilia said. And she did. "His charges never get called into question. Which would embarrass Chief Salazar who picked him for the job."

Obregon saluted her wisdom, then drained his wine glass.

"I don't get punished but the charges never get dropped, either," Emilia went on.

"True," Obregon said. "But after two years, unresolved grievances are taken off the books."

"But never out of the hallways. I get stuck with the reputation of being a sexual predator." Even as Emilia said it, she knew it wasn't a bad outcome. She wouldn't be fired or busted back to beat cop.

"I'm sure you'll be able to turn that to your advantage somehow, Detective." Obregon reached for the wine bottle in its silver cooler by his chair.

The waiter came back to take their entrée orders. Other diners stopped by their table on their way in or out of the restaurant. Obregon made a point of introducing Emilia, saying that he was having a working lunch with Detective Cruz Encinos, as if discussing a critical investigation. None of the men in suits offered their name and Obregon didn't introduce them, either.

Their entrees came and Emilia was halfway through her chicken in a spicy peanut sauce before she realized how curious Obregon was about Flores. All of his questions came at the subject of the new detective in an oblique manner and Obregon remained studiously nonchalant, but it was clear that he'd known of the young man's appointment to the detectives unit and her comments in the hearing had piqued his interest.

But there was something else lurking behind the outwardly bland conversation about a new cop and how he was adjusting to the job. Obregon was an enigma in many ways and that included his relationship with Chief Salazar. Each man had a fiefdom to protect and she'd seen tense exchanges between them in the past. If Emilia had to guess, she'd say that they enjoyed a bitter rivalry based on personal hatred. Likely there was history she knew nothing about.

Salazar had essentially made Flores a detective out of thin air. Directed that he ride with Emilia and Silvio, and when Silvio scared the kid, had directed that Emilia alone be responsible for on-the-job training. Of course Obregon would be burning with curiosity.

Emilia gently parried Obregon's questions. She didn't want to become a pawn between Obregon and Salazar. Again.

Obregon never probed too hard, however, and he didn't try to spin out the meal with dessert. Before leaving, the union boss made a point of going around to several of the tables, exclaiming over the quality of the food, and wishing the diners a pleasant afternoon. Emilia smiled but didn't say anything; this whole act was about being seen.

His bodyguards rejoined them downstairs and they strolled back to the union building a block away. More of his protective detail were in two cars; one parked in front of the restaurant and the other outside the gates to the union building. Emilia wondered if the walk was another visibility stunt.

"Was everybody in that restaurant a cop?" Emilia asked.

"Some cops, some business associates," Obregon said lightly.

Once inside the gates Obregon went directly to the white Suburban parked in a visitor spot. "I remember this vehicle," he said. "Still holding up, is it?"

"Gets me where I want to go," Emilia replied. She took out her keys and pressed the button on the fob to unlock the car, her shoulder bag in the other hand.

"A very enjoyable lunch, Detective," Obregon said.

"I appreciate the union's efforts to resolve the grievance," Emilia said pointedly.

Obregon gave a bark of laughter but then his face grew serious. He swiveled his eyes to either side and his security detail melted away. He stepped so close that his chest brushed against Emilia's. He licked his lips and Emilia felt sparks of sexual tension coming off the man. One sip from the bottle labelled insanity and she might be tempted. Sex with him would be like encountering a tornado in the dark; a spiraling blind rush. Everything in pieces afterwards.

"Is Rucker still the one with permission?" Obregon asked.

It was a reminder of one of their first encounters, the one that had set the personal boundaries between them. "He is," Emilia managed.

"Pity," Obregon murmured.

Emilia swallowed hard. He hadn't put his hands on her, yet she felt pinned in place. "Lunch was your idea," Emilia said softly.

"You can pay next time." Obregon slid away from her.

Emilia nearly fell forward as Obregon went, as if she was nothing more than iron filings; bits and pieces pulled toward a magnet and massed into a single shape against it. But she caught herself. He'd be the unfixable mistake.

Obregon gave her a nod, his security detail closed up around him, and they went into the building.

Emilia was glad she had the car to hold her up. She'd been a fool to think lunch with Obregon would be debt-free.

But she still had a job. And Kurt.

Chapter 29

"We should start with a dress," Mercedes suggested as she steered Emilia into a boutique.

"Something I can wear to Mama's wedding." Emilia looked around. Mercedes had navigated them through the dramatic atrium of the Galerías Diana mall, with its two-story palm trees wrapped in fairy lights, and into the flagship store of a fashion designer. The walls were lined with posters of Beautiful People, clothes were organized by color, and red glass light fixtures dangled from the ceiling. Sales clerks wore red aprons with the designer's logo embroidered on them. "*Por Dios*," Emilia groaned. "There's nothing in here I can afford."

"Sales racks," Mercedes said firmly. The dancer headed for the back of the store.

Emilia followed, trying to muster some enthusiasm. Getting together with Mercedes was supposed to be a treat but after the hearing and lunch with Obregon all she wanted to do was go back to the Palacio Réal, climb into bed, and pull the covers over her head. She'd left the hotel that morning, yet it seemed forever ago. By the same token, Friday seemed impossibly far off.

Mercedes was saying something. Emilia blinked and realized her friend was holding out a filmy pink dress.

"You're kidding," Emilia said. "I'd look like a hibiscus with legs."

Mercedes made a face and hung the dress back on the rack. "You need style, Emilia. You wear too many bland things like that gray suit."

Emilia hitched up the lapels of her jacket. "This is fine."

"Please. It's a gray suit with pants. The jacket looks like a box." The dancer tossed her hair over one shoulder and plucked another hanger off the rack. "How about this?"

The dress was a simple crocheted cream shift with a matching silk slip. Emilia fingered it gingerly. It was the sort of elegantly understated thing women wore at the Palacio Réal with chunky jewelry and rich men. "Maybe," she said.

"Go try it on." Mercedes pressed the dress into Emilia's hands and prodded her into a curtained dressing room. "I'll pick out a couple of other things."

The dressing room was as lux as the rest of the store, with a gilt mirror, porcelain hooks, and a chair with a red velvet cushion. Emilia dropped her bag on the chair. She took off her suit jacket, wriggled out of her shoulder holster, and hung both on a wall hook, the weight of the gun pulling the leather straps taut as the rig dangled. Blouse, shoes, trousers, and then she slid the cream dress over her head.

Mercedes is right, Emilia thought as she pirouetted in front of the mirror. The dress was clingy but not tight, cut to skim the top of her cleavage and leave her arms bare. The cream color offset the caramel tone of her skin. On impulse, Emilia pulled her hair out of its usual ponytail, shook it loose over her shoulders, and smiled at her reflection. The grim woman in the severe gray suit was gone, replaced by someone softer, sexier, more confident.

Emilia poked her head out around the side of the curtain. "Mercedes?" she called softly.

"She's at the front of the store," a male voice said. "The clerk will keep her talking for a couple of minutes."

The curtain in the dressing booth next to her opened and a man stepped out. Emilia hadn't seen him in awhile. It was Perez from Organized Crime.

He snatched up her arm above the elbow, pulled her out of reach of her gun, and shoved her into the other cubicle. "Nice dress," he said as he flung the curtain closed.

"Shopping for a friend, Perez?" Emilia asked, breathing hard. Perez had a big automatic in a belt holster under his jacket.

Perez was a short, wiry man. He wore an expensive navy suit with a subtle chalk stripe, a white shirt and a dark paisley tie. As with every other time Emilia had seen him, unless his hands were occupied, his fingers rubbed against each other with small, fluttery movements. She knew that Perez had spent years on the razor's edge as an undercover cop and the tic was his reward. He never appeared to notice.

His grip on her upper arm tightened and he shook her slightly. "What did you tell Victor Obregon?"

With her free hand Emilia grabbed his tie and twisted it into a chokehold. "We can have a conversation if you want," she whispered, her face close to his. "Or I can scream and say you're assaulting me."

Perez smiled, despite the stiff collar digging into his skin, and released her arm.

Emilia let go of the tie and he immediately straightened it, doing that little head stretch thing men do when things are too tight around the neck. "Always liked your style, Cruz," he said. "Had my eye on you ever since you killed that Esgrimidores gang banger. Took guts to run after him the way you did."

"That was two years ago, Perez," Emilia said. Long before she'd met Kurt, Emilia was enjoying a night out when a gang invaded the club. Her date had gotten the credit but she'd been the one to take down the gang leader's brother. "This is an odd place to talk about it now."

The curtain wasn't fully closed. Emilia could see Mercedes across the store, chatting with a sales person. No one appeared to have seen the little tussle by the dressing rooms.

"What did you tell Victor Obregon?" Perez asked again.

"Why should I tell Victor Obregon anything?" Emilia parried. Perez had an agenda. She had nothing. "What does he have to do with me?"

The Organized Crime liaison officer waved a finger in a classic *don't fib to me* motion. "A pretty girl cop only has two reasons for having lunch with Obregon. Either she's the fuck of the month or she's his stoolie."

"Who said I had lunch with Victor Obregon?" Emilia asked.

"Every cop in Acapulco knows you had lunch today with Victor Obregon," Perez snarled. "I want to know why."

Emilia shrugged. "He wanted to know how my partner is doing."

His head gave a barely perceptible twist, like a sci-fi robot unable to process some bit of data, as the fingers of his right hand fluttered. Perez planted his other hand on the wall by Emilia's head and leaned toward her. "Why? What's wrong with your partner?"

"I got stuck with some rookie. A kid who doesn't know anything."

"Why should Obregon care about your rookie partner?"

"Isn't that his job?" Emilia countered.

A sales associate came by and peeked into the curtain opening. "Pardon, but it's one at a time."

Emilia flung open the curtain.

"You look marvelous in that," the woman caroled.

"Doesn't she," Perez said warmly. He put his arm possessively around Emilia's waist. "I was telling her the same thing."

Anyone who saw them together would think he was a business man who'd left work early to help his younger wife shop. A new dress for an upcoming event with investors. Anything you want, *mi corazón*.

Across the store, Mercedes was still deep in conversation with the other sales associate. Part of Emilia wanted to shout to her for help; another part wanted to keep Mercedes as far from Perez as possible.

The woman smiled enthusiastically and bobbed her head. "Shall I get you a belt or a long necklace so you can see how it looks with accessories?"

"No." Both Emilia and Perez said it at the same time. He winked at the saleslady. "Let me talk her into it," he said.

The sales associate moved away. Perez swiped the curtain closed again and grabbed Emilia by the shoulders. "You expect me to believe that's all you talked about with Obregon?" he said, his voice low and harsh. "Your rookie partner? What did you tell Victor Obregon about the Ora Ciega?"

There it was. Emilia forced herself to keep breathing. "I could have told him quite a bit," she said. "How you closed down the *Pacific Grandeur* investigation. Killed Irma

Gonzalez from Customs to protect your partners. Ora Ciega being processed at the Fiesta Verde cannery in Gallo Pinto, then loaded on the cruise ship."

Perez let her go. "You got a good imagination, Cruz," he said.

Emilia took a breath, sure he was bluffing. "A finger got traded all the way from Gallo Pinto to Acapulco where it was sold as the finger of the Blessed Padre Pro. Remember him? From a long time ago? I bought it."

Perez let out a quiet bark of laughter. "What did you need a saint's finger for? Praying for a miracle?" His eyes raked her body. "Always thought God did all right by you."

Emilia ignored the comment. "After the Salva Diablo murder aboard the *Pacific Grandeur,* I traced the finger all the way back to a killing field outside Gallo Pinto. The finger had Ora Ciega embedded in the skin. Same stuff the Salva Diablo kid had in his pocket. Your clowns have been following me around, trying to figure out what I know."

She had his full attention now and kept going. "The way I see it, the Salva Diablo kid went looking for his friends. Were they mules bringing Ora Ciega up to the Fiesta Verde Cannery for you? Tried to save a bit for themselves? Or were they a rip crew who traced the stuff to the cannery and tried to steal it? Either way they had to be dealt with."

Perez stared at her without blinking.

"This kid," Emilia went on. "The only one with the balls enough to come get his revenge, try to steal some more Ora Ciega, whatever. He knew about the ship, knew when it docked in Acapulco. When he showed up, Bonilla killed him to protect the network. But Bonilla panicked and called some temp cell number you'd given him."

"Lucky guesses." Perez flashed her an unmistakable look of . . . of . . . respect.

Madre de Dios, he thought she was a good detective! Anger surged and Emilia fought it down; she had to work with his mood, not against it, convince him she was impressed. "How long did it take you to chop up the bodies?"

Perez grinned; they shared a secret. "Los Martillos wanted

to send a message to stay out of Gallo Pinto."

Bile surged into her throat. Emilia was sure she was going to throw up. "Did you film it? Post it online for the Salva Diablo to see?"

His face tightened; she'd crossed a line and the moment of confidence had passed. "I think you told Obregon your theory about Ora Ciega being smuggled aboard a cruise ship," he rasped. "Implicated a couple of senior cops. Customs officials, too."

"You must not know Obregon," Emilia swallowed hard and tried to sound scornful. "With that much information he'd move in, take it all, and not leave anything for anyone else. No one with half a brain tells him anything."

"And you have half a brain?"

"If I was going to peddle Ora Ciega," Emilia began. Her knees were shaking and she could barely hear her own voice over the pounding of her heart. "I'd cut Bonilla out of the chain. He's nervous and arrogant. A bad combination."

"Bonilla owns the ship."

"Bonilla used to own the ship. Burned himself out of the network when he killed the kid and was too lazy to get rid of the body the same night. We can't use him any more."

"So now it's 'we'?"

Emilia felt like a gambler, throwing dice when she didn't even know the rules of the game. She could only feel the rush as the wheel spun and hear the faint slap of cards that someone else was dealing. "Why bother to move the Ora Ciega out of Acapulco at all? Laws in *El Norte* are loosening up. Pretty soon your buyers are going to get it all home-grown. Your profit margin is going to fall but the risk of getting it over the border won't. Pretty soon the risk won't be worth the money and every peso Bonilla takes for using that ship is another peso out of your pocket."

"What do you know about such things, Detective Cruz?" Perez mocked her.

"Maybe I've been looking for the right opportunity." Emilia pulled her eyes down, suddenly afraid he'd seen through her lie, only to notice the sales tag of the dress dangling by her waist. The dress cost 8000 pesos. She held out the tag so he could see. "I need cash," she said.

"I hear you're running with a rich crowd," Perez said. "Namely, the manager of the Palacio Réal."

"Who doesn't like drunks in his bar," Emilia said.

"So I heard," Perez said.

"Did you hear me say I need cash?"

Pablo's eyes were assessing now. "I heard. But not enough."

"Ora Ciega is special," Emilia asserted. "The spring break crowd will be expecting something they can't get at home. Why throw away a cut on Bonilla and his cruise ship?"

His head twitched yet again and his fingers fluttered. "What can you deliver? A sales network?"

"Maybe, but I'm not sharing it with the messenger boy. Or any of the other flunkies who've been following me around." She threw down her last card, not sure it was enough to take the game. "I'll deal with the top. Or not at all."

"Only with *el jefe*?" Perez seemed amused.

"Don't make me waste any more time, Perez," Emilia said, as if she'd been the one to initiate the conversation.

Perez's fingers fluttered by his side. "I like your style, Cruz," he said. "Fine. I'll set up a meet."

Emilia knew she'd played it well but she wasn't going to take another step without Silvio. She crossed her arms to conceal her trembling. "I'm bringing in my partner. He's part of it or no deal."

The man smiled nastily. "Sure, bring the kid. About time he learned how to be a real cop."

No. "I didn't mean him--."

"I did," Perez said. His eyes slid over her body again. "Buy the dress. If things work out you can wear it when we celebrate."

He skirted the clothing rack by the dressing rooms and made his way to the front of the store. He slowed as he passed Mercedes. Emilia held her breath but he didn't speak to the dancer before leaving the store.

Emilia darted into her own dressing room through the half-closed curtain. Her gun was still in the shoulder holster dangling from the hook. She slumped onto the chair in relief.

"You wouldn't believe it," Mercedes exclaimed, suddenly poking her head around the curtain. "The clerk has four daughters and they all want to take dance lessons. They'd had some with a studio on the other side of the bay but the teacher got sick and stopped teaching. I gave her my card, told her all about the classes."

"That's great." Emilia couldn't tell her it was all a setup. No one was going to call. The dancer's card simply meant that Perez would have yet more information to hold over Emilia's head.

"The dress looks great," Mercedes said, stepping into the booth. "Are you going to get it?"

Emilia shook her head. "There's nowhere to hide my gun in this dress."

Twenty minutes later, as Emilia was telling Mercedes she had to get back to the office, her phone chimed with a text message. "Tonight. 2:00 am. Construction entrance Torre Metropolitano."

Chapter 30

Emilia pulled the Suburban to the curb, prayed he was home, and dialed the number. Silvio picked up on the second ring.

"We need to talk," Emilia said. "Something's happened."

Silvio swore. "Is this what I think it is?"

"Maybe," Emilia hedged.

"I already told you, Cruz," Silvio said. "I'm done with this case."

Emilia looked around. She'd been to Silvio's house before. It was in one of the poorest neighborhoods, where kids ran barefoot in the streets, stray dogs rooted in garbage, and someone died in a shootout every other day. But he'd lived there since his youth as an up-and-coming boxer and twice a week his wife Isabel gathered up all the homeless kids and gave them a free meal. A room in the house was set aside for Silvio's illegal bookie business. He'd started it years ago when he'd been temporarily suspended during the inquiry into the shooting death of his partner Garcia. Emilia knew that the income from being a bookie fed the kids.

"I'm parked outside," she said. "Either you open the gate to let me in or I start telling everybody who passes by that Franco has been rigging his numbers."

The connection died in her ear. A minute later a slab of corrugated metal opened and Emilia drove the Suburban into the drive. The gate clanged shut behind her.

Silvio yanked open her door. "You better have a real good explanation, Cruz."

"Listen," Emilia said.

Thirty minutes later Silvio passed an agitated hand over his crew cut. "This stinks real bad."

"I know," Emilia said quietly.

"Fuck. Fuck."

Emilia was sitting at the plain pine table that apparently served as both desk and meeting space. Half of it was covered with papers and old accounting ledgers. She propped her elbows on the table and let her head fall into her hands.

"*Rayos*, Cruz," Silvio swore. "Don't go bawling now."

Emilia heard his footsteps cross the room, open the door, and go out. She wondered if there would ever come a time when pretending to be on the take wouldn't work. First Bonilla, now Perez. Every cop in Mexico was always presumed to be corrupt.

Silvio came back in. He opened two bottles of beer by snapping the caps off against the edge of the table.

Emilia lifted her head and Silvio shoved a bottle at her. He sat down in front of the ledgers and found paper and a pen.

"Okay." Silvio got ready to write. "Perez was worried that you'd told Obregon who was responsible for bringing Ora Ciega into Acapulco."

"But I don't know who is responsible."

"Does Perez realize that you don't know?"

Emilia thought again about the strange conversation in the store. "No. I just said I wouldn't negotiate with the messenger boy. Meaning him, the *pendejo*."

Silvio pointed the pen at her. "If Perez was in charge, he would have said so. By not saying so, he confirmed that someone more senior is in charge."

Emilia closed her eyes and answered his questions. They'd done this hundreds of times with witnesses and suspects. Made them go over their story again and again, trying to find some forgotten detail or angle, ferret out something hidden in the back of the mind. She forced herself not to look at her watch, even as she felt the minutes tick away.

"Okay," Silvio said finally. "Your lunch with Obregon brought this to a head. Which says that *el jefe* is a cop, not Customs, and a little afraid of Obregon. But he's senior enough to co-opt Customs and use his clout to get that body out of the morgue."

"It doesn't matter," Emilia said. "*El jefe* could be Chief Salazar, could be somebody else. Whoever it is, we keep playing the same game I started this afternoon. Pretend I'm ready to make some extra money and I can promise a network to handle their Ora Ciega. Make more money for them than using Bonilla and the cruise ship route to *El Norte*. Find out who is at the top and take it all to Espinosa. Not like I can exactly report it up the police chain."

"How good of a liar do you think you are, Cruz?" Silvio asked heavily.

"As good as I need to be," Emilia answered, impatience finally getting the better of her. "This is a sting. The biggest takedown we've ever done. Just once, do you think you could be a little positive? Tell me I did the right thing?"

Silvio swung his head and gave her a look of pure incredulity. "You never should have set this up without talking to me."

"You weren't there," Emilia snapped. "And the last time we talked you gave the distinct impression of being a giant fucking *pendejo*."

"*Rayos,*" Silvio swore but it was more at himself than at her. "Don't go. Don't fucking go."

"If Flores and I don't make the meeting, we're both dead. Perez will figure a double cross or a badly played bluff." Emilia counted off liabilities on her fingers, one by one. "They know where I live during the week. About the hotel on weekends. Know how to find my mother. Kurt. My best friend. Flores. You."

Silvio threw down his pen. "Fuck."

"I'm going to make the meet." Emilia's chest was tight.

They stared at each other across the table. Silvio's face was grimmer than usual. He broke eye contact first.

"We'll wire you up," he said finally. "I'll stay right behind you, ready to move in if it goes bad."

We. He'd said 'we.' Emilia felt relief dance in her bones even as she glanced at her watch. The minutes were streaking by as if she was in a fast-moving time warp. "They'll be watching for me to have a shadow."

"The Torre Metropolitano, right?" Silvio picked up his cell phone which had been next to a pile of betting slips. He thumbed through the contact list as Emilia watched. "You remember the *abarrotes* shop behind the place? We talked to the owner? First he complained when vehicles blocked off the side street when they were putting up the construction barriers. Second time he said the workmen were stealing from the store."

Emilia nodded. It had been a 30 minute exchange nearly six months ago but Silvio had it right at his fingertips. "I remember. Asian guy. Sold noodle cups and clamshell souvenirs."

"Well, he's going to be open late tonight."

Emilia played out scenarios in her head as Silvio made the call. In all of them, *el jefe* turned out to be Chief Salazar, who either killed both her and Flores or arrested them on trumped up charges of peddling drugs, which would be conveniently found in her car. The trial would be a sham and she'd be murdered in prison. Or even better; Perez had snipers in the construction cranes and shot both her and Flores as soon as they got out of the car.

Five minutes later Silvio had set up his outpost in the convenience store. Emilia finished her beer and shoved the worst-case images out of her mind.

"Now we just need the wire," Silvio said. "Loyola's never going to approve the equipment. You don't have anything stashed in your car by any chance?"

"No." Emilia set her empty bottle on the table and looked around the room. At some point someone—likely Silvio's wife—had painted the walls yellow and put up some heavy cotton curtains. The wooden chairs around the table were cheap and solid, but the backs were carved into the shape of sunflowers. Silvio looked comfortable there and Emilia knew that, under different circumstances, this was a cheerful spot to watch television, drink beer, trade jokes.

Emilia watched Silvio as he scribbled some more notes. Once upon a time she'd mistrusted him. Certainly had never wanted to partner with him. Silvio was cranky, brusque, even brutal on occasion. But mostly he was a tough cop, a survivor of worse situations than this. Together, they had resources.

Emilia squared her shoulders. She wasn't some defenseless, cringing girl waiting to be slaughtered or framed.

She was going to get to the top of the pyramid, find those responsible for the slaughter at Gallo Pinto, Yolanda Lata's overdose, and the murder of Irma Gonzalez.

"Bet there's some confiscated equipment in lockup," she said.

"The evidence locker?" Silvio asked.

"That's right."

"Your cousin runs the place," Silvio said thoughtfully. "You think he'd do it?"

"The famous Sergeant Cruz?" Emilia said as she dug out her cell phone and dialed her cousin's number. "He's family."

"Can you trust him?"

Emilia smiled.

"Takes a thief to catch a thief," she said and then Alvaro came on the line.

☼

The last few hours had been a whirlwind. Emilia knew she should be tired, but she was pumped to the gills with adrenaline and nervous energy.

The evidence locker had been a surveillance shopper's paradise and Alvaro had supplied them with an even better rig than they would have gotten from the police tech team. It was confiscated cartel goods, of course, a digital dream of two-way audio with a 10 mile radius. Alvaro had asked no questions, simply met Emilia at the evidence locker, listened to her requirements, and fiddled with his database before disappearing into the caged area and returning with a steel case full of equipment. Emilia let Silvio tape the tiny microphone and battery pack to her chest right there, trying not to wonder who'd been the last person to use the equipment or how many people had died as a result.

Flores had met them at a small restaurant near the beach at Playa Tamarindo that had an enclosed parking lot. Emilia knew he'd been puzzled at her instructions to take a taxi. He'd recoiled as he'd walked into the restaurant and saw Silvio with her.

As Silvio wolfed down a plate of fish tacos and *bayos refritos*, Emilia told Flores about the conversation with Perez and the meeting at the Torre Metropolitano.

Flores's mouth formed a perfect O and the color drained out of his skin. He swallowed hard. "Of course I'm coming," he said. "I'm a cop. I'm your partner."

Together with Silvio, she outlined the plan, such as it was, to Flores. Silvio would be in the *abarrotes* store in the side street in back of the construction site. He'd be able to listen in. Emilia tried the earpiece that would let her hear Silvio and decided not to wear it. She'd have to let her hair down to cover her ear and Perez would recognize that she wasn't wearing her usual ponytail.

Once they met *el jefe*, Emilia and Flores would agree to set up an Ora Ciega distribution network catering to the *norteamericano* college crowd. The selling points would be Emilia's street contacts and Flores's college friends. With the wire capturing the conversation, Emilia would get them to implicate themselves by talking about the killing field at Gallo Pinto and the murder of the Salva Diablo gang member aboard the *Pacific Grandeur*.

It was all fake, Emilia stressed to Flores. Playacting. She wasn't really going to sell Ora Ciega but would have to negotiate a bit before agreeing to *el jefe's* terms in order to appear genuine. Once the meeting was over, they'd drive a few maneuvers to make sure they weren't being followed and meet back at Silvio's house.

Tomorrow, they'd turn the information over to Espinosa and the *federales*.

Silvio left first in order to park his car a few blocks from the Torre Metropolitano and walk over to the *abarrotes* store. He'd case the area as he went, then call with whatever information he'd picked up. Emilia and Flores would head out after that, do a little recon themselves before pulling into the construction lot.

Once in the store, Silvio would be able to cross the street and be inside the construction site in less than a minute. Of course, anything could happen in less than a minute but she felt good knowing that he'd be listening in. They'd tested the wire and loaded new batteries. The mike and her ability to lie were her best weapons tonight.

"We don't have any other options, do we?" Flores asked.

It was the calm before the storm. They were sitting in the Suburban, in the restaurant parking lot. Emilia had watched Silvio head out after tipping the parking attendant extravagantly. He played their presence as a love triangle: husband catches wife with younger lover. Silvio thought it was funny, Flores seemed confused, and Emilia didn't care. The story made their actions plausible, including why she and Flores were sitting and talking in the car.

"This is the only option," Emilia said. "We'll see this through. Get them all." She had both hands on the steering wheel but hadn't yet started the engine. Now that everything was in place, she felt calm.

There were only a few cars in the lot. The guard was sitting on a box by the entrance, listening to a radio. The Suburban was parked in one of the few spaces that wasn't lit by the mercury glow of lights built into the enclosure walls.

The moon was full, hanging low over the city like a wheel of yellow cheese. The sky was ink blue and the stars were flecks of glitter that reminded Emilia of the gold in Villa de Refugio's window. The store and the lie that had started it all.

She and Flores both wore bulletproof vests under their clothes. Emilia had changed from the gray suit she'd worn all day into the gym clothes she always kept in the trunk; tee shirt, capri leggings, and cross trainers. A loose hooded sweatshirt hid the vest but made her gun in its shoulder holster a little less accessible. She'd put her wallet and badge into the sweatshirt's zippered pocket and slid her rosary into the chest pocket of the tee shirt. She'd need all the help she could get tonight.

Flores had on jeans and loafers topped by a khaki cotton windbreaker that covered his vest and gun. "This *jefe*," he said. "He murdered all those people at Gallo Pinto, didn't he?"

"The community police probably did most of the dirty work but he ordered it," Emilia said. "Dumped the body from the morgue there, too. Had Irma Gonzalez from Customs killed because she started asking questions about the Customs officers who probably were in on it."

"Cut them all up." Flores's voice sounded like that of a small kid in the dark.

"Don't think about that, Orlando," Emilia warned. "Keep your mind focused on catching them."

Flores took a deep breath. "I won't let you down, Emilia," he said and turned to face her.

Emilia flexed her fingers; she'd been gripping the wheel so hard her hands hurt. "This isn't about me, Orlando," she said. "This is about staying cool. Not getting excited. You don't have to say much, just back me up. Don't make up anything, just follow my lead, and we'll be out of there in 15 minutes."

"I know." Flores had an earnest, yearning look on his face. "I'll make you proud. No mistakes this time. Not like when we talked to those two forgers or Gloria."

Made de Dios, he was like a child trying so hard to please. "I think when this is all over," Emilia said. "We should have a talk. About the kind of cop you want to be. What kind of choices are out there for you."

Flores blinked. "A career talk, you mean?"

Because you're suited for any career except this one. "Yes."

"Thank you, Emilia," Flores said. "Thank you for caring."

To her surprise, Flores threw himself over the console and hugged her. It was the same awkward embrace as he'd given her in the squadroom a few days ago, with his face buried in her shoulder. Emilia gave him a pat on the arm, realizing the security guard had chosen the moment to look around and that Flores had given their cover story a boost. But *Madre de Dios*, the pending career talk with Flores was also going to be about personal space.

Her cell phone rang. Flores dropped back into the passenger seat and smoothed his hair.

"The construction gate at Torre Metropolitano is open," Silvio said when Emilia answered the phone. "Nobody watching it that I could see. A few lights on around the base, same as always at night, so that tourists can see the design."

His voice sounded strong. Silvio was no defeated boxer; he was a champ ready for the ring. *Me, too*, Emilia told herself.

"We're on our way," she replied and started the engine.

Chapter 31

Emilia constantly checked her mirrors for a tail as she drove east. The traffic was light around the bay even in the touristy zones near Playa Morro. She rounded the traffic circle at the Diana monument and kept going. At the midpoint of the bay, near the CICI Water Park, she wondered distractedly what Pedro Montealegre was doing and if he'd been promoted again. They passed the three white rounded Torre Victoria towers and the slightly taller Hotel La Palapa, with its 30 floors and angled sides, as they continued into the Colonia Icacos area. Most of the high-rises along the bay were spotlighted at night, tall white columns that graced postcards and distracted the eye from the dirt at street-level.

The site of the half-built Torre Metropolitano loomed ahead as the road curved into the eastern side of the bay. When finished, the tower would be another one of Acapulco's iconic skyscrapers rising from azure ocean, defiant and modern against a backdrop of iron mountains. Its innovative spiral design had been hotly debated in the news last year. Some said it would become Acapulco's most famous landmark, others argued that the design was inherently unstable. But a consortium of investors had pushed it through.

The building would be 25 stories when done and about half had been erected. Steel and glass cladding rose into the sky, topped by a mammoth yellow crane. The whole structure was partially hidden by temporary construction barriers of corrugated steel. A picture of the Building's final state was repeated on the barriers, as if miniature Torre Metropolitanos were strolling down the street, interrupted by the royal palms along the avenue.

Emilia made the block twice, seeing nothing unusual. Lights were on in the *abarrotes* store. She called Silvio, told him they were going in. When she broke the connection she steered the Suburban into the open construction gate on the street running parallel to the Costera.

Once inside, Emilia could see that the upper floors of the partially finished building formed a raw skeleton of steel and cement. The girders gleamed red, an effect of moonlight and the glow from the uplights ringing the base of the building. The bottom stories were sheathed in dark green glass but the upper stories were still bare steel elbows jutting into the air. Each story rotated, the corners floating free, to form an overall spiral effect. The first time Emilia had seen the design in the newspaper, she'd wondered how it would feel to sit in the corner room, knowing it was hanging in midair. There would be only the pull of the center to keep the edges from unraveling and plunging to the ground in a mess of glass and electrical wires.

She let the engine idle. An orange construction elevator was clamped to the outside of the structure. Six cement trucks and an equal number of small front loaders were parked in the lot. There was space for thirty cars inside the enclosure and across the pavement Emilia could make out the silhouettes of three long trailers. Closer to the structure, piles of iron girders and concrete slabs loomed higher than the top of the Suburban.

It was exactly 2:00 am. A light snapped on over the construction elevator.

"Is that for us?" Flores asked.

"I think so," Emilia said. She hadn't said so to Flores, but she knew why the meeting had been set for the Torre Metropolitano. If anything went wrong, it would be easy to stuff their bodies into a cement truck. By tomorrow they'd be part of Torre Metropolitano's foundation.

She parked the car close to the building and cut the engine. They got out and crossed the short distance to the elevator. The orange cage was at ground level. The light flashed.

"Looks like somebody wants us to take the construction elevator on the outside of the building," Emilia said, for Silvio's benefit. The rosary in her chest pocket was heavy and the wire under her tee felt prickly, but both were reassuring.

They stepped into the cage and Emilia pulled the grating closed. The floor gave a lurch. The orange cage lifted the two detectives into the night air.

They rose high enough for Emilia to see over the construction barriers, over the lower buildings along the Playa Guitarrón, and almost to the rounded dome of Punta de Guitarrón. Bars and restaurants were open on a Monday night, music carried on the breeze, tourists were having a good time, and the ocean lapped at Acapulco's door. Business as usual.

The cage ground to a halt. Emilia and Flores stepped out onto a lunar landscape of exposed steel girders, tarp-covered mounds of construction supplies, and needle-edged wind. The building's central shaft was cloaked in cement walls. Only a few vertical beams stretched into the sky along the perimeter, ready to bear the weight of the next story to be placed on top. Otherwise the huge space was open and lit only by the ambient glow of city lights and the single bulb at the top of the elevator. Emilia made out a small wheeled cement mixer and the base of a crane.

Maybe it was her imagination, but the framework of the building seemed to shiver with the gusty breezes. Emilia walked forward, instinctively disliking the edge. Flores came with her and they were halfway to the interior walls when the elevator light went out. The empty cage rattled and began to descend. Cold snaked down Emilia's back at the thought of their only retreat being gone.

"I bought the dress," she said loudly into the darkness.

A flashlight clicked on near one of the central shaft walls. Two shadows emerged from behind the wall. Emilia couldn't make out faces.

"Right on time." The voice was that of Perez.

"I do what I say I'm going to do," Emilia said, squinting into the glare. "I'm here, my partner's here. Let's talk Ora Ciega."

"What does your partner think of your idea?" The light illuminated Flores.

Emilia pressed her hand against Flores's arm. She could hear him breathing in short little spurts. "He's with me. All the way."

"Let him speak for himself."

Flores pressed his hand over hers. In the darkness they were joined together, a team. "What my partner said," he called. "We're together on this."

The flashlight disappeared, replaced by a light on the wall behind the two shadows that threw a half-circle of dim yellow over both. Perez was in jeans and a leather bomber jacket. The other man was older and heavier and wore a suit topped by an expensive trench coat. He looked familiar. A face that had looked at her with interest when she was at the restaurant with Obregon.

Flores let go of Emilia, clapped his hands, and burst out laughing. Emilia froze as he doubled over in mirth, sure he'd cracked under the pressure.

Still laughing, Flores darted forward, navigated a pile of steel rebar, and held out his hands to the older man. "Tío José Ramón!" he called. "I can't believe it. You've played such a joke on me!"

"Orlando," the older man greeted him.

Flores embraced the man as Emilia watched in confusion. "I told you I wanted you to meet Emilia," he said breathlessly, between gusts of mirth. "But this is too much. Even Emilia was in on it." He flapped a hand at her. "You were so serious! And you knew all the time."

"Did she," the older man said, his glaze fixed on Emilia.

Flores took in a big breath, his face split by a huge smile, and backpedaled to Emilia. "Of course," he said. "I've forgotten my manners. Tío, let me introduce my Emilia. My partner and so much more. Emilia Cruz Encinos, may I introduce my uncle, Captain José Ramón Almaprieto Chavez."

Emilia forced herself to keep breathing. *Madre de Dios*, Flores's uncle was *el jefe*.

Flores went on. "He's the head of Internal Affairs and the reason I've always wanted to be a cop."

It was true. But it couldn't be. Emilia had all but forgotten that the rookie's full name was Orlando Flores Almaprieto. At any rate she'd never known the name of the head of Internal Affairs. Few cops ever did. *Is he related?* No wonder Denton thought she was a fool.

From the names, it was clear that Flores's mother and the head of Internal Affairs were sister and brother. Rigoberto Flores might be an indulgent father, but it was the uncle who'd bought the nephew his childhood fantasy.

José Ramón Almaprieto Chavez. The man behind the legendary Alma. The man who held the soul of the Acapulco police force at his mercy.

Alma, who no doubt had something on everyone from Chief Salazar all the way down to Loyola and Ibarra.

Alma, whose name had become synonymous with his unit so long ago that no one remembered any more.

"Detective Cruz." Almaprieto acknowledged her with a nod but made no other move. "I think you know Lieutenant Perez from Organized Crime."

"Yes," Emilia managed.

Alma's flunky, she thought. Organized Crime handled the bulk of the Acapulco police department's drug smuggling cases. Almaprieto doubtless told Perez which investigations-- like the *Pacific Grandeur* murder--to kill or keep.

Perez smiled, the amusement on his face as plain as if he was a ringmaster standing in the spotlight. No wonder he'd wanted her to bring Flores.

"Lieutenant Perez tells me you think we've been following you around," Almaprieto said.

We. Of course. It all made sense now. "Internal Affairs cops use identities of the dead," Emilia said, as if it was a fact she knew.

"You must be as good a detective as Orlando keeps telling me." Almaprieto's face was a mask, betraying no emotion. "How did you find out?"

Emilia felt the wind play around her bare calves. "Your unit rents all your cars from Banderas at the airport," she said.

"Very good. I'll make a note to mix up the rental companies." Almaprieto had his hands in his coat pockets. Emilia knew he was armed but she didn't know in which pocket. "Before we get down to business, tell me about your conversation with Victor Obregon."

"It didn't have anything to do with Ora Ciega," Emilia

parried. "I don't give him my opportunities."

Almaprieto switched on the flashlight, momentarily blinding her. When she brought up a hand to block the glare, he turned it off.

"Obregon could have been a deal breaker," Almaprieto said. "I'm pleased by your attitude."

He paused and looked at Emilia expectantly.

"Thank you," she said, for lack of anything else.

"When Orlando told me his intentions toward you, we had to make sure you'd be a good fit for the boy. A little private investigation to be sure you're right for him. As long as you make a few adjustments to your private life, I have no objections."

Emilia didn't understand. Was he implying she had been followed because of Flores, not because of the Ora Ciega investigation?

"This was just family, you understand," he went on. "There's no official file on you at Internal Affairs."

"Good to know." Emilia felt blind and on shifting sands.

Almaprieto raised his chin at Flores. "Orlando, say your piece to Detective Cruz now."

"Tío! I'm not ready," Flores protested.

"What's going on?" Emilia murmured to Flores. Cutting across her shock was the thought that Flores was in on the Ora Ciega scheme. Had he been planted inside the squadroom to subvert the investigation?

"Emilia, I know we haven't known each other very long," Flores began. He tried to catch her hand but Emilia pulled away.

"Tell me what's going on," Emilia hissed.

"Tío José Ramón said he needed to make sure you were a good cop." Flores caught her hand this time and held it tightly. "And a good person. I knew you were but he insisted. To make sure we're right for each other. I love you, Emilia. I want us to be partners. Not only at work. Partners in every way. Forever."

Emilia felt as if she'd been walloped by one of the bags of cement forming a lumpy pyramid by a small wheeled mixer. A moment ago she'd believed Flores might be Almaprieto's stoolie, now she should believe he wanted to be her husband? "Orlando, we'll talk about this later," she murmured and tried to extricate her hand.

"Emilia, don't you see?" Flores didn't let go. "My uncle wants us to be happy. This was the best joke ever. We'll never forget the day I proposed."

Perez made a funny sound, as if muffling laughter.

"You knew?" Emilia asked the Organized Crime officer.

"You'd better tell him about your weekends at the Palacio Réal before the wedding," Perez drawled. His fingers fluttered by his side.

Emilia finally pulled away from Flores, her heart clanging in her chest. She'd been set up. She'd thought she was being so clever, setting a trap to catch the head of a smuggler ruthless enough to order the killing field at Gallo Pinto. In reality it had been a trap for her.

She couldn't wrap her mind around it, didn't know how to recover the situation. Could she play it through and get Perez and Almaprieto to incriminate themselves? Or was the only chance to laugh about the joke on Flores and get out? But Perez knew why she was really there. Panic kept circling her brain. She couldn't think, couldn't plan her next move.

Behind her, the light to the construction elevator flicked on. The cage rattled loudly. No one said a word as it rose to their level and jolted to a halt. Emilia and Flores turned around to see the grating open. Valentino stepped out, clad in a nylon jacket and jeans. Flores gave an involuntary cry.

"Our little group is complete," Almaprieto said. "I take it you all have met before."

Emilia and Flores were trapped in the middle, between Valentino by the elevator and the others by the central building shaft. The wind whipped Emilia's ponytail against her neck and flapped the skirts of Almaprieto's trench coat around his legs. The elevator light clicked off. Valentino turned into a faceless dark hulk. For the first time that night, Emilia was truly afraid.

"I'm here because of her." Valentino's voice was loud and

raspy. "There are *federales* crawling all over my town."

"We're here to talk business," Perez said. "A new plan with less risk. Use Fiesta Verde. But not the ship. Bonilla's messed that up."

"Fiesta Verde and the ship are a good system," Valentino said. "We don't--."

"You!" Flores shouted, his outburst drowning out the vigilante leader's last words. He pointed a shaky finger at Valentino. "You killed all those people at Gallo Pinto. Chopped them up."

"Orlando, stop," Emilia whispered. "Let's hear what they have to say."

Flores wasn't listening. He whirled to face Almaprieto. "Tío, are you involved?" His voice cracked. "Are you the *jefe* we came to meet?"

Almaprieto's face betrayed nothing.

"*Madre de Dios*," Flores gasped, as realization dawned. "You're part of it, aren't you? The drugs. Those cut up bodies. You're partners with this murderer."

"Orlando, calm down," Emilia said. Her glance swung between Perez on one side and Valentino on the other.

"Tell me it's not true," Flores shrieked at Almaprieto.

Almaprieto stared unblinking at his nephew.

"I thought you were in with your partner?" Perez said mockingly.

"Tonight's not a joke, is it?" Flores began to cry as he stumbled like a drunk toward his uncle. "You'll be arrested. Emilia's wearing a wire--."

Out of the corner of her eye, Emilia saw Perez's fluttering fingers disappear inside his leather jacket. She fought the zipper of her sweatshirt as she sought her own weapon but something smashed into the back of her right arm. Emilia pitched forward, pain erupting from shoulder to fingertips. The gun fell out of her nerveless hand and was lost to the darkness. Instinct made her roll away from the source of the shot and she found herself scrambling for cover behind the pyramid of cement sacks, her right arm lifeless and bloody.

She heard Flores scream, followed by the sound of a slap

and the thud of a falling body. The wind swirled around a steel pillar to her left. Emilia heard footsteps crunch over the grainy cement and a low curse as someone stumbled in the dark. Valentino. He was close.

The pain in her arm was blinding and Emilia knew she didn't have long. She edged away from the barrier, keeping it between her and the voice, groping for her gun. Instead of the pebbled handgrip, her fingers of her left hand closed around a length of rebar. She found the midpoint so that she could lift it without either end dragging noisily on the ground. It was at least 3 meters long, heavy and unwieldy as she crept back to the barrier.

She hadn't been quiet enough and a shot rang out. Emilia flinched as the round buried itself in a cement bag a handbreadth from her face.

Valentino was right on the other side of the cement. Tucking one end of the rebar under her left armpit for balance, Emilia rose up and swung it as hard as she could, hoping to catch his hip. The rebar rammed into something solid and boomeranged away from her. She kept control, swung it again, and heard a crack.

Darkness threatened to overcome Emilia as she and Valentino fought for control of the rebar, sawing the stippled metal rod between them. Her right arm hung by her side, useless and throbbing. As a last resort, Emilia pressed all her weight down, using the top row of sacks to cantilever the rebar. The opposite end of the rod soared upwards, only to stop abruptly, as if jammed. A howl tore the air.

There was suddenly no pressure on the rod and it clattered away from her. Emilia looked over the cement bags to see Valentino splayed out on the ground, a gaping hole where the rebar had split his face from eye to mouth. Blood drained out of an empty eye socket. She scrambled over the barrier and pried his gun out of his hand.

Perez appeared out of the gloom. "Cruz!" His shot hit her in the chest.

Time stopped as Emilia spilled backwards. She landed flat like a fish out of water, gasping desperately for air around the painful compression of the bulletproof vest.

The wind clawed at her and Emilia realized she was on the very lip of the tower, where a red elbow of steel formed an open triangle in the air. Far below, another steel joint was offset by a few degrees. The next rotated even more, as the spiral twisted down the half-made structure.

Perez scrambled over the barrier and loomed over her, gun in both hands. Before Emilia could roll away he shot her again, sound like a thunderclap in her ear. Pain blanked her brain as her chest was crushed. Suddenly there was no more air in the night sky.

Maybe it was the adrenaline or the thought of dying, but Emilia managed to raise her left hand from the cold cement. Valentino's automatic was the same model as her own. The weight and heft was oddly familiar. She fired at the same time as Perez.

As her vest absorbed yet another point-blank shot, Perez overbalanced. Emilia had a breathless glimpse of a face contorted against the stars and then he pitched over the edge.

The next thing Emilia knew, a weight like an anchor was pulling her toward the abyss. Perez had both hands around her left ankle as the rest of his body swung free. His legs scissored, desperately trying to get a foothold on the elbow girder.

Emilia felt her calves scrape against raw cement as the weight of Perez's body dragged her down. She kicked feebly at his hands with her free foot. Pain radiated from her chest and blurred her vision. Her useless arm throbbed anew.

Perez got a toehold on the corner of the girder and one hand found the cement floor. He managed to rise above Emilia and grabbed her sweatshirt. "Enjoy the fall, you little bitch," he panted and heaved her toward the empty sky.

The gun was heavy in Emilia's left hand as she squeezed the trigger in the direction of his voice. The automatic fired again and again. Her teeth gritted against the pain shooting sparklers into her head. The report filled her ears and the recoil battered her shoulder into the cement.

Perez let go.

Gasping for air, Emilia watched his body cartwheel down the side of the building. Someone was screaming but she didn't know if it was Perez or herself.

"You're more trouble than you're worth, Detective Cruz." Almaprieto's voice competed with the cries and the blood hammering in Emilia's ears.

High above her, yet almost close enough to touch, the big yellow moon flickered. The stars over the ocean merged with the sparklers of pain, everything dipping and diving like Pedro Montealegre's silver dolphins.

Through the shimmer, Emilia watched as a man in a coat played a flashlight over her prone body. Almaprieto. The screaming changed pitch; there was hysteria in the sound now. It was the scream of an animal, a wild animal that was trapped and dying. Wild dogs railing at the moon, she thought dully. They would die, too.

Almaprieto's gun was dull and ugly as he stood over her.

The shot was loud.

The pain was too much. Emilia closed her eyes and let herself fall.

Chapter 32

Strange creatures hovered over her, all eyes and spectacles, the rest shrouded in green. They spoke in a language she didn't understand. Plastic hands roved over her body, stripping off her shoes, sweatshirt, and holster.

The heavy vest had molded itself to her torso. There was an immense relief when it was pulled away but the release made her scream. Her tee shirt was cut away and she saw the rosary tumble from the pocket. Emilia tried to stretch out her hand to take it. Her arm didn't move. "That's mine," she said.

Her words were lost in the frenzied motion all around her. No one listened.

The noise around her intensified even as Emilia felt her hand grow cold. The chill spread up her arm, travelled across her chest and stilled her heart. She closed her eyes.

"She was always at the top of her class," Sophia's voice said. "When she was 12 she even won a medal at school."

"What was it for?" Kurt's voice asked.

Sophia sighed. "Maybe science. Emilia was always good at science."

Emilia forced her eyes open. She was in a hospital room, with an IV drip in the back of her left hand and her right arm in a cast from shoulder to wrist. Her chest ached, but her overriding sensation was one of floating. The head of the bed was slightly raised. She could see the moving green ripples of a heart monitor screen on one side of the bed, and her mother and Kurt sitting in two metal and tweed armchairs on the other side.

"Volleyball," Emilia said. Her voice came out in a hushed rasp, as if she was a three-pack-a-day smoker. "I won it for volleyball."

Both Sophia and Kurt jumped to their feet. Sophia's smile

was the same as always, beautiful and a little vague. Kurt looked relieved and exhausted at the same time.

Sophia kissed her first. "I've met Carlos, your nice young man, *niña*."

"Who?"

"I invited him to the wedding." Sophia patted Emilia's arm.

Emilia blinked and suddenly Kurt was there instead of her mother.

"You weren't supposed to meet my mother this way," Emilia whispered. Her face felt strange, as if it belonged on a mannequin.

Kurt smoothed her hair. "Sophia and Ernesto are okay. Your mother thinks you just broke your arm. Don't worry about anything."

Emilia blinked. Her eyelids felt like granite. "Am I going to make it?"

"You're going to be fine," Kurt said softly. "Took a round in your upper arm. Broke the bone. Your vest stopped the rest but you have four broken ribs and a lot of bruising."

Questions pushed at Emilia's consciousness. *How did I get here? Is Flores alive? Did Silvio tell Espinosa?*

She fell asleep again.

The next time she woke, Silvio was in the room, sitting where her mother had been before. He was using the rolling tray that fit over the hospital bed as a game table. Cards were laid out for solitaire.

"Hey," Emilia croaked.

Silvio looked up from the cards. "You want water or the nurse?"

"Water."

He got up, pushed a button by her bed, and it slowly raised to a semi-sitting position. There was a small dresser opposite the bed. Silvio fetched her a glass of water from a pitcher and unceremoniously jammed a straw into it. "Here."

Emilia look it with her left hand. The water was cool. A few sips and her mouth felt like part of her head again. "What day is it?" she whispered.

"Thursday."

"Thursday," Emilia repeated. She'd lost three days.

When she lowered the glass, Silvio put it on the tray next to his cards. "You want the nurse now?"

"No," Emilia said. "Tell me what happened."

Silvio scooped up the cards and shuffled them. "What do you remember?"

"Valentino was down," Emilia recalled slowly. "Perez had fallen. Almaprieto was standing over me and I couldn't move. Couldn't breathe. I heard someone scream. It must have been Flores."

"Flores shot Almaprieto," Silvio said.

"Did he kill him?"

"Either the six shots or the fall killed him." Silvio spoke without emotion. "He landed right next to Perez."

"Almaprieto was his uncle," Emilia said.

"But you were the woman he wanted to marry," Silvio said. "Flores killed Almaprieto to keep him from killing you, then got you down in the elevator."

Emilia closed her eyes, trying to take it all in. Each thought emerged slowly, as if forced through a funnel. "Are Flores and I in trouble?" she managed.

Silvio shuffled the cards again. "According to the press statement from Chief Salazar's office, Almaprieto and Perez met Monday night so that Almaprieto could urge Perez to resign. Internal Affairs had investigated, found him guilty of unspecified abuses. Chief Salazar had counseled Almaprieto against a meeting, but Almaprieto obviously decided that such a senior officer deserved the courtesy."

"*Madre de Dios*," Emilia said shakily and opened her eyes.

Silvio went on. "I gave the tape to Espinosa. He believed the whole story about trying to get the Customs rosters and what happened to Irma Gonzalez, but couldn't make an arrest at Customs because no one on the tape mentioned Customs or Sarmiento or Irma." He shrugged. "Same as always. Two steps forward, one step back. I said we'd watch Sarmiento, see what develops."

"That's all?" Emilia quavered.

"Don't rush me, Cruz," Silvio grumbled. He fanned the deck of cards then just as quickly snapped the deck into a tidy rectangle. "Espinosa cut a deal with Salazar. That's the basis of the cover up. This way we keep Almaprieto's extended network from going after either you or Flores."

Emilia blinked. "What about ballistics?"

"Both Almaprieto and Perez carried the same make and model of automatic they were shot with. Looks like they shot each other. Nobody's going to bother with ballistics."

"Valentino?"

Silvio shook his head. "Can't say the name rings a bell."

"He was there," Emilia struggled to sit up. "You heard--."

"*Rayos*, Cruz. You really lost your sense of humor." Silvio reached in back of his chair, pulled out a folded newspaper. "Read page four when you feel up to it."

Emilia tried to unfold the paper. Silvio watched her, then with an impatient snort, he opened it and pointed to the story. The body of Bernardo Valentino Pinto had been found near the village of Gallo Pinto east of San Marco. A leader of Los Martillos, a local community police organization, Valentino Pinto's death was thought to be the result of a power struggle inside Los Martillos related to a recently discovered killing field near the town and the *federale* drug raid on the Fiesta Verde cannery in Gallo Pinto. Valentino Pinto's faction of Los Martillos was under investigation, according to a *federale* spokesman.

"So you--." Emilia trailed off.

"Long drive in the dark," Silvio said matter-of-factly.

"*Madre de Dios*." Emilia tried to imagine Silvio collecting Valentino's body off the top of the skyscraper and hauling it out to Gallo Pinto in the middle of the night.

Silvio interrupted her thoughts. "So you're in the clear. Flores, too."

"Wait." Emilia's brain slogged through the chain of events. "How are they going to explain a detective getting shot the same night?"

Silvio put the deck of cards on the tray table, divided them, and slid the top cut under the bottom half. "You, me, and Flores were on stakeout, trying to catch the gangs stealing from stores in the neighborhood. Drive-by shooter got you."

"Your idea?"

"One of my best," Silvio said with a hand on his heart. "By the time Flores and I got you to the emergency room, the wire was gone, the story was polished, and we were ready for prime time."

"What about ballistics?"

"Supposedly none of us got any shots off. So no need to check. Hollywood's the only other person who knows everything. I thought he deserved that. I found your gun. He took it home. Nobody's asking to look at it."

"Thanks for telling him." Emilia's left hand roved over the blanket. "Where is Flores? Is he all right?"

"That kid nearly got you killed," Silvio said with sudden heat. "As soon as I heard him laughing on the audio I knew you were in fucking trouble. All that shit about getting married. I assume you didn't know. Also that you weren't planning on dumping Hollywood for him."

Emilia reached for the water glass with a wobbly hand. Silvio gave it to her again. "He'd dreamed up this this giant fantasy of the two of us together," she said after a few sips. "Like his fantasy of being a cop."

Silvio plucked a card out of the deck and tossed it onto Emilia's blanket. "Kid admitted to me that he'd told Almaprieto that he was in love with you. He knew what was going on the whole time."

Emilia picked up the card. It was the queen of hearts. "So it was true. Almaprieto got his goons to look me over. It had nothing to do with the investigation."

Silvio shuffled the cards. "If Flores hadn't been there, you'd probably never know who'd been checking you out."

"And if I'd never had lunch with Obregon, they would never have gotten spooked."

"Looks that way." Silvio fanned the cards and Emilia stuck

the queen of hearts back into the deck. "Flores resigned on Tuesday."

Emilia closed her eyes again. Her lids felt heavy, as if a wet towel was pressing down on them. "Did you make him?"

"Nobody had to make him," Silvio said. He shuffled the cards, squared the deck, and left it on the table. "The kid wanted to get as far away from Acapulco as he could. He went to some music gig in Mexico City. Left you this note."

Silvio pulled a small envelope out of his back pocket and tossed it on the bed.

Emilia didn't have the energy to pick it up. "Did you read it?"

"It's an apology," Silvio said. "A kid's apology, as if saying 'sorry' takes care of everything."

A nurse bustled in and smiled to see Emilia awake. She told Silvio he had to leave.

"I'll let Hollywood know you're awake," he said and headed for the door.

"Franco." Emilia was suddenly weepy. He'd gotten her and Flores out of a crime scene, given the tape to Espinosa, let Kurt know what had happened. No testing her, no backing down from the fight.

Silvio wasn't the easiest man to work with but he was a damn good partner. No matter what bluster he threw at her, she knew he'd always come through.

"What?" He turned in the doorway.

"Your bedside manner is shit," Emilia said.

Silvio gave her a rare smile. "You owe me for the cards."

He left. Emilia put the envelope from Flores on the tray table next to the deck of cards as the nurse checked the various monitors. "Are my clothes somewhere?" Emilia asked.

"Let's see." The nurse opened a cabinet facing the bed and took out a large zip-lock bag with the hospital logo printed in blue. She put it on the bed next to Emilia. "Some of your clothing had to be cut off, but everything else was collected up."

Her cross trainers, with the socks neatly rolled inside, weighted the bag. With her left hand, Emilia slowly took out the bulletproof vest. Three rounds were buried in the thick material.

Emilia's hand shook as she emptied the bag, finding footgear, leggings, and the stuff from her pockets.

Her wallet.

Her cell phone.

Her badge.

Her rosary.

Chapter 33

Two weeks later, Emilia wore one of Mercedes's silk dresses along with a scarf as a sling to her mother's wedding. A mariachi band played in the church garden afterwards and the newlyweds spent two nights at the Palacio Réal for their honeymoon as their wedding gift from Kurt.

On the last weekend of her administrative leave, Emilia asked Kurt to take her back to Gallo Pinto.

"Are you sure you're up to it?" Kurt asked.

"Yes."

Kurt put on some music as they headed east on the highway to San Marco. Maná sang about a lost love. It was one of Emilia's favorite songs, even if the video was incredibly tragic.

"Thanks for doing this with me," Emilia said. "I know you think it's crazy."

"You do a lot of crazy things, Em," Kurt said. "This isn't one of them."

She'd stayed at the Palacio Réal after being discharged from the hospital and had a feeling that she'd be spending more time there and less time in the house with Sophia and Ernesto. Jacques brought her fabulous dinners, Olivas paid his respects, all the bartenders from the Pasodoble Bar visited, Raul the pianist played her a special concert one night as she and Kurt sat in the lobby, and even Christine came up with some magazines for her. Emilia was touched by it all, even as she realized it had taken a shooting to make her feel more at ease in the hotel.

There was no roadblock as they approached Gallo Pinto, although they saw two navy and white *federale* trucks parked near intersections in the center of town. Shops and outdoor restaurants were open. The small church was having an event and the adjacent playground was in full swing with kids playing on the apparatus and parents on nearby benches eating *churros*, roast corn, and cotton candy.

The road that the *federales* had carved through the sugar cane and scrubby landscape wasn't hard to find. Kurt's SUV rocked and bucked as it climbed to the top of the hill. He stopped near a stanchion the *federales* had left behind. A ribbon of yellow crime scene tape fluttered from the top like an explorer's pennant.

When Kurt opened her door, Emilia got out of the car with her shoulder bag. She walked past the stanchion, taking in the desolate scene, listening to the whisper of restless souls as they plucked at her own.

There was little left to show what the place had been. Before leaving, the *federales* had flattened the earth where they'd dug up those piecemeal graves. What stray clumps the wind coming off the ocean hadn't scoured away, the sun had beat into submission. The field was flat and empty. The only movement came from scraps of yellow tape stuck to scrubby pines or the few remaining stanchions.

There was no trace of the atrocities that had been committed. Nothing except whispers on the wind.

"Are you okay?" Kurt asked.

Emilia swallowed and nodded.

"Pick a spot," he said.

Emilia walked across the field. It seemed larger than when she'd been there with the *federales* and their tents of equipment. She found herself drawn to the cliff side. The pines and palms still hid the view but she could hear the surf far below. Two metal stanchions remained, joined by a straight piece of crime scene tape that rattled in the breeze. It could serve as a headstone.

"Here," she called.

Kurt brought a shovel and the cooler from the car. "You okay?" he asked. "Want to sit in the shade while I do this?"

"No," Emilia said. "I'll stay."

Kurt drove the point of the shovel into the ground. The dirt was rock hard from months without rain and it took a long time for him to dig the hole. Sweat was rolling off Kurt's face and arms and staining the front of his shirt before he was done. Emilia was drenched in sweat, too, her cotton sundress limp against her skin. Her right arm itched inside the cast.

When the hole was deep enough, Kurt put down the shovel and opened the cooler. Emilia took out the small package. The finger was wrapped the way it had come from the Pinkerton lab, swathed in waxy cloth and encased in a zip-lock bag with directions to return it to the Acapulco morgue.

"Do you want to say something?" Kurt asked.

Emilia bent and gently put the package into the hole. "May Padre Pro be there to receive you," she murmured.

"Amen," Kurt said. He filled in the tiny grave.

Emilia found her rosary in her shoulder bag. "Do you remember the day we went to Villa de Refugio?" she asked.

Kurt nodded. "You told me about stealing chocolate coins."

"I didn't tell you the whole story," Emilia said.

"Why not?" Kurt asked.

Emilia squeezed the rosary so hard the edges of the case dug into her palm. "I'm not sure. I've never told anyone."

He didn't respond, just waited. A gust off the ocean lifted a wisp of yellow hair that lay across his forehead and Emilia's heart stuttered.

"Everything I told you was the truth," she said. "Except the part about getting the coins. Remember I said that the big display case got knocked over? Glass everywhere? I grabbed up the coins and we ran away."

Kurt nodded.

"I thought I had grabbed a coin but what I'd really gotten was this." Emilia opened her palm and held it out for him to see.

The rosary case was a gold disk about 2 inches in diameter and about half an inch thick. The cover was embossed with the likeness of a man with an oval face and large eyes. Running along the circular edge were the words *Blessed Miguel Pro Juarez S.J.*

"It's solid 18 karat gold," Emilia said as she popped the tiny latch. The rosary inside was a delicate thread of gold chain and tiny round beads. "A special rosary to commemorate his beatification in 1988."

"This must be worth a couple of pesos," Kurt said. He took the rosary beads from her and inspected the cross and the Padre Pro medallion that joined the thread into a circle.

"It's a limited edition." Familiar guilt swept over Emilia. "Worth a fortune."

"Hey." Kurt tipped her chin up. "You didn't mean to steal it, Em."

"I never gave it back, either." Emilia pulled away from his hand, ashamed to meet his eyes. "I didn't want to. A few times when money was really tight, I thought about trying to sell it. But I never could."

"Nobody's judging you, Em."

"I had it in my shirt pocket when Perez shot me," Emilia said. "Right over my heart. The point-blank shots compromised the vest. One of the rounds impacted right over the rosary."

Kurt looked again at the case in her hand. "I don't see any dents."

"I know," Emilia said. "It should have been destroyed. But it wasn't. I wasn't, either."

"I've been on the battlefield, Em," Kurt said slowly. "They say nobody there is an atheist and it's true. You were meant to have that rosary. It was meant to be protecting you that night up on the Torre Metropolitano."

Emilia felt tears prick the back of her eyes. "You think Padre Pro saved me?"

Kurt coiled the beads back into the case. "From what you told me, Padre Pro was on the right side. Could be he's been looking out for you all this time."

Emilia blinked hard.

"You okay?" Kurt asked.

"One more thing. Help me open this." Emilia showed Kurt the tiny vial of holy water from the Vatican hidden inside the top of the case. She had never taken it out. Until now.

As Kurt held the case, Emilia pried out the vial with her left hand. She worked the cork loose and let a drop of holy water fall onto the dirt covering the grave containing the finger. As the breeze freshened, she walked across the field, scattering holy water.

The breeze stilled as she emptied the vial. The whispers faded to nothing. The air was soundless. Clean. Empty.

Kurt came up beside her and tears slid down Emilia's face. He put his arms around her.

"You were wrong, you know," Emilia sniffed into Kurt's chest.

"Impossible. About what?"

"You said the hotel was my safe zone," she said.

"That I did," Kurt said. "And it is."

"No, you were wrong," Emilia said. "You're my safe zone. Not the hotel. You."

They left Gallo Pinto as easily as they'd come, with no roadblocks or men in white tees carrying long guns. Emilia's rosary was back in her shoulder bag and she felt buoyant. Absolved. Shed of a heavy burden she'd carried for too long.

"Given that today seems to be a day for clearing the air," Kurt said as he drove. "I want it on the record that there's nothing going on between me and Christine. I'm no cheater, Em."

"I know," Emilia said. "I'm sorry. Everything was wrong with the world that night. I didn't mean to go all crazy on you."

"As long as you believe me."

Emilia couldn't stop smiling. "I do. I don't like Christine but that doesn't mean you're fooling around with her."

"Wow," Kurt said. "Such a solid vote of confidence."

"Why do you put up with me?" Emilia asked. "I'm either getting shot at or acting like a crazy woman."

"Put up with you?" Kurt flashed her a broad grin. "This sounds uncharacteristically like angling for a compliment."

"No, I'm serious," Emilia said.

Kurt's happy expression faded into introspection. "When I was a Marine, life was . . . I don't know. Bright. Sharp. On a knife edge. Lives depended on you. Things demanded more than you thought you had and you always had to find a way to come up with it." He glanced away from the road and at Emilia. "You know what I mean?"

The road unwound before them and the wind whistled through the open windows as Maná sang. Emilia nodded. "I know."

"Living on the edge is addictive," Kurt said. "I missed that feeling. Until I met you."

"So it's because I'm a cop?" Emilia asked.

"No, it's because of everything you are," Kurt said. "You're a fascinating woman, Em. I can't resist the challenge."

"Challenge?" Emilia wasn't sure she liked that word in this context.

"It's my personal challenge to uncover all your secrets, Em. Every last one."

"You make it sound like I keep things from you," Emilia said indignantly.

Kurt laughed all the way to the turnoff at San Marco.

Chapter 34

Emilia walked into the squadroom with Silvio. The cast and sling meant that she was on limited duty, but it was good to be back.

Macias and Sandor were back from the training course in Mexico City. Ibarra exuded enough smoke stink to be a chimney. Castro and Gomez were still dangerous idiots.

The only change was an empty desk where Flores had sat.

Loyola greeted her with a curt nod before starting the 9:00 am meeting. It was a litany of the same violent crimes. Everybody had a pile of unsolved. The morgue was fully stocked. Two overnight shootings. Macias and Sandor were up on the rota and took the dispatches.

After the meeting the detectives milled around with coffee and sweet rolls. It was a rare few minutes of camaraderie. Loyola didn't join in, however. As soon as the meeting was over, he went into his office and shut the door.

When the group broke up, Emilia wrapped a pastry in a paper napkin and tapped on the office door.

"Come."

Emilia went in and closed the door behind her. "Brought you a *concha* before Castro and Gomez finish them off."

"Thanks." Loyola nodded and she put the roll on his desk. "How are you doing?" he asked.

"Pretty grateful for that vest," Emilia said.

Loyola nodded again, dug some file folders out of a pile on his desk, and held them out to her. "Taking you and Silvio off the rota for two weeks until you can shoot again. Got a couple of robbery cases might be related. Looks like a ring is operating around the Fuerte San Diego. Lifting small tech items off tourists. Break it up before the mayor's office starts calling."

He hadn't offered her a seat but Emilia sat down in one of the chairs facing his desk. "Electronics? We got a lead on a fence for the stuff?"

Loyola sighed. "Nothing."

"Well," Emilia said, thinking of Chavito and the pimp's network of contacts. "We'll get on it. I've got a source down in that neighborhood."

Loyola stared at the pastry on his desk. Emilia made no move to leave.

"You heard the news?" Loyola asked after a long moment. "About the head of Internal Affairs?"

"I heard."

Loyola poked the *concha* as if assessing the amount of icing on top. "He had something on everyone. Eyes everywhere."

Emilia shrugged, but her thoughts raced. Was Loyola referring to himself? Or Chief Salazar? Or was Loyola simply demonstrating that he knew the truth about the deaths of Almaprieto and Perez? Had Flores told him before resigning?

"Internal Affairs," she said noncommittally. "Crap job."

"Rumor has it," Loyola continued. "Almaprieto had something on everyone except Obregon Sosa, head of the union."

"Obregon's pretty slick," Emilia said warily.

"I heard you had lunch with him awhile ago," Loyola said. "Was he slick then, too?"

"Yeah," Emilia said, with as much meaning as she could muster. "Pretty slick."

Suddenly Loyola threw himself back in his chair. "Look, Cruz. I don't know if that grievance was the way to go but you fucking nearly killed me. My balls were stuck in my throat for a week."

"You suggested I owed fellow officers blow jobs for not raping me," Emilia exclaimed. "You're lucky to have any balls left at all."

Loyola reddened. "Okay, so maybe not every fucking word that comes out of my mouth is perfect. *Rayos*, I didn't ask for this job."

"Well, I asked for mine," Emilia countered. "And fought damn hard to get it. If I have to fight to keep it, I will."

Loyola lifted his eyes to the ceiling. "*Por Dios*," he swore.

"You and Silvio deserve each other."

Emilia stood up, clutching the robbery folders with her good hand. "You want a cup of coffee to go with that roll?" she snapped.

"No," Loyola bit back. "I got a cola."

"So much cola isn't good for you."

"With any luck, I'll have a heart attack and someone else can have this fucking job."

It was a draw, Emilia decided, and she was oddly pleased as she left the office. They both understood that the grievance was dead in the water. Neither had apologized, although Loyola had all but said that he knew he sucked at his job. It was as decent an outcome as any having to do with personnel issues that she'd experienced in over 12 years as a cop. Still, she wouldn't let her guard down again.

On the other side of their computer screens, Silvio was slurping coffee and swearing at his keyboard. From the commotion she knew he was completing the monthly statistics report. Emilia ignored him as she opened the first folder Loyola had given her. Ten statements from tourists who'd been pickpocketed after visiting the Fuerte San Diego. All had lost cell phones and small cameras.

The second report was a raid on a house thought to belong to a local gang. Anonymous tip. No arrests but a big haul of stolen electronics.

Photos of the seized items were clipped to the folder. Emilia flipped through them. The techs had done a good job of documenting the evidence. Big clear plastic bags, like the zip-lock bag used by the hospital to save her clothes, were full of small electronics. She counted four bags of cameras in one photo. A larger photo of each individual bag followed. Each bag contained at least 20 devices.

The next set of photos were of bags of cell phones. Emilia paged through each shot, not that it really made a difference, but it felt good to be at work again, engaging her brain and trying to make sense of the city's crime.

A jolt of hot pink stood out in a bag of gray and black cell phones. The pink case was studded with rhinestones around the edges. More sparkles formed a big "Y" on the back.

"*Madre de Dios*," Emilia said out loud. "It's Yolanda's cell phone."

"What's your problem now, Cruz?" Silvio growled from the other side of their computer screens.

The trail to Lila Jimenez Lata was suddenly fresh again.

"Get your keys, Franco," Emilia said.

El Fin

Glossary of Spanish Terms

Abarrotes: snacks
Bayos blancos: white beans
Chatarra: junk
El Norte: the United States
Jefe: chief, person in charge
Madre de Dios: Mother of God
Mercado: market
Norteamericano: North American
Pendejo: asshole, jerk
Por dedazo: expression meaning "by the finger" to indicate patronage
Rayos: exclamation, similar to "oh hell"
Sicario: cartel henchman or assassin
Tumbadore: person who steals drug shipments

About the Author

In addition to political thriller *The Hidden Light of Mexico City*, Carmen Amato is the author of the Emilia Cruz mystery novels set in Acapulco, including *Cliff Diver*, *Hat Dance* and the collection of short stories *Made in Acapulco*. Originally from New York, her books draw on her experiences living in Mexico and Central America. A cultural observer and occasional nomad, she currently divides her time between the United States and Central America. Visit her website at http://carmenamato.net and follow her on Twitter @CarmenConnects.

Fiction by Carmen Amato

THE HIDDEN LIGHT OF MEXICO CITY
CLIFF DIVER: An Emilia Cruz Novel
HAT DANCE: An Emilia Cruz Novel
DIABLO NIGHTS: An Emilia Cruz Novel
MADE IN ACAPULCO: The Emilia Cruz Stories
The Angler: An Emilia Cruz Story
The Cliff: An Emilia Cruz Story
The Beast: An Emilia Cruz Story

One last thing . . .

If you would like to recommend this book to other readers looking for a new mystery series, please consider posting a review on Amazon. Return to the book page on Amazon and follow the prompts. Your comments will be greatly appreciated.

To receive monthly mystery updates with exclusive excerpts, sales alerts and book release news, please visit http://carmenamato.net and complete the form on the home page. When you subscribe, you'll receive a free copy of *The Beast*, the first Emilia Cruz story which reveals how Emilia became Acapulco's first and only female police detective.

Thank you and happy reading.

All the best, Carmen

CARMEN AMATO

Made in the USA
Middletown, DE
02 June 2016